Behind Even The Shadows

Paradox Puzzle

Molly Moles

Scriverdea Publishing

Lewisville, Indiana

Scriverdea Publishing
4886 East 1100 North, Lewisville, Indiana, 47352
Printed by IngramSpark with permission

For additional information, contact Molly Moles using the listed address or email behindeventheshadows@gmail.com. Be sure to join @BEtheShadows on Facebook (with links to other social media platforms) for author updates and fan forums.

Paradox Puzzle first edition, 2021
Third in the *Behind Even The Shadows* Series of six novels.

Cover artwork by Bekah Koen
Photomanipulation, logos, and accents by Jacob Moles
Concept editing by Janet Hughes
Map created using Inkarnate.com with proper licensure

ISBN: 978-1-951499-10-5 (paperback)
978-1-951499-11-2 (hardcover)
978-1-951499-12-9 (eBook)
978-1-951499-13-6 (Audiobook)

LCCN: 2021909520

Novels in the

Behind Even The Shadows

Series:

Cloaked Heart

Unveiling Thorns

Paradox Puzzle

Mental Tempest

Verity Pursuit

Callous Closure

~ Dedication ~

To The One Who gave me the ability to produce the work I do ~ my Lord and Creator, God Almighty. May He be glorified in all I do, and may this book — and series — be a reflection of young Christian adults striving, growing, renewing, maturing, and perfecting day-by-day to follow Him and be in the world but not of it. Standing up to the sinful nature of those who do not submit to God's commands, while at the same time, showing them they do not have to continue in hopelessness and sin.

~ Acknowledgements ~

Sometimes "thank you" doesn't do justice; and yet what else can I say except, "Thank you!" I've added a couple enthusiastic readers to this great team and am looking forward to this following growing:

Janet Hughes   Bekah Koen   Jacob Moles

Rush Limbaugh

~ Table of Contents ~

~ Pronuciation Guide ~

NOTES: Underlining: "hard" vowel. Capitals: stressed syllable.

Last Names:

Lanphren: lan-FREN

Places:

Yergo: ER-g<u>o</u>

Miscellaneous:

(Title) Apothecary:
<u>a</u>-POTH-eh-cary

(Fabric) Devoré: de-V<u>OR</u>-<u>a</u>

("Disease") Irochromolysis:
<u>I</u>R<u>O</u>W-kr<u>omo</u>-l<u>i</u>sis

(Language) Koine: K<u>OY</u>-ney

(Knife) Kopis: K<u>O</u>-pis

(Title) Neurosan:
NEW-r<u>ow</u>-son

(Knife) Seax: S<u>EE</u>-kx

(Knife plural) Seaxes:
S<u>EE</u>-kx-<u>e</u>z

(Title) Teralyn: T<u>AI</u>R-ah-lin

(Apricot in Armenian)
Tsiran: TS<u>EE</u>-ron

~ Map of Quidoria ~

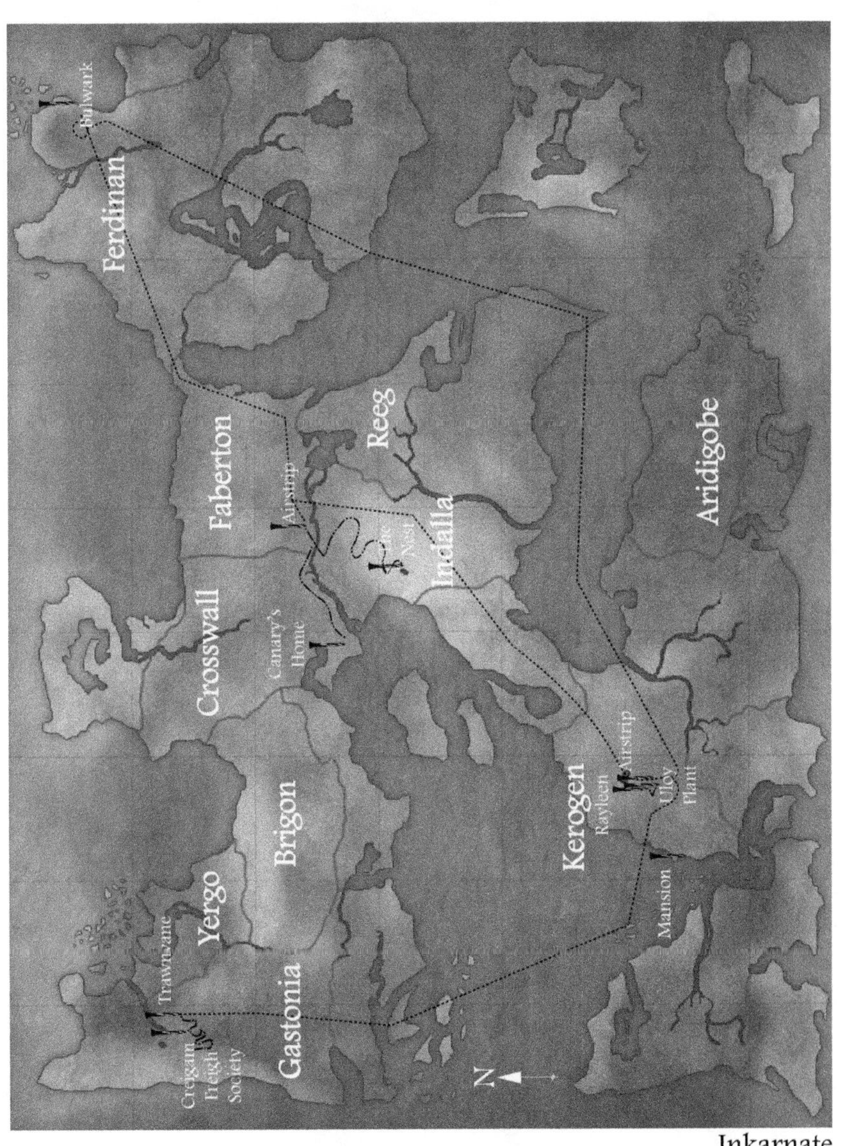

Inkarnate

~ 1 ~

A band of four sedans streaked through the countryside; all of them exact copies of each other. The haze in the air obscured the view of them almost to the point they were nothing but…

Shadows

"Has Canary— I didn't think so. What about Emissary? … Good. Then he'll be there when the first extraction team arrives. Grounder informed me of their departure about an hour ago. Make sure he knows about them and that he's on the cleanup detail. … We're still wheel-bound, but should be boarding Raven within the hour; less Enforcer. … No, they're with us. They said they wanted to be present to support Doyen when— I am well aware Confrere and Helpmate aren't part of the Veil any longer. I wasn't insinuating that by my remark. … She'll be with the second extraction team. … That concerned me as well. I'm not sure how she got the flare off if Wolf was deactivated. … No. But Doyen is— I truly don't see it as an issue anymore. She's been dealt with. … That was why I said Confrere and Helpmate came…"

This cryptic phone conversation continued, inching Destan back to consciousness. He moaned and bobbed his head as he fought his eyelids; this task being more labor intensive than what he thought it should be. By the time he gained enough of his faculties to open them, he started rambling as he mumbled: *Still raining? ~ No. No that looks like fog. ~ Well, whatever it is, it sure isn't the weather that makes waking up e— how did Fidus get here so fast? I would have thought Rocher would~ Wait! What's with the detail? Why—*

His eyes all but bugged out as he whipped his head around to look at the man he'd been avoiding for the past three months. This man, who was about fifteen years his senior, noticed the sudden movement, "Doyen's awake. I'll get with you later. — Glad to see you're awake. Try to take it easy. Mender said you need to—"

"Where's Calli?" Destan asked frantic.

"Who?"

He gritted his teeth as he tried to pull himself up, grimacing as he argued, "You know good and well who Calli is, Fidus! Don't you 'dare' try to play dumb. Where is she? What happened to the two who w—"

"The extraction teams have everything under control. Don't worry."

"Fidus? Where. Is. My. Wife?" Destan demanded; though his face looked more horrified than anything.

"She's with the extraction team," he motioned to the rear window in a casual way.

"Stop the car."

Now irritated, Fidus sighed, "We'll be back—"

"I shouldn't 'have' to repeat myself."

"Very well," he sighed as he pushed his hair behind his ear; tapping a button on the door beside him. "Pull over. Doyen wants to see her."

To Destan, it felt like the person driving just let off the gas so they could torture him by coasting to a stop; when in fact, they braked pretty hard.

Adrenaline was doing its best to keep the pain at bay as he stumbled to the other vehicle and threw the back door open.

If he wasn't hissing from this physical torture already, the mental and emotional torture he now was being flooded with would, "What in the name of— she wouldn't hurt— what did you do, Fidus!"

"This was necessary."

This simple statement which took a stab at justification didn't sit well with Destan, "Anything she did was to protect me, you moron."

"Destan, please," a familiar, soft voice tried to soothe.

And now the band of mutineers became more extensive and much closer to home, "You? But you know Calli, Tabitha. Rej. ... You know she didn't do anything to warrant this."

"It's better this way," she smiled softly. "Just calm down."

"Better?" He jerked away from her hand. "How is this 'better'? — And you! We talked about this and you promised me."

"Destan I tried." Redje defended as he jogged up and pulled Tabitha to his side. "I can only do so much. The Veil made the call."

"Fidus, I swear that you all are going t—"

"We need to get moving so we can get clear of any patrols. Where are you riding?"

Either Fidus had no fear or he didn't know about Destan's "anger issues". Plus, why in the world would he add insult to injury? What was so pressing about leaving the area: a completely rural one at that? Why was he so cold and removed from what he did?

Destan got in his second-in-command's face; almost spitting since he was hissing from pain, "Remind me why I chose you to be Fidus?"

He answered with a level of confidence that was borderline arrogance, "Because you said you could trust me in every scenario."

"Well you just showed you 'can't'. Get out of my sight before I—just get out of my sight."

With a direct order given, the man backed away and motioned to others who were standing nearby. The only ones who didn't move were the two best friends Destan couldn't believe would be party to such a heinous thing.

"Don't dare say a word. Either of you. Just leave me be. Now!" He said in a cruel tone as he got in the vehicle.

ℬ

Destan slammed the door and stared at Callimay, saying in agony as his hands shook; him terrified to touch the wound on her neck: *You made it through all that with Baleck and Ginger only to be picked off like some wild animal by those 'I' told you to call for. I—* "Calli, please. You've got to wake up. Tell me this is a nightmare. Tell me 'I'm' the one who can't see what's real. Please Calli. Please…"

The car started to move with no change in this horrific reality he found himself in. What was he going to do? He told her to fight back when she was the one like this, but how in the world was he supposed to do it? Her ability was triggered by love. How in the world was he supposed to feel that emotion right then?

Her body was beyond limp when he finally found the courage — let alone physical strength — to take her in his arms. Destan grimaced and groaned as he flopped onto the seat; and continued for a short time after as he started breathing hard. Even holding her caused him so much pain… but he had to have her close.

"Calli… please." He pleaded in a broken whisper as he fought back tears. "Calli you've got to be alright. I… I can't believe they'd actually do this."

As he continued this emotionally crushing venture, the window to the front of the car rolled down and Doctor Gerould calmed, "She was just tranquilized, Destan."

There was a striking pause as he one, tried to take in what was said; and two, tried to comprehend who was telling him this, "You? You're the extraction—"

"Long story short I got back as fast as I could when I heard Fidus: he was at his wits-end when he showed up. I knew he wasn't thinking when he called Enforcer to clear the playing field. Confrere tried when he found out, as did Helpmate, but he disregarded them because—well, you know. Thankfully Sentinel and I were able to get him to understand doing that wasn't going to fix anything. I couldn't get all the details to him fast enough, but at least he listened. And before you ask, yes, I gave him this alternate route; and I specifically made sure Sentinel and myself were the extraction team for Callimay. … The amount she got is going to keep her out for quite a while."

Well this "minor" detail would have been lovely to know about… oh, say ten minutes ago?

"She's…" Destan paused as he looked down at Callimay and then back to Doctor Gerould. "What was she given?"

There was a paused, followed by a deep breath and a quiet answer, "Five. I w—"

"Five! Are you insane, Lance!" Destan jerked back, yelling in a shrill voice. "That could've killed her. A two would h—"

"Doyen? Have you already forgotten when she was having those nightmares?" He turned around in his seat and gritted his teeth; glaring at the out-of-control man he was desperately trying to calm while giving a reality check at the same time. "I was giving her a healthy three at that point and she was breaking through it like she was just waking up from a short nap. I didn't 'want' to do it, but Fidus said a five was the only option if we were going to tranquilize her. … If it didn't work he would've had her killed."

Yet another wave of shock ripped the air out of the vehicle; though this one wasn't nearly as long-lived. There were still several emotions flying around inside Destan, but they were running out of steam fast, "H… how long will she be out?"

"I really don't know." Doctor Gerould took a half relieved, half pained sigh. "Under normal circumstances I'd say she would be out at least until tomorrow night, but… with whatever was done to her at the Society I just can't say for sure. She could wake up at any moment and only be lethargic. Then again, she could be down for a couple 'days' and be perfectly fine when she wakes up. I just don't know."

"You said Rej and Tabitha tried to—"

"Wolf contacted them and Rocher as well. Redje somehow found out quicker about what Fidus was planning and immediately tried to stop him; I mean 'immediately'. If I'm keeping things straight, Tabitha called Rocher who contacted me so we could talk him down. … You 'need' to sit down with him on the flight back to Bulwark and explain everything. You're due to come back anyway."

"I know," he sighed as he threw his head against the head rest. "Calli's fine though, right?"

"I checked her right before we left. She's breathing very shallow, but nothing unexpected. That blood isn't from anything major; the carrier only nicked a small artery because she moved after Enforcer made his shot. You know he's not keen on setting his sights on a female for any reason, so he was really frustrated when he found out that happened. — She's alright. Just rest, Destan. I'll want to check you again once we're in the air."

While he heard that last part, it didn't really register because he was so busy scolding himself and complaining as he rocked her: *I can't keep anything stable for you. First we had to jump ship at the Society, and then you couldn't go home; then we ended up abandoning the mansion… now you probably can't even go back to Rayleen. — Well we can't go back right now; that's for sure. — What have I done? How in the world am I going to explain all of this to you? How can I expect you to just come with me to Bulwark without question? How can I expect you to stay there while I'm out on missions? But how can I cope with the danger you would be in if I trained you and took you with me? ~ Why don't we address the first issue: how are you going to explain this all? You can't just brush it off and keep her in the dark anymore. ~ There's no way she wouldn't have any questions. And I won't lie to her. — Fidus will just have to deal with the reality that you're here to stay with me. They all will. I don't care what the Veil says. I just… I just don't want to— I don't want to hurt you, Calli. I don't want you to be scared. I'm sorry I never told you, but I didn't because I… I just wanted to keep you safe. I just wanted to do what my father couldn't. … I love you, Calli. I'm sorry.*

As he sat there, hunched over, he was reminded how Callimay was already putting herself in danger. That day was the perfect example. She chose to and did it gladly because she loved him so much. And the more he thought, the more Destan realized she had been doing it all along: constantly watching him to keep him from going insane all the while silently suffering through all the pain he would go through. She went so far as to track Toreon back at the Society to figure out what he was doing that one night — putting herself in every imaginable type of danger. In short, Callimay was doing all of that because she wanted to do everything within her power to protect the one she loved most.

Destan's thoughts were soon interrupted by the overbearing power of a battered body; and then even that was interrupted by the car stopping. Granted he wasn't conscious of this fact, but he'd formed the habit of pulling Callimay close to him whenever something happened or was said that startled or angered him. And he wouldn't have known about it even this time if it weren't for his wrists yelling and screaming at him for neglecting them.

A quick glance out the tinted windows revealed vague outlines of larger buildings and lights here and there; some of which he knew belonged to Raven. Sure enough, when Rocher opened the door for him, he saw the sleek, black jet sitting on the apron, ready for its owner to climb aboard so they could make the flight "home".

Something inside Destan felt trapped; like a prisoner being dragged off to an uncertain place where he wouldn't be able to escape and would most likely be the last place he'd ever see. He didn't want to get out; let alone get in the jet and go where its destination was. All he wanted was for Callimay to be safe. And after what he was told? He didn't know if going to Bulwark would indeed be a "safe" place for her to be.

All these thoughts brought forth the startling realization: Callimay couldn't help. This drastic decision made during a situation he didn't fully understand was much more dangerous than Fidus realized. Destan was sure Doctor Gerould said something, but it was most likely in the part of his defense that was cut short. With him being in this vulnerable state, was it safe for him to be around her… or on a plane?

Now he was spiraling in an altogether different way that was just as dangerous as what he was trying to prevent. But remembering what Rocher and Doctor Gerould did encouraged him in a way that helped stabilize his emotions: they protected the love of his life from the death sentence, they made sure they could be with her when he couldn't… they were doing everything they could to keep her safe because they cared for her.

Though this was a victory that was much needed, a new struggle reared its head within moments and brought everything tumbling down again: it was enough of a chore for him to get out of the car but carrying Callimay made things almost impossible. And yet, for as much as he was in pain, he refused to let anyone else touch her after the way Fidus talked about and treated her.

The first generation of cicadas had emerged in full force for the season; their hypnotic voices pulsating from the surrounding trees. Since the storms rolled through, the air smelled like the most pleasant fusion of fresh turned dirt and clear, cold spring water. All of these indicators of early summer were quite often seen as things which calmed the senses; allowing for rest and relaxation… and yet Destan's mind was so torn in two polar opposite directions that nothing less than his wife's voice would help.

He huffed and stormed past a couple individuals in all black who put their left fist up to their mouth — as if covering a cough — and grimaced as he worked his way up the steps. Rocher attempted to help, but the anger and pain in Destan's eyes halted his efforts; not even a word being said.

A growl lingered as he shifted back and forth in the seat: *I can still smell her perfume. ~ Crazy to think that was just a day ago. But, what's new: wonderful memories being corrupted with anger?*

When he opened his eyes, he saw a small group at the front of the jet. His nervous hand searched for Callimay's wedding band while his eyes darted back and forth: *As if things were hard enough. … I— this was never supposed to happen.*

The sole female in this group kept looking back at Destan as if trying to find the courage to say something to him. Once the man next to her finished talking, she whispered in his ear and then he took her hand and they walked back. Her strained voice seemed to be the only thing holding back a flood of tears, "Destan I'm so sorry about what I said. I thought you knew."

"It's my fault, Tabitha. I wasn't thinking when I heard Fidus say he 'dealt' with Calli. — L… Lance told me what you tried to do, Rej. I s—"

"You know, Destan?" He admitted as he reached over and gave a firm but gentle tug on his shoulder. "If 'I' were told Tabby had been 'dealt with' I can pretty much guarantee you I would've lost it. Everything rational in this life 'can' fly out the window when the woman you love is hurt or you don't know where she is. I get it. … And I think you better understand why I stepped down when we got married. I knew I couldn't keep Tabby free from 'every' type of danger; but I knew how to minimize it as much as possible. — Now it's your turn: you've got to decide what's best for you and Callimay 'with' Callimay. Don't worry about the Veil and Shadows; they'll take care of themselves. You've got to take care of each other."

"But I accused you two of—"

"It's alright, Destan," Tabitha took her glasses off and wiped her eyes. "I was at fault thinking you knew. Looking back, I can see how heartless and cruel I must've sounded; you thinking Callimay had been killed. In hindsight, knowing what you were thinking, you reacted so much better than I would've expected you to. … You're getting there Destan, please don't give up. Being a Christian is a growing process. There was miscommunication on 'both' sides. Everything is fine now."

"Just remember: a setback, awkward moment, or new situation that isn't handled the best doesn't automatically make you a failure or a man with no capability to learn and grow. It doesn't even automatically make what you did a sin, okay? — And thinking back to what you'd been talking with me last week about, I believe this should be a huge, real-life 'aha' moment. You 'do' show Callimay you love her; you do it even when she doesn't know about it. Doyen's far from having any high ground in that battle. Don't let him have ammo by apologizing for loving her. Now I'm not saying there isn't anything at all that needs to be addressed, but that was more of 'how' you said it. … Have faith in yourself." Redje continued to encourage; putting his arm around Tabitha and smiling, "I know we haven't been married 'that' long; but then again we remember that first year really well. And I know you're going to be going through — I'm guessing real soon — what we did before we even got married. So if you 'ever' need anything… even if it's just having someone to bounce ideas off of, we're here."

"Thanks," Destan took a relieved breath; but cringed when he saw the others in the jet, "There's so much that's got to be discussed with so many people. I'm almost— no I 'am' tapped out."

They both looked where he did and then to each other before Tabitha spoke in a soft voice, "Just do what you can. It's all anyone can ask, regardless of what they might say. You've been through the wringer. That in and of itself is enough of a reason to allow extra time."

Not meaning to say it loud enough for them to hear, Destan mourned as he laid his forehead against his unconscious wife's, "I just wish I could talk with you before I have to take care of this. I don't want you to be terrified; not knowing where you are or what's been going on this whole time in the background. … Rocher warned me almost two months ago about this."

"Callimay is strong." Tabitha got up and sat beside him; gently patting his arm where it didn't look injured. "You know she is. Keep that faith in her when you talk to her. Don't lock her out. Let her help. That's what God made us for: we help and fix what we can, where we can. We can figure things out sometimes, but the only way that happens in those 'odd' situations is if we're 'told'. For the most part we do know there are limits, things we can't fix or do; but that doesn't mean we don't want to at least know what's going on. We want to struggle with you through the uncertain times; to be in the chaos and confusion because we want to be with you. It reminds us that you care about us and love us to include us even when we can't do anything. Some may say that's undo stress to put someone under, but from what I've heard, Callimay can tell in a special way when you're stressed. Don't make her think she's the cause of it. Tell her what's going on. It might be a bit embarrassing or uncomfortable at times. I mean Redje and I still have those moments for goodness sake! Just… don't hide anything from her. Tell her what is going on: everything. I know the Veil wouldn't like me saying that, but the fact is you 'are' Doyen. As your wife, Callimay is entitled to know what's going on and what her husband is up against. So show her Doyen: leader of the Shadows, head of the Veil. Be who you are in that aspect of your life. — I know you're probably scared about how she'll react. And at first, she may very well react exactly like you think. But given a little time? Like I said: she's strong. She loves you with all of her heart. And I know you love her with all of yours."

"I do," he moaned under his breath, trying to hold back tears.

"We all have different sides to us, Destan." Redje finished as he took a deep breath, sounding as encouraging as ever. "Doyen is just another side of you, but he doesn't define you. God is the only one allowed to define you, limit you. Don't debase yourself and give up the side of Destan that is husband and protector to Callimay simply because he has to work harder now. Let him stay rooted and remind Doyen of his place; all the while still allowing Doyen to do what he needs to. I know it might sound impossible, but you know with God's help nothing is. If you remember to love Him, that love will keep flowing to Callimay. Love outlasts any emotion because it truly isn't an emotion. It just takes work… constant work."

"But I don't know if I can still be Doy—"

"Please take your seats. We'll be taxiing momentarily." Rocher said over the com.

Seizing this moment, Fidus marched back, "We need to talk."

Destan hesitated, but sighed as he leaned his head back and closed his eyes, "Fine."

"We'll head up front then." Redje took Tabitha's hand and helped her stand.

"If Callimay needs someone to hang around while you're gone, I'm more than willing to help. The Utrees are looking after Rose so we have a couple days to spare."

For some reason, Tabitha's comment pulled a weight off of Destan that he didn't even know was there, "I will. Thank you. And something tells me she'll really want to see you."

Fidus sat across from Destan and did nothing but stare him down for a good five minutes. — Awkward? — Regardless of his duties and the insurmountable questions that had to be answered, Destan was exhausted… and still mad at Fidus.

The flurry of what happened was still settling in his mind; now wasn't the time to get into the thick of things. But, putting it off wasn't going to make it go away: in a way he'd been trying that for the past three months… and look where that got him.

Unable to stand this judgmental nonverbal communication any longer, Destan spoke up as he shifted in his seat, "Before we talk about anything, I need to know why you were so bent on murdering my wife back there. What did she do?"

"What would you do if four teams were leveled by nothing but a woman's scream?" Fidus steadied himself as the jet started its takeoff. "Let alone her behavior was nothing less than some mentally disturbed person; beating at the air and wailing over a puddle of water."

"I get that someone who had no idea would be freaked out, but I 'told you' about the whole situation of us having abilities and there being others. You 'never' stopped to consider that?"

"Well excuse me for not fully understanding what that entailed. Decisions needed to be made and that wasn't high on my priority list."

Destan made a face as he tried his best to stay composed, "Well you 'better' make it a priority to keep 'all' of your intel at the forefront of your mind when making such drastic— 'deadly', decisions."

There was a pause, proving his point was more than valid.

"Well… I guess I'm not proud enough to lie about the pushback from some in the Veil about you marrying swaying my decision. I was getting sick and tired of hearing their belly-aching, and—"

"Don't pawn your decision off on someone else, Fidus. You've put up with flack before over much more serious matters." Destan leaned back and closed his eyes; sighing before he finished, "Go on."

Again, there was a pause. The tension in the air started creeping up to where the rest of the individuals were; their hushed comments to each other becoming less and less frequent.

"Seeing how the other two and her 'fought'… I've been in some baffling, awkward, and unique situations but I couldn't believe what I was seeing. Well, what I 'wasn't' seeing. Nothing made any sense with how she was acting in comparison to the Falconer and his mate: she just sat there while he worked you over. She was even looking straight at you at one point but did nothing. Then she screamed and everyone fell over like cascading tiles. In what I now know is a moment's lapse of judgment, I saw an opportunity to silence the questions surrounding your personal decision while ensuring your safety. … Confrere and Helpmate pushed hard to get me to see my irrational thought process but due to their demoted status and personal connection to you and the situation that was looming over you— yes, I ignored them because they knew her. But when Sentinel and Mender voiced the same objection, I began to open my eyes and come to my senses. I think they'll tell you it was in the nick of time. And it's needless to say that Enforcer was more than relieved to hear the change."

"I knew there was going to be a bit of an uproar when word got back to the Veil about Calli, but I didn't think you'd all lose your ever-loving marbles!" Destan winced as he pulled her closer; sounding and looking agitated. "I thought you all would be the professional, level-headed people I'd always known. Irritated, yes, but adults. Guess I was asking for too much understanding from you. … I wasn't ready to come back and explain. And still I hadn't decided how to get away without her knowing; and I was just starting to really enjoy what I had. — And no, I wasn't enjoying it too much, Fidus. … When I decided to marry Calli — to be blunt — my duties as Doyen were the last thing on my mind. It crossed my mind not too much later, but I knew I had plenty of time to figure out exactly how I wanted to handle it so everything was safe and secure for everyone. But then the encounter's date started creeping up; and then when I got your note and saw you…

I just didn't know how to tell Calli what was going to happen and yet keep her protected. I kept convincing myself if she didn't know she'd be as safe as possible... but— oh why bother. You obviously don't care."

He rolled his head over and stared outside, just waiting to hear Fidus continue, but there was blissful silence.

Once he was able to emotionally take looking at his second-in-command, Destan looked back over and raised an eyebrow, "You know now that Calli was only protecting me, right? Whatever happened as far as the others being knocked out, I take it by your lack of comment that they're alright? ... So, obviously whatever new ability Calli has found isn't deadly. And she wasn't intending to do it to them." *With it being new she didn't even know to use it against Baleck and Ginger, really.* "She was only protecting me from those two we were battling."

"One standing on the boundary wouldn't be able to tell the difference as I've said this whole time. And if I'm being frank, I'm still leery of her."

I guess I can't blame you for that. ... You'd probably be leery of 'me' if you saw what I did. ~ Was that a stab? ~ Why do you think I didn't say it out loud?

Fidus leaned in closer and said in a hushed tone; quite opposite of what they were just talking about, "I'm going to warn you, the last rumblings I heard were that a vote will be called when you arrive."

"I think everyone here knows that. ... And in fact, I expected it." Destan huffed; an ever-growing part of him wanting to tell his second-in-command to leave him be. "I've got to get things squared away with Calli first. She deserves to have a say in what 'my' decision is regardless of what the Veil thinks."

"But— fine. I'll see what I can do. ... What do you plan to do in the meantime? No outsiders are allowed into Bulwark."

"There hasn't been a vote yet. And as long as I'm Doyen, 'I' decide who's allowed in."

Unsatisfied, he shook his head as his eyes narrowed, "That's a security risk—"

"Deal with it. She's coming." Destan put his foot down as he began to glare and grit his teeth. "It's not like I'd be bringing her to Deep Dark. She's going to just be in and around my suite at first. And even if

I let her have free rein of Bulwark as a whole… I trust her more than I trust you. She is my wife. I trust her with my life — quite literally. So with that in mind, I expect you to get your mind wrapped around the fact: if you are going to have me, she's going to be right beside me to some extent."

"A complete outsider has 'never' been allowed into the Veil." He started bickering; his eyes flashing. "Are you mad? We're 'this' close—"

"I said to some extent, Fidus. Geez! But what would it matter if she was? I wasn't 'supposed' to get married in the first place and yet here we are. Just because that's the way things have been does 'not' mean that's the best way or how they need to continue. You may see her as a weakness or even a distraction but she's made me stronger, Fidus."

This comeback put some things into perspective even if it was in a bit of a brazen manner.

After a while, a stern warning was given, "It will be up to 'you' to convince the Veil — not me."

"Look. I'm not asking you to stand beside me and hold my hand. What I 'am' asking is that you respect my wishes as any decent human being would. I'm staying with her until I explain everything." Destan eyed him with the same seriousness as when he stared down Toreon. "The Veil will just have to wait. I mean they've waited for almost ten months. A few more hours or even a day or two more won't kill them."

"How did things go with your mission?"

And there went his last ounce of emotional strength; not to mention his physical endurance, "Fidus, I'll have the full debriefing at some point soon. There's nothing so pressing that can't wait until then. That's an order."

He took the firm but equally desperate hint; nodding as he got up and left.

I should've thought of that sooner. ~ Well, it's done now and you got your answer you wanted. ~ True.

It wasn't but a few minutes before they were at cruising altitude. While it wasn't horrible there in the seat, the lounge in the back of the jet had a bed… which of course sounded much better. The flight was going to be over three hours, so there was plenty of time to take a short nap. He struggled and complained as he got to his feet, Doctor Gerould overhearing this commotion and offering his assistance, "Your wrists can't take much more."

"I'm fine Lance. … I don't have to— ah, geez!" He stumbled back and slammed into the door of the lounge; hissing as he growled under his breath.

"Destan please let me—"

"No! Leave us alone."

℥

Just being where he couldn't see anyone made his circumstances much more bearable. Destan took a grunting breath as he leaned against the wall by the door, staying there for a rather long time.

When he could stand it, he hissed as he pushed off the wall, jogging to the bed on the other side of the room.

He tripped right as he got to it; his eyes bugging out as he threw his hands out to catch himself. There was silence in the air, but one that only made you want to scream. Tears streaked down his face that was burned with pain and agony; him doing his best to quickly shift his weight so he would fall beside Callimay and not on top of her.

Out of breath and his thoughts clouded by pain, Destan lay there and worked to keep his emotions under control. No one had to remind him how dangerous he could be in an enclosed space like this jet… and without Callimay to try and keep him reined in.

Before much longer, Destan took a deep and shaky breath, now knowing he was out of danger. His green eyes strained to focus as he looked up at the ceiling, so he let his head roll over to the side: *How do I— I never wanted you to know about this. I know we've been though things just as dangerous, but I want to give you a life like what Rej has given Tabitha. … I want to do what 'you' want; whatever it is.*

Destan wanted to do what he could to clean Callimay's face at least, but there wasn't any way he could. While it wasn't the end of the world by any means, this triggered a feeling of helplessness and the extension of his inability to protect her.

Hearing the voices outside, his focus shifted. He winced and hissed as he pulled Callimay to him, calling out in a weak voice, "Raven? Let me know when we're in Bulwark airspace. … And lock the door."

15

"Very well, Doyen." The plane's AI, a female, responded.

What do I do, Calli? He asked choked up as he kept watch over her. *God? I… I don't know what to do.*

For as much as this fear paralyzed him, it also drained him; drained him to the point of utter exhaustion. It wasn't until almost four hours later that Destan had a rude awakening when the jet's AI announced, "Bulwark airspace reached. Touchdown in thirty."

At first he didn't respond, but then his eyes popped open and he gasped. When he tried to move, he yelled out, looking at his clenched fists: *Why does this keep happening! Ah geez! What the— let go!*

A knock came on the door, followed by concerned questions, "Destan, what's wrong? Destan?"

"I… I'm— unlock the door, Raven." He finally conceded; rolling away from Callimay as he writhed in pain.

"What is it?" Doctor Gerould rushed over.

"It's my hands," he hissed as he rocked back and forth.

"Well, just relax them and I'll—"

"I can't!" He yelled; his eyes flashing as he shook his fists.

"Alright," Doctor Gerould put his hands out to calm him and started thinking as fast as he could. "Let me… let me try to do something to get the pain under control. Hang on."

He ran out and came back with Fidus and Redje; Tabitha standing at the door looking horrified. It took these two men every ounce of strength they had to keep Destan still enough so the injection Doctor Gerould had could be administered. While it was a fast-acting and powerful pain killer, it still needed time to get into Destan's system.

In a strained and almost terrified voice, Destan got out in between his painful fits of rage, "Get me away from Calli. I don't want to hurt her. … Do it now!"

The nonverbal communication between Redje and Tabitha during this all told a terrifying story of its own. They both knew what Destan "told" them, but they had no idea this is what it could "look" like. In a way, they both felt insensitive for brushing off what he'd talked about with them so many times. It was true that they couldn't comprehend what he was saying until they actually saw it. There was no way to describe what they were seeing.

"How much longer do you think, Mender?"

"Almost there Fidus. Just give it another minute. — Doing alright?"

"Yeah," Redje said a bit labored as he kept a strong hold on Destan's left arm.

"We'll be beginning our decent into Bulwark within a couple minutes," they heard Rocher on the com as the jet began to lean to the right. "I've been informed the Veil is assembled and awaiting Doyen."

"I'll go tell him," Tabitha said in almost a screech before Doctor Gerould could even get a word out.

She came back as fast as she could, stopping at the door as she worked to catch her breath. Redje ran over and took her hand, "It's okay Tabby. Sit down and rest."

"Dest—"

"He's gonna be alright."

"Wh… what happened?" She whispered, gripping his arm as he led her along.

"Not even Doctor Gerould knows. He said Destan yelled out about not being able to loosen his fists. … Now just sit and relax. I'll go talk with Rocher. A… are you doing alright?"

"He's okay… right?"

Redje got down on a knee and framed his wife's face with his hands, "He's fine, Tabby Bae. Sore and really sorry he caused such a scene, but he'll make it through. He specifically said that his emotions are in a much safer place now so we can relax."

"I shouldn't be so worried, but I—"

"It's alright." He squeezed her quivering hand that she'd put over her baby bump. "And even though he is able to do much more 'damage' now with what the Society did, don't you 'ever' think he can push past me and come after you. If it came to that, I promise you I would keep you safe; just like I always have. Please don't cry."

She fought her sobs as she bit her lip, "H… how's Callimay?"

He sighed as he smiled: *There's my Tabby Bae. Such a trooper.* "She's still out, but Doctor Gerould said she's showing signs of coming around… as crazy as that sounds since she got a five. — Now just stay here. Fidus said he'll call for help if something happens. I'm going to go talk with Rocher and see if he can pull some strings to get the Veil to back off for a bit so Destan can regroup. I think we both know it's best he has as much time to level off as possible. I'll be back in a bit."

ℬ

Rocher wanted to be with Destan, but maned his post and kept them in a holding pattern. Everyone was awake by now but kept quiet: they knew something happened since they weren't landing, the air in the room was beyond heavy, and there were a couple Veils missing. They exchanged concerned glances with Redje or Tabitha since they were calm; their eyes asking what they didn't dare utter out loud.

The door to the lounge was still closed; Doctor Gerould and Fidus staying with Destan this whole time. While he was out of immediate danger with regards to his emotions, he knew he could easily "relapse" if the pain from his wrists got any worse. — Yes, he was still in pain even after the shot he got. — It stood out to Fidus how calm Doctor Gerould was about this all; reminding him that he'd been with Destan longer and better understood the situation.

"You said this has happened before?"

Destan took a deep breath and closed his eyes as Doctor Gerould kept working on his wrist, sounding a bit lethargic, "Yeah, twice. The only thing I could think of that was the same both times was that I was having a nightmare." *The same one I've had for over twenty years.*

"How did you get them to release those two times?"

"I kept shaking them and then using my thumbs to try and pry them apart. — Ah! — And then I'd sit there for a few minutes and massage them and constantly move them so the pain would go away for good."

"Were these two times after you came back from the Society?"

"Yeah. — Are we in a holding pattern?" He asked confused when he realized the jet kept taking quarter turns to the left.

"Until I say we can land." Doctor Gerould nodded; finishing when Destan started staring at him, "I guess we're good. — Fidus?"

"I'll let Sentinel know." He whipped around and left.

With what happened, for as much as he wanted to, Destan knew he wasn't going to be able to carry Callimay. His suite was far too long of a walk once inside Bulwark.

But who could he trust with her?

Seeing this inner conflict written all over his face and putting two and two together, Doctor Gerould offered, "Let me help, Destan."

In a knee-jerk reaction, he whipped his head around and snapped, "No! I'll make it."

"Destan Quinton, y— you're barely going to make it that far on your own. I don't even know if you 'will' make it under your own power. You know good and well you can't carry her in the condition you are. Let me help you. … We're not against you, regardless of how things were handled. People who don't know about the serums are going to react this way to some extent; you should have seen Redje and Tabitha earlier. … Just give them time and be willing to prove again and again to them she's everything they couldn't imagine possible. … And you know I mean that in a good way."

He hung his head as he rolled over and groaned as he got up; saying under his breath, "A… alright."

Even though the man taking her was a dear friend — and a doctor at that — Destan was finicky about how he was holding her. Doctor Gerould knew he was just paranoid about keeping her safe in the vulnerable state she was in; him making every effort to adjust to how Destan felt comfortable.

Everyone glanced back when the door opened and Destan came out, a sigh of relief refreshing the air. Doctor Gerould followed close behind and laid Callimay in his arms after he sat down and was comfortable, "I'll carry her until we get to your suite. Or better yet, you can go with me straight to the infirmary and Confrere can carry her."

"He's got Tabitha to look after. I'll make sure she's alright before I go with you," he replied in a daze.

❦

Rocher landed the jet with the finesse he was known for; it being just one of the earmarks of the mastery level of which Destan constantly strove for.

With wheels on the ground, everyone was on edge; them scurrying around and filing out in quick succession as soon as the hatch opened. Rocher came out before long but only looking back for a nod of both approval and confirmation that Destan and Callimay were alright.

"Just… just don't let her go, Lance." He fumbled to say; part of him not wanting to let her go. "If you—"

"I know you're worried, but I know for a fact that no one's going to hurt her, Destan. I'll go slow so you can stay right beside her, alright?"

After checking to see if she was awake, Doctor Gerould took her. It wasn't his smartest decision, but Destan practically jumped to his feet so he could keep up; him right behind the two of them as they came down the stairs.

Doctor Gerould heard the sound of something — someone — tumbling down the steps and turned to see Destan on his knees practically; Fidus supporting him so he wasn't putting any weight on his wrists, "Let me help, Doyen."

He was hoping Destan would be more open to help, but it appeared he needed the "hard lesson" method again: *Why don't you just injure yourself so I can 'make' you stay in bed? That'd be so much easier on everyone… including yourself.*

"I may have hurt my standing with you, but I 'am' on your side." Fidus affirmed; Destan still resisting his help and trying to keep up with Doctor Gerould who started off.

Another stumble tugged at the hearts of those who were standing guard; them looking concerned and creeping forward. — It was either accept defeat and be with Callimay or be stubborn and left on the apron to welcome the early sun's rays. A classic example of the age-long internal battle man has always had to fight: humility vs pride.

❦

When they eventually got to the suite, Doctor Gerould made a point to double-check Destan's bandages and see what needed to be done, "Well it could be worse. Let's get you to the— Doyen!"

"What?" He jerked back, his voice almost shrill.

"You need to come to the infirmary."

"Not now. I feel much better."

Trying to keep the situation from escalating but unwilling to back down, Doctor Gerould reached out and took hold of his arm; sounding irritated, "Destan you've taken a pretty bad beating overall. It's not just your wrists. Have you forgotten what almost happened on Raven? Or what about the advice I gave over a month ago about you keeping yourself healthy so you could protect Callimay? Do you seriously think you could protect her if something happened right now?"

He looked at his wrists and then Callimay; finally answering as he hung his head, "No."

"We'll stay with her, Destan." Tabitha offered as she looked back at Redje; them standing at the door this entire time.

"I'll come for you if she even 'looks' like she's coming 'round." Redje nodded as Destan ushered them in. "Go get your wrists taken care of. It'll help Callimay if she sees you in a better condition than this when she first wakes up."

He sighed as he took her hand in his; secretly trying to control the pain of even that much effort, "The first sign…"

"I'll let Nexus know and come for you myself." Redje encouraged as he patted his shoulder. "Now go get yourself looked at. You need it."

Destan consented with an undertone of resentment; leaving with Fidus and Doctor Gerould at a somber and slow pace.

ℬ

The two dear friends of Destan sat huddled together by the window and kept bobbing their focus between each other and the young woman they'd both come to love, and knew meant the world to their best friend. On occasion, Tabitha would get up and check on Callimay; her face looking more and more concerned each time, "What's wrong?"

"I… I'm just worried, Redje."

"Doctor Gerould knows what he's doing. He's been taking care of her this whole time." He comforted as she sat down and took his hand.

She squeezed it as she leaned against him; interrupted by the door opening. They whipped their heads around, relieved to see Destan. He wasn't by any means what he looked like at the ball just a little over a day prior, but the pained look in his eyes was gone and he looked refreshed… even though there seemed to be a hint of pain still left in his voice, "How is she?"

"No change," Redje shook his head.

"Tabitha?"

"Yes Destan?"

"When I go for my debriefing… could you stay with Calli?"

"Of course I will, Destan. I'll do whatever I can."

"Thank you guys so much," he let a shivering breath of relief out as he sat beside his sleeping wife. "I… I'll call you when I need you."

"We'll be close by — surveillance — whenever you're ready." Redje led Tabitha over and stopped beside him. "Do 'you' need anything?"

"Just her." *Just her, God. Please. …* "Do you two—"

"Don't worry about us." He smiled as he gripped his shoulder. "We'll drop some food by in a bit. — Everything's going to work out the way it needs to. Have faith and do the right thing no matter what."

❦

For the next hour, Destan held Callimay and tried to figure out how he was going to explain to her what was going on and where she was. The Shadows didn't deal with just one small group of lunatics like those at the Society. This was a completely different ballgame than what even Callimay understood concerning the history he gave her about the Eradication and such. This battle was being waged against the most ruthless governmental group ever known on Quidoria: the Syndicate. Nothing was guaranteed in his "job" except that his life was in jeopardy one-hundred percent of the time.

As promised, Redje and Tabitha dropped some food off; being optimistic enough to have some for Callimay as well. He was grateful for their constant concern and apologized for his lack of reciprocation.

Of course they replied that they were glad to help and understood he was under quite a bit of stress from several different fronts at the time, "We know that even if caller's warning had been sounded you'd be there in a heartbeat for us. … Do you need us to stay for a bit?"

"Thanks Rej but I just need some time right now."

"I know I don't have the answers you need right now, Destan," he sighed as he took Tabitha and Destan's hands. "But I know 'Who' does. … Do you want me to start?"

"Please," Destan nodded as he took Tabitha's hand and they all bowed their heads.

❦

Once they left he was doing so much better. He ate some, but his appetite was understandably suffering because of what he had to do.

All these thoughts racing through his mind didn't help: the reality Callimay would be thrown for another loop concerning her husband; not to mention the high probability she was going to react in a "bad" way. The more he allowed this rehearsal to play out in his mind, the more he started overthinking everything. And this was only made worse when he felt her push against his chest and heard her moan.

Destan asked scared as he pushed her hair out of her face, "Calli?"

Frozen with dread, he lay there and waited those few, long minutes as she worked to fight off the sedative. As much as he wanted to hear her voice, the moment she started talking he wanted her to go back to sleep. He wasn't ready to tell her.

"Good morning," she rubbed her smiling face before draping her arms across his chest; sounding fuzzy and happy even though she was groggy, "I don't know about you, but my sleep schedule getting thrown off like that 'really' came back to bite me: what a messed up nightmare I had! You woke me up super early and dragged me out of the house while shots rang out. Tabitha, Redje, 'and' Rose had been gunned down in their yard. And if that wasn't enough, you drove like a madman into the middle of nowhere where you fought Baleck. I thought he killed you but it turned out Ginger was there and made me see the whole thing. … Oh! At one point you told me Toreon killed Tabitha, Redje, and Rose. That should've tipped me off it was a dream, but oh no, not me. And then there was this part about you locking me in the car somehow; it talking to me after I hit this hidden button in the clutch. — Now I've gotta say the pain I felt from breaking my nails to get that stupid lid open sure felt real. — Then after we fought with them for a while and I discovered a new ability, there was this guy dressed just like you when you would wear your all-black outfit. He was pretty mean to me. And then something hit me in the neck and everything went black. … Quite the 'story', huh?"

There wasn't any answer, but she didn't think much of it. Maybe he wasn't awake yet. She didn't have her eyes open since her eyelids felt so heavy but she could feel his emotions churning in a frantic way, "I didn't mean to upset you by—"

"It's good to see you, Calli. So good to see you." He sighed as he ran his fingers through her hair.

His emotions backed off, but something still wasn't right… and it didn't take her long to realize, "Your face! Y— Destan was that real!"

Lord please help me. He took a deep breath and sat up, reaching out to calm her while he did his best to keep his voice and movements low key and quiet, "Everything's alright. Just take a deep breath, Calli."

"So it 'was' real? Everything that— that means— who are you!" She yelped as she fell off the bed while trying to get away; scrambling to her feet and running to the far wall where she pinned herself against it.

"Calli it's me. Destan." He said tender as he got up and started over; still limping.

"That's not what the other man said."

"Please let me—"

"Why do you keep lying to me?" She shrieked as she slapped his face. "You're worse than Toreon 'ever' was to me. At least he was open about treating me like dirt. Y— you've gotten me to care for you and fall for your cleaver little scheme! Why are you so… so cruel!"

The slap hurt, but her words cut far deeper, "Calli I didn't lie. I haven't lied to you once this whole time. I'm sorry if you think I did. — I didn't offer all this information because I wanted to protect you. Doing this type of job isn't safe, Calli."

"What did I say about keeping me in the dark?" She said furious as the look on her face changed. *What are you doing! He could hurt— 'kill' you if he felt like it! … We've gotta get out of here. Now!*

She saw the door and dashed there; throwing it open. Callimay was crying, so she couldn't see that well; but when she turned to see who was talking she just couldn't believe it, "T… Tabitha? Redje? Y… you were dead! I saw you on the lawn!"

"Oh thank goodness you're alright," the sweet voice of the friend she knew couldn't be alive called out as she ran over, a bright smile on her face.

Scared to death, Callimay took off in the other direction down the long hall with high ceilings and natural stone walls. The way it "felt" they must be in a hotel or resort… which meant at the end of the hall would be a staircase leading to the lobby and freedom.

But as she got closer to the end, she didn't see an exit sign or a door for that matter. And then there were a couple younger men who rounded the corner and stopped dead in their tracks when they saw her. Callimay froze for a moment, seeing what they were wearing: their outfits looked like that man she remembered seeing!

Things kept spiraling out of control. She pushed by them, not knowing where she was going and not caring; she just wanted away. If she kept running long enough, surely she'd find an exit and be able to get out. — This building had to have a door somewhere! — Her vision started blurring and her balance gave way; her tripping and stumbling into the wall before falling.

When she regained her faculties, she wheezed as she got to her feet; more hysterical each time it happened. Why wasn't there any door for a staircase? Where was she!

Was this whole escapade of any good? Deslan could outrun her without even using his ability, and probably even with him injured. How could she think she ever had a prayer of getting away from him?

After what felt like an eternity of running through this endless maze of halls, her not hearing anyone following her, she came across an exposed flight of stairs that led to a door. The moment she opened it, a blaring alarm sounded, "Unauthorized entry. Unauthorized entry. Level one, quadrant three. Unauthorized entry. All available personnel report. Blood moon threat. I repeat, blood moon threat."

Callimay looked back in fear at the small group of people who rounded a corner and locked their stern, piercing gazes on her. "Blood moon" must mean something horrible; their drawing knives made her feel like she was some deranged animal that was being hunted.

She whipped her head around and saw the outside world. At least out there she'd have a chance.

It was still dark, but she could smell salt water in the air, knew the ground was stone of some kind, and there was not a tree within any reasonable distance. Even though she didn't know where she was or which way would lead to safety, she knew standing still was much more dangerous. So, she took off for the distant tree line. Already feeling exhausted scared her even more, but she just couldn't give up; she was too close to where she could find a hiding place.

Not too much later she collapsed; her neck starting to throb where she recalled being hit by something before she lost consciousness. What hit her? Was her grogginess due to it? Was it a drug dart? — Hitting the cold stone ground wasn't in any way pleasant, but she repeated it a couple more times as she fought and clawed to get to safety.

She made it to the grassy area right before the tree line but didn't know there was a ravine between her and it. Callimay tried to keep herself from yelping in fear, but she was caught off guard.

This last tumble was it; she didn't have the strength to get back up. By this point, she could hear someone running toward her: *Don't say anything. Don't move. Try not to breathe so hard. ~ Maybe they won't see me. ~ We've got to hide!*

A quick glance around showed a crevice in the overhang of the top of the ravine. She pulled herself to it and pinned herself against the ground wall; hearing the person above her panting and heaving. There wasn't any sound for a few seconds… and then they dropped down right in front of her, making her clap her hand over her mouth to keep her yelp from being heard. Her efforts didn't work; the person starting to search for her in a frenzy.

At first all she could see was from just above their knees down… but when they put their hand at their side she knew who it was: *Destan!*

He looked just as terrified as his voice sounded; him gripping his side as he hobbled back and forth while wheezing, "Calli? Calli please! Calli I won't hurt you! No one will. I promise. They just don't— Calli! Calli let me explain. Please!"

Closing your eyes never made you invisible, but what else could she do? She heard him plodding back and forth and then silence: *He's staring right at me. I can feel it!*

Nothing happened.

Slowly but surely she opened her eyes and saw she was alone. Callimay slumped her shoulders and tried to catch her breath; looking like this was the first breath she'd taken since she fell where she was.

This reprieve didn't last, though. Two others dropped down together quickly followed by almost a half dozen more. — What in the world? There wasn't any sound that would suggest any person was running in that direction; let alone this many!

There was a woman who spoke up in a rushed but calm and highly professional manner, "Doyen's headed for the trap, I'm sure. That's the first place he'd want to cross off the list."

"Agreed. She can't be far. The verge hasn't been tripped." A gruff voice Callimay recognized — one of the original two who jumped down — called out to the others. "Fan out in a mile radius, leaving the trap to Traceur and myself. Have your beacons set to receive. If you find her, activate it. Report back at caller's warning regardless. We don't need to add insult to injury."

A roll of hushed acknowledgements swept the group which had grown to almost two dozen at this point.

The black-laden individuals then dispersed, not a trace of them within a few seconds. They vanished — noise and all.

Just

Like

Shadows!

Once she felt like no one was nearby, Callimay started to come out of hiding. But then another individual jumped down, followed by another, "Where could she have gone, Redje?"

"Not far. Not in her condition, anyway. And we both know Destan can't last that long either." He replied worried as he started rushing around. "Stay close. We don't have much time before caller's warning. I just wish we could've gotten out sooner—"

"Where are you doing? We should catch up with Destan." She asked as he started searching not but twenty feet from where Callimay was hiding.

"Tabby you know just as well as I do that Callimay isn't the type to run when she's scared… well, at least not if she has a place to hide."

She grabbed his arm as he started to kneel right where the woman they were searching for was, "But didn't Destan say she 'had' on a few occasions? And then when we were inside? Redje I don't think she's here. The poor thing looked so terrified."

He sighed and gave his wife a hug, sounding like he was trying to calm himself down, "Alright. We'll do it your way. … I just hope we find her before anyone else does. By the threat level they assign— we've gotta act fast, Tabby."

"We need to get Destan away from the trap. He's in no condition to be around it."

Redje said determined as he took her hand, "Come on."

Now Callimay didn't want to leave. Every time she tried, someone else came along. She didn't know how many more scares she could take and not be found.

Ten minutes passed and nothing happened. No one new showed up and no one came back. There wasn't even the sound of a bird or woodland creature to be heard the entire time. So, feeling more confident and rested, she crawled out and took off.

Callimay was still sore and disoriented, but her adrenaline was at max capacity. She still had no idea where she was and whether or not she was heading in a direction that would take her to safety or not… or if there was anywhere safe to go. The air around her felt so humid while at the same time cold; a strange fog clinging to everything in sight. This misty barrier made her feel like someone was hiding behind each tree; especially after seeing everyone disappear like they did. It was unnerving how stealth and fluid they moved.

It then dawned on her that she'd seen Destan move like that on a few occasions and it made her that much more upset with him: *Calli?*

Not that he could "track" her by using her ability, but she didn't want to hear his voice. She didn't care if she never heard it again or saw his face. At this point, Callimay didn't want anyone near her. There wasn't anyone left to trust.

She looked up to the sky as she mouthed something; seeing it was beginning to show signs of daylight. It would be getting easier for her to move, but as she looked around, something felt vaguely familiar about the area: *Oh no. I— this is where I—*

"Callimay," a familiar voice called out. "Oh thank goodness we found you!"

ᛏ

Her head felt like it was being whipped around as she started waking up; Callimay reaching out, searching for something solid she could grip. It was the only way she knew to get this turntable feeling to stop: her forcing her mind to understand it was stationary.

But what — who's hand — she found wasn't what she wanted. She gasped and bugged out her eyes, seeing Destan sitting beside her, "Get away from me!"

"Calli please," he said choked up as he had his hand shoved away.

She moaned as she stumbled toward the window wall that led to a balcony, Destan running after her to keep her from falling off. He was almost sobbing as he wrapped his arms around her; partially because he was in so much physical pain but mainly because of the emotional torment he was in, "I love you, Calli. I always have. And I always will. Nothing's changed. Please. Just— let me explain things. If you still hate me after that then fine, I won't make you stay; but please give me a chance. Please, Calli. I'm begging you."

She fought him for a while and then started to calm when she saw him crying. Callimay heard his labored breathing and remembered at that point what he'd been through; and yet she wasn't about to let her guard down. She closed her eyes and looked away, asking in a quiet and harsh tone, "Where are we?"

"Ferdinan."

Where you have 'friends' in the government. … Makes sense. She rolled her eyes as she sighed.

Destan took a big, deep breath and looked her in the eye; trying to sound calm and confident, "Before I say 'anything', I need you to be sure in knowing nothing's changing between the two of us. You're my wife and I love you more than my own life. I know this is all new and frightening, but I'm still here. I still love you. Okay?"

The response he was given only made his emotional torture worse: stone cold silence.

"W… we're here in Ferdinan because it… Calli I… we're… we're where the Bulwark of the Shadows is. You remember the button I told you to hit when I was fighting Baleck? That was a distress signal: a flare. Since I 'called for help', my fellow Shadows brought me here where it's the safest for—"

"What happened? Who are you?"

"I don't know everything yet about what all ended up happening; but I do know that Ginger and Baleck are gone."

"'Gone' gone?"

"Yes. — And then, as I understand it, you were given a high-dosage tranquilizer because they were scared of you." *Well, 'are' scared.* "Once they got everything taken care of, we all flew here as soon as we got back to Rayleen. … Calli? Calli this is truly what my 'job' is. I…" Destan stopped and tried to figure out how to say what he now knew he should have told her before he even asked her to marry him; cringing as he grieved, "I oversee a network of people across the world who are dedicated to protecting those of us who are left-handed; willfully disobeying the International Law every, single, day. — Doyen, the name on that note that you thought was just bad handwriting? Well, it wasn't a mistake. It is my official title in this organization. Your good friend Fairove was correct about me having a 'fancy' name. I'm so glad he didn't overhear you saying Doyen. And he was right about my coat. 'How' he knew I'm not sure, but so many people are Informants that it's hard to keep track. — What you've been calling my duster is actually my veil. It's what a special group of us in the Shadows wear. We perform various missions of espionage against the Syndi—"

"Wait… what?" She shook her head and pushed him away. "So you're telling me you're the leader of a group of spies? You go around killing Synd—"

"Calli, we don't go around killing Falconers and members of the Syndicate for sport or like some spy organizations do. We do everything to avoid that. That's never our mission. We'd just be acting like them if we did." He tried to explain as he followed her back inside.

"But you just said Baleck and Ginger—".

"That was only done because I was in immediate danger. … Like when we were in Faberton."

"Fab— you mean 'they' were the ones who killed Toreon and Webb? … Was that man who found us the same person I heard that night?" Callimay asked terrified as she stumbled backed; hitting the wall. "How long has he been following you— us?"

"He wasn't the exact one who pulled the trigger that time, and I'm not sure if he's the one you heard or not. And… he's been mirroring me since April when Rocher was injured."

"Who are you!" She screamed as she burst into tears; wailing as she gripped the wall.

"Calli?" Destan begged as he hobbled over. "Calli I haven't changed. It's still me. I'll always love you no matter what. Please believe me when I say that."

"Why didn't you tell me about any of this?" She staggered to the other side of the room; trying to stay away from him.

"I… I just wanted to protect you. I thought… I thought it would be better this way: that if you didn't know you'd be safer. I didn't want you to worry about all of this on top of everything else. I was doing this all so I could keep you safe. I was doing this because I love you."

"I… how… why… w…" she stuttered as she slid down the wall and buried her head in her hands.

Destan wanted to take her in his arms and hold her but he could tell she was hesitant when he kneeled beside her. There was now a clear boundary of comfort that she'd put up; one he wasn't allowed in to. While she was letting him stay closer than he thought she would, he felt as if he were a million miles away from her.

He was the cause of this pain she was going through. He was hurting her on one of the deepest levels. He basically threw her off of White Cove again… and she was violently reacting to his actions — or lack in this case.

But as it was then, he couldn't blame her now. The only thing he wanted at that moment was for her to not feel alone and scared. How was he supposed to show her, though, if she wouldn't give him the chance to?

A few minutes passed; the two of them worried and torn in different ways over the same reality. Callimay had calmed from the hysterical high she was in which made Destan feel better, but her being quiet equally concerned him. When he was about to say something, she mumbled under her breath, "How long have you been a Doyen; or whatever you call yourself."

"I've been a Shadow since I was sixteen. I was made a Veil when I turned twenty and then handed the reins of Doyen when I turned twenty-two."

She began to shiver as she asked in a timid voice, her eyes stricken with terror, "How many people have you… killed?"

"None, Calli. God's blessed on that front the entire time."

Another moment of profound silence.

And yet this silence wasn't so weighty. There was a glimmer of hope he could see. She was slowly processing everything in a more rational way. Her willingness to ask questions was the biggest relief to him — she was talking to him, "Why did you join?"

"I guess you could say it's a family business since both my mother and father's sides were involved in it to some extent for quite a while." He explained as he let his small smile jump out; opening his hand to her as he continued, "As bad as this might sound, I wasn't given a choice to join — it was just something expected of me. Now I never resented it or felt at any point that I didn't want to join. In fact, I was itching to get into it: when Rocher asked me what I wanted to do with my life I said I wanted to stop this stupidity the Syndicate was spreading." *I know I used a different word instead of stupidity, but that's the past.* "But for as 'good' as that motivation was I found out over time that it wasn't right. I had reality splash me in the face like the ocean on the coastline not but a week into it: the first solo run I was sent on. It was to retrieve a politically high-profile teenage girl whose twin sister was mistaken for her and executed just days prior to drop. Her mother was even executed for trying to defend her. With her father's role in the government and his connection to the Shadows he didn't want to leave and lose what he felt was so important to the livelihood of his daughter. So, he called us to take her to safety. She was frightened out of her mind when her and her father showed up at the drop point — and rightly so. But when I saw the look of desperation that her father was doing his best to hide, the fear in his voice as he said his goodbyes, and the tears he shed after she was far enough away she couldn't see; I realized this was so much more than 'proving them wrong'. Actual lives were — are — at stake; innocent people of all ages are being murdered. Families are being torn apart because of this seclusion, secrecy, and fear. I realized I had an obligation that couldn't be taught. There was a reality that was only seen in the eyes of those who were living through it. I never saw it because I'd been 'protected' the entire time. I didn't know what it was like to 'live' really. What I dedicated myself to had the potential to impact the world to teach them to help others; not just 'don't do wrong'. I found in that brief encounter that there was so much good that could come from being a Shadow. ... And you know what? That girl I helped save? You know her."

"What?"

"It's Tabitha."

"You're kidding me."

"She was the one who made me stop and think about things; about God. Rej did too, but what I saw with her and her father — knowing they were Christians — scared and left me in awe. They were scared, but then they weren't. It was odd, but so captivating."

"So... so this is like the underground railroad from our ancient history class?" She asked with uncertainty in her expression and tone; her eyes getting wider as more things started falling into place.

"Not 'exactly' the same, but there are similarities." Destan nodded as she gripped his hand.

Callimay shied away as he put his other atop hers, rushing over to the window and pacing back and forth.

At first Destan followed her, but stopped when he realized what she was doing. These next few minutes were going to be hard, but he had to let her decide for herself. She wasn't screaming at him — so there was that — but the look in her eyes made him concerned. Was his openness too late in coming? Did he end up destroying what he thought he had been working so hard to preserve and protect?

There wasn't any change Destan could see, and he just couldn't bear to listen to her. Minutes slipped by, one by one like the endless waves that could be heard below them. Unable to wait any longer, he asked in a strained and quiet voice, "Calli... Calli, what do you want me to do?"

She stopped and looked up with a worried expression, like what his Calli would from hearing his voice like that, "What do you mean?"

"Do you want to stay here or go ho—"

"Fidus and Sentinel are on their way, Doyen," a voice called out.

He cringed as he closed his eyes and sighed: *Why now! We were 'just' about there! Really! I just—* "Alright Nexus. Contact Helpmate and tell her to report here."

"Affirmative."

"Who..." Callimay shrieked as she pinned herself against the wall. "Who was that? Or 'what' was that?"

So close! So close and yet so far. Not that it mattered now, though. All he could do was start over.

"It's alright," he came over and reached out to brush the side of her face; her flinching and pulling away. "Easy, Calli. It's me. No one's going to hurt you. I promise. … That was the— well I guess you could call her the 'switchboard operator'. That's what you call the phone liaison in Faberton, right?"

She was still timid, but nodded as she tried to hold back tears and keep a stiff upper lip; the poor thing looked like a frightened child.

Destan took a step back and gave her some space, hoping with everything that he would have enough time to at least gain her simple trust back before he left. He just wanted her to see he hadn't changed toward her; that he still loved her.

Precious moments slipped by: Callimay reeling from the hard slap of reality she'd been given while Destan was trying to keep himself from being torn apart by his two duties which didn't feel compatible.

He inched closer, asking worried, "Calli? Calli I have to go for a little bit but I promise you I'll be back just as fast as I can. … Tabitha's coming so she can stay with you. That is if you'd like her to stay."

Silence. Cold, dead, tormenting silence.

"Ca—"

The pain of her running into him so fast hurt like none other. She clung to him as she sobbed, not uttering a single word. There was the lingering reality that she wasn't sure about this all when Destan went to stroke her hair and she flinched, but she stayed with him.

A lonely tear of pain dragged down his face, but her making that decision and showing him that he was still her "safe place" made it worth it. He knew this wouldn't last long and held every second he had with her dear: he had her back in his arms.

Then the dreaded sounds of heavy footsteps came.

Destan grimaced, the pangs in his heart searing his chest as he let her go and hobbled to the door. He spoke with the man Callimay remembered seeing before she passed out; Rocher being there as well. They were stoic as they spoke in hushed tones; Rocher not even acknowledging she snuck up and was huddled behind Destan. Well, not until Tabitha showed up.

After a brief comment to Destan, Tabitha came in and offered a hug to her dear friend, "I'm so glad you're awake, Callimay."

She clutched her arms across her chest and turned; avoiding looking at her, "Hi."

"Calli?" Destan called out.

"Yes?" She whipped around and ran to him.

"I love you." He smiled and gave her a kiss. "I'll be back in a bit. How about y—"

Please don't go. She cried as she gripped his wrist.

I… I have to, Calli. I'd take you with me but I can't. I'm sorry. I won't be long. I promise.

"A… alright," she bowed her head and stepped back, letting go. "Oh no! I… I forgot all about y—"

He calmed her as he waved the two men at the door on, wiping his distraught wife's face, "I'm banged up but I'm alright."

"But I—"

"If it helps you feel safer, to grip my wrist like you did, then I'll gladly deal with the pain."

"But you're crying. It hurt—"

"I want you to feel safe and know you can come to me for protection no matter what's going on, where we are, or how good I feel. Okay? … Okay. Now I'll be back in a bit. Tabitha said she'd stay around as long as you need her to." He paused, part of him still not wanting to leave.

"Is something wrong?"

"I… Calli, are you okay?"

Fidus called out, the irritation in his voice making the air quiver.

Callimay stepped back and looked away as she wrung her hands, not saying a word. And yet this was her nonverbal way of screaming that she wasn't happy… and he knew it.

"I… I love you, Calli. You can talk to me while I'm gone if you need to. … Does that sound good? … Calli?"

His name was called out again, Callimay closing off even more.

Doyen started vying for "top spot" inside of Destan; he already got him to forget that he was stanch about staying with Callimay until she felt safe and knew what was going on… but the leach wasn't satisfied until he had his "host" under his thumb completely. It wasn't until

Fidus stormed up and started talking in a cruel tone that Destan's mind was made up: Callimay turned away and scurried to the other side of the room as he turned away and shut the door.

℈

In a way she felt betrayed as she curled up next to the window; as far away from the door and every human being she could see. It appeared every one of Destan's "friends" wasn't who she thought they were. Well at least that appeared to be the case with Redje, Tabitha, Doctor Gerould, and Rocher. Was there something else they were hiding from her to keep her "safe"? What more astonishing bombshells could they drop on her? Why didn't she notice anything "wrong"? There had to be something: *Am I just 'that' stupid and naïve? ~ What was there to be suspicious of? ~ I've always known there was something… well, something 'off' about Destan. And I'm not just talking about the clothes he wore; though you've gotta admit things make sense now about that. ~ I'm not arguing that point, but what was 'off' about him? What happened to always wanting people to be their own individual self? I thought that's part of what drew you to him? ~ Well I just thought— I don't know!*

Tabitha hung back for a while, knowing the best thing she could do was let Callimay have complete control of the situation; she needed to have some sense of control over things around her. It was the least she could do.

There was a haze over everything outside since it was cloudy and raining. The foaming waves endlessly rose and fell, crashing into the jagged ocean-front at the base of the cliffside directly below. Callimay silently cried as so many things ran through her mind. It was almost an hour before anything was said.

So much for Destan only being gone for a "little bit".

Callimay let a sigh drag off her lips as she stared at the endless ocean that lay before her, "Why did Destan have to leave?"

"Well, he has to get back up to speed on things since he is the leader of the Shadows and he's been gone for over nine months. I'm sure he'll have a few meetings at some point to brief everyone about what's all happened since he left."

"Like what?"

"I'm not sure about what they'll talk about 'entirely'. One thing I know will come up is you."

"What about me?" Callimay asked worried as she looked up for the first time.

Tabitha sat there for a moment, looking worried before she spoke, "Well, you see, there's an 'unwritten code' in the Veil: none of them are supposed to marry. It's suggested to any Shadow, but being in the Veil is extremely dangerous. Having a spouse is seen as a distraction and—"

"Burden," she finished, sounding equally depressed and furious as she stood.

"Oh, Callimay. Don't 'ever' think that Destan sees you— Callimay? Callimay wait!"

Deja vu started weaving its endless cloth as she bolted for the door and threw it open; running out into the hall. The only difference this time was that she had someone more vocal following her. Tabitha was slow to her feet, but did her best to keep pace with the terrified young woman who was sprinting down the hall, "Callimay! Callimay please come back!"

It took her less time to find the door she found last time; the same warning and alarm sounding when she opened it. She didn't care though. This time was different. She wouldn't get caught: *There has to be some boat or ship nearby. If I can find a safe way down to the beach I'll be able to flag them down.*

That was a good theory, but it became quite apparent that a theory was all it would be: this cliffside was identical to the one at the mansion with no pathway to get down to the beach… which didn't even exist.

Callimay looked back in fear but no one was there. — There was still a chance! — She made a mad dash for the tree line but collapsed; her vision blurry and her legs like soft rubber. Did they give her something that caused her body to shut down if she tried to escape?

What she feared came true: she could hear the sound of someone running toward her, "I'm not going to hurt anyone! I'll leave and never tell a soul about this place. I just want to go home. Please!"

The heavy sounds she heard vanished. Callimay yelped as she looked up and saw Destan standing there, scared and out-of-breath —

just like herself. He was gripping his side as he wheezed; the turbulent wind tossing his hair everywhere.

She cried as she scrambled to her feet and staggered into his chest, "I wanna go home. Everyone hates me and thinks I'm some—"

"No one hates you, Calli." Destan took a deep breath and did his best to soothe her. "Everyone's just on edge because I'm injured and you're new to them. That's all this is, Calli. It's okay."

"You asked me what I wanted: well I want to go home. I want everything like it was before. I don't want them to take you away from me. I don't want them to change you and me be left alone. I want you for myself. I want to be back in Rayleen and spend time with Rose and Mrs. Manning. I just want it to be the two of us. I just… I want to live! Live with you! Baleck and Ginger are dead. They were the last two that you said we had to worry about. We can relax now. We ca— yes, I'm probably being selfish. But don't I have that right as your wife to want to be with you? Don't I have the right to be with you?"

After he cradled her against his chest for a few minutes, he spoke in a caring tone while trying to hide his winces and groans, "I'm not going anywhere, Calli. And no one will make me leave you. It's my choice. Remember? … Let's get out of the weather. I don't want you getting sick on top of everything else. Come on."

℥

Destan came back in and down the stairs to where there was a rather large crowd of people who were all standing like statues, staring at him. He huffed from being out of breath as his eyes began to burn with anger, "I said: stand down! Go back to your details. … Now!"

Everyone began moseying in different directions; eventually clearing a path for Destan. Callimay kept her eyes closed most of the time, but opened them when she felt an overwhelming amount of tension from him. She glanced around and saw a few men standing by a door that had some type of emblem on it; they all had the same kind of coat on as he did. Nothing was ever said, but their searing eyes spoke volumes as the two of them kept walking past them.

As he rounded the corner that put them on the hall that was where his suite was, Redje and Tabitha perked up and jogged over; Destan calming, "We're fine. Everything's fine now. If I need you I'll have Nexus find you."

They both nodded and left even though Tabitha didn't look like she wanted to.

Destan took Callimay in his suite and encouraged her to lie down; him collapsing next to her right after she did. She gasped and sat up when she saw and started to feel how much pain he was in, "Oh no! I… I'm—"

"It's alright, Calli," he smiled as he put his hand on her shoulder, taking a few deep and labored breaths. "Just… just let me rest for a little bit. — Nexus?"

"Yes, Doyen?" The female voice responded.

"Lock the door, would you?"

"Done."

"Just rest Calli." Destan said groggy as he motioned for her to lie beside him. "I'm. Here."

ℌ

A few hours later, she opened her eyes and saw Destan sitting next to her. He smiled so sweetly when he said, "Everything's alright, Calli. You're safe. I'm here."

"Are you sure you're alright?"

"I'll be just fine. I've got to go for a little while, alright? Tabitha said she'd come stay if you wanted her to."

"Again?" Callimay asked depressed as she bowed her head.

"This is the last time, I promise." Destan assured as he put his hand under her chin.

"It would be nice to have someone here… I guess." She sounded so deeply hurt. "How long will you be gone?"

"Hopefully not even a half hour."

Callimay followed him to the door and noticed his veil slung over the seat nearby. She picked it up and offered it to him as she rubbed the leather between her fingers, "Don't you need this, Destan?"

"Hold on to it for me while I'm gone. Can you do that?"

"Alright. … Destan! I—"

"Yes, Calli?" He asked concerned as he rushed back in the room.

"I love you," she whimpered as she stroked the front of his shirt, not looking at him.

He smiled so sweetly as he tilted his head and brushed her cheek, "I love you too."

She dragged herself over to the window and curled up on the floor, clinging to his veil that was drenched in his cologne. That scent was so special to her and made her forget everything for a few moments.

As she sat there, slowly rocking from side to side, she heard footsteps, "Thank you for coming, Tabitha. I'm sorry I ran off. I… I—"

"You were scared. It's alright."

"I shouldn't think Destan could be so easily swayed, though."

"You had a bit of a bombshell dropped on you today. You found out about another side of Destan that you had no clue existed. I can understand why you would begin to doubt things."

"D… Destan said he rescued you?"

There was a pause; Tabitha's expression changing. She finally answered as she pulled a chair over and sat down, "Yes. Yes, he did. — I'm afraid I can't sit on the floor like you can… and be able to get up quickly, that is."

"I'm sorry."

"I realized the second I started sitting down that it was a bad idea, but gravity had me at that point so there was no turning back. Just… warn me if you're gonna bolt on me, okay?"

With no response, it was up to Tabitha to keep the dialogue going, "Destan's really changed over the years. He used to be so quiet and reserved. He barely spoke to me the entire run."

He's still like that, actually.

"I mean, I could barely see he was there at the drop off point since he was wearing all black and it was the new moon."

"He got you during the night?"

"That's part of the reason we're called Shadows. We do the vast majority of our work during the night hours to help keep it as inconspicuous as possible. The Veil, especially, has to operate under the cover of darkness to keep them safe. — Destan's hair was a bit longer back then. And I say that trying to be nice." Tabitha laughed even louder as she switched topics again. "I don't know if he just was going through a phase or if me constantly making fun of him finally made him cut it."

"You mean he had a mullet!"

"And proud of it! Actually, I'd say it was borderline rattail, but that's splitting frog hairs. ... But anyway! Like I said, he was different back then. Even before I came along he was different. At least that's what Redje told me."

"Huh?"

"I'm sure you know Destan hasn't been a Christian 'very' long. Redje was actually the one who studied with him at first. He's told me stories about Destan when he was younger... I thank The Good Lord that Destan was willing to listen. What he almost— that's all in the past now and I'm sure he's told you all about how he got out of his old life and was Immersed. — You know, I can even tell how much he's changed from last fall to now. You've made him stronger, Callimay. You really have. You've made him stop and think about things he normally wouldn't have. He's understood the whole time his actions can have consequences which can affect others, but he's oftentimes ignored himself and just thought of others. Now he has a wonderful reminder in you to make sure he does take that extra effort to think of himself and know someone thinks enough of him to worry. Thank you. He's all the better because of you coming into his life — no matter what others may say."

"Thank you, Tabitha. — So... what happened to your sister exactly? Destan said something a—"

"I'd rather not talk about it. I... I'm sorry." She rubbed her arm and shook her head in an almost violent way. "There's just too much that's ra   I just can't."

"I didn't mean to—"

"I know you didn't. It's okay." She took a shaky breath and tried to smile. "I just— it's best if I don't talk or think about it. Okay?"

The only thing now audible was the occasional voice out in the hall and then seagulls and sea spray outside. While Callimay had so many questions, she knew it best to keep things to herself... but she wasn't good about hiding it, "Destan didn't tell you much, did he?"

"N... no."

She took a shaky breath and surrendered, "I'll tell you about the run… but nothing else."

"I don't need to know!" Callimay washed the windows with her hands as she turned around. "I won't lie and say I don't 'want' to, b—"

"He was super serious the entire time; and like I said: we hardly talked." Tabitha stared outside, her face washing out and her voice becoming almost a whisper. "He was always checking things around us, making sure I was okay, and never left my side. He was like a 'big brother' if you will. — I remember at one point he was up for about three days straight when we were between safe houses. For the longest time I couldn't figure out how in the world he did it."

"So I was right," Callimay mumbled under her breath.

"Right about what?"

"When we escaped the Soc—" she stopped dead in her tracks, her eyes bugged out with fear.

"It's okay. That's all gone; no one's coming after you from there anymore. They're gone. … And I already know about what happened." Tabitha assured as she tilted her head and grinned. "Destan told Redje; so naturally Redje told me. Now Destan told me later too, don't hear what I'm not saying."

And now she felt guilty: *Why would you think that? ~ I… I don't know what to think right now.* "Well… when we escaped, Destan was up for almost three days straight. At least I thought he had; he never answered me outright either way. I didn't know how in the world he could do such a thing — let alone while he was shot — but what you just said makes perfect sense. … I felt so guilty for making him do that while I rested and slept. He was shot and the poor t—"

"You didn't make him. Destan 'chose' to. It's part of his being to protect others. It wasn't something his training taught him. It's just who Destan is: the kind of heart God gave him. And I am convinced that's what turned the tide when he was studying with Redje."

"So that's what you do mostly: find left-handed people and move them to where they'll be safe?"

"More or less. We all have our functions. Like Redje and myself: we're guards of Rayleen's Safe Haven. And then Destan's got his high-profile position while Rocher and Doctor Gerould…"

"You're just protecting everyone." Callimay rambled in a hushed tone as she looked out the window. "And in the way you're doing it you have to be extremely careful who comes in."

"Very." Tabitha sighed as she nodded.

"So that's why no one is sure if I can be trusted!"

Tabitha hesitated; bobbing her head to-and-fro, "I 'guess' you could put it that way."

"Destan has another name everyone calls him by…" Callimay tried to recall, snapping her fingers.

"Doyen."

"That's right. — Does 'everyone' have a special name?"

"Yes."

"What's yours?"

"Helpmate. Though before Redje and I changed 'jobs' when we got married it was Nexus."

"Why did it change?"

"Because my role changed. A Shadow's name is given to one, protect their true identity; and two, give a code name for their 'job' within the Shadows. So, when Redje and I got married I wasn't the networker anymore. I was the guard's helper."

"So Redje's changed too?"

"Redje 'was' Fidus, but now he's Confrere."

"Fidus?" Callimay asked as she wrinkled her forehead. "That's what the other man's name is, isn't it?"

"I think I know who you mean, so yes. Fidus is the title for the second-in-command."

"Redje was Destan's right-hand-man!"

"Those two worked so well together on missions. There wasn't a better and more effective team of men here than those two. … I knew how much Redje loved me when he told Destan he was stepping down. Destan was devastated at first, but he was so supportive and happy for us once that initial shock wore off. I think he just thought of me as 'one of the guys' and didn't realize Redje and myself were more than 'friends' and 'co-workers'. But being a perfectly content bachelor, what was he supposed to think? Everything was working out great with the three of us for so long; why change it?"

"So… Destan never wanted to get married?"

"Left in a group of men, doing what they love, I don't think there would be 'any' man that just 'wanted' to get married. They need 'her' to come along and remind them there's someone worth fighting for; not just some 'thing'. — Destan was immersed into his role as Doyen and so he completely conformed to the standard that was given for such a role. He hadn't found anyone who would make him question his outlook and behavior. And I don't think he ever looked… because he hadn't met you."

He never looked once? … "H… how do you become a Shadow?"

"Well, it kinda works out where they find you more times than not. But there is a type of 'application process' to get in. If you're selected, you come here to Bulwark to complete your training." Tabitha gestured to the room. "Once you've completed the regimen — and passed your final — you're given your beacon and assigned your title and detail."

"What's a beacon?"

"It's what you could call your diploma." Tabitha pushed her hair away from her ear. "You see this scar?"

"Scar?" Callimay got up and walked over; leaning over a little so she could see better. "What scar?"

"It's there." She laughed as she took her best friend's hand and put it up against the side of her head. "Do you feel that little bump?"

"Yeah. What is it?"

"That's the activator for my beacon. It's an implant that's put next to your ear — whichever side you choose — and when turned on it'll send out a homing beacon only Shadow beacons can pick up. It's how we make contact with each other no matter where we are in the world. It can also be used for a distress call if the Shadow can't call for help."

"Yours must be ringing in your head like crazy!"

"It doesn't stay on all the time." Tabitha laughed as she rocked back in her chair. "That bump is the activator like I said. You can control when it's on or off."

The air in the room was much lighter, but when Callimay saw what was on the floor where she'd been, she became depressed again.

After she sat down and took Destan's veil in her hands, she asked, "What about getting into the Veil? What happens with that?"

"That's a whole different ballgame. You're 'asked'. There's no point-system to get in. — What are you holding?" Tabitha asked concerned as she jumped out of her seat.

"Destan's dust— I mean veil."

"That's Destan's?" Tabitha almost shrieked, her eyes getting bigger.

Callimay had a moment's flashback to what happened between her and Fairove; fear creeping in, "What's wrong."

"Where did Destan say he was going?"

"He didn't say." Callimay shook her head as she scrambled to her feet. "He just promised me it would be the last time he would be gone. I asked him if he needed it and he said no and told me to hold onto it for him until he got back. — Tabitha, what's going on?"

"I… I might be wrong."

"Tabitha. What's. Wrong!" Callimay asked horrified as she gripped the leather collar; its usual creaking and groaning sounds being louder than ever.

"I'm… I'm not allowed to say."

"Tabitha!" Callimay dropped the veil and grabbed her by the shoulders. "If this has anything to do with Destan I need to know. I'm his wife. What is going on!"

"If Destan doesn't have that on while he's meeting with the Veil, he's surrendering his rights and is putting himself at their mercy."

She screamed as she jumped back, "Why would he do that!"

"He's got to be stepping down for you, Callimay. It's the only thing I can think of." Tabitha cringed as she bowed her head. "The only thing is, since he went in there without his veil he's letting them choose his 'fate', if you will. I guess he did it to make sure they make him leave."

"I never told him oh no!" She gasped as she turned back and grabbed the leather coat. "This is all my fault. I've got to get to him."

"Callimay, wait!"

"I've got to stop him, Tabitha!" She started to cry as she opened the door, calling out in a loud voice, "I didn't mean what I said. Not after what I know now. — Destan!"

Breathing heavily and shaking, she ran into the hall and closed her eyes, trying to remember which way Destan came back and where she saw those men with veils.

After a moment she darted off.

"Callimay! Stop!" Tabitha screamed as she ran after her. "You'll die if you step foot in there! Callimay!"

With no response and knowing she couldn't keep up with her, she mumbled to herself in frustration as she ran back into the suite, calling out in desperation, "Nexus! Get Confrere on this line… now!"

"Just a moment." Nexus replied calmly.

"Tabby?" Redje asked concerned. "What is it?"

"Destan didn't take his veil with him. I think he's meeting with them right now. I told Callimay what I thought he was doing and she's trying to stop him from leaving." She panicked; still trying to catch her breath as she leaned against the back of a chair. "You've got to stop her, Redje! You know she'll die if she steps one foot in there!"

"I'm on my way." He answered as the line cut off.

℔

Before long, Callimay came to the end of the last hall and saw someone with a veil go in a room. She closed her eyes and took a deep breath, relieved to know where she wanted to go. As she looked again, she saw Redje round the corner at the other end of the hall — much father from the door — and could hear him call out, "Callimay! Don't go in there! Destan will be fine. Just wait for him outside."

"But I don't want him to do this!" She cried out as she bolted.

"Callimay, you can't go in there!" Redje yelled as she got to the door. "Callimay stop! Listen to me! I know what I'm saying!"

Unwilling to listen, she wheezed and groaned as she pushed with everything she had to get the door to open. Redje was closing in; her panicking and starting to scream and throw herself against the door.

It finally gave way and it smacked against the wall of this dark room. She stumbled in and slammed against a railing of what turned out to be balcony. Still trying to gain her bearing since it was so dark, she glanced around as she heaved. Her eyes finally adjusted and she saw Destan standing in the middle of the round room below her.

"Calli!" He almost screeched. "Calli get out of here!"

"Destan don't do this!" She cried as she ran to the stairs on her left, Redje trying to grab her arm.

"Confrere I'll take care of her!" Destan blurted out when he saw his best friend where he shouldn't be. "Leave. Now!"

He didn't want to obey the order, and Destan was grateful for his willingness to do what he was to help, but he let go of Callimay's sleeve and slipped out before the door shut.

As she came down, she saw two men standing guard at the bottom as well as two behind her. They quickly converged on her with their knives drawn, and were just about to grab her when she heard a familiar voice order, "She holds the veil of Doyen. Stand down."

They stopped dead in their tracks and backed away from her into the darkness of the room. Callimay shivered from seeing that and stood there frozen with fear.

"Calli, what are you doing!" Destan scolded in a hushed tone as he rushed over, still hobbling.

Still watching where the individuals disappeared to, she gulped and ignored her husband's angry question. It wasn't until he gripped her arms that her focus was diverted; her whipping her head around and yelping as she pulled away.

Seeing her violent reaction, Destan backed off and tried to calm her as quickly as he could, "Easy, Calli! It's me. It's okay. … W… why did you come in here? What's wrong?"

"I know why you left this," she cried in a whisper as she pushed his veil against his chest. "I don't want you to do this. I know you're doing it because I said I wanted to go home but I changed my mind."

"Ca—"

"What is the meaning of your interruption, young lady?" a different, booming male voice addressed Callimay.

As she turned, she saw what looked like viewing boxes situated on a raised portion of the floor all the way around the perimeter of the room; two of them were empty at the time. The room was dimly lit and felt eerie to Callimay in light of not only its natural appearance but what she just witnessed and then earlier by the tree line. And to add to this unsettling ambience, it was as if some kind of mist hung in the still, stoic air.

"I…" she gulped as she looked to the elderly man who appeared to be the one addressing her. "Wait! I know you! Well I think I do. Y—"

"I'll ask you again — and only one more time — what is the meaning of you interrupting?" He growled as he fixed his piercing gaze on her.

"I… I brought Destan his veil."

"Calli don't call me that."

"Don't help her, Doyen." The man warned, causing Destan to step away from her and bow his head.

"Don't you 'dare' tell my husband what he can and can't do for me! And what's so wrong with me calling my husband by his given name?" Callimay stormed down the rest of the steps and over to where this man was; looking him straight in the eye before looking around at everyone when she heard several gasps. "Doctor Gerould? Rocher!"

"Deal with the outsider." Someone called out. "She—"

"I thought you were supposed to help people like me? I'm a lefty, Southpaw… Derelict. Why do you want me gone, or dealt with like that person demanded? Why am I seen as some evil person for addressing people I know by their names?"

"You are the one who came into this sacred gathering uninvited." The elderly man reminded, not fazed in the least by her bold comments and actions. "It is not our responsibility—"

"Yes, I burst in, but I only did it to stop my husband from making a rash decision. I came to speak with Destan… not you." Callimay demanded as she pointed a motherly finger at him.

"This is unheard of!" "Why is she permitted to stay?" "Why has she not been dealt with already?" "Who is she to be given an audience?" Were questions and demands which began to fill the air as she came back to Destan who was still mortified; his hands quivering as he reached out to her.

"Everything surrounding this vote is something the Veil has never encountered." The elderly man silenced the room as he put his hand up; grumbling as he glared at the young couple on the landing of the staircase. "Allow the young woman to speak with Doyen for a time."

Callimay turned to Destan as he started rambling nonsensical words in whispers to her. She couldn't understand how he could act so submissive when he was the leader. How could one person's warning cause him to completely back away from her? But, she had something else to take care of at the moment, "Destan 'please' take this. Tabitha explained everything to me; or at least enough for me to better understand things. I… I want you to stay. I'm sorry that—"

He gasped and shoved his veil back toward her, "Don't let go of it."

"Why not?"

"I…" Destan tried to figure out how to explain as he rested his shaking hands on her shoulders. "There's… Calli, it's… that veil is the only thing keeping you alive right now. If I take it away—"

"But you're the leader? At least every leader I've ever known is the head of what goes on in a group. What's this about me dying by being in here? I haven't heard one soul say anything 'secretive' and I most certainly can't see anything in here."

Destan hesitated as he glanced around and then back to her, "During a vote, things are different. And since I didn't come in with mine, I don't have any authority. But even if I do take it, I… I can't protect you."

"But why not! Destan what's wrong? Why are you acting like this?"

He raked his hands through his hair as he walked in a small circle, trying to talk as quiet as possible, "I… I've given up my role as leader. You said you wanted to go home and so I'm making sure we can."

"But I don't want you to." She pleaded, now teary-eyed; angry with herself for making things so difficult for him. "I know I said that earlier but I wasn't thinking clearly. I was just reacting. You knew that. I know you knew that. I'm sorry, Destan. I… Tabitha told me what you did for her; and I know you've done it for countless others. Destan I don't want you to stop. I know you want to be here. You wouldn't have kept it a secret from me if you didn't want to keep doing it. I understand now that you were only trying to keep me safe while still doing what you knew you could do to help those like us. I know you didn't lie to me. I'm so sorry I accused you of that. … But you don't have to do any of that any more. I want to help you. I don't care what I have to do; I'll become a Shadow if that's what it takes to be by your side. I know that would mean I'd give up some things but I love you more. And all I want is for you to be happy and for me to be with you. That's all I want. I don't care where we are. I promise, Destan. … I'm sorry I acted the way I did. I just—"

"You've had ample time." The elderly man announced without any care or concern. "And now that you have spoken with Doyen you may remove yourself from this arena without any repercussions. Consider yourself fortunate that I am being so merciful."

"I demand to stay!" Callimay gritted her teeth as she glared at the older man; terrifying Destan even more as she stormed back to him and all but got in his face. "Destan's my husband. I deserve to know what's happening. He didn't commit some evil, heinous crime by marrying me and I'm not some slave girl you can order around… or a Derelict you can blackmail and bully for your pleasure. — Do any of you know what Destan went through for me these past nine months? Do you understand I need him just as much as he needs me after what the Society did to both of us? This may be me putting myself up on a pedestal, but do you know the only reason Destan's here is because of me? He would've gone mad and killed himself long ago! Your leader is handicap in a way now. … And I'm the only one who can help him."

A wave of gasps could be heard in the room as she paused; the expression of those she could see now being ones of fear or doubt, and a certain individual having a smile of support grow.

"Actually I take that back. It's not me entirely." Callimay corrected as she turned and looked at Destan, her voice back to its soft and tender nature as she reached out to him. "Destan's love for me is what saves him each time. I guess it's not me pleading with him to calm down that ends up changing his mind. It's his heart that convicts him of his love for me; and more importantly, God. Nothing can erase what is in his heart. No one can do that to anyone no matter what they try. Love can't be erased just like it can't be faked. — I know you all may see me as a distraction, a burden, a weakness, or whatever term you want to give me; but Rocher even told me that I've changed Destan for the better. Just ask him. And I've heard Doctor Gerould say similar things as well, isn't that right? … I know that dangerous positions warrant special precautions to help protect the persons involved, but at the same time, having the kind of help that only a spouse can give makes those times so much more bearable and even worth fighting through."

"That's quite enough, young lady." The elderly man demanded in a firm and loud tone as his fists clinched tighter and tighter with each word; ending what he obviously saw as her public display of sedition. "If you wish to remain a pest, so be it. — Let us continue our work and hold the outsider accountable for her actions; freeing ourselves of any responsibility in the matter. A yes vote is to uphold Doyen's declaration and exclude him from the Veil completely. A no vote is to refuse his declaration and uphold him in the position as Doyen. This must be a unanimous vote."

"Set the timer," she heard a familiar voice — Fidus — call out.

"Destan?" She turned and saw him push his hair back and bow his head. "Destan, what's going on?"

He quivered as he wrapped her in his arms: *Shh, Calli.*

The floor they were standing on lit up with the shadow of a clock face. Callimay jerked her head up and saw a giant clock above them. The hands weren't moving at all and she doubted it was telling the correct time. She then scanned the room and noticed everyone had their backs turned to them; their heads bowed.

Dead silence.

And then the second hand broke it as it began its trip around the clock face.

Destan brought his wife's wandering head to his chest and held her close. Callimay could feel his heart pounding and his hands shaking more and more as they held onto her tighter and tighter with each passing second. He was extremely nervous… terrified, actually.

After the second hand finished its second trip, it stopped. All the lights went out. Destan pushed Callimay back to arms-length and stood there with his eyes closed, head bowed, and his shoulders slumped. He was breathing heavy.

She whipped her head around only to find everyone was still facing away from them.

This waiting and silence became too much for her, Callimay frightened so much that she began to tremble as much as Destan was.

He let go of her and slowly looked up; pushing his hair back again. While he stopped shaking, he looked like he was out of breath; his eyes were as wide as when he saw her come in the room.

A few moments later, everyone turned around and looked just as austere as they had.

"You heard the vote, Doyen?" Fidus inquired.

"I have." Destan confirmed as he looked over to the one addressing him, sounding more confident.

"What was the verdict, Elder?"

"It appears her emotion-jerking 'story' swayed a multitude. Doyen is upheld in his position. There were no yes votes." The elderly man sounded a bit frustrated as he huffed; but shook it off and proposed, "Now comes the issue of what to do with this young woman."

"As Doyen I am allowed to make a direct order concerning any issue, Elder." Destan spoke up as he put both hands on his veil Callimay was clutching; letting out his tiny smile and nodding to her.

She let go and watched as he effortlessly put it on and subtly motioned for her to stay there. He then marched over and took his position with the rest of those wearing a veil around her. The smile he had was only for her, his public expression still lending itself to that of fear and uncertainty about what was happening.

"That is providing there isn't a three-fourths majority to overrule you." Elder muttered in just a loud enough voice for Destan to hear him. "Don't think you're some high and mighty king, immune of the laws you enforce on others."

"Callimay Berchoff," Fidus addressed; letting the other two continue their own squabble if they wanted to while trying to make headway on the more pressing matter than that of egos.

"But how did you— my last n—"

"You said you were willing to do whatever was necessary to remain with Doyen, is this correct?"

"I did."

"You went as far as to say you would become a Shadow to remain at his side?"

"Yes."

"I will be the first to admit I was infuriated to learn of your presence in Doyen's life." Fidus recalled as he took a deep breath, tapping his fist that was loosening on the railing in front of him. "But I have come to understand a bit more as to the reality that a person can function in the same role as another but require a completely different approach and foundation. Doyen told me on the flight here that you made him stronger. During an 'attack' he had on the flight, his sole concern was for your welfare and safety. I do not claim to have full confidence in his past choices, but I will concede what I mentioned earlier and affirm my confidence in his actions from this point forward. My only request is that in changing how Doyen conducts himself he does not stray from the purpose and foundational principles of the Veil and Shadows."

"I want to help Destan in that." Callimay confirmed as she looked back at him, smiling as she finished, "Like you said: things may be different but I know we have the same goal — to help others."

"This is extremely unconventional, but the situation is what it is and we must find a way to function as is required." Fidus hesitated as he appeared to look toward Rocher and Doctor Gerould for support. "In a logical extension of what all our votes have been, I believe we have acknowledged even though we may not agree that Doyen's conduct from this point on — within reason — will require support from an individual who is currently an outsider to us. From what I personally witnessed, I trust her comments about the depth of Doyen's situation and how she is intimately intertwined with his continued survival. … So, I propose we allow Doyen's wife to begin her training regimen. And beyond that, upon receiving her beacon, allow her an audience to be added to the Veil."

Oxygen was going to become scarce in this room before long from the several gasps voiced throughout his comments.

"Note that I said she must receive her beacon to be allowed the opportunity." Fidus clarified as he looked around the ring of people; finally resting his gaze on Elder. "And as I stated, I have personally witnessed one of Doyen's episodes that she spoke of being able to curb. For us to continue in our work, we must lay aside our differences and give Doyen the support he is in need of to remain alive. Commander would not wish us to bemoan — in her words — the predicament we now find ourselves in. We have voted to uphold him as Doyen and so we must be purposeful and quick about our handling of how to resolve this 'deviation' so we can continue on."

"Votes must be heard by the individual being voted for or against." Elder reminded; sounding like he'd found an easy out. "That is not just some 'tradition' that I'm willing to bend on."

Why would you nit-pick on this point when you voted against an equally important code? I just don't understand why you fuel your feud with Doyen. It's as if you enjoy this. "Since I spoke up for her 'I' will act as her beacon. I believe it to be quite clear what my vote would be. As usual, Doyen will be the officiant for the vote. — Doyen?"

He stood there, his mouth gaping open for a few seconds as he tried to find an answer; nodding after the overpowering silence registered.

"Very well," Elder grumbled as he motioned toward Callimay.

Do you want to do this! Destan's eyes practically bugged out as he stared at her.

Yes. I'm sure. She smiled as she clasped her hands behind her.

Destan's voice cracked as he called out, "Reset the timer."

Callimay's joy was drained because of the strained tone of her husband's voice… and the fact he turned his back to her: *W… wait! What do I do?*

Just close your eyes and look down like last time.

"A yes vote will be to afford— each Shadow is required to have a title." Elder interrupted himself. "You cannot be referred to by this title 'officially' until you receive your beacon, but it would be best for you to learn our ways now."

"Liaison," she blurted out; and then explained in a quieter tone, "Tab— Helpmate explained to me how the titles are chosen."

Took that right away from my father.

It's who I am.

I'm not complaining.

"Very well then, a yes vote is to afford 'Liaison' the opportunity to enter a training regimen to become a Shadow; and… grant her an audience with the Veil upon receiving her beacon to be put up to a vote of addition to the Veil. A no vote would be to completely exclude her and force her to leave Bulwark — forever." Elder eyed her as he turned around; the last to do so. "This must be a unanimous vote."

"What!" Destan almost yelled as he whipped around.

"If there is a no vote now, there will be no sense for her to be up for a second vote." Elder clarified as he and everyone else turned around. "Take it or leave it, Doyen. I know I speak for a super-majority when I say this."

So, if someone says no that means I… Callimay gulped as she tried to hold back tears.

Don't give up hope. Destan tried to console as he looked at her in a longing way. *I… whatever happens, 'we' will be together. I promise you.* "Fine. We'll do it your way. — Start the timer."

Everyone turned their backs to Callimay and Fidus so the process which just took place could happen again. She looked at Destan with desperation as he closed his eyes and turned away from her; the lights going out at the same time.

Just close your eyes, Calli. He said a bit choked up. *Everything's going to be fine.*

Promise? She cried.

I promise.

Fidus faced Callimay with his head bowed and eyes closed; her mimicking him.

Just as last time, the floor became the shadow of the clock face overhead and it began to slowly tick by the one-hundred and twenty seconds. Callimay's hands began to tremble at her side; her heart beating in sync with the clock and getting louder with each passing second. She understood why Destan was out of breath… she was starting to feel that way herself. The unknown of everything started to terrify Callimay. Did she really think this through?

Finally, the two minutes were over. She whipped her head over to Destan who hadn't turned around.

Destan?

No response.

She looked at Fidus, asking in a broken whisper, "What happened?"

"Welcome to the Shadows, Liaison." He cracked a smile as he whispered; patting her arm. "I have no doubt you will succeed."

Everyone had since turned around and faced Callimay and Fidus.

"You know the vote, do you not?" Elder turned his nose up.

"I do," she nodded as Fidus walked back to his position.

"What was the verdict, Doyen?"

"Cal— Liaison has been awarded the extraordinary chance to prove her worth to the Veil." He replied almost breathless; staring at Elder with leery bewilderment. "It was a unanimous yes vote."

"You will begin your training regimen in the morning. With the condition stipulated, I think it best to pair you with a member of the Veil." Fidus gave Callimay what sounded like her first debriefing and detail. "You already know three in this room as well as two who were previously among our ranks; with the profound connection one Veil — in particular — I put forth Doyen as your trainer."

Nothing was said by anyone one way or another.

Content, Fidus announced, "If there is nothing more concerning this issue which any Veil deems necessary, and Doyen has no objection to the detail, let it be known I relinquish all my entrusted authority back to its rightful owner: Doyen. Let is also be known he will from this point forward carry all of the duties and responsibilities that have been delegated to various Veils during his absence that were also his own."

"It is known." Destan responded in his usual formal tone; and then paused for a moment before finishing, "The silence that has fallen leads me to believe my fellow Veils are eager to continue their details… let the veil be removed so the shadows can be seen."

And with that, all the lights were turned on. Destan stood there for a moment and stared at Callimay, and then ran to her and rushed her out of the room.

ћ

Once they opened the door, they saw Redje and Tabitha huddled together. Tabitha shrieked as she ran and hugged Callimay, trying her best not to cry, "How in the— oh thank The Lord you're alright!"

Destan staggered over and reached out to the wall to steady himself before he leaned his back against it; taking a deep, shaky breath as he rubbed his hands across his face.

"Tabby, let's let them be." Redje hinted as he took her hand and motioned to Destan.

She nodded and gave her one last hug, "I'm 'so' glad to see you."

"We'll see you two later." Redje kept a calm, quiet tone as he took Tabitha's hand and turned to leave.

Callimay now looked at Destan and knew he was a nervous wreck. She didn't want to say anything to drive him overboard, but then again, he needed to be reminded to keep calm, "A… are you hungry?"

He sighed and slid down the wall so he was now sitting on the floor; he still had his eyes closed and looked frozen stiff, but Callimay could notice his hands were beginning to tremble.

She dropped to her knees beside him; reaching for them. Whether it was because he wasn't expecting it or he was in pain, Destan jerked away from her touch.

"I… I'm sorry," she said ashamed as she laid her hands on her lap and bowed her head.

It was obvious to anyone he was still breathing hard and terrified. This was all her fault: she let her emotions take precedence to the wisdom and knowledge of others in an instance where she had no clue what was going on. It appeared she had done more damage than good… she wasn't being Liaison. And the worst part was, Destan had withdrawn from her. Why, she wasn't completely sure; but she knew part of it had to be because he was mad. Here he was, doing something to make her happy, and now she said it wasn't what she wanted.

Some people came and went, looking perplexed and slowing for a moment as they walked by; but most of the time, Destan and Callimay were alone. It was nice to not have interruptions that could send him back to square one — he was calming down — but the deafening silence was becoming too much for her to bear.

"Let's go get something to eat." He finally responded as he stood and offered his hand to her. "And then some rest. It's been a long few days. … You'll be going through a lot of training for a while, I guess, so any rest you can bank will help."

"Alright," she tried not to cower as she took his hand and followed.

They walked for a little while through the empty, winding halls; Destan plodding along at a slow pace with Callimay lagging a bit behind him still. Neither of them said anything of any kind: not a sigh or a grunt even.

There was, however, this underlying emotion of pain in him which worried her. He didn't "look" to be in pain but as Callimay looked down she saw his wrists. They were bandaged and it wasn't difficult to see his left one was beginning to bleed again.

It hit her again what he'd been through physically; what they'd both been through in only what… two days?

Why in the world did I... I'm sorry Destan. Callimay cried as she rubbed his hand, and then finished in a timid voice, "Your wrist is bleeding. Do you need t—"

"It's fine."

"But—"

"I said it's fine!" He snapped as he stopped and stomped his foot on the cement floor as he whipped around to face her.

Callimay cowered as she winced, trying to stay as strong as she could and not run: *It's not his fault. I've done so much damage that he's confused about what I want while still being in so much pain from what Baleck did.*

Destan stood there for a bit and then groaned, not saying a word while he calmed down. He eventually turned and kept on walking at the same speed.

After what felt like hours — which in reality was only five minutes — they came to what looked like a small restaurant. He stopped and turned to her, "Would you like to stay or go back to the suite?"

While his tone was much better than earlier, it was still curt enough to make her bow her head and be brief, "Whatever you would prefer."

He nodded; his voice sounding softer now, "Calli? Is there anything specific you want?"

"No," she shook her head; not lifting it to look at him.

The individual who took their order looked a bit stunned, but soon they handed Destan the sack with what was going to be the first real meal the two of them had in over twenty-four hours. — On that front alone, anyone could understand why Destan was acting like he was.

His gait and overall body language suggested he felt better. Knowing this gave Callimay a bit more opportunity to look around her as they strolled through the maze of halls. His grip on her hand was loose, which was understandable since it was his left hand; but if he felt her hand slipping out, he would grip it and then slowly loosen it again.

❧

Not but a moment after he shut the door, Callimay started getting things ready. She ran over and pulled a second chair next to a table over by the window, trying to be as quiet as possible. Her mind was going at the speed of light as she tried to think ahead so Destan could rest… and hopefully avoid him getting upset again.

At one point she looked back and saw him standing there, staring into nothing; like he did so many times back at the Society. She took a deep breath and crept over, gently putting her hand over his fist that was clutching the bag their food was in.

His hand melted as she barely brushed against it. He looked down as she took the bag and just stared at her. Callimay smiled softly and then hurried back to finish getting things ready.

Everything looked complete, but then it didn't. She stared at the food with a puzzled expression on her face, looking at the meals that were spread out. Something was missing.

The lightbulb went off, her whipping around to get the important, missing items: silverware.

"Calli?" Destan blurted out, sounding nervous.

"Yes?" She stopped and looked back, sounding nervous herself.

"I… I love you so much." He hesitated and then ran over and scooped her into his arms. "You didn't have to do that back there."

"I'm sorry I—"

"It's alright now. You're safe… everything's alright. … Just— just listen when someone tells you something. Especially about the way things are done around here. Alright? I don't want to have come this far only to lose you. Okay? … Okay. I love you, Calli."

~ 2 ~

Callimay woke up early the next morning only to find Destan still asleep: *He's beyond exhausted. ~ It's hard to believe that only two days ago you were~ I'd rather not think about that right now. It's... just not right now. All that matters right now is he needs his rest.*

She checked his wrist and then sat there for a while and looked at him in such a longing way. How he dealt with everything the past few days proved he was keeping that beast inside contained and under control. He was able to do and be so much more than a caged animal ready to strike like his father believed. Liaison was key to this, but like she said: it was still his conscious choice that made all the difference.

After making sure he was comfortable, she slipped out into the hall and focused to find Tabitha: *I hope I'm able to figure out 'where' she is. ~ Why not just 'ask' her? ~ I don't want to scare her! What if she goes into labor because of it? ~ She's not 'that' far along, silly. ~ No. No I won't do that. If I can't figure it out I'll just start walking. Surely I can ask someone for directions to get back here if nothing else.*

Before long, she found herself lost; but with no one to ask for help and still no clue where Tabitha was. She could hear her but what she heard wasn't helpful.

What about asking someone in there? Callimay noticed some type of observation room to her right. *Well... I guess I could— oh! There's Tabitha! ... I really don't want to do this.*

After bickering with herself and trying with no success to open the door, she tapped on the glass to try to get her attention. That didn't go as planned. Someone else quickly came over and did something to darken the windows so she couldn't see in anymore.

Callimay closed her eyes and sighed as she surrendered: *Tabitha?*

She was deep in thought, so obviously Tabitha wasn't expecting to hear someone ask for her; let alone use her actual name. There wasn't anyone close by that was talking with her, so she leaned back in her seat and rubbed her face: *I'm losing my mind.*

No you're not. I 'did' ask for you.

She gripped the armrests of her seat and whipped around, finding Callimay peeking inside. — It was a one-way window now. — Tabitha shook her head and took a few moments to catch her breath, after which she looked around for a few moments before she came out.

Her reaction wasn't what Callimay expected; her exclaiming in the kind of whisper Rose used… which wasn't one, "What in the world!"

"I didn't know how else to get your attention since no one else would help."

"That's— so you really can? Talk to people in their minds, I mean."

"I know you're scared of me. I just… I wanted to talk to you and I didn't know how else to get your attention without 'bothering' the others more than I did. I know they still don't like me."

"I'm not scared of you, Callimay." She ushered her down the hall.

"You didn't say that word exactly or out loud, that's true. But I heard what you thought."

"I… I… I didn't know what—"

"Don't worry. I know you're not 'scared-scared' like some would be. And believe me, you're not the first and won't be the last." She put her hand atop her best friend's and smiled.

"What did you want to talk about?"

Callimay looked around a bit and then bowed her head as she fiddled with her shirt's hem, "Should I leave? I mean, am I doing more damage by staying? Fidus advocated for me, but I could tell he was reluctant about it… and he was the most 'encouraging' person in there. I don't want to make Destan's job harder by—"

"They're the ones causing damage." Tabitha looked over her shoulder and glared back at the room she was in. "They don't like the thought of someone trying to do something 'different' even though it's not wrong."

"But if that makes Destan's job harder…"

"I understand what you're thinking, but think about the alternative: how would you handle living in Rayleen by yourself? 'Maybe' seeing your husband once a week on Sundays; providing he could make the what… five-hour flight home in time? How do you think he would handle it? The time away from you?" Tabitha challenged as she leaned against the wall, tilting her head. "I admire you for being selfless, but being selfless doesn't mean being destructive… because that's what it will be: for you, your husband, 'and' your marriage. You two need to stay together no matter where you are. You vowed before God to stick it out with him. And even though it might not be something you thought of at the time or even knew about being possible, all the backlash and ridicule he is given is included in that promise. — Now I know you're not trying to run away and hide, but just think about it a little more. You've just found out about this and it's going to take time to sort through all the emotions let alone the facts."

A few Shadows walked past as this cold splash of reality washed over and sunk into Callimay, Tabitha "saluting" or greeting them; depending on whether or not she knew them.

Now having more wisdom to make a better decision, she took a deep breath, "I don't know why I never thought of it that way. … I guess it could be seen as me being selfish: going home and leaving him alone. — I know that's not what you said I was doing, but I can see how easily it could be taken that way. And I don't want to do that to Destan or have someone — him — even think that. Yes, this is all new to me, but in a way I'm not surprised. It makes sense for him to be doing this."

"And…"

"May I ask you what I originally wanted to?"

"Sure. But why don't we walk while we talk?"

"Okay. — I'm supposed to start my training today to become a Shadow and I wanted t—"

"What?"

"If I'm telling you something I'm not supposed to, I'm sorry. I won't feel bad if you tell me to stop and I understand I really don't know much of anything. — Fidus gave me this option to become a Shadow. And with it came the extension that once I am given my beacon," *whatever that is,* "I can go before the Veil to be added to their group."

"So you can stay here with him." Tabitha nodded as she hummed in an agreeable manner while she stopped and turned. "Fidus is coming around quicker than I thought after what he said— but that's good! And thank you for warning me, but I don't see a problem with you telling me that."

The calm that embraced the air was so welcoming and comforting; the smile on Callimay's face much freer and natural than before, "So… is there anything I need before I start? Something to help make Destan's job easier?"

"Well I think what you first need is some lessons on our codes of conduct. His name here is Doyen… 'only'."

"I don't see why I have t— okay. Alright. 'Doyen'." Her face pruned up as she pursed her lips. "Is there anything I can do to make 'Doyen's' job easier? Ugh! I hate how my mouth tastes after saying it."

"It's strange, I get it. But it's also fun as well. Believe me." Tabitha winked as she started off again. "But as far as 'helping him' goes… well, if you want to 'impress' him while at the same time show the Veil you're serious, I think some new clothes would be a good way to start. You need some anyway. I should've gotten something. I'm sorry."

"I would like to brush my hair, but other than that I'm fine. … Though I won't turn down a change of clothes." She picked out a clod of dirt from her shorts. "But why 'new' clothes? Are you talking about a uniform or something?"

"Yep. Even I have one… it's just that it doesn't 'fit' right now. — It actually hasn't fit since four months into my pregnancy with Rose." Tabitha laughed and sighed at the same time. "But anyway! Does Doyen know you're gone by chance?"

"No. But he's still asleep so it's okay."

"How do you know that?"

"It's kinda hard to explain. He's still thinking of things since he's dreaming, but not consciously so it's muffled."

"O… kay." Tabitha shivered a bit. "W… what can he do? He never told Redje outright; let alone me. Or at least put it in terms we could understand very well."

Callimay almost laughed as she snapped to, "Well he— everything, really. Not that he can right now, but he could."

"What's that supposed to mean?"

"He has his own ability of super speed and heightened strength, but he's able to gain abilities from others. Destan— 'Doyen' can do what I do, teleport, he has various vision modes, and can alter his appearance to look like someone else. I don't think he got anything from Hyra; and I don't know if he gained anything from Webb, Baleck, or Ginger—"

Tabitha stopped and shook her head and hands, "Hold on there. You're telling me he has the ability to clone others?"

"Their abilities, yes." Callimay nodded; sounding proud. "His father actually formulated the serum he has because of Destan himself. He named it Challenger. Though he never intended—"

"Amazing," Tabitha stared off into the distance as she shook her head slowly; then asked curious, "Challenger?"

"Yeah."

"Well isn't that a 'coincidence'. Challenger was his title before he became Doyen. It was his father's as well."

"You mean Destan's father's title was the same as—"

"In that case the title was kinda… passed down as a sign of respect. — Here we go! We'll get you ready in no time."

𝕾𝕯

The shop Tabitha brought her in looked like a high-end clothing store with a small hair salon. Well this was quite the odd type of store to find in a place like this! But that shock didn't last long because all the clothing was black. This fit in with the feel of the place perfectly.

And yet, as she looked around, Callimay noticed something was missing that she now knew was very important, "Where are the veils?"

"They don't keep those out because they're tailor-made for each individual. Getting it is kinda like an 'initiation ceremony' if you know what I'm talking about."

"Oh. Okay. … What if someone's gets damaged or lost? Can they get a new one?"

"To lose one's veil is to show you don't care about the Veil." Tabitha warned; still talking in a hushed tone. "You're never supposed to go anywhere without it unless your detail deems its absence necessary. And as far as if it's damaged… I've never known someone to have that happen to the point it was a problem. It sounds reasonable enough, but I really don't know. They're made of a grade of leather that can take an enormous amount of wear and tear."

"Oh." Callimay sighed as her shoulders dropped.

"What's wrong? Why would you ask about that?"

"It's just… Destan's veil has a bullet hole in it. Two, actually. That's why he had that sling on for a month. — I don't know if he ever said anything about it to you or not. — I can tell it's bothered him ever since. He never said anything aloud, but I found him a couple times out on the deck, holding it and staring at the holes and stains; talking to himself about how he wished they were gone. I tried my best to clean it, I really did… but I could only get so much of the blood off since it soaked into the hide and dried. And there wasn't any way I could scrub away bullet holes; but that didn't stop me from trying to get them patched." She almost cringed as she rubbed her arm. "I was… I was just wondering if he could have a new one made. Maybe it wouldn't, but I think it would help him."

"Well…" Tabitha tried to keep things as positive as possible as they walked around the different displays and racks. "Maybe if we explain the situation to Outfitter we could see about getting him a new one."

"Do you know why Destan's doesn't have sleeves? Everyone else that I remembered seeing did."

She paused for a moment, her eyes glazing over a bit as she stared off in front of her; and then sighed, "It's because his father was a Veil and fell in the line of duty."

"But he died—"

"Yes, Destry went there to help," Tabitha hushed as she glanced around; speaking in a whisper now. "But he was also a Veil at the time. They used his position to gain information to help get those who were left-handed out of harm's way. That veil Doyen's wearing is actually his father's. It was inherited just like his title was. — The Veil's code stipulates when the original bearer dies and if their 'inheritor' is added to the Veil, this inheritor undergoes what's called the Right of Respect. The leader of the Veil quite literally rips the sleeves off the veil mere moments after the person has been veiled. It's to show that the inheritor is following in the footsteps of their family and it also shows honor to the fallen Veil. ... Now I've only known this right to take place twice. And the other time the veil wasn't functional for the inheritor, so the right was completed and the veil retired. — They may seem very... well, 'mysterious' as to why they do things the way they do, but most of it is understandable because of the danger those in the Veil are in. That, and they uphold traditions as if they were law condemnable by death."

"Destan never told—"

"Don't tell him I told you, Callimay. He's had enough ridicule and public shame placed on him because of it. And it's a constant reminder of what he personally witnessed; one he's not allowed to get rid of. — I've never seen the right performed, but when Destan came out of that room... it were as if someone had taken his heart and ripped it out of his chest, then threw it on the floor for all to see as they mocked him." Tabitha almost hissed as she gritted her teeth. "Really? I see the right as a humiliation more than a sign of respect. I know it's done to respect the life given, but the life that has to bear that respect should be worth more. It makes no— I started rambling, I know. I'm sure he never said anything because you didn't know about this all. And since you found out he hasn't had time to say anything. And then I highly doubt it was something he deemed an 'urgent priority'. ... Please don't mention it; let him tell you. I'm sure he'll tell you when he's ready."

"Alright," Callimay promised as she noticed someone coming into the room.

"Well it's about time, Outfitter. I was beginning to wonder if you'd come out of retirement and took off for who knows where!"

"Helpmate! What are you doing back in Bulwark?" The heavy-set man asked as he laughed joyously.

"Long story."

"New recruit?"

"Yes sir." Callimay nodded as she clasped her hands behind her; standing as tall as she could.

"I didn't know you were taking on regimen duties with your family growing..." Outfitted began to ask as he peered over his glasses at Tabitha; unable to miss the fact she was expecting.

"I'm not her trainer." Tabitha made a face as she rolled her eyes. "Doyen is. I'm just helping her get a few things to start."

"Doyen! … Is he back?"

"Have you been under a rock or something for the past day and a half? You slept through the blood moon threat?"

"We had one?"

"Oh good night."

"Apparently I do live under a rock." He contorted his face as he stroked his scruffy beard; shrugging as he finished, "Oh well. I take it the threat was disposed of."

"Oh everything's fine." Tabitha rolled her eyes as she rubbed her temple. "No need to worry yourself."

"Good. — Well we need to get this young lady into something appropriate so she can look presentable for Doyen; as well as make sure she is able to function at the high level I'm sure he'll expect. … And we'll need to see about that hair of yours." Outfitter commented as he grabbed a book, pointing back at Callimay without looking. "I'm afraid you won't last with those long locks."

She looked down at her hair that hadn't been touched by a brush in two days; gripping it in her hands as if scared.

"She doesn't 'have' to cut it, Outfitter." Tabitha calmed; seeing how much it hurt Callimay to hear that. "She can go with my style."

"Don't want to cut it, huh?" He raised an eyebrow as he turned back around.

Her voice came out like the whisper of the breeze through the trees; her stroking her free-flowing locks, "I'd prefer not to."

He nodded in approval as he turned a book toward her, "Well, I admire you for that. Most would just chop it off so they didn't have to deal with it or take the time needed to do it 'right'. — So! Which would you prefer? These are top-level and what I would suggest being worthy of any student of Doyen. Being trained by him is a rare thing indeed! … I actually don't think he's trained anyone."

Callimay browsed through them at first, but slowly became sucked into what she knew: clothing design. It still bugged her that each and every drawing was black. They were all different, yes, but they were still all the same. How boring! And then they were all long-sleeve shirts with a semi-bulky collar and black pants with varying numbers of pockets or stripes on them.

The more she looked at them, the more Callimay didn't like them… and it wasn't because of what she was objecting to earlier.

"Well, Callimay?" Tabitha asked a few moments after she closed the book. "What do you want to try?"

"Is there anything else that you have? I mean… is this it?"

"N… not really," Outfitter stuttered as his eyes bounced back and forth between a shelf behind Callimay and the book which was pushed back to him.

Catching this cue — and hearing what he said to himself — Callimay trotted over to the shelf and picked up the top drawing she saw. Yes, the outfit was black, but there was something different about it. It looked new, fresh, modest, and… well, like something Callimay wouldn't mind wearing, "What about this one?"

"Oh, that's just some of my personal doodles." Outfitter laughed in a nervous tone as he rushed over and took the page along with the others away from her. "They're not approved yet and only approved ensembles are allowed for Shadows."

"I'm not a Shadow, officially." Callimay reminded as she bent the page so she could see the drawing. "And I really like it."

"Well…" he scratched his head and contorted his face, wanting to justify letting her have it. "It is true that whatever you have as a trainee doesn't have to be approved… and you do like it?"

"It's the only one I can see myself wearing."

That's all he needed to hear, "Why not! It'll serve the purpose you need during the regimen. And maybe by then I'll have it approved or find a close substitute that is. — I 'should' tell you that it will take me a day or two, but I couldn't stand not finishing this one. What size?"

"Well, since I don't know your sizing standard, why don't we start with medium?" Callimay suggested.

Tabitha cleared her throat, interrupting the conversation before Outfitter disappeared back to his stash, "What about shoes? You've got to have something on your feet, don't forget."

"Umm…" Callimay whipped her head around, immediately locking on a pair. "How about these?"

"Those!" Tabitha and Outfitter asked in unison; their expressions and vocal tones matching.

"Why not? They're a bit heavy, but not bad. I'll get used to them."

"Those are regulation, grade A Veil boots." Tabitha gulped; unable to believe what was said as far as a possible con of the boot. "Only those who've trained for at least a year can wear those without twisting their ankles during a run; let alone be quiet enough for any mission."

"Well, I guess I don't have to." Callimay shrugged her shoulders as she set it back down and began looking at the others.

"You mean you could run in these?" Outfitter asked stunned as he came over and pointed at them. "And be quiet about it?"

"I grew up in the hills and I have run in shoes similar to these… quite often. The only thing was: mine were taller and stilettos… and I guess lighter as far as weight goes, though. As long as you walk on the ball of your foot, you can be really quiet."

"You're kidding me." Tabitha tried to keep from laughing.

"No, I'm not. The heel on these are what… maybe three inches? And the heel is really chunky so there's added stability right there. My stilettos were six and a half inches."

"You're sure?" Outfitter cautioned as he glanced at the sole of the boot; noting the number on the sticker.

"I won't place any blame if something does go wrong. Size eight… medium width if you have it."

Outfitter surrendered as he turned around and plodded to the back, "It's your ankles, I guess. If Doyen says otherwise, I would definitely come back for a different pair."

Once he disappeared, Tabitha whispered, "Did you know those—"

"No! They just caught my eye is all."

"And the ensemble…"

"All of the others reminded me of the girl who shot and almost killed Destan." Callimay admitted as she started to space out; then switched the conversation, "So what's this about my hair?"

"It has to be kept out of the way so it doesn't get caught on a tree branch or whatnot; but still loose enough so if you're signaling another Shadow it doesn't look suspicious." Tabitha explained as she escorted her to one of the chairs in the other area. "And with your bangs the way you have them it'll work out perfectly. — Now this book shows the different styles available. Mine should be toward the back somewhere.

It's been a while since I've looked in this book so I… ah! Here it is. Very secure and yet still flowing."

"If you could show me how to do it, I guess I could do it." Callimay bit her lip. "Maybe."

"Not the greatest at styling your hair, are you?" Tabitha smiled as she nodded; flipping through the book again. "Why don't we look for something a bit simpler, sound good?"

As they kept going through the different styles and talking, Callimay noticed something else that was odd, "Why are all the pictures with dark or black hair?"

"It's another code: everyone who isn't stationary or in black widows has to have dark brown or black hair so they truly are a shadow during a run. Your hair is boarder-line… but don't worry about it right now. If Doyen likes your hair the way it is, then I think you'll get by."

"So what about your hair? Yours is such a pretty, deep auburn color. Did you get to keep it?"

"Well, it was black until Redje and I got married." Tabitha reminisced as she looked down at her hair. "I didn't think about it when I made my decision, but regret it even to this day. My hair has actually never gone back to its original color or 'felt' the same. It was a vibrant and lighter red… and it was really curly and soft. Redje says that it's soft and a beautiful color, but this is nothing like what it was my entire childhood." *But it does make looking in the mirror more tolerable now. So it's not all bad.*

"What about Destan? Do you know if his hair is naturally bl— never mind. His dad had black hair. What a stupid question."

The page flipping stopped within a couple minutes as Tabitha pointed, "What about this? Do you think you could style this yourself?"

"Can I try it now and have you help me? The way you do Rose's hair leads me to believe you know a thing or two about such things."

"That wouldn't be a problem at all! Outfitter probably got lost looking for those boots so I'm sure he'll be a while."

Tabitha's hands were so tender as they started working away to make Callimay's hair look just like the picture. For a moment, the memory of the first time Mrs. Berchoff did her hair came back. Why? She couldn't quite understand.

"What the— was this all a prank?" They heard Outfitter call out. "You've gotta be kidding— alright, very funny 'ha, ha'. Now—"

"We're coming." Tabitha laughed as she motioned to Callimay. "We'll finish it after we get your ensemble squared away."

🕉

After a few tries with different sizes, Callimay soon had her black ensemble completed and her hair fixed appropriately. Tabitha peaked around her best friend's shoulder as she nodded in approval, "I think it'll work just fine. You did a great job with your hair. All you need is a little practice."

"What are these for?" Callimay questioned when she noticed the sleeves that were along the sides of the pants.

"They look like— Outfitter?"

"What?"

"Mind explaining all the bells and whistles on this ensemble? We don't want her walking around with the incorrect weaponry, do we?"

"Heaven's no. Forgive me for not having a list ready. Those you're fiddling with are built-in sheaths for hummingbirds." Outfitter started rattling off. "The blouse sleeves have hidden — single hummingbird sheathes — and then the boots? Umm... I think those are the mini spikes, but they might be standard size."

"Since when did sleeves get sheathes?" Tabitha sounded upset.

Outfitter jabbed as he shook his finger at her, "Since you left."

"I pave the way for these newbies, I tell you what. I had to use hair pins or risk having a spike in my hair... and now they get actual throwing knife sheaths. Kids now-a-days. Spoiled little brats. ... Oh! Outfitter, I have a question."

"I'm listening," he acknowledged in a raised voice as he walked to the back.

"Have you ever had to repair a veil?"

"Excuse me?" He backed up to the door and looked over; his forehead severely wrinkled. "Repair a... a veil?"

"Yeah. Doyen got himself in a bind and his veil suffered."

"Doyen!" Outfitter gasped as he came back out. "When did this happen? How? Who?"

"He's fine." Tabitha calmed; now regretting she opened this can of beans. "I was just curious if you ever had or were allowed to repair or make a new one for someone if it was damaged."

"That's… that's never happened." Outfitter tried to think; shaking his head as he rubbed his beard. "I… I'd have to check about any code concerning such things. I could let you know—"

"I'm not going to be staying much longer so you can let Callimay know when you do."

"O… kay."

"Surely you heard the rumors about Doyen being married, right?"

"Who hasn't?"

"Well…" Tabitha exaggerated as she motioned to Callimay.

"No!"

"Guilty," Callimay raised her hand; trying to be light-hearted.

"Well of course I'll let her know as soon as I find out!" He immediately agreed; his expression changing. *The wife of Doyen liked my own concept! Maybe she can get him to switch to a newer ensemble for himself. That old rag he wears is of no use to him…*

ℬ

As the two of them walked out, Callimay jerked back and gasped, "I've gotta go. Destan's awake."

"First left, first right, and at the end turn left." Tabitha waved as she called out to her.

"Thank you!"

Callimay ran the whole way and stopped at the door just long enough to catch her breath. She cracked it open and snuck in; being ever so quiet. From what she heard he wasn't "awake", so she was hoping he hadn't gotten up yet.

But, as she shut the door, she heard his booming voice, "Callimay Rose Nevrille. Where have you been?"

"Destan!" She screamed as she turned around and jumped back, dropping the bag her clothes were in.

"And what in the world are you wearing?"

"I… I've been with Tabitha and Outfitter for the past… I guess for the past two hours." Callimay admitted as she glanced down at the watch she had on and then right back to him. "I went to ask Tab— I mean 'Helpmate' if there was anything I needed to do before I started training. She said that doing this would help my standing with the Veil if they saw I was serious about having an actual ensemble from t—"

"Don't 'ever' leave without telling me, Calli." Destan sounded more worried than upset as he took her in his arms and held her close. "I was— just don't leave like that again. Okay?"

After he was satisfied, he asked as he put her at arm's length and looked her square in the eye, "You don't 'have' to do this. This isn't some class like even physics was for you. It's much more physically and mentally demanding… even your Veil regimen will be an entirely different— Calli, are you sure about this? This could take in upwards of two 'years'. You'll constantly have to train and work…"

He felt and saw the shock from how long this was going to take settle in, but she sounded determined and calm, "I want to be with you, Destan. And this is my only choice if I want to. … I'm ready for this. — So! What's my first lesson?"

"Learn to call me by my title," he tapped her cheek and turned around, hiding his smile from her.

"Yes Destan." Callimay nodded quickly as she clasped her hands behind her; and then corrected herself when he turned around and flashed his eyes at her, "Doyen! I meant: 'yes, Doyen'."

"That's better," he nodded as he turned back around; trying to keep from laughing.

Destan?

"Yes?" he looked over his shoulder; sounding curious.

"Do… I mean… will I… will I 'ever' be allowed to call you Destan again?" She wrung her hands as she bowed her head; her voice sounding crushed and scared.

"Oh, Calli," he turned around and kneeled in front of her. "As far as I'm concerned you just have to use that when we're around other Shadows or Veils… or when we're out on a mission. I wouldn't be able to stand not calling you Calli so I'm not going to expect you to always refer to me as Doyen. I rarely call Redje, Tabitha, Rocher, and Doctor Gerould by their titles… even around others here."

She smiled as a few tears jumped ship and slid down her cheek.

Destan wiped her face and then stood as he rubbed her arms, "I think for your first day I'll teach you about our codes of conduct and the history of the Shadows and Veil. I say that more for myself really… I'm still feeling that once-over Baleck gave me the other day. For his age, he had great form and reaction time."

"Are you sure you're alright?" Callimay rushed over and reached out to him. "Is there something I can do?"

"Another thing you need to remember is that this won't be the last time I take a licking. I'm not telling you to stop caring, but you need to realize me having cuts, bruises, or being sore is going to be 'normal'. And you need to know that I can take it. … Okay?"

But why! Why would— how can you live like that!

"Calli?" Destan tilted his head as he lifted her chin. "Calli I'm just sore right now. I really only said something because I know with the way my emotions can escalate and cause bigger issues… and I don't want you shell-shocked when it happens again."

"But why does it 'have' to happen?"

"Fighting for your life means you're going to take a beating in one way or another. I'm just hoping I can take it all so you stay—"

"I've got to be able to fight for myself, Destan. You even said that a couple days ago." Her voice strained as she tried to hold back the rest of her tears.

He stood there and closed his eyes, knowing good and well what she said was true: by his own definition and admission just two days ago, she was — for certain — going to be hurt one way or another by those who were evil. Yes, he could take the brunt of a physical beating for her, but the fact remained that she had to know what to expect so she could withstand it when it came in "real life". And she could still feel everything he went through.

☙

For the rest of the day, he taught her what he was allowed to at the time and what she needed to know concerning how the Shadows came to be and what they were doing. Remembering that she loved history made this teaching really easy for him. In fact, it made it so easy that the day slowly morphed into one of their lazy ones they would have back in

Rayleen: her curled up in his arms, sitting and looking out at their new view; neither of them saying anything.

"I'm sorry everything's been ruined, Calli." Destan apologized as he leaned his cheek against her head; stroking her hair.

"Well… I always wanted to see the world." She sounded rather light-hearted as she fussed with a loose string on his one cuff. "I didn't get to see it on the way here, but…"

"Always my optimist." Destan smiled as he put his hand under her chin, resting his forehead on hers.

Callimay assured as she gave him a kiss, "I loved our special evening at the ball. No one can 'ever' take that away from me. Thank you."

"I—"

"Elder has requested your presence, Doyen." Nexus informed; having the exact same timing as Rocher did for so long.

"Now, now?" Destan asked irritated as he threw is head back in frustration. "Can't he wait a while?"

"Now."

He growled as Callimay crawled out of his arms, "We never get—"

"Hey," she framed his face with her hands and make a bit of an exaggerated expression. "Don't make me calm you down."

"Alright," he sighed as he closed his eyes; and then smiled and finished, "Liaison."

"You!"

"What?" Destan exaggerated as he made a face back.

"I… oh you know I can't stay mad at you." Callimay surrendered and plopped down in front of him.

"I'll be back… when I get back. Elder's unpredictable, so I don't know how long this will take." *I don't know what in the world he wants to see me for.* He took a deep and almost labored breath as he grunted and got up.

"D… Destan?"

"Yes, Calli?" He grunted again as he put his veil on.

"Could I go with you? I won't go in! I just… want to be with you."

"It's probably best that you don't right now. Things… just not right now. Okay?"

"Okay."

Destan smiled after he gave her a kiss, "I'll see you as soon as I can. Love you."

"I love you too."

🕉

After he left, Callimay went back to the window and sat down. She tried to find something to entertain herself with but she wasn't as resourceful as Rose always was: *There's got to be something I can do. … Maybe I can go see Tabitha? ~ She was working when you saw her this morning. ~ True. … And her and Redje might be eating dinner right now. — It was fun having them over or us going over. I… I miss~ Now don't start. Try to think about now. … Wait!* *Destan?*

So, you decided to come anyway, huh? He smiled as he kept walking. *What can I do for you, 'Milady'?*

Tell Rocher I said hi. — Will you be back in time for dinner? Or would you like to pick some up?

Oh. I guess I forgot about that, huh? Oops! … Since it's Elder who called me — like I said before — I doubt this will be a quick and easy fix or discussion, so how about I see if Rej and Tabitha are available? … Calli? Calli I'm sorry I didn't think about missing—

But Nexus said Elder 'requested' to speak with you. The way you're talking it sounds like it was a command. Why?

It's one of those: it's worded as a request to sound like you're being nice and allowing the other person to decide what they want to do because they are your superior when in reality it's a command.

But you're the leader. Why is Elder allowed t—

If anyone has a problem or issue, they're allowed to 'request' to talk to me. Things can go wrong and they need to be fixed… and I don't know every detail about things to anticipate some things that do end up going wrong. — I'll admit Elder's a frequent flyer when it comes to his requests not being 'emergent' issues, but he's not doing anything 'illegal'. Just 'super' irritating; which is normal for him. I'm gonna try my best to keep myself in check, okay?

Oh. I'm sure you'll be fine. — Well, back to what you said, I'm not really hungry right now. And I don't know if I'd enjoy myself being with them by myself. She sighed; sounding depressed.

I really am sorry, Calli. … I'll bring something with me, I promise. — I've gotta go. I'll let you know when I'm able to talk again. It's best if I don't space out when talking with him; or I'll get that lecture too.

Alright, she sighed as she closed her eyes and lay down.

A little while later she woke up and started wandering around the spacious studio; the noise of her heels reminding her of the mansion's marble tile floors. Callimay sighed as she ran her hand across the stone wall, sad she wasn't "home", but still able to be glad at the same time: both her and Destan were safe.

She couldn't help but notice how the few pieces of furniture matched so well; made from the most immaculate black resin, mirror-like platinum edging and accents, and some pieces covered where needed with the softest of pure black leather that was embossed with the same emblem… the one from the car!

The only desk in the room was rather understated; its desktop not much larger than a writing desk. It only contained four drawers, two on each side. Both top ones being smaller in size than the bottom ones.

Callimay curled up on the plush leather seat and fingered the drawer handles; finally opening the top left one: *Typical drawer for any desk. … Are these gel pens! ~ He'd be able to afford them, that's for sure. ~ This glides like water on glass! And just look at the rich color! ~ Ha! I could tell it was still shiny. I knew that'd happen! ~ Surely it washes off. … See? It's fine.*

Once her infatuation with the writing utensil was over, she looked in the drawer underneath it. Again, it was another typical drawer for a writing desk: file organizer. This one was pretty immaculate and yet jam-packed at the same time. Callimay contorted herself so she could read the tabs; slamming it shut when she saw the word "mission" on one. She was scared to look behind her, worried Destan or someone else would be there to scold her for looking at them, but she was alone in the room. And how could anyone be mad? The drawer wasn't locked. How could she know what was inside was a secret?

Now calmed from her momentary scare, Callimay swiveled the seat to the right side of the desk and opened those drawers.

Things now began to get interesting: this side was definitely not what you'd expect in any "normal" writing desk. If it were a spy's desk

— which it was — it'd be normal, but it startled her nonetheless. Two sheathed knives were the only occupants of this drawer. It appeared they'd been untouched for quite a while since an outline of dust was left in the drawer when she picked them up. Rubbing the sheath to get the dust off proved they were black leather… stamped with the same emblem as everything else in the room. The handles were a black resin with what looked like a galaxy of stars trapped in them. She slipped one out and saw the black, mirror-like blade that was engraved with scrolling and writing. Callimay tilted it so she could read the writing.

Remember Challenger: every Veiled battle in the Shadows is worth fighting…

Curious since there was an ellipsis at the end, she laid that knife on the desk and took out the other one.

…because you have two hearts waiting for you in the light.
~ Lylah and Destan

These were your father's! Callimay gasped as she started fumbling; almost dropping the razor-sharp blade on herself.

She still had the sheath in her one hand; and as she flipped it so it was right side up, she saw a little piece of something fly out and skid across the floor. Whatever it was, it was a dark color, so she kept her eyes on it to see exactly where it went.

Callimay set the sheath down without looking and darted over to where the little escapee flew. At first she was concerned it might be sharp, but the more she looked at it the more it looked like a piece of paper that had been tightly folded: *Huh. I wonder what it could be. … Whoever did this really knows how to fold paper. Goodness! I don't know if this has 'ever' been unfolded. … This is like those fancy little trinkets I remember Trever saying he brought back from Ferdinan the one time. What were they called? — Wait a second. This handwriting looks familiar. ~ You're right; it does look familiar. Hum… oh! Those capital letters. They're slanted but nothing else is. Destan's father wrote like that.*

I'm hoping this is never read, but if it is that means the fight isn't over. Elder isn't who he is leading everyone in The Shadows and Deep Dark to believe he is.

The Shadow Boxes contain everything needed to complete this black widow.

Canary was reassigned, so I am down to utilizing what resources I have.

Elder "cannot" be allowed to stay within the Shadows in any capacity. In fact, he can't be allowed to stay alive. Don't underestimate him; he is more powerful than anyone can imagine: he is the Origin of a kind of evil only matched by the devil himself.

What! She shrieked in horror as she reread what was written. *I… who… Elder? Wasn't he— and what's a Shadow Box? Who is Canary? What evil has Elder done to deem him worthy of capital punishment? And why did Destry refer to him as Origin? That was Baleck!*

Callimay scrambled to her feet and fumbled as she put the knives back in their sheaths and threw them "and" the note in the drawer; somehow hoping the frightening truth associated with them would vanish if kept hidden. She sat there plastered against the seat, heart pounding as she tried to make sense of what it said.

There was another detail that didn't make any sense. Yes, she knew what a shadow box was; but this was "specifically" capitalized. So whatever this object was, it wasn't what she knew a "normal" shadow box to be.

The lonely drawer on the lower right side was all that was left that could possibly contain the answers she was looking for. — Destan had to know about this; he didn't appear to like Elder. — Maybe it did, but Callimay was frightened to see what secrets might lie within. It could be that there were no answers… just more questions.

Her curious nature won out. And then it didn't. The drawer was stuck. Was this a warning? Should she— it gave way.

"Calli don't!" Destan yelled as he slammed the door.

She yelped as she jumped back; falling out of the chair, "I'm sorry. I didn't mean t— I was just curious—"

By this time he was beside her, helping her up. The look on his face suggested her knee-jerk reaction wasn't quite right, "I'm sorry I scared you. I didn't mean to yell— you didn't do anything wrong. I just… I haven't opened that drawer in almost two years. It… it's just been easier for me to leave it that way."

Callimay glanced back at the papers and trinkets that looked like they were thrown in it.

"There was a box of things from my father left here for me. I got tired of seeing the box day after day so I tossed everything in here and kept it closed. A 'nice' and 'honorable' way to preserve my father's memory, I know. I just couldn't take it at the time."

"I'm sorry." She felt horrible and rushed over to shut it. "I'll stop—"

"No. No, it's alright. You didn't know." He took hold of her wrist; and then paused before he finished, "No, let's clean it out. It needs to be. … Would you help?"

She nodded as she clasped her hands in front of her, trying her best to smile at Destan who appeared distressed.

Before too long, they had most of the contents of the drawer on the desk… and surrounding floor. — How in the world did that all fit in such a small drawer!

As Destan picked up a magazine, he froze. And then a few seconds later, his hand jerked as he forced the magazine toward Callimay; him not taking his eyes off of what was in the drawer. It was another short period of time before he moved again; this time reaching in the drawer.

When his hands reemerged, they were cradling something rather small. As he moved his hands, she could see it was a box of some kind. It was shiny, so the logical thing would be to assume it was made out of metal… which made sense since the overall design — that she could see — matched everything in the room.

Destan sat down, still in somewhat of a trance, and pushed some things aside to make room for it on the desk. The box made a hefty metallic "clack" as it made contact with the desktop.

Quiet and curious, Callimay came up beside him and sat on the armrest, putting her arm around him as she looked at the box. It had something etched into it that was broken up… just like the puzzle box from the mansion!

He felt the top, and then started shuffling what turned out to be panels… again, just like the puzzle box from the mansion. When he got done, he flinched and took a quick, deep breath.

"What?" Callimay asked worried.

"This is the original seal of the Veil. … I… I've never seen one of these boxes before. Never. — And… yeah, it's solved. It should open. I don't understand what's wrong."

"Well, maybe it's just finicky: the pieces have to be 'just right'?" She tried to keep him calm as she rubbed his back; suggesting after a couple minutes of him fuming to himself, "Would you mind if I looked at it?"

Without saying anything, Destan handed it to her. What he called a "seal" looked like a mini picture of him standing on the cliffside at the mansion on a windy day: a man wearing a "veil" that was snapping and flapping in the breeze: *You don't think? ~ It's got to be: Destry's Shadow Box! ~ But didn't his note say box'es', plural?*

Doing her best to hide her reaction since she could feel him staring at her the entire time, Callimay started turning the box so she could see all the sides. She finally turned the box over and saw there were symbols on it that were scrambled and scattered across the bottom, "I think there's another puzzle."

After a few moments of working, he whipped his head up to her; his eyes looking horrified. His lack of explaining what was causing this reaction from him prompted her to ask, "What do those symbols mean? Is it solved?"

It appeared he took the first breath that he had since he found the box, "It's spelling 'Challenger' using the alphabet of an ancient language of the Homeworld. … Only a couple dozen families around the world still use it here."

"Which one?"

"Koine Greek… what the entire New Testament was originally written in, actually."

"So that's what it looks like?"

A few moments lapsed before what Destan first said sunk in, her eyes bugging out, "Challenger!"

"That's what I thought as well. But there's a couple problems: this is just a transposition of the letters, not the actual Greek word for challenger. And then the usage of Greek at all… we don't use it since it's so rare. Yes, not many know how to read it but it'd be a dead giveaway if found. Japanese is so common as a second 'language' for writing that we use it instead. … I just don't understand."

Destan kept at it as he muttered to himself and finally unscrambled the pieces.

All he had to do now was slide the last piece up to complete the puzzle… but he hesitated. A part of him was scared to see what was inside the box since this was attached to his father. He really didn't want to go through that right now; he wasn't ready.

Callimay knew he was fighting inside of himself — it being nothing but a worsening stalemate — so she reached over and pushed his hair out of his face so she could see his eyes. Destan looked up at her and opened his mouth to say something, but just couldn't get it out.

"We can leave it for right now, don't worry. We'll put it in the top drawer and look at it later… when you're ready."

He took a deep breath as he closed his eyes and handed the box to her. She rubbed the side of his face as she smiled; leaning over to give him a kiss.

When she shut the drawer, Destan got up and left the room. Not so much as an "excuse me" said.

All of a sudden Callimay felt a spike from him. She ran into the hall and saw him storming down the hall and disappearing into a room. His emotions were continuing to escalate this entire time so Callimay ran to where he was as she tried to keep in touch with him mentally.

As she opened the door, she heard him grimacing and hissing, "How in the world am I supposed to move on completely? Do I have to erase your memory altogether? When will the torture stop! There's nothing good left for me to—"

He was punching a heavy bag, but didn't have anything on his hands. With the force he was exerting, Callimay ran over and grabbed his forearms so he wouldn't hurt his wrists. She unfortunately made the painful mistake of standing in front of him and ended up getting the wind knocked out of her when Destan overpowered her.

As the air left the room, he came back to himself and yelled, "Calli! Calli I'm so sorry for— Calli!"

She was curled up on her side, wheezing as she tried to catch her breath with her hand that kept clawing at the floor beside her.

Before long, the shock of the pain wore off and she started slapping the floor; her eyes bugging out as if to scream at him.

"I'm glad to see you got right to it, but don't work her too 'hard', Doyen." Fidus cautioned as he came in and shut the door. "At least not on her first day."

"Calli. Calli stay with me. Calm down and take a deep breath. I know it sounds impossible but you can do it." He ignored the ill-timed comment made by his second-in-command. "In. Out. Follow my lead. In… out."

I can't… I can't calm down. I can't… I can't breathe!

Yes you can. He tried everything he could to be calm for her; doing everything to keep his self-scolding at bay. *Focus on breathing. How do you do it? Look at me. Watch me: in, out. In… out. In… out. … There you go.*

Callimay was on her back now, her hands trembling as she tried to hold his arm; her trying to "catch up" on breathing.

Fidus made another comment, reminding Destan he was in the room. He whipped his head around and snapped, "When did you get here and why are you here?"

"When I walked in the room and not a second before. — Helpmate and Confrere asked me to relay if I saw you that they're leaving for Safe Haven at the end of the day tomorrow."

"Make sure Nexus notifies me before they leave for the airstrip."

"I'll see to it," Fidus nodded as he opened the door to leave; stopping and turning back for a moment, "You'll get used to that feeling, Liaison. Just keep working. It'll get easier and more tolerable the more you do it. Keep it up."

"Calli… Calli I'm sorry I— why can't I keep myself under control better!" He couldn't retrain himself and scolded himself as his attention bobbed between her face and her quivering hands.

Destan please! You getting mad at yourself is 'not' helping me any. … 'I' was dumb enough to step in front of you, okay? I know good and well I'm not immune to being a 'victim' of your anger. It's my fault.

~ 3 ~

The next morning was a rough start for Callimay, but she did agree with Fidus that she needed to get used to being "sore". Though not suggesting she needed to get used to being punched, specifically.

And then at breakfast she was reminded of another change, "Why can't we spend the day with Tabitha and Redje?"

"Because you're in your regimen."

"Well… can't we do both at the same time?"

"Calli, you can't just buddy up with some of the 'upperclassmen' for a day to get your assignment done. This isn't 'school'." He tried to be reasonable yet firm. "I'll try to plan things today so we can grab a bite with them before they go, okay?"

She wasn't thrilled about what he said; but this glimmer of hope was all she needed, "Let's get to it, then!"

Doyen didn't approve of how joyful and carefree she was acting: hanging off his arm as she smiled and continually asked questions. And then Destan was angry with Doyen trying to take over. Needless to say, this battle was easily noticed: *Destan? … What's wrong?*

I… I'm just learning to— just learning to balance the way things are going to be from here on out. He took a couple deep breaths as he stopped and closed his eyes. *It's nothing you need to worry about.*

I just don't want you to get angry. She sounded worried as she rubbed his wrists with the softest touch. *I… I love you.*

After another deep breath, he opened his eyes and looked down to her; smiling, "Thank you for reminding me."

They walked hand-in-hand the rest of the way, Destan opening the door for her to the room he'd been in the day before, "How about a

84

retake from yesterday? This time I'll intentionally and 'safely' introduce you to this side of the regimen."

She froze as he walked to the back of the room and took his veil off, "Right now?"

"Being able to protect yourself is the number one priority of any Shadow or Veil. I know the codes of conduct were kinda thrown at you as a do-or-die expectation, but if push came to shove they'd say protect yourself at all costs no matter what. … It'll be alright. I'm here, no one else. We'll start with blunted versions of what you'll use so don't worry about hurting yourself 'or' me, okay? … Calli?"

"A… alright."

"Calli? Calli if you can't do this—"

"No, no! I…" she paused as she tried to figure out how to best word what she was thinking. "I guess I never thought about having to fight someone. I mean I kinda have, but I just used my abilities… and I still can't figure out 'how' I did it. And then if I had to kill—"

"As long as there is breath in me I will 'never' let you be in that situation where you have to make that call. … Ever." He looked her square in the eye as he held her by the shoulders.

She stood there and put her shaking hands on his arms and worked to calm herself down; Destan making sure to give her as much time as she needed. He knew good and well that she had no clue what she was really getting herself into, but he also knew she wouldn't quit. It was on him to keep things paced so she wouldn't be overwhelmed, and yet keep up with the set regimen and show her what this lifestyle entailed.

"Okay," Callimay took a deep breath and smiled. "I'm ready."

"I'll be here the whole time to help, alright? … Okay. Let's get started. — The Shadows utilizes a variety of combat styles because the Syndicate likes to diversify their skills so no one can predict what they'll do. They think we're pretty stupid but that's beside the point. We'll start with a very simple hand-to-hand." Destan explained as he took a step back, now in a defensive stance. "There are several ancient forms we've chosen for their effectiveness without utilizing weapons that disturb the silence we operate under. The Syndicate uses most of them as well, but we do have a few that are… well they're special because of their secretive and ancient backgrounds. I'll eventually teach you all of them since you'll be going through Veil regimen as well, but the main thing to concentrate on at first is to learn to defend yourself. It's our code to stay on the defensive: only initiate engagement when absolutely necessary. Once you've done them all, decide which discipline you want to utilize as your standard form. — And don't ask me which one I like best, okay? I'm so much taller than you that mine most likely won't be a favorite of yours anyway. — Pick the one that is most comfortable for you. With that said, knowing all the forms to some degree will make it possible for you to anticipate what your opponent will do when you encounter them. And then last on the list? Everyone else will tell you to 'not' adapt to your opponent, but I'm going to tell you 'to' do it while I train you so you can learn easier. … Info dump?"

"A little," Callimay replied a bit nervous as she did her best to mimic how he was standing.

Once they had been working for a while, she relaxed to the point she started asking questions. At first he wouldn't answer because he wanted her to focus, but then he started to realize she wanted to hear "him". She was in need of reassurance and an outlet to help her keep calm. So, he started pulling double-duty: focusing on her questions while at the same time focusing on how best to explain and show her these different skills. Of course there were a few he couldn't answer due to the shroud of secrecy with the Veil, but he assured that she'd find out when the time was right. — His confidence about her getting into the Veil was another point of confidence for her: he believed she was going to finish this and get in.

Things seemed to all fall into place at one point: her all of a sudden stringing a couple simple skills into a sequence. After she did this a half dozen times without him prompting her to, Destan ran with this to see how far she could go. He knew it was going to be basic skills only, but he was becoming curious to see what she would do: if she could begin to improvise on the fly.

They were in mock-combat for a few minutes without any break; and by the end she looked fine. He was more than satisfied with what she could do and put his hand out to give her a high-five… but instead was blindsided by Callimay pinning him to the ground.

"Destan!" She shrieked as she jumped back. "I thought—"

"It's my fault," he put his hands out to calm her as he sat up. "I didn't say anything about being done."

"I'm sorry!"

"Calli, it's fine." Destan almost laughed as he rubbed his cheek. "I've had much worse than being caught off-guard by a little girl who has just learned how to properly slap someone."

"What!"

"You hit like a girl," he shrugged as he sat there and started to grin. "And that's to be expected… because you are."

"Destan Quinton…"

"Yes, Callimay Rose?"

"Why do I even try. — And before you say anything, yes, I know it's time for lunch."

"Good!" He slapped his legs and then jumped to his feet. "Let's go. I'm starving."

Callimay sighed and rolled her eyes as he grabbed his Veil; making sure she looked civil when he turned around. He strolled over and offer his hand; smiling the entire time. She started to reach out but hesitated, "You're not going to pay me back for that… are you?"

He chuckled as he rubbed her cheek, "No. Although, part of your regimen is to learn how to outdo me. You're going to have to beat me."

"Huh?"

Is she ready for this? ~ Well you went and opened your big fat mouth so now you have to. … "You're going to have to punch me. In fact, you're going to have to get me to the point I yield to you."

She shook her head furiously as she jerked her hand away, "There's no way I would 'ever'—"

"Calli. I knew about that being part of your regimen. It was one of the first things I thought of when Fidus put you up for consideration. And since I knew that, I knew I 'had' to be your trainer. There's no way I'd ever let someone else to lay a hand on you. — But it's true: I'm going to become your opponent, not your trainer, not your husband. You're going to have to hit me and… and I'm— Calli, you don't have to do this. We can go home to Rayleen. I 'will' walk away from this if that's what you want."

"But we've already discussed this."

"I know we did, but you didn't know about this. — I guess it's my fault for not saying anything, like I've done before. … I guess I just didn't think of it being a problem because I'm your trainer." Destan sighed as he took Callimay in his arms. "I'm not going to 'make' you do this. We 'can' go home."

"You can't leave. They need you." Callimay sounded upset as she tried to keep from crying. "And if I want to be with you then I 'have' to do this. They've made it very clear that I can't stay with you all of the time unless I do. Just talking with you isn't enough anymore. I want to actually be 'with' you. I said I was willing to do anything… I guess I didn't think anything included fighting you and possibly hurting you."

Destan opened his mouth to say something, but just let out a heavy sigh and laid his chin on top of her head. The more he thought of it, the stress from every exercise she had to complete was going to be emotionally hard on both of them… in the hardest of ways. Things were going to get more and more difficult each day. They were most likely going to get frustrated with each other because he was going to have to show her the firm and strict leader he was as Doyen when he was her trainer.

"No matter what happens during this all," Destan soothed in his deep, calming voice as he held her. "Remember that I love you with all of my heart. Remember that I'm not forgetting. And Remember there isn't anything or anyone in this world that will ever change that."

Time stopped for a while; the sun bursting through the clouds for a little while and flooding the room with its encouraging warmth.

When a cloud that was too thick obscured it, Destan wiped Callimay's face and tried his best to finish what the sun started to do, "We don't want everyone thinking I don't love my wife and make her cry all the time, do we?"

"No," she smiled as she began to laugh.

"There's my Calli."

As they made the trek to the foot court, what happened kept Destan's mind occupied: Callimay had all but mastered the entire first three tiers of skills for this first form of hand-to-hand combat… in only one day! This was completely unheard of for someone who didn't have a background in some form of combat already. Her ability to adapt to what he was teaching her and implement the exact same skills with such ease and confidence was mind-blowing.

℈

To think Callimay was going to slow down for the afternoon session quickly proved to be a laughable thought. But how in the world was she doing this?

Destan kept asking her if she ever did any type of self-defense course but she always told him that the only "fighting" she ever saw was in the old spy movies she sometimes got to see on Saturdays… when she was allowed: *This just makes no sense. How is she able to 'anticipate' me if she's never truly seen or done it? I'm the one with that ability, not her. … But, I have to admit she was like this before gaining her ability. ~ Does that 'really' count? I mean… well it isn't 'that' different I guess. So what is it? ~ Maybe God just gave her the special, natural capability to learn fast… kinda like what I've been able to do my whole life. But I've gotta say: she's ten times quicker than I am.*

Destan was so preoccupied with this that he stopped early. They were well ahead of where they needed to be — she pretty much had this simple form mastered — so why push things?

This didn't make much sense to her since he didn't say "why" he did it, but Callimay wasn't about to complain: they got to spend a couple hours with Tabitha and Redje before they left.

"If you need anything, anything at all…" Tabitha offered as they all walked outside; it pitch black out.

"I'll know who to go to," Callimay smiled as she gave her a hug; finishing what her best friend started saying. "Thank you so much. Knowing you two are there for us means everything."

"Best you get used to hearing this," Tabitha sounded caring yet somewhat motherly at the same time. "It's how Shadows say goodbye: may the new moon continue to rise on you, Callimay."

"Contact me if anything changes." Redje reminded as he soft-slapped Destan's shoulder. "You're always welcome to come back to Safe Haven for a short spell if you need a break."

"Make sure to be on extra alert the next few weeks. I don't know if Baleck and Ginger got any or gave any information about where we were to the Syndicate." Destan broke the light-hearted feel of this send off. "I wasn't conscious for the whole thing and Calli did say Ginger left for a little while at one point."

Redje nodded as he took a deep breath, "I'll be sure to."

"Tell Rose we said hi and we're sorry we left without saying goodbye." Callimay added as her eyes started to get glassy.

"She's going to be heart-broken that her 'Desan' isn't going to be back for a long time."

"Oh, we'll be back, Rej. Don't you worry your feeble, old self about that." Destan jabbed; though he still sounded serious.

"Huh?" Callimay asked a bit shocked; Tabitha mimicking her look.

"I can't just abandon the side of me that is tied to Rayleen that 'the public' knows about. It would draw unnecessary attention. Especially now." Destan explained to the small group as they stood on the apron. "The rest of the balls will continue as planned; and so we'll be back for the week of each one and then come back to Bulwark in between until winter sets in."

"Well then. I guess we'll see you in a few weeks!" Redje smiled as he put his arm around Tabitha and started off; waving one last time as they looked back.

~ 4 ~

Even though things were so different, unfamiliar, and sometimes downright frightening, Callimay pushed through and was all eyes and ears to soak in as much information as she could: *I can't constantly be asking questions. ~ But isn't that you saying you're a burden to him?*

The next day they continued working in the combat room, shifting gears since it was almost as if he were giving a refresher course to a seasoned Shadow. Destan debated with himself a bit, but decided to introduce her to the Shadow's standard weapon of choice — the Seax.

She never said anything, but immediately recognized the shape of it: it was the exact same ones as those she found in his desk… his father's knives. As he showed her the correct form when holding one, she asked rather coy, "So, do all Shadows carry these?"

"Most do because they're sturdy and yet on the smaller side." Destan nodded as he walked behind her and nestled his face close to hers to fine-tune how she was holding the blunted knife. "Sorry Calli. I didn't mean to startle you. Something looked funny so I needed to see exactly how you were holding it. A… are you alright?"

"Do you?"

"Do I what?"

"Do you carry these?"

"But I… on occasion, yes." He sighed as he took a step back; not completely satisfied with her dodging his question. "I prefer to use just my hands and confiscate whatever my opponent may have. I've used that exact strategy with both Toreon and Baleck, actually."

The pause in his voice caused her to look over, "What is it? Am I still not holding it right?"

91

There was a moment where you could almost see what she said flow in one ear and right out the other before it jumped back in; him shaking his head, "Huh? … Oh! No. No, I'm fine. … I mean 'you're' fine. You can relax for right now. — Calli are you alright?"

"Yeah."

"Okay. — It looks like your ensemble is equipped with sheaths for a pair of Seaxes as well as a slew of hummingbirds and mini spikes."

"What 'are' hummingbirds?" Callimay asked confused as she looked at him over her shoulder. "Outfitter talked about them but I never asked him what he meant."

"They're an extremely small throwing knife." He explained as he walked over to an open cabinet. "Only Veils carry them. … Did you pick those boots on purpose?"

"No, I didn't." Callimay defended as he let a bit of a smirk jump out at her; unlocking the case he took out of the cabinet. "I just liked them the best. Everything else was so bulky or boring. These looked so much nicer. And I assure you, I can run in these with no problem."

Destan looked at her for a moment as he opened the case; and then busted out laughing.

"What?"

"You picked them because they weren't 'boring'… not because of their function." He could barely contain himself. "Oh Calli, you've got so much to learn. I know your job was more on the look of things, but form and function did come into play even in your work. Right?"

"What else was there to look at when picking them? They're shoes that cover your feet. All shoes do that and the ones at the store were all boots and relatively the same. How else was I supposed to pick out shoes? … That's why I picked this ensemble: I liked it."

Destan continued to laugh; this second wave almost doing him in, "Your ensemble isn't chosen for its looks. It's chosen for its function."

He had to wait until he could continue without laughing; explaining calmly, "Each ensemble is designed for a certain purpose. — Just like I'm sure you know certain suits or dresses are. — Those who are what we call 'stationary' don't require all of the bells and whistles that a Veil would require. And by the look of things, yours appears to be grade A Veil material. I've never seen that style before, though."

"Outfitter said it wasn't approved, but he consented since I'm just in training. He said he would try to get it approved by the time I finished or have something that would substitute."

"Figures. He gets bored easily. After running free for so long, being confined makes him fidgety. — He used to do quite a bit of fieldwork back in his heyday… 'quite' a bit. But things changed and he's found himself stir crazy. He's tried time and time again to get me to come in and change my ensemble."

"Why?"

"Because he's bored, I guess. At least I can't figure out why else he would be pestering me so much. — So," he took a set of small throwing knives out of the case. "First things first: these are 'real'. Okay? Second: they slip in your boots like this. Only the loops are visible so it just looks like part of the—"

Oh, that looks 'so' much nicer. That metal accent is just perf—

"Callimay!" Destan snapped as he threw the rest of the knives down and grabbed her by the shoulders. "This isn't funny! Your ensemble as a Shadow and Veil is your first and last line of defense: it houses your first line and then functions as the last resort. This isn't just a uniform to know you're a part of some click like at the Society. There's no room for error. The smallest mistake is unforgivable. It could mean you or someone else dies. Stop treating this like a joke and some social club!"

Callimay stood there in shock; she wasn't trying to downplay everything to "social club" status. She knew and was becoming even more aware of the fact this was going to be dangerous. All she was trying to do was be herself like she had been.

But it was quite apparent that wasn't going to fly anymore.

Regardless of what Destan said, their life together was changed: he was treating her different. She was sure he still loved her but it wasn't enough for her to submit to him as his loving wife; she had to be obedient as someone inferior to him. Every decision she did or didn't make was going to be scrutinized without mercy. He couldn't treat her like he had when he was teaching her physics. He couldn't even treat her with the patience he had when she was learning to drive. There was no room for error now. She lost her Destan who was care-free and jovial… the man she had to fight to find and keep. Now he was back to his old self that she first met: cold, cutoff, somewhat cruel, and seemingly heartless.

"Yes, Doyen." She gulped as she bit her lip and bowed her head. *God? Please help me right now. Help Destan. We—*

"We'll come back to those later. Take up your Seax, Liaison." He ordered as he turned and stood across from her, taking his stance.

ֆᎠ

Lunch was miserable, this poisoned atmosphere following them wherever they went. The edge in his voice faded but he was direct in how he addressed her with no reassurance or encouragement.

She tried once to get him to "loosen up" but that backfired in the most miserable of ways. It took her everything she had to keep from crying; what Mrs. Manning encouraged her about being tested to its limit. She didn't know if she'd survive.

For the afternoon and evening, Callimay hardly said a word. Anything she did say was only an acknowledgement of what Destan was demanding.

After a while of him constantly criticizing every little thing she did, she couldn't stand it any longer. She threw the Seax against the wall and ran out of the room as she screamed.

It was difficult for her to catch her breath as she ran down the hall; her sobs that violent.

When she got back, she slammed the door to the suite and wailed as she crumbled to the floor, "God help me! I can't do this! Please! Don't let me lose Destan… not again! … Please give me Your wisdom to know what 'needs' to be done. I… I don't— please help Destan. Help open his eyes and heart again. It's in Your Son's Name I pray these things, amen."

By this time she had quieted and only had muted sobs jump out every now and again. The emptiness of the room that announced its presence from her sobs echoing made Callimay desperate, "Nexus?"

"Yes?" She replied monotone.

"Can you reach Tabi… Helpmate? Please? It's very important."

"Pick up the private line in the room and I will contact Helpmate."

"Where is—"

"It's by the computer screen," she almost huffed.

Callimay scrambled to her feet and ran to where it was. She braced herself against the desk and then curled up beside it, trying to keep calm as it rang for an eternity.

Please, Tabitha. She cried as the darkened room felt like it were closing in on her to swallow her up. *Please pick up.*

There was a moment of silence, followed by the groggy and quiet voice of her best friend, "Callimay?"

"Oh Tabitha," she sighed in relief as she began to weep.

"What's wrong?"

"I've lost him. He's gone. I don't know what to do."

"Lost? Lost who?"

"Destan's gone!" Callimay cried louder; her starting to become hysterical. "I don't think I can do this."

"What happened? Where are you? Are you hurt?" Tabitha jumped up as fast as she could and started pacing the floor.

"Tabby… why are you up?" Redje asked as he rolled over and turned the light on.

"Shh! I can't hear." She waved her hand as her eyes got wider.

"…but he thought I was making a big joke about everything and just snapped. I was just being my fashion designer self; not mocking his authority or the—"

"Call Destan right now." Tabitha put her hand over the mic so Callimay couldn't hear her.

"Why?" Redje asked concerned; then paused when he saw his phone light up, "H… he's calling me. — Hey. What's going on?"

"I can't find her." He blurted out, sounding frantic. "Nexus said she was in the suite but I can't see her anywhere; and no one else has—"

"Slow down. Can't find whom?" Redje calmed as he got up and left the room.

"Callimay!" Destan almost yelled; his green eyes wild with just as much fear as anger while he stormed back and forth in the hall. "She ran out when I got mad and now I can't find her."

"Well, wherever she is Tabby's on the phone with her. I don't think she's physically hurt. Now, 'emotionally' I—"

"You heard her voice?"

"It was muffled, but yeah."

Destan took a deep breath and put his hand out to the wall to support himself, "She's alright?"

"Physically, I think she's just fine." He reminded in a calm tone as he peeked back in the room at Tabitha who nodded. "Now mentally and emotionally is something completely different."

"Rej… I…" he fumbled as he threw his back against the wall. "I don't know if I can do this."

"Just tell me what's going on."

He sighed painfully as he leaned his head back, trying to get his thoughts together, "You said my love for Callimay would change who I am as Doyen… well I just found out it's not. We were working basic hand-to-hand today and— maybe I did push things. She adjusted so quickly and accepted things, but maybe I went too far: since she was advancing so far so fast I introduced her to the weapons that completed her ensemble. She didn't quite understand I was being serious when I explained how they were made to look like part of it; and even 'I' was laughing about everything at first… but then I flipped out when she made a joking comment to herself — not even out loud. After that I did nothing but pick every little thing she did apart and constantly belittle her. I… I even shoved her away at lunch. I knew this was going to be hard for both of us but I really thought our love was going to get us through. Do I not really love her? Have I been lying to myself this whole time… and her?"

"Destan, stop." Redje gritted his teeth as he came out into the living room. "If you didn't love her would you be on the phone with me right now? Would you be half out of your mind with worry?"

"What's happening then! And you didn't see the fear and loneliness in her eyes. It's like I threw her over White Cove all over again."

Redje sighed as he sat down in his recliner; sounding much more somber, "Not in her, but I have, Destan. The first time I laid eyes on her I had my heart set on Tabby. Why do you think I broke my precedent and pulled rank on Synchronizer so I could train her? I wasn't about to let any other person be that close to her. … It all made sense to me at the time to do it that way, but I found out that first day how naïve I was in letting my emotions cloud my better judgement. I struggled so hard with how to balance the two for the longest time. On one hand — the side that had fallen in love with her — I wanted to do everything for her; but on the other — Switchblade — just wanted to treat her like another Shadow. That side of me knew I couldn't marry since my job was too dangerous. He dominated me so much; and yet each time I noticed I would try harder and harder to break him. I would tell myself things would be different. But each time it wouldn't be until I saw that look in her eyes that I could hear Switchblade laughing at me and my pitiful efforts to change. For the longest time I couldn't understand why I was letting that happen, but then I realized: 'I', Redje, wanted her to quit. I wanted to save her from the life I was leading. She'd been through enough with her sister and mother, and I loved her so much. Pushing her past her limit was the only thing I could think of to get her to quit. And yet I died inside every day when I saw that terror and fear in her eyes from my brash efforts to detour her. Every day I hated myself for what 'I' was trying to do. It wasn't Switchblade at all. I was only using him as the fall guy. I didn't want to take responsibility for what 'I' was doing. 'I' was making her mind up for her, telling myself that she really didn't want this life and I knew better."

"But we're married, Rej. I can't keep treating her like this and not expect our marriage to suffer from it. She's already given up so much to stay. I can't keep doing this to her!"

"Did you hear what I said?"

"I can't lose her. If I do this one more time I'm afraid she'll leave."

"Destan Quinton Nevrille!" Redje raised his voice as he stood up; and then took a deep breath and sat down, rubbing his face. "Just listen to me, alright? I know when you're charged it can be hard, but I need you to focus on what I say: do you 'want' her to do this? Do you 'really' want her to become a Shadow — and possibly a Veil — like you?"

Silence.

"I get why she agreed to this, but we both know she had, and still has, no idea what she's agreed to. And knowing that I can pretty much guarantee you what I was doing is what you are doing: trying to play the bad cop so she'll quit; so she won't get hurt." He explained as he saw a curious little hand creep around the corner of the hall wall. "Rose? Sweetheart, you need to get back to bed."

"I wanna be which you, Papa." She mumbled as she rubbed her eye. "I skeared. Why you yewl?"

"Destan, hold on a second." Redje sighed as he put the phone down and brushed her hair out with his hand. "Papa's sorry he scared you. I was just trying to get someone's attention. But Papa didn't do it in probably the best way, did he? … You've got to be absolutely quiet while I'm on the phone, alright?"

"I pwomise," Rose nodded as she crawled up into his lap and wrapped her little arms around his big, strong one.

"Okay. — Sorry, Destan."

Rose perked up when she heard the name but didn't say anything when Redje looked at her to remind her of the promise she made.

"I just don't know what— part of me 'does' want her to quit, but the other part doesn't want to deny her what she wants. I'd quit, but then things are progressing so well that I just… maybe I'm trying to decide what she wants. I don't know!"

"You said you were joking with her before you snapped?"

"Y… yeah." Destan admitted as he hung his head; a few tears racing to his nose and jumping off.

"Take this or leave it since I wasn't there to see for myself, but I'm wondering if you are trying to find balance in this all: keeping 'her' happy while making sure 'you' don't forget how serious things are."

"But I only feel like I'm treating Calli like she's dirt. I know she can tend to be a bit too optimistic about things, but I also know she understands this is serious. Maybe not to the level you and I do, but I'd never say she's totally oblivious. … She's tried so hard to please my demands today, and when she stormed out I finally saw that she tore herself apart to appease me. But she's not failing me. 'I'm' failing 'her'. I'm supposed to be stronger and help her. I just don't know what to do!" He said in anguish as he tapped his fist against the wall.

Redje rubbed his face and sighed; Rose looking up to him with her big, brown eyes that almost quivered with worry, "When I was at my wits end I asked Mr. Utree as well as my father what to do. And do you know what they 'both' said? … They reminded me we're human no matter what we're trained to do: creatures of habit. Once we get one train of thought in our minds, we can run that horse into the ground until it dies… and if we're super dedicated, we can take the time to dig it up because we don't think it's buried deep enough. What does that all mean? Sometimes it can be hard for us to adjust and adapt because we find it hard to accept a new way of doing things. — I know you've 'trained' Callimay before, but those were 'simple' things that didn't have any 'danger' associated with them. This type of training is going to require a completely different approach 'after' you figure out whether or not you're willing to let her keep doing this. If you can't convince yourself of that in your heart, you won't be able to train her at all. Believe me. It doesn't work that way. It never has and it never will."

Silence.

Rose raised her hand, and then asked in a sad voice when Redje nodded, "Ez Desan cwying?"

"I don't know, Sweetheart. He might be."

"May I tewl him I wuv him? Pweeze? I miss him."

He smiled as he put the phone to her ear, "Talk slow and be gentle."

Destan started sobbing when he heard her tiny, tender voice reach through the phone and give him a hug, "Desan? Desan I wuv you. Cowimay wuv you two. I no she does. We awlways hear four you know madder what. … Pweeze doan cwy. Is otay, Desan. Is otay. … I no know what wong, but I no dat God tan hewp. He verwy stwong and He awlways no what's white. … Desan?"

"I love you too, Rose." He sniffled; unable to stop his smile from spreading across his face when saying her name. "Thank you."

It sounded like she kissed the phone, and then he heard her and Redje talk for a little while before he got back on the line, "Destan?"

"I forgot I need to talk with God about this all before I make up my mind. … But if I 'do' decide to stay, how am I supposed to change? What did you do?"

"Regardless, you need to know you've already adjusted other parts of your life to fit into your new mold of you and Callimay. If you think back — really think about it — you'll notice you have. Doyen just hasn't been 'fitted' yet. You're not beyond hope when it comes to adapting and changing, Destan. It's just that Doyen hasn't. And if I'm going to be upfront: he hasn't even had a fighting chance. … Just remember it's not going to be an overnight thing. You've got to be willing to stick it out in the long-run; and remind Callimay on a regular basis what is going on and let her say how she feels. — 'I' have faith Doyen will figure it out. Give him time. Give 'yourself' time."

While this encouragement was so helpful, his strained voice still felt hopeless; him sliding down the wall as he finished, "I can't afford to lose any with Calli. I can't afford to be off on my timing. I can't afford to mess up continually like this. I… I can't afford to lose her. I've felt like I have a couple times and— I just can't go through that emotional pit of torment again, Rej. I can't. And I know she can't, either."

"You need to learn from your mistakes, but you've got to learn to leave them there: in the past. You've got to decide that each day you will do better. We're supposed to die to ourselves daily, Destan. Trust Callimay like Tabby said and be honest as well as realistic with her."

"What do I say?"

"Tell her what you're telling me. Tell her you're worried. Tell her you're not sure about things. — Show her you're human. — Now I'm not saying tell her you're giving up. Just because you're worried doesn't mean you're giving up; and just because you're human doesn't mean you're doomed to fail. You're at a crossroads of sorts right now, and now is the most critical time for you. 'You've' got to decide if 'you' want to stay and let that trickle down to the next question of letting Callimay stay. … And let me say if you decide to walk away and come back to Rayleen you're not a failure. If anything, you're strong and wise to see what is best and act on it no matter what others may think. … Destan? You need to remember that you 'can' make good decisions when it comes to you and Callimay. I mean, you married her, didn't you? Wouldn't you think that was a good decision? You're a good, Godly man who's making great strides to become the best husband you can possibly be; one who's fighting to make sure his old man of sin stays dead. — Now I could go on and on, but I don't want you to see my words as undo pressure or an absolute expectation."

"You're fine. Y… you're helping me think things through."

After a little while, Redje finished while Rose snuggled closer to him as she started to drift off, "Your wife is your helper given to you by God. Callimay wants to help; I know she does. She just needs help to know what you need help with. You need to tell her what you want."

"But what she wants is more important. All I need to know is what she wants. I just want her to be happy. And the only way that can happen is if I know."

"Now take this with the brotherly love that is intended, okay? — You two talk and talk with others to help them, but somehow I get the impression that you forget to talk with each other. You know you need to help each other and even yourselves just as much as other people, right? Doing is great, but you need that special time to talk; get things in the open and ask for help. Listen to how she feels and don't be afraid to tell her how you feel."

"I don't want to burden her with my insecurities."

"Do you seriously think she doesn't know there's something 'there'? And I'm not even talking about her ability. Would her knowing about them make those insecurities worse?"

"I… I just don't think it'd be a comfortable situation for us."

"Let me give you this encouragement: it won't be." Redje grunted a bit as he got up and started back to Rose's room. "Not right now, anyway. You've got to build that trust so it 'can' be. You're scared how she'll react and she's probably scared how you'll react… and I think that unknown factor is starting to tear you two apart. Don't base your fear off of assumptions."

"But how? I mean I want her to talk to me, but how do I get her to understand that?"

"Talk, to, her. You've both been through a lifetime of emotional drama this week; let alone the last few months. — If you decide to stay, I think the best thing is for you two to build your foundation of trust 'first'… then continue with the regimen. You've got to trust each other to the point that fleeting emotional outbursts don't uproot your relationship. And you need to have that freedom to be stern with her and her not think you're nit-picking her to death or being downright mean." Redje tried his best to be encouraging while brutally honest at the same time. "Destan? Are you there?"

"I wish everything were easy for her. She's been through so much."

"Marriage, just marriage by itself, isn't easy. It's rough… 'really' rough sometimes. I hate to say it; but I've been foolish and let my voice raise, I've let harsh words fly at Tabby, I've slammed a door or two in her face, I've misinterpreted what she said and placed blame, I've let our communication breakdown. I've let Switchblade, Fidus, and even Confrere creep up in me. But I have — and I know you do too — a loving and patient wife who submits to your wishes even when she knows there's one million different ways that are easier, puts up with your stubbornness by watching you storm out and slam the door behind you, and bears under the loneliness when you're trying to fix things by yourself. When she's the one lying by your side at night? The only one who can say, 'I love you' in a way that gives you strength, and the loving and warm embrace that makes you feel in control? You remember the wonder and beauty that marriage is. You remember the wonder and beauty you saw in her when you first met. And so, you fight harder to make sure you're not storming out on her, blaming her, or raising your voice to her. In short, you learn to be patient and wait. You learn to listen first and talk second. — Callimay strikes me as the one who always sees the silver lining. She looks for the good in everyone and works herself, maybe to a fault, to death to pull it out of them. That might put her in a place where she overlooks dangers, but don't see optimism as something evil. You telling her, reminding her what's going on, isn't swinging completely to other way, either. You're just trying to protect her. Realism isn't pessimism."

This last statement brought things full circle for Destan. He sat there and rubbed his face as he started working through things, talking out loud in a calmer tone, "Does she even want to talk to me anymore?"

"I—" Redje hesitated when Tabitha came out. "Just a second. — What is it?"

"Destan needs to talk with Callimay; she needs him desperately. The poor thing is half out of her mind with fear of him leaving her. She just wants to know he still loves her. She's been practically begging me on the phone for the past minute or so. I really think she's having a nervous breakdown."

"Where is she?"

"Callimay? Callimay, where are you? … No, no! It's alright. I just wanted to know. — She's in the suite next his desk."

"Rej?" Destan asked a bit concerned when he didn't hear anything for a little while.

"Callimay 'does' want you. Tabby just told me she's begging for you to be with her and talk to her. She wants to know you still love her because she's scared half out of her mind you're leaving."

"Where is she!"

"She's in your suite by your desk."

Destan dropped the phone and stared at the wall across from him. Callimay was just on the other side of the wall he was leaning against this entire time! — When he originally looked in the suite, he just glanced without looking around the door.

The next second, he scrambled to his feet and flew in the room; his phone skidding further down the hall as his veil flipped it to the side.

When he threw the door open he could hear her wailing. He raced over and wrapped her in his arms even though she started thrashing.

"I'm sorry, Calli!" He tried to console; his voice sounding agonized as he began to cry. "I love you so much. Please forgive me."

Now knowing who it was, she stopped her desperate attempt to defend herself and melted in his arms. She quivered and shook as she fell silent and let him rock her, "I love you more than anything or anyone, Calli. I'm not leaving you. I know my actions aren't a good reflection of that right now, but I'm trying. I'm trying to change. I'm sorry. You'll never lose me; I won't walk away. I promise you."

When they looked at each other it was easy to notice the pain and fear in each other's eyes: they were both emotionally broken. The reality of what they had been through in such a short time of their lives hit them both like a ten-ton wrecking ball. So many things that were left unaddressed, pushed aside, suppressed, forgotten, and hidden began to pull and tug at the two of them to rip them apart. It was starting to feel like they were strangers to each other; that their love was washing out with the tide.

Destan looked down and saw the glistening of her rings; closing his eyes as he quietly confessed, "I have taken you, Callimay Rose Berchoff, to be my loving wife for my own to enjoy and protect. Through the storms and calms, need and plenty, weakness and strength, illness and health… I have vowed to love and cherish you as the rare jewel you are until my heart ceases to beat and I am called home to our Father above. … Calli I… I don't…"

At first she was touched to hear him recount his marriage vows, but when he started pausing and sounding more and more uncertain; fading out when he finished with such negative sounding words… was he leaving? Was he telling her he couldn't fulfill his promises to her anymore? That who he truly was couldn't allow him to be who he promised? Was he saying this side of him was too powerful and quenched the love she thought they had worked so hard to form?

His silence was speaking volumes; his avoidance of looking at her answering every question she had. She was alone again.

Callimay let her hands drag as they fell off of Destan's shoulders; her clutching them to her heart. She couldn't breathe; her heart breaking inside of her as it was being ripped out.

In fact, she began to question if she ever truly had Destan. Had he lied to her so well while things were fine so she was blinded to the red flags she should've noticed? Was it true that she became too trusting and allowed her heart to be consumed and destroyed beyond repair?

Destan's voice cracked in desperation as he broke the murderous silence; looking up at his beyond distraught wife, "I don't… I don't want to break those promises. I want to keep them more than ever with what's going on. I know they weren't ones I made for that day alone: I have to keep them each and every day. — Calli? Love was never something I truly tried to understand until you spoke that four-letter word to me. I don't even think I truly enjoyed life until you came into it. … I didn't know what it meant to truly protect someone until I saw you needed it. I never noticed the storms I was in until you showed me what the calm could be like. And even though I had plenty, you showed me how needy I was. Through what others saw as weakness, you showed me the kind of strength that forever endures. You sacrificed your own health to heal my sickness. … I know good and well I promised through any situation in life that I would keep you as my sole focus: my priority. To protect you until my dying breath because you are so precious and rare that I can't 'ever' afford to lose you. I promised to recognize I'm not alone anymore and come to terms with the fact that means I need to adjust my life to reflect such. To see how special you are and that anything I do or say should scream that to the world so there is no doubt. That I have no right to break it when things are inconvenient or hard for me; the only one strong enough to break that vow being God Himself. I have no right to walk away and leave you alone. I have no right to push you aside, blame you, treat you like a servant, ignore your wants and desires, make assumptions about what you want to hear from me, or hide anything — and I mean 'anything' — from you. I have the free will to choose… and I still want to choose you. Please let me, Calli. Let me be the husband you deserve. I know I need to work harder to fulfill those promises and avoid all those things I have no right to do. … I wish more than anything that I could go back and change what I said and did today. … I… I belittled you and made you feel like dirt. I know I did. And I know you've given up so much to be here with me. I know it hurts your heart to let go of some of those things. You do everything to make me happy and please me; and I know how the tiniest of things I may critique can cause you grief because you think I'm unsatisfied and telling you that you failed. I'm not, Calli! I'm so sorry if I come across that way. If anyone is failing it's me. I'm failing at communicating with you. You've known for so long how me conveying my thoughts isn't a strongpoint I have… but I know I need to tell you this so you understand 'why' I acted the way I did; regardless of how awkward it might sound or how difficult it is for me to get out. — Now I'm not trying to justify myself, I'm just trying to help you understand what I'm having to work through. — I was upset that you were being so carefree and light-hearted about how your hummingbirds worked with your boots; thinking you were missing the point of why they're made to look like part of the hardware on your boot. I failed to remember that I was laughing and playing along just moments before. … I know I was being hypocritical by snapping at you: saying only 'I' could laugh it up. I'm supposed to be stronger and I wasn't. I'm sorry, Calli."

He took a few moments to regroup as well as let that first round of apology sink in; and then continued, "Redje doesn't think I've got my mind made up whether or not 'I' want to stay and that it's making me not want you to do this. That I'm trying to bully you into quitting. … And the more I think about it the more I know he's right. Some small part of me is terrified that something's going to go wrong and I'm going to lose you: that being here isn't safe for you. I 'know' it's the safest place in the world for us, but some small part of me can't believe that, and I don't know why. It's bugging me like none other but I don't know if I'll ever know why I feel that way. Maybe it's just my excuse to get us away from here. To get 'you' away from here. — After I snapped that last time and you left; I… I got scared that I didn't love you. I knew I was letting Doyen lead and I was seeing you as someone below me; someone who wasn't as good as me. So, the side of me that isn't Doyen started to doubt us. But even that didn't make sense. I'm not that kind of leader. I don't 'rule'. I just— maybe because of how you found out about all this caused me to— I'm not making much sense, I know. It doesn't make complete sense to me either. Calli? Calli I want you to do what you want, but at the same time I don't want you here. I don't want you to be alone, and I most certainly don't want to be by myself here, but I know what I'm doing here — if it works — will make our lives so much simpler. There's this battle going on inside of me that isn't allowing me to train you like you need. I keep bouncing back and forth and my emotions can't keep up. And I know that's hurting you. I… I'm sorry, Calli. I really am. I'm sorry I jumped into this without making sure I was ready; or you were. I thought I was and thought it wasn't a big deal you didn't understand, but— Calli I'm not sure what to do."

No response.

But it was okay, he wasn't worried… for some reason. Getting this out in the open was helpful. He wasn't scared.

"You're my bright and glowing ray of sunshine, Calli. You're my optimist who is always encouraging me to do the right thing. Don't lose that. It's one of the millions of reasons I love you. … I can't afford to lose you in any aspect of the word. I'd die inside if I did. I almost have a couple times and thought I did once. I don't want to go through that emotional torment again. I don't want to be here without you. I need you, Calli. Please tell me what I need to do to make things right. Please tell me how to gain your trust back. I want to talk with you. I want to understand you better. I know I did it after everything with Toreon calmed down; and I'm remembering how wonderful it was. Please… just… please don't give up on me. I might have slipped back, but I'm not giving up. I love you, Calli… I do. And I always will."

She was struggling with this complete emotional swing as well as the fact she almost repeated what almost got herself killed: she completely misunderstood what he was meaning and started thinking about what this apparent bleak future would hold. Reality was far from that nightmare she was concocting! He just was scared to talk to her; too scared to open up because he was scared to lose her. It was still a challenge for him on all sides of this situation; but he wasn't telling her goodbye. His silence wasn't that of rejection. Destan was fighting within himself to pour his heart out to her so she knew how he felt.

Callimay cried as she buried her face in her hands, "I'm sorry!"

Destan reached out as he calmed, "You don't need to—"

"No, I do! I was thinking horrible things about you and us. I… I thought you were getting ready to tell me goodbye. I thought you were going to tell me you hadn't considered this part of your life when we got married: that you couldn't fulfill your promises to me. I assumed since you didn't say anything more that you just didn't want to hurt me by finishing what you started. I thought since you didn't look at me you were scared to see me when you said it. I doubted you. I doubted us. I doubted you ever loved me and lied to me this whole time. I started thinking you'd been trying to find an excuse to leave me and now you'd found it. I'm sorry, Destan. I… I have to confess: a small part of me has always felt that way. I was too scared to say anything when we first got married, but then things seemed to work themselves out so I just put it aside. Now, I— I'm sorry. You probably hate me now for even thinking that. I don't b—"

"Calli I don't hate you! I never could. And the way I treated you, you really had no other choice. There was no other logical explanation for me being so distant. You didn't know and I didn't care to tell you for so long. And I didn't make things easy for you to be open with me. I'm sorry for all the pain I've put you through. I could blame it on so many things but it doesn't matter. I had a choice and I chose the completely wrong option. You should never — ever — have to endure that again. Please tell me if I'm making things hard. Things are hard enough as it is. I don't want to add to it in any way. I don't have any right to."

"I'm sorry I said you were worse than Toreon and that you kept lying to me," she sobbed as she threw her arms around his neck and laid her cheek against his. "I know that hurt you so much. I should've never accused you of sinning against me when I knew good and well you hadn't. — I love you so much, Destan. And I don't ever want you to leave me. I always want to feel you near me. I just… I want to be with you. Everything else doesn't matter. I'd give up having a place to call home if it meant I still got to be with you. … And I knew deep down all along that you couldn't be like that: lying to me and not caring about me. Things just kept happening that would make me entertain that thought enough so it stayed. If anyone's sinned, I guess it's me."

The truth hurt both of them, but at the same time it was healing. They finally understood each other on a new and deeper level. This lingering tension between the two of them was resolved. Now they could make made better choices and have the freedom to speak with each other about those decisions. It didn't take the danger or trials that were sure to come in the near future away; it didn't even give them a guarantee that they wouldn't have to go through a situation like this again. But it gave the two of them hope that they were fighting together… on the same side now.

While they didn't speak for a while, this kind of healing they began was best achieved without a word said. But before long Destan asked as he pulled Callimay back so he could see her face, "Do you want to stay? I want to make whatever you wish a reality. I just need to know."

"Tell me first what you want."

"Like I said, I 'want' to keep doing my work here, but I don't want you to 'have' to stay here with me and go through this regimen… but I don't want you to be alone in Rayleen while I keep working." He sighed as he rubbed his neck; and then put his finger to her lips as he finished, "But when it comes down to it: I just want you to be safe and happy. I want to give you a life that you can look back at when we're old and gray and tell me 'thank you' and 'I love you'. So, whatever I need to do to make that happen I 'want' to do. No hesitations, no questions. If you want to go home to Rayleen and start a family of our own, I'll throw this veil in Elder's face and not look back. I 'can' walk away from this. You are more important to me. … If you want to stay, I'll do everything I know to prepare you and make sure we're together. And I'll work my rear off so our relationship is stronger. — Now, what do you want?"

She reached behind him and opened the top desk drawer: *I can't leave and have a clean conscious about this. … I found your father's Seaxes the other day and there was this paper that fell out of the one sheath. Something terrible is going on here, Destan.*

He read the note that was written in a rushed manner — it almost looked like his father's hand was trembling as he wrote it — muttering in a disgusted tone, "How on… what is he… why?"

"That box you found the other day. Do you think it's what your father mentioned?"

They both looked back at the drawer and stared at it; the sounds of them sniffling interrupting the silence every now and again. He folded and unfolded the paper a few times before he reached in the drawer. The room started filling with this feeling of worry as he flipped it over, revealing the one misplaced piece. He laid his finger over it, but hesitated; looking at Callimay with what almost looked like terror.

"I want to do this, Destan. As long as you want to, I do." she nodded as she reached over and put her hand on his. "This is what I want: to help save those who need the help that I know I can give… and to do it with you."

There was a high-pitch snap, but it didn't "open". It wasn't like the other boxes Destan had. He could feel the lid move, so he slid it back to reveal not only what they were looking for, but some things he thought were lost forever.

His hand quivered as he reached in and pulled out his mother's rings. And then there was a small wooden paperweight that had his name jaggedly carved through the pristine, hand-carved seal of the University of Kerogen on it.

Destan's whole body began to quiver and tremble, yet it was so rigid and stiff as he began to remember things connected to those items. His gaze was fixed in such a way that he was too frightened to look away from those small items.

Callimay wasn't expecting there to be so many "personal" items in there. This wasn't at all what she was expecting. She knew seeing these things put him in turmoil; and she also knew his knee-jerk reaction was to run from the pain of those memories. So she reached out and began to wipe away the tears from his pain-stricken face: *Destan?*

The tone she used when speaking that one word was all it took to pull him out of the trance he was in. He closed his eyes and let the tears gush forth; dropping what was in his hands at the time. His arms trembled violently as he reached out for her and she took him in hers to comfort him.

She softly cradled his head next to hers as he continued to weep bitterly. Callimay understood the pain he was going through because she knew what it was to find something after so long that brought back all the pain and anguish of the loss of a loved one. His heart was breaking all over again; it reliving every scarring memory.

I'm here, Destan. She rubbed the side of his face as she held him closer. *I know it's hard. Don't be afraid to cry. Don't be afraid to remember. The past—*

Why can't it stay there, though? He cried in frustration as he worked to keep himself under control. *Why does it torment and haunt me when it comes back? Why can't it just go away and stay away if it won't 'play nice'? Why can't I remember any of the good? There had to be some. But— all I remember is the pain. I don't know how to let go and move on. I… I'm not like you, Calli. I can't find the good when there's so much bad.*

"Oh, Destan." She sighed teary-eyed as she brushed his hair out with her hands and then framed his face. "I wasn't always like this. For so long I was wracked with pain and loneliness. All I could see was the bad. I wasn't moving past the pain… I was wallowing in it and allowing it to consume me. I even cut myself off from everyone because I couldn't bear to see how happy others were. It made me feel like they didn't care I was in pain; almost like they were happy to see me in pain. I even became angry and resentful for a short time and made myself lonely. They weren't leaving me, I was pushing them out. … It wasn't until I found a letter my mother wrote me that I was reminded: what I remembered was my choice, what I chose to see as important was my choice, how I felt was my choice. She had loved me so much and done everything to help me even though she was hurting and trying to heal. She reminded me that this wasn't just about me and how I felt; it was about how I could help others going through what I went through and show them to not give up. She taught me that there was a love that would never leave me no matter what happened to those around me I so deeply loved. The words she penned reminded me I wasn't alone. There was still good to be taken from what happened. I just had to be willing to make that hard decision to let her go; to leave the past where it was. I had to admit to myself that part of my life was over; to remember it but to see that what I had right then was so beautiful and precious… and what was ahead could be so bright of a future if I wanted it that way. — We are so very much alike, Destan. We truly are. I can tell from the look in your eyes that you know exactly what I'm talking about. I know you want to move on. I know you want to put the past where it is and belongs. I know you want to enjoy what you have now. I saw that when we were in Rayleen. But that was because you chose for yourself to make it that way. You did it because of me… but that's not enough because you're not right now. You're placing blame on memories that are what they are. It's not their fault, Destan. You've got to make the decision to fight the pain, push through it, find the good, and lay the past to rest. You've got to do this for yourself. Not me. You've got to want better for yourself. And in so doing, you will make things better for me. … Letting them go doesn't mean you don't love them. It doesn't mean you didn't care. But they wouldn't want you in this pain, Destan. They wouldn't want you to not live your life full of happiness and joy. … Maybe I'm not making any sense now, bu—"

"You are," he slowly nodded and rested his forehead on hers as he closed his eyes. "It's going to take me time and effort to get to — and stay — where I want to be. Just like with everything else."

They sat there for a little while longer so he had time to process everything. The topic had shifted from what he originally had planned, and yet it applied: he had to keep working to make change stick… in any area.

Destan could tell Callimay was fighting to stay awake, and so he left everything on the floor and carried her to bed, "I think we both deserve and need a good night's rest. We'll talk about this more in the morning after we've had some rest and can spend some time in prayer."

She nestled her face close to his, "We'll get through this."

He replied after he kissed her, "I'm going to put those things away and then I'll come to bed."

The lightning still flashed through the pouring rain, illuminating the room for an ever-brief moment each time. Destan dragged himself back to where the note, box, and such were; swiping some sensor that made the windows darken. He knelled down and started putting things away, ending with the box. There was another memory stick in it, but that wasn't what caught his eye. The bottom of the box was white. As Destan felt it, he could tell — and even hear — that it was some kind of paper. He reached for the light switch on the desk and jumped back when he saw the name written on it.

And just like that, he wasn't tired. Destan sat down and attempted to get the paper out, but it was the exact same size as the bottom. He reached down to his boot and took out a different type of small throwing knife and used it to loosen the stubborn paper; making sure to not damage it.

He glanced back to Callimay, who was passed out, and then opened the envelope.

Destan,

If you get this letter that means you're at least eighteen now. I'm sure you've grown into a strong and independent young man. Your role here in the Shadows — and when the time is right, the Veil — is so much more important than you realize. Take courage during the hard times and remember your mother and I are with you.

Remember that your "mummy" loved you dearly. I remember the day I came home and she cornered me; practically wailing about not wanting to lose you. She was frightened out of her mind when you told her that you didn't want to use your right hand since "it didn't work" after you tried several times to draw with it. But since you picked things up so easily by just watching; I hoped you would be able to watch the two of us and "learn" to be right-handed.

God just didn't make you that way; He made you stubborn for a purpose: I had a lesson to learn. You could learn everything else by just watching for a little while and then do it like you'd been doing it for much longer than you have even been alive. But when it came to breaking you of that, you fought harder and harder each time.

I soon realized that I was trying to change you because of what other people thought. But I couldn't stand by and do nothing. You needed protection. And a kind that at the time I wasn't capable of giving.

Just when I was about to give up hope finding someone to trust, Mrs. Jackman (Commander) and General Harmon Willgun (Elder) contacted me. They were a God-send… or so I thought. I immediately joined the Shadows when I found out about their mission and was soon added to Deep Dark. — It wasn't referred to as the Veil at that point in time.

There wasn't much I did at first, but then my first official "detail" was assigned: Elder pulled strings on his end and got me into the research department of the Faberton government. Lylah wasn't happy with my secret purpose for being in Faberton — nor the public reason — but understood it was to make life easier for all of us. Especially you.

Elder, Canary, and myself worked day and night to glean information and organize rescues and runs to save as many left-handed people as possible; getting them to Safe Haven in Ferdinan. We operated under covers that allowed us constant contact with each other while fulfilling our independent roles.

At first Elder was a true comrade-in-arms; but when he found out what I was doing with Chameleon he flipped like a popover: starting to pry into the serums and manipulating them. His reasoning for ordering me to stop with Chameleon was because it wasn't what the Shadows' mission was. I tried to explain that it was just a temporary fix — of sorts — until we could complete our mission, and it was a special case. He didn't like hearing any of it; everything falling apart at that point.

I am hoping everything is fixed and Elder disposed of before you get involved, but I just don't know if I can. Chances are I didn't complete my detail if you're reading this. But maybe someone else has and you're just now getting this. Or, maybe I didn't destroy this letter before you found it and I am still around. I can only hope and pray at this point.

Regardless, I know you're in quite a bit of pain from seeing what happened to your mother. I hoped for so long that your young mind would forget it, but from what Rocher's told me, it's forever burned into your memory. I'm so sorry you went through all that. I'm so sorry your young eyes had to witness the cruel nature of what the world is really like: the extremes those in it will go to so they can have their fix or win an argument. And I know you thought you lost me that night, too, and this has to be a shock to you.

You can thank Canary for me surviving that nightmare.

There isn't a day that goes by I don't regret not keeping my two most prized possessions as far from danger as possible. I know there is no way to eliminate "every" evil or protect against "all" danger, but I did have the choice to keep you two from what happened. And in each instance I chose the wrong path. I'm sorry, Destan. I grieve and morn her lost each day and I hope you never have to see the woman you love how I saw your mother.

It's my deepest wish that I can come home to Kerogen and be with you to at least give you that closure, but I can't. Not yet. I'm still fighting. Fighting in hopes that you don't have to.

I know the Veil is strict and unwilling to change — and mostly for good reason — but Destan, don't let them become your life. Choose what "you" want; don't let others do that for you. You don't have to stay here forever. Now I'm not saying drop everything and grab the first girl off the street to marry so the Veil won't take you. What I am saying is that you need to think for yourself. You need to decide what's worth fighting for and never lose sight of it.

Don't be afraid if you ruffle the "fur" of other people. And with your spunk, I don't see that being an issue for you. Just learn to control and channel it. Don't make the mistake and view authority as something which needs to be undermined and brought down just because it's over you. But at the same time, don't see it as an easy way to get what you want and manipulate others; letting them take the fall for your mistakes. Learn to respect those in authority the way you would want to be. And if you choose to become Doyen, remember you were once under that authority: treat everyone like you wanted to be… not how you might have been. Work with your fellow Shadows and Veils. Lead by being a servant. Teach with patience and understanding, remembering you were once there yourself. Stand strong against those who aren't doing the right thing. Defend those who are.

I'm going to be all fatherly and sentimental now, but hear me out: I fervently hope and pray you find a jewel like I did in your mother. I know the Veil frowns upon that in every way, but I beg to differ as a whole. You can lose focus of what is important if there's no one helping ground you. That's why my Seaxes I always carry are engraved like they are. It reminds me there was someone so special standing beside me though it all: supporting and helping me whenever she could. You need to realize though that you have to accept her help for it to do any good. I know there's been so many times that I should have and neglected to. Don't make my same mistakes but don't be in fear that you "will" make the same mistakes. Accepting failure before you even start will most likely doom you to that end. Have faith in yourself. Take the good out of the bad, but remember if you are not careful, the bad "will" repeat itself.

May the new moon continue to rise on you and keep you safe, Destan. Godspeed in your runs. I hope to be back in Kerogen before too much longer and raise you the best way I can. If that unfortunately doesn't happen, remember I have always loved you. I believe in you.

Your Father,
Destry Quinton Nevrille ~ Challenger

Destan leaned back in the chair and stared up at the ceiling. Like the last time he read something his father wrote, there were so many questions he now had. It was now completely apparent Destry didn't die when he thought he did. He knew about him being a Veil and his work while at Faberton was for such — obviously — but he survived the fire. Canary saved him. He was alive and at Bulwark for years it seemed! Rocher had to of known. Why didn't he tell him!

And what was this "Project Chameleon" all about? Why was Elder so against it? How did it interfere with the Shadows' mission?

Adding to it all was the bombshell drop: Elder was related to Baleck and apparently the head of governmental research in Faberton!

Callimay was right: the deeper they got into this the more confusing and dangerous it got. He thought she didn't know what she was getting herself into… well "he" really didn't know what he was getting himself into. How could he know that going to the Society was going to open this cleverly disguised scheme. Destan wasn't even going there with the intent of doing anything for the Shadows; they just monopolized on it when they found out he was going: *Father… what is going on!*

The thunder became more frequent and was beginning to disturb Callimay. Destan quickly folded the letter and started to put it back in the envelope when he saw there was a picture still inside.

He didn't remember it at all, even though he was in it. His father was wearing an ensemble quite similar to what he had on at that very moment… and his veil which still had its sleeves. Destry was sitting in a chair laughing at a very young Destan who was standing in front of him looking perturbed. There was a little girl wearing a frilly orange dress standing next to Destan who looked to be about his age; holding his hand and giving him a kiss on the cheek.

Destan chuckled to himself as he looked at the equally awkward and laughable picture. The little girl reminded him so much of Rose. She seemed to act just like her: hanging off his arm and begging for his attention and affection.

More of a reflex than anything else, he turned it over to glance at the back. There was a note from his father.

I don't know if she's (smudged words) get her to Canary.
Her name is Callimay (smudged words) The last I know
(smudged words) Quaverly, Faberton.

"Calli!" Destan shrieked as he whipped his head around.

"What?" She asked startled and sleepy and she sat up and looked around. "What's wrong?"

He didn't reply.

She plodded over and looked at what he was doing, "Destan, please come to bed. We'll talk about this all in the morning."

"Calli… I…"

"It's not going anywhere," she took the picture out of his hand and put it, along with everything else, in the drawer. "We're not going to be thinking clearly. At least 'I' won't. Please come to bed. Please?"

His broken words didn't make any sense, so he followed her back and tried his best to go to sleep.

~ 5 ~

It didn't feel like it was but an hour or two since Destan closed his eyes, but he did it to himself. Groggy and grumpy, he rolled over to get up and saw Callimay was getting breakfast ready. She was in her ensemble already and looked like she was reading some receipt; after which she took a container out of a bag and put it with a couple others.

In some ways everything seemed so much better, but in others it seemed so much more confusing. On one hand, the wall that was between the two of them was gone in regards to them feeling free to speak with each other; there was a stronger cord of trust being woven together. But on the other, Callimay was someone he knew when he was young; and someone his father knew. Why didn't he remember her? The picture wasn't anything he remembered happening. Then Canary fit into all of this somehow. Destan knew who she was but never met her since she had been in a black widow mission in the Syndicate's high ranks for years… before he even became a Shadow. And then what about his father's mentioning her as his "savior"? How did her saving Destry's life "happen"? Destan was there until seconds before the house collapsed… that alone should've killed him.

"Good morning." Callimay smiled as she turned and saw him sitting on the edge of the bed. "Did you get any sleep? You were up so late last night. I can keep things warm if you need to get some more rest. I don't know what you have planned since it's S—"

"Do you know anyone named Canary?"

She raised her eyebrow; sounding sarcastic, "Is this some kind of trick question?"

"No."

"What's wrong, Destan?"

"It's what I found last night."

"Let's at least eat first. Okay?" She tilted her head as she turned his face back to her smiling one. "Then we'll figure all of that out. Please?"

He sighed as he wrapped her in his arms and kissed her, "Alright."

Still, he was distracted the whole time during breakfast. He pushed his food around the plate for forever and kept glancing back at the desk and then back to Callimay.

She did her best to keep an eye on him without "intruding" since she knew it had to do with what he found last night: something connected to his father and his painful past.

But this silence wasn't something she wanted to hear after what they went through the night before, so she asked, "So what are we—"

"When do you remember first meeting me?"

"You know that." She made a face as she giggled. "Orientation day."

"You're sure?" Destan tapped the tabletop in a nervous manner.

"I'm fairly certain I would remember if I met you before. You're not the forgettable type."

"Well what if it wasn't recent that you met me?"

"What do you mean?" Callimay asked confused; part of her starting to worry. "Is something wrong?"

"My father wrote me a letter, and with it was a photograph of the two of us when we were young."

"How do you know it was me?"

"He knew your name. — Your name isn't very common, Calli. — He even mentioned Quaverly."

"Well, I don't 'exactly' know that's where I'm from." She corrected as he got up.

"Just look at it. You've told me yourself that Rose looks like the spitting image of you when you were her age."

She followed even though she was highly doubtful about it all. It was really late when he saw it, so chances were he read it incorrectly. But, she took everything in stride and politely took the picture.

At first glance she didn't notice anything shocking; and she really didn't think it was her in the picture. She became a bit more critical of examining the picture when she saw it did indeed say "Callimay" on the note, but almost half of the text was smudged beyond recognition, "There's too much missing to— wait! That dress. It was the one I had on when I rode the train to meet— how! I don't remember this! … Who's Canary?"

"The only Canary I know is a member of the Veil. I've never met her, though. As I understand it from the letter, she worked with my father during his stay in Faberton." Destan explained as he handed the paper to her.

"Your father wrote this to you," she handed it back and shook her head. "It's not my place to—"

"It's alright, Calli. I 'want' you to read it." *Then I won't be the only one confused.*

His second offer met some resistance, but she eventually took it; being careful as she opened it. There was a knock at the door, so he went to see who it was while she kept reading.

"This was left in Euro, Doyen," a middle-aged man informed as he handed Destan his duffle bag. "No one else claimed it so I assumed it was yours."

"Emissary? What are you doing here? I thought you were—"

"My detail is completed. I actually got back the same day you did. I'm in your debrief session tomorrow before I put in for reassignment zoning. … Hey, I was just as shocked as you are that I got pulled so quickly, but I guess that's the way things go sometimes."

"O… kay," Destan replied confused as he checked inside the bag.

"Oh! I found this in the hall. Figured you probably dropped it."

"I did." Destan sighed as he took the phone. "Thanks for not stepping on it."

"It's good to see you're on the mend." Emissary gestured to his arm. "Nasty hit they laid on you a couple months back. Callimay didn't know if you were going to make it. Glad you did. I would've never heard the end of it if you hadn't."

"How did you—"

"Destan, I— Trever?" Callimay jerked back when she saw who it was. "What in the world are you doing here?"

"Hey," he winked as he nodded his head. "Surprise!"

"You two…" Destan began to question as he became tongue-tied.

"When we were in Faberton. Remember my old friend?" Callimay explained in a dumbfounded tone. "Well… this is him."

Destan threw his hands in the air, "I give up. … You've known her this whole time — five years was it you were stationed there — and didn't tell me?"

"She would barely talk to me. How was I supposed to get her in contact with you or know you were 'interested'; let alone bucking the system and searching?" Trever defended; a little bit of sarcasm finding its way into his tone. "And I had been there seven years, Doyen."

As if she just realized where they were, Callimay waved her hands in front of her, "Wait… wait a minute. Why are you here? Are… are you a Shadow?"

"I do believe you've had an epiphany." Trever laughed as he leaned against the door. "I was wondering how long it'd take you to catch on."

"So that means— you were in Faberton on a mission?"

"She has wisdom beyond her years sometimes."

"But… what were you doing there?"

"It isn't allowed for a Shadow to divulge such information about their details to a trainee, oh dawnfluff." Trever quipped as he patted her head.

"Well 'excuse' me," Callimay exaggerated.

"Let me know when you two are done." Destan rolled his eyes and began to walk away.

"I'm done." Trever snapped to. "I just wanted to give you that and make sure you were doing alright. The last time I saw you I didn't know what to expect."

"Sorry things went the way they did that night." Destan calmed as he turned and nodded. "Thanks for keeping Calli company and doing everything you did. And I appreciate you retrieving this for me. … How long are you in rezoning?"

"At least two weeks. I'm seeing about transferring to the detail in Indalla. Things are getting a bit sketchy there."

Destan glanced at his watch and then apologized as he nodded his wife over to the other side of the room, "I almost forgot what day it is. — Calli? There's a Bible on the one shelf there. Could you grab it? — We've got to get to Assembly, Emissary."

"You're welcome to join us," Callimay chimed in; a full grin across her face as she jogged over.

"Naw, I'm good. I'll see you later." He backed up and shook his head before "saluting" Destan.

ℬ

There was a bit of a bounce in Callimay's step as they walked along hand-in-hand; similar to their first Sunday in Rayleen. She was thrilled there was a group there they would be Assembling with. Well, at least she assumed that since they were actually going somewhere and not just staying in the suite.

If nothing else, she was glad to be out and about with Destan.

Where they went wasn't too far from where Tabitha and her went to get her ensemble; her dumbfounded yet again when she saw who was standing at the door, "M… Mr. Utree?"

"It's so good to see you two. Helpmate and Confrere let me know the moment they could about what was going on." He perked up and came over to greet them. "How are you?"

"Adjusting, thankfully," Destan took a much-needed breath of relief as he gave him a hug. "It's good to see you, Overseer."

"So… so w— how many people from Rayleen are Shadows?" Callimay interrupted; her looking a bit dazed.

"Less than I think you are assuming now." Mr. Utree smiled as he turned his attention to her. "How are you doing?"

"Well, like Destan said: adjusting." She rubbed her arm as she sighed. "I'm doing much better than I was the first day or so."

Mr. Utree ushered them inside as he kept talking with them; him noticing how much his "familiar face" seemed to be helping Callimay, "I know from the times I spoke with Doyen that this wasn't how he envisioned 'breaking the news' to you about this noble effort we're — specifically he's — part of; but it encourages me to see that you both are standing strong under this immense pressure."

There was a short pause, the two of them exchanging glances before looking down. Picking up on this, Mr. Utree continued, "You 'are' standing. I know you are. Maybe not running like you were in Rayleen, but your forward progress is still evident by Callimay being here."

Another round of silence was offered as the two of them looked at each other and then allowed a breath of relief to sneak past their lips.

Feeling more confident and seeing an opportunity, Callimay asked out of the blue, "Would you be able to stay for lunch?"

He smiled as he put a hand on her shoulder and then Destan's, "You beat me to the punch this time. I'd be thrilled to join you two; and for as long as you need and want. — Oh! Excuse me for a moment."

Mr. Utree rushed off and came back with two books, "Roselyn wanted to be sure you had these."

"Thank you," Destan took a deep breath as both he and Callimay took their Bibles; the air around this threesome feeling so much lighter.

"Tell her we 'both' said thank you." Callimay's eyes began to water as she clutched the leather-bound book close to her chest.

❦

That time spent away from everything gave them the clarity they needed to make one of the biggest decisions of their life. Things were put into perspective so that they could focus on what was important; prioritizing everything else as needed.

Even though what they discussed most of the time was "serious", Destan made a point to make sure his end of things were kept positive.

And this positive undertone quickly became contagious; Callimay starting to smile more often and even laughing a couple times. That joyful sight and sound was all Destan needed; and he hoped was at least a start for her.

At one point Trever showed up, Callimay not taking no for an answer when she invited him to sit with them, "I'm sure whatever you need to do can wait a few minutes."

"I…"

"Whatever anyone says," Destan calmed as he leaned back in his chair and looked over. "Just tell them 'I' said you could be late. Okay?"

"I— alright." He sighed as he shrugged his shoulders.

When he sat down he looked awkward, but Callimay wasn't about to let his mood affect her, "So how long are you staying?"

"It all depends on how long it takes me to get a new detail. I'm really shooting for Indalla, but I know it's not easy to get a position there since it's so close to Crosswall. That and with the new lockdowns it's hard to get in there in general." Trever fidgeted as he explained.

"The way things were the last time I went through there hinted they might." Destan sighed as he rubbed his forehead. "I'm sure you'd be a great help to the detail there. I'll put in a word for you."

"Thanks," he said a bit uneasy.

"Wewl how wong aw you staying?" Callimay tried to get out; looking embarrassed and jumping up from her seat when she couldn't. "I so sawry. I didnu—"

"I get you're excited, but I didn't know you'd turn into Rose." Destan joked as he tried to calm her. "It's okay."

"Desan, some sing… some sing's wong." She looked panicked.

Trever asked concerned as he and Destan jumped up to her side; Mr. Utree not far behind them, "Callimay? What's wrong?"

"I… Iza don't feewl…" she reached out for Destan to steady herself as all the color in her skin drained.

She looked disoriented and confused; it sounding like she was beginning to wheeze.

"Calli!" Destan gasped as he grabbed her.

"What in the name of…" Trever gulped as she began to convulse.

"Nexus!" Destan yelled as he picked her up; catching the attention of everyone else in the commissary.

"Yes, Doyen?" She responded in her normal, calm tone.

"Alert Mender and the team last night. I'm on my way there now." Destan ordered and then ran out. *Hang in there, Calli.*

Without saying anything, Trever and Mr. Utree followed… but there wasn't anyone to follow. Destan disappeared! They looked at each other for a moment, but took off toward the medical wing.

⸻

Destan got to the medical wing just after Doctor Gerould did. He laid her down and stepped back even though he didn't want to let her go.

"What happened, Doyen?" Doctor Gerould asked in a calm yet loud voice as the team hooked Callimay up to the various monitors.

"We were finishing up eating lunch with Overseer and Emissary when she all of a sudden started talking with a lisp. She grabbed my arm and then within seconds she turned gray and collapsed; starting to seize like this."

"Where did she get her food?"

"We shared the s—"

"She's going hypoxic." Someone mentioned in a raised voice; everyone responding in unison… something bad was happening.

All of that "commotion" became too much for Destan to handle. He ran out of the room and stood across the hall, staring through the glass door at what was going on. Someone was calling out to him, but he couldn't stop looking at Callimay long enough to respond.

"Doyen? Doyen what's going on?" Trever asked as he got to him. "Why did you—"

"Emissary, I need you to go back and confine everything. Get with the lab so they can analyze the food. … Now!"

"On my way."

The one thing he needed to "not" do was jump to conclusions and place blame. And yet what did he do? He latched onto what he his father said and ran wild with it: *Elder did this.*

But why? What would he gain by killing Callimay?

For the first little bit, Destan was a nervous wreck since everyone was running around — they really weren't but he thought they were.

Mr. Utree stayed with him but didn't pry. By the look on his face Destan didn't know what in the world was going on anyway.

One by one the medical team left until it was just one nurse and Doctor Gerould with Callimay. They stayed for a while and then he came out, "I don't mean to sound flamboyant or exaggerate things, but you got her here without a moment to spare. — Our initial analysis doesn't show any poisonous chemicals in her system, but some don't take that much. The other labs should be back in a bit and will give us a definitive cause. … Where in world did she get her food?"

"We ate the exact same for lunch… literally." Destan sounded desperate. "I wasn't that hungry so she shared hers with me since the servings were so large."

"Hum. … What about breakfast? What did you have then?"

"I… I don't know. I woke up and she was laying everything out."

"Did you eat the same thing?"

"No. We had our own meals. What's going on, Lance!"

"My first thought is that the food workers just need a refresher on proper handling… but if you haven't been affected at all then it must be from what she ate for breakfast."

Just then Trever jogged up, "They've got it all. At least everything I found still there."

"I need you to go to my suite and do the same thing." Destan didn't miss a beat.

"Make sure you tell them to check that first." Doctor Gerould imputed as Trever turned to leave.

"Got it."

"Are you proposing this was a target?" Mr. Utree asked in a hushed tone as he glanced around the empty hall.

"If Doyen isn't showing one sign of it, then it 'had' to be what they ate this morning. And since you said you had separate meals, she unfortunately got the wrong one."

"I didn't see you or Callimay out this morning when I was getting breakfast. When did you get yours?" Mr. Utree continued to ask; sounding more inquisitive than concerned.

"Like I said," Destan tried to catch his breath and calm. "I woke up and she already had things laid out on the table. What time? It was 0723 when I looked at my watch."

"That's odd. I was there from 0615 until just before 0800." Mr. Utree thought out loud as he adjusted his glasses.

"Well, until you can talk with Callimay I think it best to lay this all to rest." Doctor Gerould calmed as he glanced back and then to his watch. "Until those labs come back there's not much else to do."

"I wish I shared your confidence," Destan's shoulders dropped as he leaned against the wall.

Doctor Gerould folded his arms across his chest and sighed, "I'll say this much: this isn't food poisoning like everyone thinks of. I'd state my reputation on it since there wasn't anything on the preliminary labs. This was a target using a highly toxic poison. There is no reason to go after Callimay so it 'was' meant for you, Doyen."

"But how would—" Destan interrupted himself as Trever ran up. "Did the lab get everything, Emissary?"

"Everything was gone when I got to your suite. I asked those who would've been stationed during the time, but they both said they didn't see anyone."

"Overseer, Mender? Don't let Calli out of your sight." Destan flashed his eyes at them as he took off.

He realized if someone had gotten into the suite and cleared everything they could've very well started to snoop around. They would've had more than enough time to. — With him fixated on Elder being the one who was doing this he knew all the evidence he had to work with was left where anyone could find it.

ℬ

As he came in, the room was so put together that you would have never guessed anyone had been in there. He raced to the desk and threw open the drawer: *Oh thank goodness.*

The box was still there and had the memory stick and note in it. But, as he looked around, the letter and picture were gone. Destan looked everywhere but there wasn't anything to be found.

At one point he stopped himself and closed his eyes. He muttered a few words and then nodded before he jogged over to one table.

With nothing to show for his efforts, he came back and slid into his chair at the desk and laid his hand on the left side, activating an interface, "Nexus?"

"Yes Doyen."

"Patch my computer here in the suite into the video feed for this quadrant." He ordered as he logged onto the computer.

"One moment. ... You should have it."

"Send me the names of the details on this corridor from the past four hours along with their report times." Destan continued as he scanned through the footage.

"On it."

Come on... come on... he mumbled as he searched for the correct time frame. *Wait? What? No, no, no. There's no way! That doesn't match... what the...*

The footage from the hall showed no one but the scheduled details at their allotted times. But! At 0712, the footage from the suite showed someone handing Callimay a couple sacks of food and a carrier of drinks. And as it just so happened, the person stood just so the camera couldn't see them… and it appeared they muffled their voice in some manner. Angered with this discrepancy, he kept scrolling through to see if the timestamps were off somehow or there was any indication the feed was set to loop.

Nothing suggesting tampering of any sort. The person was just invisible; a true shadow. There wasn't even any record of someone getting anything "to go" from anywhere in the commissary!

He shifted his focus to see who cleaned up the suite and was infuriated. Destan couldn't believe what he saw: Trever gathered everything into a trash bag and then took it to the incinerator before lunch… and he did it in such a way to ensure no one was around to see him, "That liar! He knew what was going to happen a—"

"Mender just told me your wife is coming to." Nexus announced.

Destan waved to the screen to shut it down, "I'm on my way."

❦

After checking the hall, he jumped to the end so he could get back quicker. He knew he did it practically in front of Trever and Mr. Utree, but was hoping they would forget about it because of everything else.

When he got to the door he paused, seeing Mr. Utree sitting beside her and Doctor Gerould over at a table: *Keep it together, Boon. Come on. Deal with the Nark later. Calli needs you right now.*

As he opened the door, a wave of uncertainty washed over him; scaring him.

"Destan?" He could hear Callimay calling out in a moan. "Destan where are you?"

"I'm here, Calli. I'm right here." He answered out of breath as he rushed to her side.

"Destan?"

"Calli… Calli, I'm right here." He took her hand and pushed her bangs out of her face. "Calli, look at me. I'm right here. … Calli?"

Doctor Gerould sighed as he rubbed his beard, "She woke up like that a couple minutes ago and hasn't stopped."

"What is right before you had Nexus contact me?"

"Y… yes. Why do you ask?"

"I spiked," Destan sighed as he flopped into the chair Mr. Utree had since vacated. "Y… you don't think that did any damage, do you?"

"Well…" Doctor Gerould hesitated. "Since she responded to you I'm inclined to say that's a good sign. I'm hoping this is just a lingering side effect of whatever she's fighting off. I doubt you did any damage."

"Didn't you figure out what it was? Have those other labs not come back yet?"

Both Doctor Gerould and Mr. Utree glanced at each other; making Destan even more nervous.

"Results from the lab didn't show anything. Not a trace of anything that would cause this. I don't know what's going on. There should have been something… even the tiniest trace. 'Something'! But there wasn't even any—"

Worried someone like Trever was in the lab, Destan blurted out, "Can you perform the test here?"

"Yes…" Doctor Gerould dragged out. "But I don't—"

"Do it." Destan ordered.

He knew Mr. Utree wasn't one to take the sight of blood and needles very well, so Destan didn't give him leaving the room a second thought.

Within a couple minutes, Doctor Gerould came back with a small machine and a blood draw kit.

Callimay's voice has since faded out. Her eyes were still open and lips moving, but she wasn't "there". She didn't even flinch or notice she had been stuck with a needle. Destan's heart began racing, fearful of what was happening. Doctor Gerould injected the blood into the machine's reservoir and turned it on.

A few minutes later, the reader he had on his hip buzzed. He started scrolling through the information; Destan gripping Callimay's hand as he gulped, "Well?"

"I… I've never seen anything like this. … Whoever did this altered the poison so it would mimic the look of— let me check what the lab sent the first time. … They were fooled just like I almost was."

"What is it?"

"Whoever did this knows much more about poisons than I do. — They made the poison cloak itself, taking on the appearance of her white blood cells; her immune system. I thought it strange her WBC came back so high… but I remember from before that it was in the high 9s even then, so I dismissed it." Doctor Gerould neglected to speak in a way Destan could truly understand. "The only reason I saw it was because I caught one that was 'uncloaking'. I don't really think we have the time, but if I could do a scan of her CNS I'm sure I'd find a hotbed of these little leaches."

"Whatever it is, can you stop it?"

"I'll need to talk with Apothecary. She knows more than I do."

"How long is going to take? Calli's getting worse."

"I can ask her while I'm on my way down. She's the finest pharmacologist I know so I doubt it'll take her long; not with the situation we're in. I'll go right now… that is if you want to try this. It's the only thing I can think of to counteract it."

"It won't hurt her, will it?"

"I can't guarantee that, but with the alternative in mind the odds are pretty much even."

"A… alright."

"I'll be back as fast as I can."

The twenty-seven minutes that passed felt more like twenty-seven years. Callimay was barely moving her lips now and her eyes were almost closed: *Heavenly Father, 'please' be with Calli. She needs Your healing hand. I know I've asked for this before, but I know You don't mind that a request is repeated. I… I need her, Lord. Especially right now. Please be with Lance and Apothecary. Give them clarity of mind to find what will work; and let them find it quickly. It's in Your Son's Name I pray, amen.*

ᚠ

Doctor Gerould rushed back into the room a few minutes later with the nurse who was with him earlier and started opening different little packages and getting what looked like an injection ready.

"To get to her nervous system quicker I'm going to inject it into her spine directly. Since she's unaware of pain, this 'should' be relatively easy. At least that's what I'm hoping. — Did you get the twenty-one?"

"Yes, Mender." The nurse confirmed as she continued to work.

"What did Apothecary say?"

"She obviously objected to it being done so fast without testing it first, but agreed there wasn't any time given Callimay's state."

"How do you know she can't feel pain? I thought you said you couldn't guarantee—"

"Admittedly a blood draw isn't always noticed, but the way you're gripping Callimay's hand right now I'd think it would be causing her 'some' level of discomfort at least." Doctor Gerould observed as he gestured to the bed.

"Oh Calli!" Destan jumped when he realized what he was doing.

He kept working until the nurse came over; him rushing to the other side of the bed. Doctor Gerould leveled it before he gripped one of the sheets; instructing Destan in a stern tone, "I need you to watch her head as I roll her toward you. … Okay, now help me move her legs and shoulders so she's curled up in the fetal position. … Now. Your job while I do this is to keep her still. And when I mean still I mean 'perfectly' still. I know I said she's not aware of pain, but I'm going directly for her spine. One wrong move and I 'could' paralyze her. — Are you ready, Neurosan? — Alright, Doyen. Here we go."

Destan knew Doctor Gerould was trying to take the good out of Callimay's lack of movement, but it was plain to see this was a telltale sign she was deteriorating quickly. He took a deep breath and tried to keep focused on the good — like Callimay would. She was still with him, she was still there; it's just that she needed help… desperately.

Seeing the needle he was going to use made even Destan cringe. Usually such things didn't bother him, but seeing it happen to Callimay was completely different. He knew this had to be done so he gritted his teeth and didn't say a word.

As Doctor Gerould took his gloves off, he took a deep breath, seeming to let out the tension he'd built up over the past hour, "From what Apothecary said, the first thing you should notice is that she gets her mental faculties back. The counteractant is in her CN— central nervous system, so it will clear out all of the activated poison before spreading to the rest of her body to search for it. The sensation of touch will probably be the last thing she gets back. This is all in theory, of course. And she said Callimay may need a booster if she starts to relapse from the counteractant not being able to identify the cloaked poison. She'll also need bloodwork done every couple hours to make sure it's not wreaking havoc on her native immune system."

After he made a call, Apothecary came over and spoke with Doctor Gerould for the next few minutes as they watched her vitals.

Nothing really changed, but she didn't appear to be improving. Destan was trying so hard to hang on to hope, but he just didn't know how much longer he could last. They "just" rounded the corner where things were looking bright again. Why did it always happen this way!

"Destan? Please don't cry," a weary voice sighed. "What is— I… I can't feel my arm!"

"Calli!" He exclaimed as he threw his arms around her and let a broken sigh of relief out. "You're going to be alright. I know you're scared, but it's alright. Just give the counteractant time."

"W… what happened?"

"Just relax for a few minutes. I promise I'll tell you, okay?" He calmed as Apothecary came over.

"Doyen? Are you alright if I break protocol and use Liaison's identity?" She asked in almost a whisper as she motioned for him to come over to her. "I just do not want to taxi her any more than necessary right now but I don't want her to hear you tell me."

"Of course. It's Callimay."

"Thank you." She nodded and then turned her attention; smiling as she asked, "Can you tell me your name, please?"

"Callimay Ne—"

"And do you know where you are?" Apothecary cut off as she leaned over and flashed a light in Callimay's one eye.

Callimay shied away as much as she could and closed her eyes as she winced; Destan almost jumping over and grabbing Apothecary's arm, "Don't do that! You'll give her a migraine."

"It's my fault, Doyen. I didn't tell her." Doctor Gerould intervened. "She needs to check her eyes, though."

Destan was reluctant to let her near his wife now, but they eventually found common ground and she finished her examination.

By all indications, it appeared the counteractant was doing its job without doing anything "extra"; but she strongly suggested Callimay have a full body scan to ensure things were indeed progressing in a positive direction for the long haul. A technician came in after this discussion and took some blood; reminding both Destan and Callimay they would do this every hour for the rest of the day, and then at least twice a day for the rest of the week.

"I hope I've got enough blood for all of those tests." Callimay tried to sound jovial, but her eyes showed how worried she was, seeing the amount of blood in the vials.

She's got a point. Is that written right? He wants 'all' of this done each time? The middle-aged woman's eyes shifted back and forth, her taking her reader off her hip.

After a little bit, she looked up and bit her lip, "I thought Mender put in for a full panel in addition to the special lab, but that order is for tomorrow's first draw. So, all except for that one there will only be one vial… and it'll be half the size of these."

Destan started to tense up, worrying about this "slip" because of what happened with Trever. Callimay picked up on this and asked once the technician was gone, "What happened?"

Someone poisoned your breakfast. There obviously wasn't anything in mine so either you ate mine or someone's really trying to make me angry. — Who brought you the food?

I don't know people's names yet. Why would they poison—

The only thing I can think of is Elder. I looked and looked, but the picture and letter are gone.

They're in my back pocket. At least that's where I remember putting them. I shoved them in my pocket when I saw Trever while we were at the suite. I never took them out.

You're sure you didn't recognize the person? He asked as he took her in his arms and lifted her. *Did they have something over their mouth that you could see?*

Everyone pretty much looks the same to me, Destan. Callimay sighed as he laid her back down. *It was just a guy that looked kinda like you. … I don't recall him having anything on his face. Why?*

Did he say who he was?

She thought for a while and then tried to shake her head: *No.*

I could hear the person say something, but I couldn't make it out when I listened to the footage. What did he tell you?

Well, he said you ordered breakfast the night before and then told me the receipt had on it what each container was and who it was for. I thought that was a bit strange for them to have it 'that' specific, but when I got them out I realized why you had them do it.

What?

"You don't like grape nuts in your yogurt. — Who am I kidding? You don't like yogurt at all." Callimay laughed; sounding like her jovial self now. "And don't try to say otherwise! Yes, you ate it that one time, but just because we were too lazy to fix anything that morning and there wasn't anything else in the house. — I was surprised you ordered it for me at all. It was sweet of you to."

"I never ordered breakfast." Destan shook his head; his voice almost cracking from the shock he was in.

"Then ho—"

I don't know, Calli. If they specifically said that meal was for you… then that means 'you' were their target.

I thought only trusted people were here?

I know I wasn't running off of much before, but this is all making my assumption about Elder doing something sound 'much' more realistic. Hopefully this stick will give us answers. Destan slipped the device out of his pocket and looked at it. *I can't access it here. Everything's tracked and monitored by the Veil, so he'd have unbridled access to it.* *Though even that can be hacked apparently.* *When we get back to Rayleen we'll look at this. In the meantime, we're just going to have to keep going. We don't want to tip Elder off that we're on to him… regardless of whether or not he did this.* *Which means I can't say anything to Emissary right now.*

She worked to take his hand; having a half disgusted, half worried look on her face, "I can move it but I can't feel it at all. I'd say that makes my skin crawl, but I wouldn't be able to feel it if it were."

"It's good to see you're bouncing back so quickly!" Doctor Gerould sighed in relief as he knocked on the opened door. "Once we get this body scan done — shouldn't take more than an hour — Apothecary and Illuminary will both read it so we've got a better understanding of how you are doing internally. If that's clear, then you can leave if you want to… just don't wander off or do anything too strenuous. — Now I do want to stay on top of those hourly draws for the rest of the day. You can stay if you'd like, but I won't order you to."

"Understood. Bedrest for the rest of the day."

⅋

Mr. Utree showed up a while later and talked with them — though more with Destan since Callimay was so exhausted. He had an equal amount of concern about what happened but knew there was more going on, "You know who's done this, don't you?"

"Not really. But—" *Can you hear me?*

The initial and quite literal knee-jerk reaction didn't surprise Destan, but he was grateful Mr. Utree took it in stride; nodding.

Just think to yourself. I'll hear you. — I'm not sure, but I've got a very short list of suspects.

Evidence?

Circumstantial and what is physical is possibly going to be deemed inadmissible. I 'do' have the video feed from this morning, but there are glaring inconsistencies in complementary cameras. Destan grumbled as he sat there and rubbed Callimay's hand; trying his best to stay calm.

Who's made the short list?

He took a breath so he could think before answering: *I know this has bitten me before by not telling someone about something I know about… but I don't want to whitewash someone if they're not guilty. No matter how certain 'I' might be or what I've discussed with Calli already. I'm trying not to jump to conclusions even though I really don't see how I could be.*

There is nothing to be ashamed of for holding back until you are certain; I understand.

"How long will you be staying?"

"Well, I do have several studies and prayer meetings starting on Tuesday afternoon; so I'll be leaving here late tomorrow night." Mr. Utree looked at his watch and then stared at the wall; eventually looking at Destan, "I'll do whatever I can during the time I have here to help. Just tell me what you need."

~ 6 ~

Destan carried Callimay back to the suite at the end of the day; Doctor Gerould as well as Apothecary more than pleased with her progress and the results of the scan. Things were calm, but that pit of worry in each of their stomachs wouldn't leave; Callimay even too scared to eat anything.

Monday morning was rough when it started: Destan spazzing out when it appeared Callimay had relapsed.

But everything turned out alright: her hand he squeezed beyond what he should have was just complaining.

"Doctor Gerould never said I 'had' to stay in bed, you're the one who said that." Callimay bickered as she flipped the blanket off.

"It doesn't matter who said it." Destan shook his head and pulled it back over. "You're not getting—"

"Debriefing is in five, Doyen." Nexus interrupted. "Bradly room."

He growled under his breath, "I'll be there." *I wanted to spend the afternoon with Mr. Utree, 'not' in meetings.*

It was inevitable something like this would happen, though. Time moved on without regard to his situation.

The thing that bothered him the most was he never remembered being bothered like this before. It were as if everyone was going crazy since he got back and needed his help every step of the way. But then again, he hardly spent time in the suite while he was in Bulwark before. He was always out and about, checking on things, observing, assisting, having personal meetings when he saw people… he had no reason to keep him away. But now things were different. Doyen was beginning to change ever so slightly. Hooray for the tiny victories!

"If I do anything it'll just be to get some water or something small like that." Callimay promised as she put her hand over his fist, rubbing it as she finished, "Alright?"

No response.

"I can lock the door while you're gone, right?"

"Well… I can." Destan made a slight correction as he got up. "You're not in the database yet. Nothing with interface with you and I doubt Nexus will take a command from you. So, the only way the lock on the door would be for me to—"

"Would I be able to open it from inside if I needed to?" She watched him mess with the interface beside the door.

"Yes. Just— you're safe in here, Calli. Don't leave. Not until I figure out what's going on. If something comes up just tell me — and you know what I mean by that. It won't be suspicious if I'm not completely present at this meeting, so feel free to talk with me all you want. I might just get bored and start talking with you, come to think of it."

"It's one of 'those' meeting?"

"Yeah," he chuckled as he turned back.

"I love you, Destan." Callimay rested her head on the top of the headboard as she wiggled her fingers to resemble a wave.

Destan sighed as he leaned against the door he had opened, "You know how to make things miserable for me, don't you?"

"What?"

"It's not bad, Calli. Not bad at all. You just make me feel miserable when I leave a room and know you're not going with me. … But don't you ever try to make it easier for me, got it?"

"Okay. I'll try not to." Callimay blushed, and then perked up as she called out, "Oh! Destan?"

He whipped around and asked startled, "What!"

"I… I just wondered if Mr. Utree was still here."

He took a moment to catch his breath and then nodded, "Yes. … Do you want to talk with him?"

"I was thinking when you get back we could talk with him again. I'm kinda tired right now, so I might rest for a bit."

"I'll check with him and see what I can get worked out. — Oh! You haven't had anything to eat!"

"Right now I don't know if I could stand to eat anything." She let a shiver run through her. "I'm tired like I said, so don't worry."

"Rocher's supposed to be bringing food supplies sometime today. If you can stand waiting—"

"I'll be fine." She smiled and waved him on. "Now quit stalling and get to your meeting."

๖

A couple minutes later Destan crept back in the room. Callimay was fast asleep; her body exhausted from the battle it barely won. Seeing her looking so peaceful made him feel more at ease.

And yet part of him didn't want to leave her alone. Having the memory of how she looked yesterday was frightening. But, he knew if he waited much longer Nexus would ruin this restful atmosphere.

So, he quickly adjusted the bedspread and left; being ever so quiet as he shut the door.

When the lock engaged, he looked around at the hall he'd been in on a regular basis for the past eight — almost nine — years. He had come to recognize in general how things "felt" or "looked" different to him since Callimay came along, but this was the most striking moment he'd had thus far. Never before had he felt how cold and lonely this hall was; how hallow his footsteps sounded as he continued on his way. Each person he passed looked like a shell in a way; something was missing in their expression. But what?

This realization hit him hard: *Has it always been like this? So sterile and cold? Have I been blind this whole time thinking others felt the deep connection to what good is being done? ~ Just because someone doesn't visible show it doesn't mean they don't feel it though, Boon. ~ True. But still, things aren't what I remember them to be. Everyone looks… different. ~ You rattling the cage so you could fly the coupe probably disturbed quite a few. ~ No one but Veils would know that; and they wouldn't dare say a thing like that to any Shadow. … I guess I really haven't paid any attention to things and people around me.*

For as much as this difference in his world preoccupied him; Destan's thoughts kept returning to Callimay. The fact Doyen couldn't focus made Destan feel like he was making progress. He was careful though to keep in perspective that he needed to make sure he was consistent in how he was treating her; not just clinging to her since she had a scare…. only to pull away once things calmed down.

When he rounded the corner, the door was already closed. He groaned: *Hopefully Elder doesn't find out about my 'tardy' appearance. Ugh!* "Good morning, Shadows. I apologize for being delayed."

Everyone stood and faced him before he motioned for them to be seated. The first time Destan looked around the room he didn't notice him, but once he sat down at the front of the room he saw Trever sitting in the back row. Just his presence was unsettling. It took Destan every ounce of self-control he had to keep from confronting him about what he now knew he did.

In the next few moments, Destan shifted to full-on Doyen mode. He rolled through the motions he always had during the beginning of all debriefings and then sat back and let the other Veil present take over.

While this one was no different than what he remembered these meeting to be — long, dull, boring, and pretty useless — he noticed a strange shift in who the predominate authorizing member of the Veil was. Not that it was wrong for this duty to shift without his knowledge, but why would this Veil in particular be so vested in this facet of the Shadows' mission out of everything else?

This wandering trail of thought drowned out each person's reiteration of what was on their paperwork right in front of him. It was truly just a formality; though there were occasionally questions that either the Shadow or Destan had about something to clarify for the record. And it looked like today could be one of those where this was necessary; though this would need to be taken up with the Veil themselves, not the Shadow assigned.

But things got even more confusing when it came to Trever's debrief. Something was off in Destan's mind concerning him anyway, but rather than being like everyone else, there wasn't an authorizing member of the Veil who assigned him to this detail at all! There wasn't even any clear definition given to account for him being where he was stationed for the length of time he was. And then all he talked about was nothing but observations of the local community. It was pointless that he would be there for seven years with no true purpose. He wasn't a Veil, so there was nothing needing to be kept secret from everyone else in the room.

Needless to say, Destan wasn't the only one confused. The looks on everyone's faces — and even the comments they made to themselves — proved there was something truly wrong. Even they could hear what Destan saw in his report: why were there so many blatant holes? He wasn't even trying to cover up the fact he did practically nothing of any use while there.

And yet Destan's confusion turned to deeper suspicion because of what he saw him do the day prior.

At the end of this cringe-worthy debrief, Trever asked — as did every Shadow in their turn — in a coy tone, "Are there any gray areas that need clarified?"

I can't lie. Destan stared at the obvious holes in his report; feeling everyone else looking at him as if to beg him to ask the obvious. *But how in the world am I going to make this seem like I'm not singling him out for—*

You're Doyen. Callimay interjected in a matter-of-fact tone. *Just ask the question like you always would.*

Destan jerked a bit; keeping his head bowed, *Doing alright?*

Almost one-hundred percent. There are these little patches in my fingers and feet that still tingle or haven't gotten their sense of touch back, but other than that I'm fine.

He looked up from the papers to Trever who was still waiting for him to answer. Destan took a deep breath and tried his best to stay professional and calm while he asked the questions Trever had to know would be raised, "I don't see an initialing or a signature of any authorizing Veil assigning you to this detail. It could be a bad copy I have, but could you clarify that for me now? … And your detail isn't clearly stated to show your purpose for such a long-term one."

Trever's eyes began to dart back and forth as he tensed up; Destan being able to "feel" this change in him. This shift prompted him to listen to what he was saying to himself. It took no time to realize Trever was frantic by the tone of his voice: *How do I tell him without letting everyone else know? I can't just let that all out with everyone here. I should've made something up and put it down.*

Hearing this desperate try at a cover-up, Destan decided to defuse the matter so he could speak with him in a controlled environment; one free of any "collateral damage". He just had to keep things pointed directly at the paperwork and not veer off into what happened the day before, "Like I said, I could have a bad copy. I'll consult your initial paperwork to compare and see if something was dropped."

"Very well." Trever nodded; his voice a bit shaky. "Are there any other items needing clarified?"

"Not that I see." Destan shook his head as he browsed through the pages. "If there is anything missing that comes from your initial paperwork I will contact you."

"Understood," Trever nodded again and then made a beeline back to his seat.

After a few more debriefs, everyone was dismissed… much to the relief of Destan, "You still don't prefer these much, do you, Doyen?"

"It — for the most part — is a waste of time, Auditor." He leaned back in the chair and pushed it away from the desk. "Now I'll grant that in Factor, Rebel, and Emissary's cases this was very appropriate. — Speaking of which, do you have Emissary's original paperwork?"

"I forgot you said anything about that, yes I do." Auditor snapped her fingers as she jogged back.

It only took her a minute to log back in and shift the files where he could reach them. Destan grunted as he dragged his hand across the desk to drop the holographic file on the computer he was working at, "Just want I've 'always' wanted."

"I've got more if you want them right now."

"No! No, I'm good!" Destan shook his head furiously.

Auditor laughed as she stepped back, nodding her head as she finished, "Let me know if you need anything else. I need to get the rest of these processed and filed."

"I will. — Oh, by the way: how did you get to Faberton so quickly?"

"Emissary contacted me because of my background in the medical field. He knew the doctor Callimay was speaking with would notice your veil so he needed someone else available on the inside to help." She turned back and explained. "I'm rather curious as to why he left that whole encounter out of his report."

"How did Emissary know that?"

"The doctor's an 'official' member of the Syndicate: Informant. And if I remember correctly, he's one that has been with them for a 'long' time. He doesn't do the amount of work he did in the past, thankfully. I think his age is catching up with him in more ways than he realizes. — I apologize for trying to get you out of there like I did. I didn't know Callimay was your wife."

"You weren't the first. … Thank you for the information."

"You're quite welcome." Auditor nodded as she turned and left.

Armed with this extra little tidbit of information that was left out, Destan began pouring over the paperwork and compared it to what he had. They were both the same — half blank, practically! He couldn't understand how in the world it wasn't caught. Granted, the initial paperwork would've been processed around the time Commander was murdered, but this wasn't any reason to let something so blatant lapse.

"I just couldn't say anything earlier," he heard Trever admit as the door opened.

"Well, we're the only ones in here now." Destan set the paperwork down and motioned to the computer. "No one is supposed to keep anything from me, so… what's going on?"

"That order was given to me by 'two' members of the Veil, but completely separate and independent of each other. They both instructed me that no one else could know."

"I take it though, by your coming here that you're willing to divulge to me who they are?"

"This was all tied to Callimay so you deserve to know." Trever began as he knocked his fist at his side.

Destan tried to remain calm as he interlocked his hands and rested his elbows on the armrests of the chair, "I'm listening."

"I honestly can't remember now who contacted me first, but I remember they were really close to each other. — I always remember it being odd they both wanted the same thing and got with me right around the same time, but anyway. — Both Elder and Canary gave me information on a girl named Callimay Berchoff. Elder said her behavior had been suspicious, but was quite vague as to what that behavior was. He instructed me to keep tabs on her and look for signs of her being left-handed. Canary, on the other hand, instructed me to look for specific items to see if they might be in her possession; and told me if I found them to stay and keep watch over her until she could get to her herself. … Both of them swore me to secrecy and told me to stay until I was contacted with further instructions. At the time I was recovering from that stent I had in Aridigobe — the bad case of Moon Von's Fever I contracted — but I 'do' remember Elder telling me to pack right that moment and go. … It took me a while to get my baring straightened out, but I started looking into what Canary asked first since it sounded like the easier thing to track down. The first day I went to Callimay's house I saw one item Canary spoke of. After a while I went to the house to search of the other items but that one was all I could find. It was a while before things worked out for me to get in contact with her, Canary saying that one item was enough to warrant me staying. — Figuring out Elder's end took quite a bit more work. I couldn't find a thing to suggest she was left-handed and yet I had to admit there was this aura about her that made me feel like she was. Elder wasn't thrilled about the lack of progress I was making but he told me to keep digging and even prodding to get her to slip. I really can't figure out why he was so bent on proving she was left-handed; telling me to act like a Falconer basically. It's not like we think being left-handed is a bad thing. — After Callimay left for the Society I let them both know, but didn't hear anything. When the authorities showed up at the house a few months later and kept it under surveillance for a few months after that, I knew something was up. And then of all people 'you' showed up out of the blue— don't ever scare me like that again. I really thought you were a goner; especially with that Informant 'helping' during your surgery. But, Auditor told me it wasn't until after that all that he found your veil. … Last Tuesday afternoon I got a message from Elder, pulling me that very moment. I know he's been one to want things done in the moment when he asks, but I'm starting to get sick and tired of his 'rush, rush' mentality. I tried to reach out to Canary and find out what she wanted, but I got nothing and really didn't want to deal with Elder's flack. Come to think of it, I actually haven't heard anything from her in… gosh! It's been about five years." Trever confessed; his tone as well as his off-the-cuff comments suggesting he wasn't hiding anything. "I swear that's the truth, Doyen. Do you understand why I couldn't write anything down or say anything earlier?"

"Have you ever met Canary? Face to face, that is?"

"No. She's been on her black widow mission before I even came on."

Destan wanted to ask about that morning, seeing now that Trever didn't appear to be solely on Elder's side, but he could be playing the rebellious toad… bating Destan to find out what he knows, "Well, thank you for clarifying that all. That answers all of my questions I had with regards to your paperwork."

"What are you going to do?"

"Well there was nothing 'wrong' with them asking you to do what you did, so nothing."

"How is she, Doyen?" Trever asked concerned as he grabbed his arm while he walked past.

The sudden nature of his question and reaction could've been answered quite differently, but Destan kept calm and replied, "She's just about recovered. Still tired though, and she has blood work to get done for the rest of the week."

"Any leads?"

Destan growled as he clinched his fist: *Geez! You should know best of all, you lying scumbag.*

"I know I won't be here too much longer, but let me know if I can help in any way while I am here." He offered as they left the room; him not waiting for an answer as he continued, "She's like a little sister to me now. I knew there'd never be anything between the two of us from the start, but I didn't mind. One: it wasn't a liberty I could take, and two: she made it quite clear early on I wasn't her type. But we kept a sibling-type relationship that made me somewhat close to her. Never knew what it was like to be the big brother type, but I've gotta say I enjoy it. Especially since she's the little sister I get to have. — I'm just glad she's alright. And I know you'll keep her safe. Sorry about the fluffy nonsense there."

Who 'are' you? Destan stood there in shock as Trever left. *You've got to be a double, but which side are you landing on?*

ॐ

144

Destan tip-toed in his suite, relieved when he saw Callimay fast asleep. The plethora of paper bags on the counter and table suggested Rocher came by at some point: *Well at least we've got food now.*

After he checked his watch he started putting everything away; leaving some things out to fix something to eat for lunch.

While he appreciated Rocher's offer to take on this "small errand", the fact that he always got paper bags when he shopped for groceries annoyed Destan… slightly. Okay, okay. The snapping and cracking sound they made every time he pulled something out drove him nuts.

But, that was all soon done and over with.

He was going to get lunch started, but seeing how peaceful Callimay looked made him pause; he didn't want the smell of food to disturb her. Rest really wasn't that horrible of a thought either.

She was still wearing her ensemble which reminded him she didn't have any clothes with her and it dawned on him that he'd never seen her wear an all-black outfit before. He was so used to it for himself but it looked wrong on Callimay. She always had something cheerful in color on. In a way, it was as if she were becoming him… the part of himself that he was beginning to hate.

Destan sighed as he brushed her hair away and took her hand in his. Even though he could see it since he knew it was there, the fact was you could barely see the scars from her fall over Lookout Point.

Curious, he pushed her unruly hair away from her neck. The scars from her processing were just about gone, too.

Even though she was lying in a sea of black, he could tell she was holding something other than the bedspread with her one hand. The closer he looked, it was something long and it had a distinct satin look to it. He reached out and felt the heavy leather he had come so accustomed to recognizing.

Doing everything he could to not disturb her, he slipped it out of her grasp. Sure enough, it was what he thought it was: a veil. The more he looked at it, the more he thought it looked exactly like his — even down to the ripped seamline around the armholes.

"You're back?" Callimay asked groggy as she rubbed her face.

"I'm sorry I woke you."

She yawned as she started looking around her, "It's alright."

"What's wrong, Calli?"

"I had it right— oh. You found it."

He handed the veil back to her, sounding stumped, "What is this?"

"I…" she hesitated; biting her lip.

"You can tell me, Calli." He reassured as he sat up and rubbed her arm. "It's alright."

"The second Wednesday after we moved to Rayleen I found you outside, sitting on the deck." She sounded sad as she looked down and away; almost wringing her hands. "You looked so sad. You had your veil on your knee and you were staring at the stains and holes. I knew it meant so much to you since you wore it all the time so I… I tried to wash it while you were gone the next day. — I tried so hard, Destan! I really did. It's just that it had been long enough that the stains were set. I couldn't get them all out. It was hard enough for me to do what I did — remembering what happened that night. … I went to the tailor's and tried to find out if he could fix it when you were off flying the one day, but he said there wasn't any way to patch it. I knew he'd say it, but I just had to try. — Then I found you out on the deck a couple times after that and heard you say that you wished they were gone. Hearing how sad you were made me feel horrible. I tried the tailor's again to see about making another one, but he said the leather used wasn't like anything he had. I knew you wouldn't want one that felt different—"

"Oh, Calli." He comforted as he put his hands on either side of her face, so touched by her concern. "I'm not so attached to this that I would get upset and sad that it was damaged. They're meant to take a beating; this leather was chosen for that very reason. And I wasn't saying that because I wanted it to be like it was before; I was saying that because I was reminded of all the pain 'you' went through. Maybe I wasn't wording it that well, but I was talking to myself about taking those memories away from you so things could be like they were before. When it came down to it, seeing those reminded me of how much I wanted to make things better and safer for you. I wasn't thinking about myself. I'm sorry you thought that from what you heard; but I'm more sorry that you didn't feel like you could come to me and talk to me about it. … I admit I was a bit shocked to see it hanging out on the deck, still wet, when I got back that afternoon. I should've asked what was wrong when you were upset for the rest of the evening. I… I should've talked to you."

By this point, Callimay was crying. She crawled across to him and curled up in his gentle but strong arms, "You were worried about me? Not about your veil?"

"I'm always worried about you, Calli." Destan sighed as he rested his chin on her head. "Things get damaged or lost, but you can replace them because they're things. I can't let you get damaged or lost. I'd never find another you and I don't want to. I love you, and you alone. Please don't cry, Calli."

"I'm not crying because I'm sad," she continued to sob. "I'm crying because I'm happy."

This struck him as a bit strange… well, actually "very" strange. Of course it was well known to him how Callimay's emotional nature was still foreign to him at times. He wasn't accustomed to a single reaction being connected to more than one emotion — especially crying. He had made leaps and bounds the past month — and that past week — but this whole concept of talking with her about everything and learning to navigate her emotional responses was going to take time and effort on his part. But it was time and effort he was more than willing to put in.

"As long as you're alright."

"I am." Callimay nodded as she began to calm down. "So… you don't want this new one?"

"We haven't decided whether or not to stay; in which case if we go it won't matter. Yesterday afternoon was leaning really hard one way, but I think after what happened we should make sure. Sound good? Mr. Utree should still be here, so let's talk with him, huh?" Destan flicked his wrist so he could see his watch. "Nexus?"

"Yes, Doyen."

"Tell Overseer to report here to the suite as soon as he can."

"Got it."

"I know it's 'our' decision to make, but if I'm drawing the correct conclusion from what you mentioned this morning, you want his counsel on the matter too." Destan took a deep breath as he got up; fussing as he looked back, "Now just stay in bed. I'm perfectly capable of fixing a meal that's edible for the two of us."

"I'll take it easy," she shooed his hands away as she tried to get up.

"Callimay Rose Nevrille… I… I'll sit on you if I have to."

"We already went through this: Doctor Gerould didn't put me on bedrest, 'you're' the one who said that." She bickered as she shooed his hands away and made a face at him.

ẞ

The afternoon was time well spent. Destan was right: in light of what happened the day before their opinion on the situation as a whole shifted. They spoke with Mr. Utree for a while and then spent the evening together; putting their "stamp of approval" on their choice.

It wasn't an easy one to make; Destan standing there that evening, rubbing his veil that was slung over his chair. He wanted this change, but part of him still hesitated.

Remembering what Redje said, he knew he needed to be fully committed or it wasn't going to work. So, he took a deep breath and stepped back; letting that small smile out, "Are you ready?"

She threw her arms around him and snuggled close, "We can do this, Destan. Both of us in our own, individual ways. I know we can. It'll be awkward at first, but we've got each other and everyone else who loves us supporting us and trusting our decisions."

"I love you, Calli." He sighed as he held onto her tighter. "So much."

Having her reassurance about their decision, and then his reminder of how much he cared for her, made the room almost burst with new life. They knew all along that talking things out was the best way to accomplish anything; but this was the first time they did it about something so impactful. Now knowing how it felt to be open like this, knowing this is what trust "felt" like, they regretted not doing it sooner!

For the longest time, Destan was the first one to let go; but this time it was Callimay who had to make that decision. She fussed with the collar on his shirt and smiled, "I need to go get that blood work done so I'm ready. Raven should be ready to go, soon… right?"

"I know you said you wanted to and you were sure, but this is a big decision, Calli. Maybe I still sound unsure, but I guess I'm just not used to this talking thing… I just want to be absolutely certain this is what you want."

"I'm certain and I have faith in you. Doyen's going to do the job he's supposed to without destroying my husband. I'm not losing you. And I'll still get to see you and we'll get to spend 'us' time whenever you're free." She rubbed his face; her voice so tender and loving. "Destan?"

"How did I ever find you?"

"Come on. I don't want to miss seeing Mr. Utree off."

ჽ

It was strange as they made their way to the airstrip that there was so much "going on" after dark; but it wasn't so late that it was completely unheard of. Mr. Utree was nothing but encouraging as they all said their goodbyes; reminding them he would be sure to come back as often as he could to check on them.

Once the jet was gone, the stillness of the night was calming and reassuring as it blanketed the area, "It's odd how the moon somehow calms everything; saying it's safe to go to bed."

For as tender of a comment as that was, Destan sighed, "You're going to find out sooner or later, so best you know now: that orb of light isn't beautiful. At least not to a Shadow. Quite the opposite."

"Buy why? It makes everything visible." Callimay defended as she gestured around her. "I don't see why that's such a bad thing."

"While we can do some things during the day, most of what we do is during the night because it is easier to get around without being seen: why we wear black. But when that moon's full or super bright like it is tonight, it makes it near impossible for us to do anything."

"So I'm guessing you sleep during the day?"

"Now you know why you couldn't find me for the rest of orientation day," Destan broke that small smile as they started back for the vehicle.

"What?"

"I'd been up since Saturday afternoon to make sure the one ball I'd be missing was all taken care of; and then to get things with Fidus and everyone else squared away. And then when I saw the kind of 'kids' I was gonna have to put up with for several months… I was beat."

"Kids?"

"Not you," Destan tried to explain; knowing he'd backed himself into a corner. "Actually you were the one who kept me going for as

149

long as I did Monday; but dinner knocked me off my feet. Food coma is no joke."

By this time it was easy for Callimay to see he was blushing. Him recalling things from when they first met, or even any memory for that matter, showed that soft side of him she loved so much: *I'm so glad he's able to stay like this, even if it's just around me and for brief moments. ~ He is kinda irresistible when he blushes, isn't he?*

"Anyway," he cleared his throat. "The usual hours a Shadow and Veil keep are the complete opposite of 'normal' people. I think that's going to be a large adjustment for you. Sleeping during the day isn't easy at first; but we'll get to that later. You need your rest tonight."

ℬ

"Well you weren't in there long," Callimay perked up as she scrambled to her feet. "How did it—"

"Come on," Destan huffed as he looked back while the door to Deep Dark shut; him then reaching for her hand.

"Is something wrong? Why are you walking so fast?"

"I don't want them to catch me so they can change their minds."

She sighed as shook her head, "They weren't too happy, were they?"

"Let's not talk about it, okay? I… I just need to forget about it so I don't get too upset. I don't want you to— let's just head back."

"Well," she tried to keep positive; taking his hand with both of hers as she smiled. "I'm glad that no matter how much they complain or grumble they're willing to give you time to rest for yourself; regardless of my condition. Yes, you're Doyen and you have responsibilities to everyone else, but you're also human. I mean it's only been a week since your bout with Baleck. Your body still needs time to recover."

This time her tender comment was better received. Destan stopped and turned to her; sounding so loving as he brushed the side of her face, "I said it before, but I'll say it again: how in the world did I ever find you, Calli?"

There was a wonderful break where nothing was said. And then when they did start off again and talk, it was nothing that dealt with the Shadows or Veil. Somehow Destan turned everything off — in a manner of speaking — and let the rest of their evening be theirs.

~ 7 ~

Long before the sun made its grand entrance for the day, Destan was up, keeping a watchful, loving eye on his sleeping wife. In a way he couldn't fathom how time and time again she showed how much patience she had and that she was willing to sacrifice everything she had to make him happy.

For as much as they did go through in the last week, her willingness to listen, hear, and accept "who" Destan was left him speechless. And then her desire to join him? What wife did that just like "that"?

He remembered his comment the night before about the balls and realized even though they were an escape for the two of them already they were going to become even more so now. What a blessing the next one was mere weeks away! It was something Callimay enjoyed, but it was something Destan knew she was completely safe in attending and he loved seeing her enjoy life in that way.

Before long, his focus switched to his workload he left the night before. It was going to be handed, well, "tossed" at to him without any reservations. Fidus may have stood up with him about Callimay, but that was all he was willing to do it appeared.

This frustrating reality fueled his desire to work off as much of this tension as he could so his emotions would keep steady.

ॐ

Once he was in the hall he had Nexus set an alarm so he'd know when Callimay was awake. She wasn't one to show emotion, but he could notice the hesitation in her voice when she agreed. Destan always knew those around him were human; and yet he was reminded again of that

151

startling difference he noticed before: people who he'd never known to show emotion were beginning to, while others who had were shifting in how they expressed it or shutting down altogether.

Even though he was sore, he was glad to get back into the swing of his workout routine. He'd done his best to keep on top of it even while at the Society, but stopped. For as much as he was hated and despised, it appeared there were certain girls who reveled in pushing the envelope and being his "fan club" on such occasions.

But, one thing he couldn't do no matter where he found himself was his blade exercises. While he didn't carry many on his person, he made sure he was deft with as many kinds as possible. Some still required a partner, but his body reminded him he still had limits: much like when he was training for Toreon at the mansion.

His phone started buzzing in a strange manner, Destan smiling as he stopped what he was doing to turn it off: *Well good morning, my beautiful sleepyhead.*

I overslept?

No. I wouldn't leave without you knowing or telling you I love you after a goodbye kiss. I just needed to work some things out and get back to training so my muscles won't forget what they're supposed to do.

Train? I thought it was called 'regimen' here?

Bad choice of words. I'm not using my abilities, I promise. I'm just down the hall in the combat room doing 'normal' workout exercises.

Am I allowed to come see you, or are you coming back?

"Well seeing as how I can see you outside the door, why don't you just come in." Destan laughed when he looked over to the door — seeing who was standing there — and got up from the bench. "You didn't have to 'run' down here, woman."

"I'm not going to get much time with you today, so I'm not going to lose one precious moment I have right now."

"I'm all sweaty, Calli," he warned as she flew into his chest.

"I don't care," she said a bit muffled as she snuggled closer.

Destan sighed as he shook his head and held her close, "I love you."

"I love you too."

⚭

Callimay fixed a quick breakfast while he cleaned up and then sat right next to him as they ate. In a way, she was acting like Rose: all fidgety and staring at him with her huge, brown eyes that begged for his attention. It was a sweet reminder that he was loved so much, but the closer he got to finishing breakfast brought the reality of what he'd have to do.

She felt this slow drift in his emotions, but also knew they weren't where she needed to intervene.

He tapped his fork on his now empty plate a few times before taking a deep breath and setting it down. Destan plodded toward the door and then stopped when he looked over to his desk. In a manner of speaking, he perked up and went over to where the new veil was. He picked it up and stared at it for a while before strolling back and kneeling in front of Callimay.

"I've been thinking…" he glanced down at the leather coat and then back to her. "This veil I have right now has seen its fair share of 'active duty'; I think it's time it was retired. I'll ask about it and see what everyone else thinks. 'I' don't see any issue, but this falls under the realm of what is known as the Right of Respect which was set in place long before I came along. … The fact is: this isn't my veil, it was my father's. The Right of Respect is observed when a Veil who died in the line of duty has a family member who attains to their status: the new family member inherits their predecessor's veil. The Right states that there must be a reminder to everyone that this person is the legacy of one who paid the ultimate price. When the inheritor is given their veil, the leader of the Veil removes — to put it nicely — the sleeves of the inherited veil to show the loss and to remind everyone to never forget the loss. … It wasn't easy going though that, Calli. And it's something I hope I 'never' have to do."

She heard this from Tabitha and it made her weepy-eyed then; but to hear Destan's voice strain and see the look on his face… it was almost too much.

Seeing how she looked and knowing how she felt, he took her hands and did his best to sound chipper, "It's time I move on from the past. As much as I remember the pain about my father from this veil, when you explained to me what this one was for I realized there was a small part of me that wanted it close because it was from him. … But as always, you've helped me see a deeper truth: I need to be who I am for myself and for you. Thank you for reminding me, Calli. You've helped me find a very fitting way — and one that harmonizes with what I believe the Veil would appreciate — to show his memory the respect it deserves while finding the strength to be able to more on."

He kissed her on the cheek after wiping the tears away, and then sighed when he felt his phone vibrate, "Now I've gotta go. I won't be back until lunch, so I was thinking I could find someone to take you on a tour of Bulwark. Sound good?"

"Can Trever take me?"

"No!" Destan snapped back.

"O… okay."

"I… I'm sorry." He calmed as he closed his eyes and took a deep breath. *Calli? I… I don't want to say too much right now, but there's just something I'm having to deal with when it comes to Trever.*

Does it have to do what you talked about the other day?

No, but yes? I just need to find out what's going on first.

Callimay smiled as she gave him a hug: *It's okay. I know there are things you can't tell me yet.*

"I got with Auditor a bit ago to see if she could, but I haven't heard back. If she can't… then I guess you get to choose what you want to do. I know there's not much here in the suite…"

"I'm sure I can find something to do. You did say there was that one book I could read."

"Always a ray of sunshine."

"I love you, Destan."

He was just about to shut the door when he opened it and asked, "Are you alright, Calli? I mean, you still want to go through with this? I know I shouldn't keep asking, but—"

"I'm sure," she nodded as she put her finger to his lips. "It's alright. You're just thinking of me. I know. … Destan?"

"Yes, Calli?" He asked as he opened the door again.

"Be careful," she threw her arms around him. *Watch out for Elder. I don't know what your father meant by what he said, but… 'please' be careful. Please."

"I promise you: I'm going to do everything within my power to keep you safe. And I know in order to do that I have to first keep myself safe. I'll be careful. Okay? … Alright. I'll let you know when I'm on my way back for lunch."

☙

Most people want to skip past things they already know — especially in what could be called a history book — but Callimay enjoyed it. History, by far, was her favorite subject in school: *I wish they had this in our 'real' history books. It sure would make things crystal clear as to 'why' this all started and 'how' the Syndicate came to be. … But then that would prove how idiotic and evil this all is. Propaganda.*

Calli?

Oh! Hi! How are you doing?

Pretty good. He chuckled as he started writing again. *Auditor said she will be there shortly. … I'll tell you now you'll recognize her.*

As who and from where? Callimay rolled her eyes as she slapped the book closed.

She was my nurse in Faberton.

Is there anyone I 'won't' know here?

Now let's not get all riled up. Auditor's really nice. And you know good an well there's 'several' here you don't know.

In the silence Destan could both see and feel her piercing gaze: *Yes, the note she left did say 'Doyen' on it. … Calli? Are… are you alright?*

Yeah, she sighed as she moseyed around the room.

That sigh wasn't the type he'd heard before, and by what he could feel of her emotions he was pretty sure what the problem was now: *Lunch is only in… three hours? … Yeah, three. That's not that long.*

Still food-driven, but he's making the effort. *What do you want?*

Oh. I get to choose?

You always do.

I'm just kidding. Whatever you fix will be fine. — I've gotta go.

Callimay slouched; sad their conversation was cut off: *I love you.*

Love you too.

Not but a couple moments later a knock came to the door. Callimay opened it and sure enough there was the nurse she remembered seeing.

155

Even though that was a time in her life she wanted to forget, Auditor was tied to the happiest part of it: when she knew Destan was alright.

"Good morning, Liaison. Doyen said he would let you know, but let me introduce myself: Auditor," the middle-aged woman smiled as she nodded her head as if to bow almost.

As much as Callimay wanted to give her a hug or shower her with thank yous, she remembered what happened the last time she answered the door. "Good morning," was all she could muster as she clasped her hands behind her.

"Doyen said I was to escort you around Bulwark while he's occupied." Auditor continued in her professional tone that couldn't hide a distinct accent. "Are you ready or do you still have something to tend to?"

"Oh no. I'm ready." She waved her hands as she stepped out; and then froze when she felt the door shut, "Oh no!"

"What is it?" Auditor asked concerned.

"The door's locked. And I can't—"

Auditor half-chuckled as she tried to pat Callimay's shoulder; her jerking away, "I'm sorry, I didn't mean to scare you. ... There'll be plenty for you to see until Doyen returns for lunch, don't worry."

"Alright," Callimay dragged herself along; still mad at herself.

ℬ

In no time at all, the self-scolding that was infecting Callimay vanished. Auditor was indeed very nice even though she was formal. And yet this formality wasn't coming across as to make Callimay feel inferior. In fact, the way she treated her was more of how someone of equal standing — a co-worker — would. What a relief!

While she'd been on a guided tour before, there was something different this time... and yet she couldn't put her finger on it. It was a shock to find out just how much was housed in this Bulwark that was "buried" in this stone cliffside — the slate walls weren't installed: they were real — but that wasn't it. And then when Callimay asked a question and Auditor answered it without any hesitation, the lightbulb went off: *She's willing to talk with me, and is genuine about being happy to talk with me. ... Maybe everyone else just needs some help.*

156

Maybe I do just need to give them more time. ~ One person can make an impact, but it never hurts to have 'backup'.

As they walked past the door Callimay knew led to Deep Dark, she could feel Destan was very close; her heart feeling so warm and fuzzy. She wanted to say something to him so bad, but didn't want to cause him any grief. Even though he was good about multitasking in that way, he could get lost in their conversation just as easily as she could.

"Why is Bulwark called 'Bulwark'?" She asked after a while; hearing that term over and over.

"Commander was as much for formality, titles, and the usage of what some might call eclectic or difficult language as I think anyone was. Nothing would keep her from staying true to herself and her strong belief in holding to one's heritage but she never bound herself to her native tongue alone. So, she dubbed this place with the 'eclectic' while still rational title of Bulwark instead of what the vast majority of people would associate the title of where an organization is based."

"So even everyone's titles…"

"At first she was the one who chose every single one." Auditor nodded as she ushered her down a flight of steps. "It was a minor detail many didn't see as vital and didn't use for a while; but opinions on the matter quickly changed after what is known to us as 'the quandary'. It was the unfortunate circumstance where we experienced our first casualties: the individuals used their names during a mission and a skilled Informant relayed that information to the closest Falconer and… well, it's now one of the strictest codes. — I must say your choice sounds so very fitting. And I know I haven't been around you very long, but from what Doyen has said concerning you it's a perfect fit. I even believe Commander would be proud to call you Liaison. Which reminds me: I do want to apologize for my conduct in Faberton. Emissary didn't speak a word about you when he contacted me. So when Doyen kept going on about you and demanding I take him back I thought he was delirious. But when he kept refusing after I told him about the Informant I surrendered. I'm sorry, Liaison."

"You didn't know." Callimay smiled; her voice quivering a bit as she fiddled with her sleeves. "There's nothing to apologize for."

"Are you alright?"

"I… I just have a hard time thinking back to that all."

"I guess I'm sticking my foot in my mouth, huh?" Auditor sighed as she stopped and gave a sympathetic smile; trying to think of something encouraging to say. "Well… as I was saying about your title: Doyen's comments over the past couple days have been very telling about how much thought you must have put into that choice."

I just blurted it out, really. And it's not something I 'chose'. "Wait. Des— Doyen talks about me while he's working?"

"The times I've been around him, quite often. There are times that call for strict formality and such, but even then, I can tell his thoughts wander when certain topics are brought up… or even a phrase that he associates with you."

This was such a sweet thing to hear, but at the same time, Callimay knew her presence there was causing issues for Destan. She hung her head and mumbled, "I'm not wanting to be a—"

"Oh, you're not the kind of distraction that is bad. It's actually refreshing to see a different side of Doyen that is so tender. I've known him to have that caring side from what he does for others, but to see it so focused on one individual so consistently… I haven't seen that level of devotion in a man in quite a while." *'Quite' a while.* Auditor stared off in the distance with a melancholy look.

"So how long have you known Des— Doyen? Doyen. I meant Doyen. I 'am' trying to remember, really I am. I'm sorry." Callimay clapped her hand over her mouth.

"You've only known him by that name and it does closely correlate to his title. You'll get used to it soon, I'm sure. It's just me here, so don't worry. — I was actually here when the original Challenger, his father, was here; and I must say the first day he stepped foot in here I thought for sure I was seeing him come back from the dead. He is quite literally the spitting image of him. Not just in physical appearance, though. The way in which he holds himself and how he acts is a pure reflection of his father. I know his time with him was cut short and in a drastic way, but some things are just part of a person: it's who they naturally are."

"If I'm prying, I understand if you don't want to, or for whatever reason can't answer this, but… since you knew Doyen's father, you must have known Commander, correct?"

"Yes and no. Commander was alive, but didn't come to Bulwark that often. Elder took care of everything here even though all final decisions came from Commander."

"At the ball, Roch— I mean Sentinel said she passed away suddenly. Did she…"

"That's something I don't know if anyone will ever know for sure. It was completely unexpected. Sentinel told us she was found in her house, slain. Resources — maybe too many — were poured into discovering who did it." Auditor sighed as she stopped in front of a door. "Nothing was ever found, sadly. It's been a cloud over Sentinel ever since the case was enclosed."

"Why would he be so emotionally tied to this?"

She looked around and then leaned in as she whispered, "Commander was Sentinel's sister… well, his sister-in-law. He treated her like his sister in every sense of the word, though. It was well-known back at that time; but for some reason, as time passed, it has been hushed. I think for Sentinel's sake."

Oh, poor Rocher! Callimay cried as she tried not to gasp too much. After what happened with Destan's parents and then— how has he kept going?

"So!" Auditor clapped her hands together before panning on down the hall. "This quadrant we're in right now is where all the Shadow's quarters are… with some exceptions. Speaking of which — I can't see Doyen approving — but are they assigning you to a room?"

"Not that I know of."

"Good." She nodded, sounding much more chipper as she started walking again. "We'll skirt by the laboratory and detention quadrants before heading back up. Any questions right now?"

"Well… did you ever meet Canary? I've heard that name mentioned a couple times, but even Doyen couldn't tell me more about her."

"As it turns out, Canary and I are very close; only on a professional level, though. She came to us just after Doyen's father did. She was extremely good at stealth and tactics… the reason she was added to the Veil and put into black widow missions so quickly." Auditor said a bit somber. "She's been off-grid for almost twenty years now. And she's so deeply planted that we rarely hear from her."

"What's she like?"

"She was always soft-spoken, but had this fire in her nonetheless. In a way she was like a passive alpha: willing to go along providing her authority wasn't questioned." She thought back as she slowed to an eventual stop. "I think that was because she had such a large family — twelve and 'all' boys. But then again, I haven't seen her in so long that she very well may have changed. Being where she's at can very easily chance a person… good or bad."

"Where was she from?"

"That's something I couldn't tell you even if I did know." Auditor smiled as she patted her arm. "Let's keep going. Can't say I'm the biggest fan of this quadrant."

The tour continued for as long as Auditor could stretch it out, but as they stopped in front of Destan's suite she apologized as she checked her watch, "Well, we're back a bit early. I could stay until—"

"Thank you, but I'll be alright. I might go to the combat room and work on a few things." Callimay smiled as she looked to see if maybe Destan was around.

"I'm free for some of the afternoon if you would like to talk some more. I could take you up top since I'm sure you don't have a pass yet."

"That might be nice. I'll check with Doyen to see if he has anything scheduled for me to do this afternoon. I can get hold of you through Nexus, right?"

"See? You're picking things up, Liaison. Keep at it and know we're here to help."

❧

Callimay moseyed to the combat room and took the hummingbirds she still had in her boot out. Destan didn't show her how to use them yet, but she had the basics of knife handling. It was drilled into her from that first, stressful day in the combat room.

The rings were perfectly sized for her fingers and they slid out of their sheaths so effortlessly. She then remembered Outfitter said her blouse also had places in the sleeves for them. At first she wondered if he forgot to include them, but realized they weren't on the outside: they were on the inside of the sleeve cuffs. She tried to figure out the best way to do it without hurting herself; her contorting her wrist and arm this way and then that.

Finally, she slipped one in and felt it snap into place as if there were a magnet or some other metal piecing in there to hold it. It was a good thing too, since it would most likely fall out with it being inverted all the time: *But I didn't ever 'feel' any metal. How—*

Calli?

Yes, Destan? Callimay replied joyfully as she whipped around; part of her expecting him to be at the door.

I'm on my way. … I could feel you earlier. Enjoy your tour?

Auditor is very sweet.

Good. — What's for lunch?

Well…

What? Did you burn it?

No!

Not have an ingredient you needed? He sounded confused.

Callimay laughed: *I'm… well I'm… I locked myself out again. I didn't stop to think if I left I couldn't get back in.*

Oh, my poor Calli! Destan tried his best not to laugh. *I wasn't thinking. That's my fault.*

I'll get something ready as fast as I can, I promise. She sat down outside the suite and fiddled with her hummingbird.

I don't want you hurting yourself, I'll help.

She looked over when she heard what sounded like someone running and scrambled to her feet; Destan was all but sprinting down the hall. All she could think of was that something was wrong, so she ran to him. Callimay was still scared, but when she saw his face she understood: he was just happy to see her. The second he was close enough, he swept her off her feet and held her close.

There was no denying she felt like it had been a lifetime since she saw him; her tour only did so much to keep her mind off of him: *Come to think of it, I guess I haven't truly been away from him for a long period of time on a regular basis. I know today was the first day, but I also know this is how it's going to be for a while.*

It hit Destan that being apart was still hard on him. When he went to Rayleen that one Friday he felt fine and was able to function; not feeling a constant tug for him to go back since he knew he'd be able to get back. But when Sonnie reminded him how he talked about Callimay the entire time he was there, he had to admit to himself he wasn't fine. He did feel that tug, he was concerned about being gone, and in a way he felt lost without her nearby.

And for him, at least, there wasn't anything that needed to be said; they didn't even have to be doing something together. Just knowing she was right there and could be with him wherever he went, that was his comfort zone he didn't even know he'd developed. Now it was pulling on him stronger and making things more difficult for Doyen… and in a way he didn't want it any other way.

♄

While the kitchen at the mansion was spacious and had everything you could ever need, it didn't have the bells and whistles this one had. But Kerogen was more for tradition than being on the cutting edge of technological advancements so it wasn't "that" shocking.

Though, it was quite the feat in that it packed everything from the mansion's kitchen into a room the size of one of the smaller closets there. And then all these bells and whistles brought a learning curve for Callimay she wasn't expecting.

Laughter was an audible emotion rarely heard in Bulwark, and yet it was building in the air in and around Destan's suite. Not too much longer after it started, he ran over and opened the door to the balcony, flapping the hand towel he had as Callimay darted out.

One thing he forgot was an unused oven — even one that's been left closed that entire time — can still accumulate dust; and with as long as he'd left it unused it was no wonder the distinct smell of burning dust quickly forced them out of the room.

Smelling the salty air grabbed them both the second its scent brought back memories; them freezing for a moment. The next sense to captivate their thoughts in this reminiscing trance was sound; the sound of the waves below them and the seagulls all around. There was a pang of sadness in both of their hearts for a moment, but the strong bond of love between the two of them soothed this fleeting agony. They took the effort to remember things in a positive light; seeing the good

— and bad — for what they were and appreciating they had what they did at that moment. Memories held power; a power they both knew could be the undoing of a person or a source for their strength. Having each other made that power work for them; not control them.

Nothing was said and yet everything was understood. There were times verbal communication was vital… and then there were times like this where it wasn't needed. At least it wasn't needed when both individuals felt the same way.

Destan struggled with the concept of being married at first, but he had his eyes opened for him when he almost lost Callimay. And yet being at Bulwark and his wife standing in front of him in official dress while still being her smiling and happy self… he unveiled another layer of what it meant to be married. Love wasn't something that was straight-forward; it constantly molded and remolded how you saw life and how things impacted you.

This deep, thoughtful, loving look in his eyes tugged at her heart; Callimay sighing as her smile softened, "We'll make it. I know we will."

"Well duh. I'm sure the smell is out of the oven now."

Silence. And of the kind that just couldn't believe and yet at the same time should've expected that reply.

Laughter broke out again, though mainly from Destan.

While it was a bit annoying he felt that comment deserved a punch line, it was a relief to Callimay to see that she still "had him". That didn't stop her from "fighting" with him a bit before she surrendered.

They talked off and on for the rest of the time, part of Callimay wondering how much longer she had left: *He's been back for just about an hour. ~ Oh please don't call, Nexus. Please. I'm not ready to be alone for the afternoon. Not yet.*

"I'm sorry you can't come, Calli." Destan sighed as he dropped the spatula into the pan and rubbed his face. "If I had my w—"

"I'm not complaining! Please don't think that. I'm—"

"I… I just hate you're in such seclusion right now… again. The whole reason I'm here is so you don't have to be and look at what you're— and then to be looked down at—"

"Hey, look at me 'mister grumpy'." Callimay exaggerated as she framed his face. "We can't control their reactions. Remember? I'll get my privileges soon enough and then they'll have to either speak their mind to my face or brood to themselves."

"That is if you still want this life," he mumbled under his breath as he started plating what he had.

"Destan. I…"

"I'm just having a moment, Calli. I'm sorry."

"I want my life with you. And wherever that means I have to go and whatever that means I have to do then so be it. I'm alright with this, Destan. Our life has changed, but we're still together. And we still get to go home to Rayleen for the balls, right? We still get a little time for ourselves; like right now, even. Granted it's not like what we're used to, but it's better than not getting any at all. … Destan?"

"Y—"

"Elder is asking for your ETA, Doyen."

He threw the pan on the counter; the sound of that and the impact of his hands against the counter scaring Callimay. She reached out for a moment, but stopped: *Destan? Destan it's alright. The food's ready and so we can eat real quick and you can go.* "He'll be leaving in a few minutes, Nexus."

"I'll let Elder know."

"Our furlough can't come soon enough." He growled as he started to spike; his breathing getting quicker and heavier by the second. "I'm getting sick and tired of—"

"Just give it a little time." Callimay crept over and wrapped her arms around his one that was still as stiff as a board. "Don't let him control you. Don't stoop to his level. I'm right here."

"I know," Destan sighed as he closed his eyes and turned so he could bow his head on her shoulder.

S

The circumstances they parted under weren't what either of them hoped for, but each took it in stride and did their best to help the other. It hurt Callimay to watch Destan storm down the hall — and it wasn't just because she was in physical pain from her tie to him. No, it hurt because she had to watch him struggle through this effort to balance his workload with his "home life" and there wasn't a thing she could do. Add on top of that, the person being the biggest deterrent was also someone his father was leery of to the point he was justifying ending his life. Here it was day one and Callimay was beginning to doubt everything… like Destan was not but an hour ago.

Because of this lackluster emotional state, she stood and stared at the sink full of dishes for a good five minutes before even thinking of putting water in it. The water rippling in the sink as the seagulls sang to her made Callimay forget where she was; which also made her forget why she was feeling like she did… which was a good thing.

After taking a short nap, she woke up to someone knocking on the door, "Oh! Hello, Auditor."

"I was close by so I thought I'd drop by."

She did her best to fight off a yawn, but couldn't help it, "I'm sorry. I know I s—"

"If you need to rest I understand."

"Oh, no." Callimay tried to stop a second one from starting. "No I took a nap already. I'm fine. I'd enjoy spending some time 'outside'."

"Very well then," Auditor smiled as she led on.

♉

Prior to them leaving, Auditor stopped where Callimay remembered finding Tabitha the one day. There was quite a bit of discussion had, but they soon left by a different exit than Callimay used the two times she ran out. The wonderful thing was: this time there was no blaring alarm or group of people racing after her.

Seeing all the trees around them made Callimay pause. The tree line wasn't right next to where she left, "H… how did we—"

"There are several different entrances to Bulwark so that if daytime maneuvers are necessary we can use the canopy for cover. The one you used was the closest as well as the only one you would be able to get to. Do you remember trying to open some doors that just wouldn't budge an inch?"

"Y… yes."

"Well, those were halls that led to these kinds of doors. Without a beacon they won't unlock."

"Then why did that one?"

"You heard the alarm." Auditor tried to make light as she strolled through the densely wooded area. "It's not unguarded, but we do on occasion have individuals come in who are not Shadows or Veils: trainees, persons of interest, detainees, and so on. That isn't the entrance they use for security reasons, but there are times…"

Callimay nodded as she moseyed along; trying to shift her mind toward things that weren't connected to Bulwark and the Shadows.

During this all, Destan kept tabs on her and would stop what he was doing to watch her whenever he got a moment. In a way he felt like a little kid trying to check for any adults while taking a cookie from the jar. And sure enough, he was caught like a child: one time he didn't notice Elder walked up behind him and was scolded for neglecting the task at hand. He tried to defend his actions, saying nothing was going on at the time, but his efforts were met with nothing but cruel backlash. This all drove him overboard — him becoming infuriated — which caused Callimay to get concerned: *What's wrong?*

I… I'm just trying to be patient with others who don't understand and don't seem to want to put the effort in to understand what you mean to me. Destan sighed; working to calm himself as he looked back at the screen. *You look like you're enjoying yourself.*

You can see me?

Turn to your left. Okay, I mean 'your' right. … A little more. There. Destan sighed rather painfully; and yet still sounded tender. *You're beautiful, you know that?*

I love you, she smiled softly in the direction she now knew the camera had to be.

I love you more. I… I gotta go. I'm sorry, Calli.

It's alright. I'll see you later.

⅁

Before long, Auditor was called back, so it was off to the suite for Callimay. It still felt strange to walk through the halls by herself, but what made it worse was hearing footsteps behind her.

The people who were behind her on these few occasions would look at her with this strange expression and continue on their way; obviously confused at her reaction. But the last time was different. Her skin was crawling… and she'd only felt that feeling once before. She whipped around and was just about to scream when the person pipped up, "Hey there!"

"Oh! It's you." Callimay tried to catch her breath.

"What are you doing out by yourself?"

"Just walking back to the suite. What about yourself?"

"Not much. Pretty low key right now. — Glad to see you're doing better. What happened scared the living daylights out of not just me, but Doyen and Overseer as well. I'm really glad to see you're alright."

"Thank you… what is your title?"

"Emissary," Trever reminded as he half-laughed. "So you've decided to do things the right way, huh?"

"I'm trying to." She huffed; and then finished on a more tender note, "Thank you, Emissary. I appreciate it. I really do."

"Got any time free right now?"

"Well," Callimay looked at her watch. *Oh, that's right. Destan doesn't want me around him. ~ Well it doesn't matter because you do need to get back.* "I should be headed back to get dinner started."

"Don't blame you. After a scare like that I'd cook my own food too. Well… I'll hopefully see you around before I leave."

"When 'are' you leaving?"

"Still not sure," Trever shrugged his shoulders as he backed up and waved. "Take care."

ẞ

When Callimay got back, she gasped on horror when she saw how the place looked. Who in this "fortress" hated them so much that they'd ransack their "home"? Why was her coming causing everything to fall apart? How was it that no matter where the two of them were, danger and frustration always waited to pounce?

Destan? Destan, can you hear me? She yelped as her eyes began to dart around the ransacked room.

No response.

Destan, please! Callimay asked a bit more frantic.

Still nothing.

"Nexus?"

"Yes?"

"Could you get hold of Doyen? 'Please'? I know he's busy but I need to speak with him right now."

"Let me see if he's available. One moment." Nexus trailed off; still sounding monotone.

Callimay ran to the door and shut it, but quickly found she couldn't lock it, "Nexus?"

"Yes, Liaison?"

"Could you please lock the door?"

"I will need Doyen's approval for that, and I can't reach him."

"Please keep trying! Please!"

She felt completely vulnerable since anyone who really wanted to could waltz right in. Callimay had the couple throwing knives, but she didn't know how to use them correctly and they were so small.

Wait! Callimay gasped as she dashed to the desk and fumbled to get the one drawer open. *Oh thank goodness they're still here.*

Somehow her hands calmed so she could handle Destry's Seaxes without hurting herself; slipping them out of their sheaths and placing them in the ones on the sides of her pants. She wasn't completely proficient with them, but she knew enough and thankfully could still remember some of it.

As she looked around the desk, the Shadow Box was tossed onto the floor along with what looked like a million other papers and those discs she remembered seeing in the other drawer.

Destan? Callimay asked again; repeating it every so often.

Part of her knew she needed to check and see if she was alone in the suite, but the other part refused to let her stop shaking so she could move. It wasn't much of a surprise to see the kitchen was ransacked as well. Knowing what happened to the food the other day, Callimay's thoughts jumped to the someone who came in "spiking" the food.

Out of the fearful aura that was closing in around her she heard Destan call out over the com, "Calli?"

After she got her initial yelp and gasping fit done, she blurted out almost hysterical, "Destan someone got in and has ransacked the entire suite. Everything's thrown everywhere."

"What!"

"Someone's torn the place apart. — I'm scared, Destan. Nexus said she wouldn't lock the door without your approval."

"Just— I'm coming, Calli. Hang tight." He said flustered; the muffled sounds of him moving something in the background hinting he was knee-deep in work at the time.

"Please hurry," she began to cry as she crouched by the desk.

Hang in there, Calli. I'm coming.

There was an overpowering moment of silence before the door started to open.

She screamed as she grabbed one of the knives and thrust it in front of her, "Who is it!"

The door kept opening ever so slowly; no response.

"I know you're there!"

Long, slender, gloved fingers slowly emerged around the edge of the door and made that gut-wrenching slow roll as they one by one gripped the door. The only thing was, she couldn't tell who it was because she was standing on the other side of the door.

Feeling how out-of-control her emotions were, Destan jumped once he was out of sight from everyone. He saw someone running around the end of the hall but couldn't tell who it was. And even though he wanted to follow them he knew he needed to check on Callimay.

"There's no sense in you standing there, I know you're there!" Callimay repeated in her shrill voice; gasping when she saw, "Destan?"

"Are you alright?" He asked worried as he ran over. "Who was it?"

"I… I don't know," she began to cry; her shaking hands unable to hold the knife any longer. "I was still shocked from everything… and… I kept trying to get you, then Nexus told me she couldn't, and then the door started to open—"

"I'm here. You're safe now."

"Are we 'ever' safe?" Callimay asked in a voice that broke his heart.

What she said was true: the most secure place on the planet he thought there was… it was turning into a deathtrap.

🕉

Unaware of the situation, Rocher and Doctor Gerould showed up a little while later; walking in while chatting when they saw the door opened. But upon hearing Callimay whimpering, they paused and stood there frozen with confusion and concern.

Unfortunately, the first thought that ran through their minds was: Destan lost his temper. The look of wild anger and fear in his eyes which burned at them suggested so, but this type of carnage was not in line with what they knew the destructive nature his "condition" to result in. His reaction appeared to be more along the lines of protecting his wife, really. But why was Callimay so distraught? What happened?

"Rocher? Go check to make sure no one else is in here or something hasn't been t— someone broke in and did this. I don't know any more than you do right now." Destan's voice sounded more desperate than demanding. "I'd go myself but I don't want Calli— please?"

He left that moment without a single question; Doctor Gerould the only one left. Yes, he'd seen — as had Destan — places much worse than this, but it happened "inside" Bulwark.

All this doubt and confusion made the desire to know who Destan suspected earlier grow… who was the traitor among their ranks?

Can you hear me?

What is it, Lance? He replied a bit annoyed.

Who is it that you've got doubts about? After seeing this, there's no doubt in my mind someone's out to get you two; whether it's just to get you to leave or… permanently rid themselves of you altogether.

The look on Destan's face hinted he didn't feel this was the time to get into such things since it was taking all of his focus to keep Callimay calm; but he replied: *At the time it was just Elder, but it now appears Emissary is an accomplice. Well, to some extent.*

Elder? His eyes widened as he took a step back to think; sounding determined as he finished: *What do you want me to do? Let me help. They're not just against you, they're against everything we stand for.*

"I would in no way have the assurance that any one thing within this room is not laced; as bewildering and frustrating as that comment may sound. There is nothing tampered with to cause immediate danger, but…" Rocher came back; his demeanor of the type Destan had only seen a handful of times before. "For your immediate wellbeing, I would implore you to seek accommodations elsewhere until this situation is ramified. I will call for a detail to begin isolation procedures."

"Callimay can stay in my quarters since it would be closer to Deep Dark if something came up." Doctor Gerould stepped up as he came to her side to comfort her.

"I don't want to leave her, L—"

"Are you through with your little escapade, Doyen?"

He gritted his teeth as he hissed; moving in front of Callimay so he was shielding her, "I've got more pressing and important things to tend to right now, Elder."

"Well it's good to know you see your duties that you dropped as being worthless."

Destan snapped back as he looked up to where the camera was; moving Callimay again so she was behind him, "I will be back when I feel I can and not a moment sooner, Elder. That's an order."

"Sentinel is on his way and I'll be heading that way in a minute or so." Doctor Gerould tried to keep things a civil as possible; if for no other reason than to help keep Callimay calm.

There was a scoffing huff followed by a voice that voiced his eye roll perfectly, "Very well."

Doctor Gerould put a firm hand on Destan's shoulder and warned, "Laying your suspicions aside, you 'know' not to get him riled."

"We've discussed that all. He knows good and well—"

"Destan?" A tiny voice quivered as shaking hands reached for the lapel of his veil; drawing both his and Doctor Gerould's attention.

"Let's get you somewhere you can rest easier, okay?" He melted, sounding so loving and tender as he wiped her face.

❧

The walk there started out slow, but part of Destan was becoming more and more unsettled. He finally picked up Callimay and carried her the rest of the way; Doctor Gerould keeping pace with him the entire way.

They stopped at the medical wing first so the bloodwork she needed to get done for the evening was taken care of before they made their way down to where she would be spending the night.

It wasn't as welcoming of a place as the suite was — no windows to the outside world — but with it being a smaller room it felt safer somehow; and yet it only felt this way when Destan was holding her.

While he didn't want to leave, at the same time he needed her to understand she was safe now, "Look at me. … Whoever did that only got in because the door was unlocked. That's the 'only' reason. You're safe here, I promise."

Sobs jumped out whenever they pleased as she worked to do as he said; nodding as she buried her face against his and gripped his hair.

"I know it scared you and everything's different here — and I'm not trying to downplay that — I just…" he paused when he pulled her back and looked in her eyes. "I'm sorry it took you so long to get hold of me. I started getting wrapped up in everything and I forgot."

"You were focusing on your job. I know it's hard right now for you to find balance. And I also know there's no way you could know this was going to happen… and maybe I did overreact."

As he closed his eyes and took a deep breath, he groaned as his forehead wrinkled; him struggling to say, "I don't want to leave you."

"I… I don't want you to either, but I know deep down I've got to learn to protect myself. You can't always been there for me and things can happen anywhere or anytime."

Destan stood there for a moment before dropping to his knees in front of her, "I'm not trying to tell you to act like me, Calli. I know I've said this before, but I still feel the same. Your initial reaction to a situation will be different than mine will be; and when that situation isn't expected it's going to take more effort on your part sometimes just like it is for me, just on the polar opposite type of situation. … Calli?"

"I love you."

He let out a deep and almost labored sigh, "I… I'll see you in the morning. I love you Calli."

✆

Being alone in another man's apartment, as she thought of it, wasn't the most comfortable situation to be in. Destan locked the door so even Doctor Gerould couldn't get in, so there really wasn't anything to be worried about. And beyond that she felt she was intruding on his personal life. He told her to make herself at home, but she didn't want to critique and examine all of his belongings to find out more about his life outside of a doctor as well as a Shadow.

And yet part of her was so curious from seeing several items from a very distinct culture. He was from Faberton as she understood it, so these must be gifts from a close friend or relative from Indalla: all the bright woven textiles and broad-brimmed hats.

With nothing else to do and her body depleted of its adrenaline, she lay down and started to drift off... and then was wide awake. It sounded like his apartment was on the "main road" with all of the foot traffic outside: voices being heard as well as doors constantly opening and closing.

Where did all of those people come from? It didn't look like a busy place when they first came; and it most certainly didn't sound like this when Destan was here.

As quickly as all those sounds came, they left. Could it be those were individuals "coming in to work" or "heading home for the night" like a shift change? At least that was the only logical thing Callimay could think of. And then looking at the clock as well as remembering what she read and Destan told her, that's the only thing it could be.

But even with the constant buzz now gone, something else surfaced that made it difficult for Callimay to get to sleep. It had been months since Destan hadn't slept with her, and being in a strange environment only amplified this. As she tossed and turned, she realized she still had one of Destry's knives, so that gave her some comfort... but it still wasn't the same.

Out of the darkness came sweet, tender words: *I miss you, Calli.*

There was a pause as she opened her eyes and stared out for a moment; her fumbling: *Y... you what?*

I said I miss you. Now get some sleep. I'll see you in a few hours.

She was going to reply but was so stunned that by the time she thought to, she knew he wasn't paying attention.

Callimay lay there for a while in a daze. She kept trying to think of an instance where he had, but she couldn't remember him "ever" telling her that before. — Granted, they were never apart that often or for that long. The longest was one that Destan only remembered since she was in a coma the entire time. — All along she'd missed him so many times but never said anything since it wasn't truly for that long a time; and she felt like she would sound clingy by saying it. But when it was said to her, that wasn't at all what she thought. This was Destan telling her exactly how he felt, no overreaction or clinginess at all.

℔

Please tell me I'm not the only one seeing this. Destan stewed as he clinched his fists. *Come on, Boon. Calli just fell asleep. No need to get her worried all over again. ~ If I just knew 'who' this Nark was I could take care of it right now. I'd have~ Breathe. …* *Lance?*

I see it, Destan. I haven't got a clue how Elder could do this, but he's one of the very few who would have unbridled access to do it. …What tipped you off on him anyway?

My father. He… he left a note saying he needed to be disposed of because he said he is 'the origin of a kind of evil this…'

While his trailing off wasn't something Doctor Gerould appreciated, the profound shift in Destan's demeanor and expression hinted as to why this happened. By the time he got out of the room to ask what was going on, there wasn't anyone there to ask. Destan vanished.

A few minutes passed before Doctor Gerould felt someone tap his shoulder and then nod toward a room across the way.

"Why did you leave?"

"I had to make sure 'this' wasn't missing." He showed him a small, silver box. "Did anything come back yet?"

"Nothing's shown any signs of being laced; and whoever did it made sure no fingerprints would be left."

Destan rolled his eyes as he stretched; rubbing his neck. "Not 'that' surprising. It'd be something a trainee would mess up and do. — No other word on the feed discrepancy?"

"Traceur and Nexus have poured over it; nothing." *What's this about Elder being evil and your father saying he needed to be killed?*

Destan became flustered as his eyes got wide, *I'm not sure and we need to stop talking about it right now.*

"I hope you're satisfied," a person fumed as they burst into the room. "We've left Tindal on hold for three and a half hours because your wife—"

"Don't even start." Destan slammed the table as his eyes began to flash. "It's not like I 'had' to be there. Tindal said you were perfectly

174

capable of getting the info she needed from the get-go. … So why didn't you do 'your' job, Elder?"

"She changed her mind right after you left. There was one code I couldn't remember and it just so happens 'you' are the only other one who has it, 'Doyen'." He pursed his lips and looked him square in the eye. "Now put this fantasy to bed and get back to the work you swore you would finish."

Destan normally would've had an off-the-cuff remark ready as he stormed by, but something in him held back. Something about Elder didn't "feel" right to the point it worried him. It could very well be driven by his distrust of him since reading his father's note; but this was more than just a hunch. Similar to how he could feel Callimay's emotions, Destan could feel something inside Elder that was brewing: toxic and dangerous. But what?

℔

The rest of the night was one problem after another. He'd had nights like this before but never did get used to the constant barrage. Thankfully no one was confrontational about anything; it's just that under the circumstances it felt more overpowering and in his face. Before, he could hide the anger and let it sit; but that wasn't going to work now.

And so, when he knew he'd reached a breaking point, he started to reach out to Callimay: *Don't do it, Boon. I know why you are, but her knowing you're this upset isn't going to help her any. The last thing you need is to have her running in here again. Just take it easy and step back. Lance and Rocher will understand and cover for you.*

As if knowing he needed some space, Destan saw both men he mentioned walking over when he opened his eyes.

"Go check on Callimay," Doctor Gerould nodded on as he patted his shoulder. "Or at least go outside for a few minutes. The fresh air would do you good."

"Have no reservations, we will remind any who object of the reality with which Liaison shook them with a few days earlier. Take leave of the situation for a brief time, Sir."

"A… alright," he sighed as he rubbed his face; glancing around.

175

"Really, Doyen. I'll talk with Elder." Doctor Gerould promised in a whisper as he motioned to the door. "Go on."

ℬ

Caller's warning sounded, so Destan finished what he was doing and left; running the entire way. Callimay was passed out with his father's knife clutched in her hands in front of her. Even though the lingering sigh hinted at a different thought, there was the sliver of a smile that peeked out: *I knew I kept those knives for a reason.*

Being as quiet as possible, he slipped the knife out of her grasp and then laid down beside her. He fiddled with her hair a little and then gave her a kiss and settled down to rest.

A few minutes later he heard her stirring and then felt her roll over and curl up beside him; laying her hand over his heart. She'd never done this before while she was asleep, so he smiled as he reached over and brushed the side of her face, "Sleep well?"

There wasn't any response, so he took her hand in his and closed his eyes. Doctor Gerould was going to be back before long, but he just couldn't bring himself to wake her: *He'll understand.*

Sure enough, the door opened a few minutes later. Destan got up and came out, sounding groggy, "I'll take her by the medical wing before going to the suite."

"Make sure you actually go to bed."

"No need to be all fatherly, I'm not going to fight," he yawned and rubbed his face; dragging himself back into the bedroom.

He stumbled into the foot of the bed, jolting Callimay awake. She gasped as she sat up, but calmed when she saw Destan smiling. The first thing she noticed was his eyes; her voice sounding pitiful, "Why are you still awake? Come lie down. You need your rest."

"Lance is back and just about as bushed as I am. The suite is safe now so let's go back." Destan reached one hand out to her as he picked up his father's knife with the other. "First though, we need to stop so you can get your bloodwork done."

"Alright," Callimay nodded as she took his hand and hopped up and to his side.

~ 8 ~

After thanking Doctor Gerould, the two of them left; having to get through the "traffic" of shift change. It was noisy and crowded, but she was still waking up and not fully aware of her surroundings. She really didn't even flinch when she had her bloodwork done.

By the time they turned the last corner to get to the suite, Callimay was awake. Destan was dragging himself along; doing everything he could to look like he was doing alright. She put her arm around him and continued on, worry beginning to grow in her: she didn't know how in the world he was going to be able to function for so long and somehow keep going if it was always going to be like this. He might have done that in the past, but now? Was this a safe thing to do?

When she tugged on him because he was walking past the suite door, Callimay noticed he had the new veil on. Yes, it was the exact same style and the exact same type of leather, but it looked nothing like his father's… and all in a good way.

While this was a happy thought, the fact she had to remind him this was where they had to stop hurt her. She'd never seen him this tired and worn.

❧

The suite was bathed in warm sunlight and smelled fresh; the two of them taking the time to breathe a sigh of relief. For as much as this place was new to her, she knew it was her "home".

"I need to lock the door first, Calli." Destan pulled back and shook his head. "I know I forgot where I was outside, but I'm doing better."

"Can you sleep with it being this bright?"

177

"If I 'need' to, yes. But thankfully I don't have to worry about it in here." He smiled as he tapped part of the interface on the wall. "See? The only thing I can't really block is the seagulls, but a little ambient noise never hurt anyone."

There was a long pause as he finished working with the interface; Destan looking to her with a concerned expression, only to see what had to be the exact same expression on his face, "What's wrong?"

"I… do I need to fix you any… I don't know."

"Easy," he reached out and laid his hand on her neck. "I know this schedule's new and weird, but don't spaz out on me, okay? … I usually would want something, but I'm tapped out."

"Did something happen?" She asked worried as he walked on ahead of her.

"I got close there once, but I was able to go for a long walk and keep myself from getting too bad." Destan admitted as he flopped onto the bed. "And then things in general were hectic. But, it's all over now."

He could feel she wasn't sure what to do, and opened his eyes as he repositioned himself so he was more comfortable, "Don't worry about keeping me awake, Calli. You know I'm a heavy sleeper. I'm only going to sleep for a few hours anyway so we can get back to your regimen."

"But you're too tired to—"

"I can live off of that amount of sleep, believe me."

"Your eyes don't say so."

Destan groaned as he sat up and took her hands, "Calli? I am adjusting to the way things are shifting, but there are some things that don't need it. Or at least I'm going to give this a go for a few days to see if this will work. … Okay?"

Her complaining or trying to argue with him wasn't going to prove anything right now: *Just let him sleep for as long as he wants and then you can figure everything out.* "Okay."

~ 9 ~

Nothing came up missing and nothing was tampered with even though the place looked like someone was indeed searching for something. It puzzled Destan why the one who did it skipped past the Shadow box. He was shocked when he saw it, so any other person there would have the same reaction… at least that is what he thought. Not that he was complaining, though. He was glad it and the contents were safe and sound.

Even though it puzzled him, it was just as frustrating that there was nothing to go off of and no way to prove who did it. He kept it as hush-hush as possible when it came to Callimay — the "unresolved" nature of this incident — but couldn't personally let it rest.

The Veil, for the most part, shared his confusion and frustration; but with nothing to go off of they moved on. Or at least it appeared they did. Destan hoped they were backing off to help the person feel secure so they would cut out all of the "precautions" they were taking. They had to slipup at some point; so laying low was the best thing to do.

As always, he had his suspicions, but Trever had an alibi this time. Knowing this treacherous group was an actual group and not just some livewire person? He needed to find out who was all involved and as soon as possible.

℥

Their new schedule was working and began to "feel" comfortable for Callimay. She was satisfied with amount of sleep Destan got on a daily basis and was comforted that his emotions were more stable each day; so, she consented to the eclectic nature of their schedule.

179

Aside from initial frustration and failures when learning a new technique or skill set, Callimay's speed at retaining and implementing what he was training her was unlike anything he thought possible.

Wanting to make sure he wasn't imagining things, Destan asked Redje and a few others if they experienced the same thing; them all saying there was only one they recall being that quick to learn: himself.

One evening, he was about to say something about this "anomaly" as Rocher referred to it at one point, but stopped himself when she mentioned, "It's only been what… a little over four weeks since we started? Not even a short month! I can't understand why I'm doing so well. Do you?"

It hit him when she said "not even a short month" that she'd always been this way. This was her: *Why did I forget about that? ~ You've had more pressing matters on your mind lately. And now with that mystery solved, things should work out even better. ~ Why? ~ She's able to adapt and learn quicker which means she will finish her regimen faster. ~ I thought you were the logical one and not the one to run off with fancy ideas? ~ I'm not. I'm being serious and logical. Look at what she's accomplished in such short amounts of time: advanced Algebra, mid-level physics, and driving. Why would it be any different now? ~ Maybe I'm just wanting to 'see' that, so I'm fooling myself into—*

He felt a soft hand on his back followed by a timid, sweet voice, "Destan? Destan, are you alright?"

Her ability to calm him and bring him back outweighed any other ability she had; and it reminded him that everyone was special in their own way, no matter if it was viewed as fantastic to others. He smiled and took a deep breath as he looked over his shoulder, "I'm fine, Calli."

"I… I know I'm not allowed to know much, but I'm here if you need to talk."

"I know you are, Calli. Thanks for reminding me."

❦

In what felt more like a few days, she completed the required amount of combat and weapon training so she could advance to the terrain portion of her regimen. Callimay was thrilled she now got to be outside; even if it was only at night.

But unlike what she expected, the night air never lost the sting it gained from the sun during the day. Needless to say, her endurance wasn't anywhere near Destan's... and for some reason she wasn't overcoming this "learning curve" like she had with everything else.

"The weather isn't a 'learned skill', Calli." He called out so he could be heard above the crashing waves. "We can stop if you need to."

"No," she took a labored breath as she grabbed his hand and came to his side. "I've got to do this. You've already gotten in trouble a half dozen times for helping me. And don't deny it! I heard Elder."

"How?"

"It was hard 'not' to. Why does he yell so much? ... Anyway," Callimay diverted; feeling his emotions beginning to climb. "Why don't you have a harness?"

He brushed off as he turned to her; his grin vanishing as he consoled, "I won't fall. Okay? That's why it's called free soloing: you're 'free' to go wherever your hands and feet can get you. 'You' have a harness because you're learning. Are you ready?"

Everything in her was screaming "No!" but she stepped forward and let Destan help her into the harness: her trust in him stronger than her fear. Keeping her eyes on him was the only thing capable of keeping her from running. Well, that and hearing his voice the entire time.

The area they were in was almost a secondary cliff; the ledge under them being a good ten feet wide. Callimay would have to really kick out or actually jump to fall since she was climbing only a foot off the ledge.

As she reached her foot over to the footpath, her grip finally gave out and she started to fall backward. She'd practiced falling before, but she expected it every time. The only reaction she had was to scream and thrash her arms around.

Destan was right beside her and held her as she trembled, "Shh, Calli. It's okay. You're alright."

"But I—"

"It's okay. ... Well. Finally got that first 'real' fall out of the way. ... It's not that bad, right?"

"I almost d—"

"No you didn't, Calli. — I know being out here is different, I'm not saying that. — Just calm down. I'm right here. I've got you. It's okay."

❦

While Destan was gone, Callimay would work on the "book" portion of her training regimen. She would often times call Tabitha and Redje and have them help when they had time. Having their help was so special, but it was also an excuse to see how things were going back in Rayleen and even talk with Rose on occasion.

One evening during the week before they were headed back to Rayleen, Callimay asked, "Have you ever been to or know what the upcoming ball is? I've been meaning to ask Destan but I always forget."

"It's almost here! That's right!" Tabitha gasped as she clapped her hands together.

It can't come soon enough; Destan needs a break from this all so bad. He says he's okay but I can tell it's wearing on him.

"I've been a few times, yes. As far as what it's for? As much as I 'want' to tell you, it would be more meaningful if Destan did."

"O… okay." Callimay's forehead wrinkled as she tilted her head and raised her eyebrows.

"And I can imagine how busy you'll be when you get back, so if you would like me to go to the tailor and have them get your dress done I can. You can send me whatever notes or pictures you can find and I'll see that they get it."

"I don't want to burden you."

"Oh, it's no burden. It'd give me an excuse to go. I have so many dresses that Redje's forbidden me to go for 'a while'… whatever that means." She giggled a bit as she rolled her eyes. "But this wouldn't be for myself."

"Okay then. I'll send you something by week's end. Are there any special things I need to keep in mind?"

"It has to be some shade of green — whatever shade you want. And then it's best if you use a textured fabric. I always loved velvet."

"Green? Alright." Callimay replied a bit confused as she started taking notes. "Velvet sounds a bit heavy for the summer, though."

"Oh, believe me," Tabitha assured as she took a glass of water from Rose. "The tailor has this amazing velvet that is 'so' light. You'll forget it's velvet. — Thank you, Sweetheart."

"You wewcome, Mama." She grinned as she put her cheek out for a kiss. "I wuv you."

"I love you too. Now off!"

"Have you ever tried a pre-pleated fabric?" Callimay tapped the pen to her lip.

"No. No I haven't."

"There was this one dress I did that was… you know? I think I'll go with it. If the tailor doesn't have that fabric then I'll give the velvet a shot. — By the way, do you know if it's a girl or boy?"

"Yes, but we're holding out until they're born." Tabitha smiled as she shook her head. "Rose doesn't even know. God love my Sweetheart, the chatty baby wouldn't be able to 'not' tell if she knew."

"I understand. … Do you or Redje ever wish you would've stayed? Here, I mean?"

"Now that you're here we're mentioned in passing to each other how much fun it would be for the four of us, but we're so happy with everything the way it is. And we still have fun times to look forward to until you two can join us on a permanent basis. 'That' is going to be more fun than any mission could be. — I remember how Redje was stir crazy when we first made the switch; but he never wavered. Funny story, even though it's true, we actually got in trouble for missing our shifts in Deep Dark one time because that was when he proposed. I told him I wasn't going to give him a yes or no until we had it straight what each of us expected from the marriage. And he said he wasn't moving until we settled it. … I'll never say we've never hit bumps and come across hills along the way, but having that foundation we started with kept us grounded and guided our decisions."

Hearing what Tabitha was saying made so much sense. It made Callimay want to go back and do the same with Destan. Maybe things would have been easier for the two of them.

Seeing the look on her friend's face, Tabitha quickly clarified, "Now don't go thinking you and Destan did it wrong. No two couples are alike, no matter how much they have in common. And if you really think about it Callimay, would you've changed your mind if you knew everything at the time? … It may have helped keep things a bit more even keel, but you two have stood through more in just the short half year you've been married than some couples do in an entire lifetime of marriage. You're so strong together; and continuing to grow. Don't tear yourself apart because you did things differently from someone else or what you think is the optimal way. I think we can all look at our lives and see that there are things we would want to change just for the sake of doing it 'better'. God gives us memories so we can remember the past but He doesn't want us to long for it even if it is to change it so it's better. We learn from everything that happens in life. — Look and see what an amazing and beautiful marriage you have right now and how God is working through the two of you in your own special way."

A few sniffles kept a reply from being voiced for a while, but it eventually made its way out, "Thank you, Tabitha."

"I hate to be the one to switch topics, but isn't it about time for you to go workout with Destan?"

"He just said a minute ago that he'd be a little late."

"How's that all going?"

"I've never done any type of 'true' exercising, so this is quite the experience for me. Having Destan obviously helps it go by faster and even makes it a bit easier; but my muscles sure don't appreciate it."

"It's a learning curve, that's for sure." Tabitha smiled and sighed as she sat back. "What is it? … Oh. — Callimay? I've gotta go. Redje needs some help."

"Take care," she waved when she saw him poke his head into the camera's view. "Tell Mrs. Manning I said hello."

"Will do." Redje nodded as he returned the gesture. "Tell Destan I'll call him tomorrow if I've got a minute."

~ 10 ~

**W*e're going home in just two days! I can't wait to see—*

Focus, Calli. Destan scolded as his hair whipped around. *You're 'way' too far off the wall. Turn your right knee out.*

Without looking she knew what his expression was; and he had every right to look that way. Today was her first major test. The only "anchor" she had for her harness was Destan's grip and the fine ocean spray wasn't making his job easy; she knew that.

Now with her attention where it was supposed to be, he went ahead to check the next set of ledges and grip points. The metal ones were slick enough that halfway across the most challenging section Callimay slipped and swung out and away from the cliffside. Destan gripped the rope tighter as he tried to keep his voice steady: *There's a grip just above your left hand!*

She fumbled to grab it; now swinging back to where she was originally. Callimay knew his grip wasn't going to last forever, so she reached out for the first ledge she could find; plastering herself against the cliffside as she tried to calm down.

Something slapped her shoulder, traveling down to her leg, startling her. Destan called out, the spike in his emotions scaring her to death; but not as much as what she saw, "Destan!"

Somehow the rope broke. The sudden lack of opposing force sent him flying backward; him dropping about fifteen feet before making hard contact with a sloping edge of the cliff.

He yelled out as he grabbed what he could to hold on, sounding like he was in so much pain.

I'm so stupid! *I'm coming, Destan!*

185

No! He snapped back as he pulled himself up. *Don't you 'dare' come down. Stay put.*

But you—

Stay, Liaison! That's an order! He flashed his eyes at her as he grabbed hold of the cliffside and started back up.

For as much as she could be hurt by his snapping at her, Callimay knew Destan was only trying to make sure she was safe.

She watched him the entire time, breathing a sigh of relief when he got to her side, "Are you alright?"

"I'm going up first. I'll stop at the first level spot I come to and help you up. We'll do that until we're back up to the main walk."

"Alright."

Part of her was a tad annoyed with his constant coaching as she inched her way to him, but she knew that fall shook him. She was still scared when she slipped off but she had a failsafe… he didn't have anything! And with whatever happened, she didn't have anything either which couldn't be helping his mood at all. If there was ever a time that required her to focus: now was the time.

She looked up and nodded to his last comment; taking mental note of what "path" she planned to take. It wasn't going to be a straight shot to the top, but it was going to be safer.

They continued this inchworm-type climb back up; the waves seeming to feed off the adrenaline racing through the two of them. Of course this did nothing but make them even more concerned and wear on their emotions that much more. But they were so close now; Destan was up on the main walk! All she had to do was keep it together for at most, two more minutes.

Knowing this, Callimay made the premature decision to reach up before she was close enough. The next ledge she grabbed felt good, so she pushed off with her foot.

Snap!

"Destan!"

"Calli!" he leaned over farther to reach her hand.

The next few second felt like they went by in slow motion; her sliding down the slick and narrow stone plane they were on just a minute before.

But even though it felt slow she couldn't react fast enough; grips and installed ledges passing her by one by one as quick as a flash.

Finally! She caught the edge of what turned out to be the last ledge. Her legs were hanging off and she was struggling to pull herself back up since her grip wasn't that great.

This whole time, Destan was calling out as he raced down. Seeing how close he was gave her the strength she needed to hold on, but something wasn't right. She had a feeling something bad was going to happen; but it had nothing to do with her physical surroundings. It was her mind. Something didn't "feel" right.

For as disturbing as this was, the sound of cracking caught her attention. The ledge she had a death-grip on was pulling out and breaking off the cliffside!

"No, no, no! No don't! — Destan!"

"Calli!"

The next few seconds were a blur.

Because of the shock he was in, Destan stayed where he was and did nothing but look to where his wife had been. He still heard faint noises, but couldn't make out what they were from the overpowering sound of the sea. They weren't screams… so was she still there? There's no way she would fall without screaming. Well, unless she hit something.

He called out.

No answer.

He tried a bit louder.

Those same faint sounds started again.

Calli?

Destan? Destan help! I can't hold on much longer.

I'm coming, he sounded out of breath as he started down again.

Hurry. *I don't know how much longer I can last. I'm too scared to see how far away he is. ~ It's okay. You tried. God won't hold this against you. ~ I've got to last as long as I can.* *Destan please hurry!*

That feeling of something being off came back as she kept coaching herself: *My right hand's slipping. I know it is. ~ Just let go. You can't keep it up. It's alright. ~ That's wrong. I know it is! I… I know it won't be much longer before Destan gets here. It feels like an eternity, but it's probably only been a couple seconds.*

Her "logical self" became demanding, constantly encouraging her to let go but Callimay fought back. She'd let herself believe that lie once before: *I won't do it again!*

Let. Go. The now male voice ordered. *Quit trying to be all righteous and give into what you know is your only way out. Don't think yourself so high to be beyond my control. … You can't fight me forever. I will either break you or kill you.*

Elder! Callimay gasped when she saw his face in her mind's eye.

She felt something grab her wrists and heard a voice but couldn't understand who it was. Still in shock from what she just realized, she screamed as she gripped the ledge as tight as she could, "No!"

The voice repeated, sounding as calm as it could while still firm, "Calli I've got you! You can let go now."

"No! I won't let g— Destan?"

"Can you get a foothold at all?" He asked as he braced himself.

After swinging her legs around, she grunted, "No."

"It's alright," Destan tried to calm himself and her at the same time. "But you've got to let go. I can't pull you up until you do."

Part of her still wasn't trusting, but she looked up and saw his face: *It's okay, Rose Petal.* "A… alright."

As she let go, she felt like she was beginning to fall, causing her to yelp and scream.

Destan was calm, though he wasn't completely prepared to support her weight when he himself started to slip. With as tight as he was gripping her wrists, he knew she had to be in pain; but he also knew if he loosened his grip — since she wasn't holding onto him and her skin and shirt were soaked — she'd slip right through his fingers.

It was a struggle since Destan's shoulder was bothering him from the fall he took, but before long he had her up on the ledge. She scurried to the cliffside and plastered herself against it and him. But for as much of a relief as it was to have the immediate danger taken care of, they still had to get back up top. He knew she was exhausted, but staying there wasn't going to do any good.

He patted her arm and nodded toward to the main walk: *Do you think you can make it?*

I can try.

I know this isn't much and it's gonna make things awkward, but it's better than nothing. Destan started unhooking her harness. *Let me get this hooked to me first— I'll get it, Calli. Just rest.*

She wanted to keep helping, but her quivering hands couldn't hold on to anything the way he needed. All she could do was stand there and wait for him to finish.

It took a bit to find a spot where there was a double path of grips, but soon they started up at a snail's pace. Her wrists stung with every movement she made, but the fear of what might happen if she stayed there kept Callimay going.

Before too much longer, she braced her arms on the main walk and got out in between labored breaths, "I don't think I can pull myself up."

Destan raced to get the makeshift double harness off and shimmied up without saying a word. Then, with a firm hold, helped her up.

Callimay didn't waste any time; pulling on his hand as she took off, her not stopping until they were on grass. She wheezed and cried as she fell down and rolled over, him dropping to his knees and taking her in his arms, "I'm right here."

Even though his hold on her was so comforting, she couldn't get over what happened: *Elder's… he tried to get me to… he tried to make me think my only way out was to let go.*

What!

Elder tried to convince me to commit suicide! He tried to kill me! Callimay cried as the two of them turned; hearing several voices calling out to them.

"I would have been up sooner but I couldn't see because of the spray." Trever called out as he kneeled.

"What happened?" Doctor Gerould welcomed a distraught Callimay into his arms.

"Somehow Calli's harness broke and then as she worked her way up to me, part of the cliffside broke off. — One of the ledges on the second tier broke." Destan said a bit winded as he ran his hand through his soaking hair. "They need to be replaced… check all of them."

"I'll get a detail together," Trever nodded and took off.

"Have Traceur and Auditor go with you. If Nexus has a problem with it, tell her to get with me later." Destan was quick to reply.

"Got it."

ℬ

After they got inside and settled down — Doctor Gerould checking Callimay — he took Destan aside, "This is the third incident now of one nature or another since she's been in Bulwark."

"And you think I don't know that!"

"The Veil needs to know about your suspicions."

You seriously think the Veil is going to care about these 'incidents'? Especially if I say Elder's got something to do with it? Destan scoffed as he marched to the other side of the hall. *They've been on me for the past two weeks because of how I've been training Calli. This would do nothing but send them over the edge. I'd never hear the end of it and they'd never do anything about it anyway. They don't care, Lance.*

There are those of us who do care, Destan. The whole reason we're here at all is because we care. — And no matter who is involved, a Nark is a Nark. Even Elder's high standing won't save him. … You have a majority on your side and you know it.

A profound and doubtful silence filled the air; the young man leaning against the wall as he sighed: *I wouldn't be so sure after what Calli said a—* "Did you find them? Were there any others?"

"There wasn't even a chipped one in the lot; the natural grips included." Trever shook his head slowly; sounding baffled. "Are you sure she didn't just slip and fall?"

"I saw the one pull out of the cliffside myself!" Destan all but jumped off the wall and grabbed him by the shirt. "What did you do this time, Nark!"

"I didn't do anything, Doyen." Trever defended; sounding sincere and concerned as he was slammed against the wall. "We combed the entire stretch three times; Traceur will tell you the exact same thing. There wasn't one missing."

"Why you—"

Destan? Destan, what's wrong?

His expression froze as his eyes widened as far as humanly possible. It took him a little bit, but he got his fists to relax so he could let Trever go, "I… I'm sorry, Emissary. I… I just—"

190

"No offense taken." *If I were in your shoes I'd react the same way. Even I'm worried about her.* "Are you sure it was the second tier?"

"Yes. At the far boarder at the bottom."

"Oh. … I thought we took those out two years back?" Trever began back peddling; well, lying to be accurate. "I… I'll go check again."

℔

Destan's reprieve from anger was short-lived, him fuming when Trever came back and said every single ledge was still intact. He stormed out and looked for himself, but came back in with a gaping mouth and yet another apology to give: *I 'know' I saw the one— what is going on! There's no way that—*

"Since you have her out on the ledges without a harness, Doyen, I think it's time Liaison undergoes a combat spar." Elder confronted him as he sauntered over.

"She's in no shape right now."

"Don't brush off my words like you can some female squabble." Elder grabbed his arm and hissed. "I'm sick and tired of your neglect which has devolved into your labeling a Shadow — who took his lot with us before you did — as a Nark without so much as a charge laid against him. Have you no loyalty?"

Destan yanked his arm away and glared, "What about yourself, Elder? Where are 'your' loyalties?"

"Don't try to blur the issue. Fidus will be by tomorrow afternoon to see the two of you spar."

"Spar? Tomorrow!"

"What?" Elder scoffed as he raised an eyebrow; a familiar and terrifying gleam in his eye. "Have you indeed lied and let her continue without proper adherence to the regimen?"

"It's not that and you know it." Destan did everything he could to keep his fist at his side. "With the way her wrists are—"

"With her slipup today 'I' need to have proof you're not giving her mere surface-level training. You would not lower your high standard of honesty and deny you 'are' expediting her regimen; will you? … And don't think I'm the only one who believes this. You have no choice."

Destan gritted his teeth and started breathing heavily.

"Be grateful I'm allowing you to spar with her. I could've said 'I' was going to be her opponent… in which case I believe she would have preference of being a cliffhanger over that of my opponent." Elder let that gleam in his eye come back as he walked past. "Though, that will come soon enough."

ℬ

His nerves were raw and it was getting more and more difficult for him to keep his emotions in check. At one point Callimay had Destan put her down and she walked alongside him the rest of the way to the suite; rubbing his fists and doing everything she could to calm him.

Seeing the tears streaming down her face from the pain she was going through with his emotions made him feel bad enough, but "feeling" her wrists being just as bad as his were when they first arrived at Bulwark… it broke his heart. She was putting herself through double the amount of pain just so she could keep him safe.

While this would have been lost to him a few months prior, he couldn't help but notice it now. Having that extra "portion" of her ability now helped him see yet another reason to try harder so her load was lightened. And even though they were both shell-shocked and needed time to process it individually, they needed to remember each other and help in whatever way they could: like Callimay always did.

Both of them had enough with seeing the ocean, so he blackened the windows and turned on the lights; making a big fuss about her not doing anything with her hands, "I know what that feels like, Calli. Just let me do it."

"I'll be okay."

"No. I know what's going to happen: the second your wrist feels weight it's going to be unrelenting in its screaming until you let go. Please Calli. Please let me do this."

"But you—"

"I know, I know." He calmed as he had her sit down. "I know I did. But — and don't take this wrong — I can handle the pain. I'm used to it… kinda."

The look on her face was more telling than what she answered with, "Seriously? I've had migraines for as long as I can remember. And

192

then— I'm sure it's going to hurt, I never denied that, but I can work through it."

"But you don't 'have' to, Calli. Please let me help you. Please." He laid his offer on the table one last time.

"You're overdue, Doyen."

"I… could they just—"

"He'll be there shortly, Nexus." Callimay sighed as she gave him her "calm down" look.

I'm not leaving you.

"Destan, what can you do right now? It's not like either of us have an appetite of any kind. And I'm not training right now."

"I almost lost you… again." He started to raise his voice and then let it crumble as he flopped onto the bed beside her. "You know exactly how that feels, Calli. I know you do. … I just can't walk away and leave you after what happened."

"I know things are getting difficult, but it's only another two days until we're in Rayleen. Remember? — I'm not trying to downplay anything. I know it's hard."

I don't think I can even stand to look at Elder again.

Destan, please. She winced as she tried her best to not do anything with her hands, but wanting so bad to take his fists in them. *We don't have any proof that is tangible and supported: the note really isn't anything substantial since your father's gone and it's rather obscure. We've got to hold out until we get to Rayleen. Please, Destan. Just a little while longer. … Just take it one night at a time. And in that, just take it hour by hour. I'm still here. And if you lock the door you know I'll be as safe as I can be while you're gone.*

"Calli, I… Elder stopped me when I left and he's pushing issues that the Veil just doesn't have time for. Trainee regimens are left to the trainers. No other Veil's ever had the issues I keep getting pinned against the wall with."

What are you trying to tell me?

"Doyen?" Nexus asked, Elder's condemning voice barely audible.

"I… I'm coming. — Just rest tonight." He hung his head; and then pushed her bangs out of her face, "We'll talk about it when I get back. I promise. You need your rest right now."

~ 11 ~

Finding out what was her "prerequisite" for leaving couldn't be described as a joyous occasion, but the way he explained it, this wasn't the challenge she remembered being told about. What a relief!

Doctor Gerould fitted her with special braces, but warned she needed a couple days of complete rest before she tried to do anything of the caliber of a spar. This was going to make them two days late from what their plans were, but at this point Destan was willing to stay until the day before the ball so Callimay could enjoy herself; limiting as much as possible the pain he knew she was in.

She woke up early and had a terrifying feeling of nervousness wash over her the second her eyes opened. Callimay did her best to slip out of bed, but quickly found she wasn't the only one who was nervous: Destan was standing out on the balcony, the fleeting rays of the sun unable to do anything to calm and comfort him. The wind toyed with his hair that looked depressed… if that were even possible. And on top of everything the blank stare in his eyes showed he was trying everything possible to shut off his emotions. If he didn't, he wasn't going to make it through this.

"Are you alright?" Callimay asked in a timid voice as she crept up beside him.

No amount of effort was going to keep his emotions suppressed when he saw her face; him smiling as he opened his arm to her, "I'm better now. How are your wrists?"

"So far so good. — Do you want to wait to eat?"

Destan nodded as he took a deep breath; glancing at his watch, "Fidus should be there in five so let's just head over."

They fought their own battles as they dragged themselves to the combat room: Callimay unsure if she could view Destan as her opponent and Destan concerned he would forget who he was sparring with, Doyen taking over. This was his wife, not just another trainee!

As they came in, he noticed the cases on the back table and walked back, "Let me open yours before he gets here."

While the set she had were the standard Seaxes, the set Destan had were... different, "Are those what you would carry?"

"No." Destan shook his head as he frowned. "These are actually one of the very few ones I hate."

"What are they?"

"They're a type of Kopis knife; but serrated on the backside. That's why I don't like them. — I guess 'hate' is a pretty strong term to use for something that's inanimate, huh?"

"What do you—"

"I'm glad to see you two arrived early." Fidus greeted as he entered the room; sounding positive and looking almost happy. "So since we're all here I don't see why we can't go ahead and begin. That is, if you are able, Liaison."

It's just like our exercises, Calli. Destan sighed as he reached for her set and handed them to her. *Just try to block Fidus out. It's just the two of us.*

So... I get a kiss when we're done? She tried to mask the sting of pain she felt as she took them.

Way to give a guy motivation to have a fight be as short as possible! I'd rather be clipped and pinned right out of the gate. ... Now there's an idea!

Destan Quinton Nevrille! That'd be lying!

I know.

"Liaison?"

"Oh! I... I should be fine, Fidus." She snapped to as she let go of her now-sheathed knives and looked at her wrists.

"Good. To your post then," he motioned as he settled in his observation post.

I love you, Calli. Destan groaned as he walked away.

Well don't say it that way.

Always my ray of sunshine.

I love you too.

"And… begin." Fidus sat back; his eyes narrowing a bit.

At first it looked like they were just playing a nursery game of patty cake — their "battle" with mere pillows at the mansion was ten times more intense than this! This reservation was easily and quickly noticed by Fidus; ramifying itself in his body language and inner chatter.

Both Destan and Callimay knew this and resigned to the fact: they had to just get it over with so they could get on with the rest of their day and get ready to head back to Rayleen.

With this new determination and goal in mind, the two of them soon forgot Fidus was there and began acting as if they were in the room alone. This switch in focus gave Fidus the proof of retention and application Elder had been suspicious was lacking. As far as he was concerned he saw quite enough to appease Elder; but he noticed how the longer they worked the more intense they both became. So, he decided to let it go just a little bit further.

And a little bit more.

Oh what's one more minute?

He wanted to see how far Destan was willing to go.

They each had extremely close calls but both had lightning-quick reflexes to defend each offensive move. In a way, it looked like they were dancing by how they were in complete sync with each other! This level of mastery was beautiful to watch and what was striven for, but that's the point that baffled Fidus the most: this level of mastery took years. How was it humanly possible for her to be performing at this level this fast?

A few moments later the sound of metal smacking against metal was exchanged for the shrill and piercing screams of pain.

"Calli!" Destan exclaimed as he dropped his knives and rushed to her side. "Calli, what's wrong?"

"I didn't halt the spar, Doyen." Fidus called out as he got up.

She was still screaming out in pain and wouldn't let Destan touch her right leg she was clutching. He was confused as to what happened;

Fidus' comment not helping matters any. Destan tried and tried to get her to tell him what was wrong but soon noticed where her hands were was bleeding!

He whipped his head around and saw how the serrated side of the knife he was using on that pass was bloody. Terrified, he grabbed them and looked closer… only to find they were both sharpened. The only logical thing was to check Callimay's: they were completely spined.

"How does this happen?" Destan demanded as he thrust the sharpened knives into the wall. "Both sets are supposed to be spined!"

"I… I don't know." Fidus replied shocked as he hung up his phone. "Mender is on his w—"

"Who prepared the room?"

"I did. But I swear that both sets were spined. I tested them like we always do after what happened with Neurosan."

This whole time, Callimay lay there rocking back and forth as she hissed and cried out. Her hands were streaked with blood and it was beginning to drip off them and onto the floor. Destan was trying to comfort her, but she was so wracked with pain that she couldn't be.

Just as Destan was about to ask what was taking Doctor Gerould so long, he ran in and took an immediate assessment of her injury. To alleviate as much concern as he could, he explained everything he was doing: applying a tourniquet on her leg. Callimay was fighting him even touching her, so Destan had to hold her down; her yelping and crying out as she begged him to stop.

This all pushed Destan to the brink; but he wasn't out of line to attribute this "accident" to Elder. After the discussion he had with Callimay about what happened on the cliffside, he knew this was his doing. And with him also knowing it was more than just Elder doing these little acts of sabotage, he didn't know whether to believe Fidus.

It was almost to the point that Destan didn't care if there was any evidence he could show anyone else. He knew what Elder was doing and what his intentions were.

In a fit of fury, Destan slammed his fist against the floor.

Doctor Gerould quickly gave Callimay a sedative so they could move her and her be as compliant and comfortable as possible. The moment she calmed, Destan gathered her into his arms and bolted; jumping once he was out of their sight. This time it was Fidus and Doctor Gerould left to figure out what happened; though it really wasn't a surprise to Doctor Gerould.

"I'm right here," he did his best to comfort her as he laid his forehead against hers while laying her on the bed.

After he got there and checked her leg once more, Doctor Gerould shook his head, "It's just too deep for me to do here. She's going to have to go in for surgery. If not, she's just going to keep losing blood."

Destan's heart sank. He couldn't say no, but at the same time he didn't want to let her go where he couldn't. And then part of him knew he could've prevented this: he knew deep down something was wrong when he saw those Kopis knives. In a spar, the trainer always utilized their preferred style of knife. He should've taken the moment needed to at least make sure they were spined… if not switching them like he wanted to.

"Destan? I can't have her consent because of the medication I gave her." Doctor Gerould came up and put his hand on his shoulder.

"You know I can't say no and I can't say yes either." He replied in agony. "I… I… there's no other way?"

"I wish I could do everything right here, Destan. I know why you don't want this, believe me I do. It's just too deep. She needs more than just sedation."

"I… just don't take too long."

With that consent, Doctor Gerould nodded to the person at the door. They took off and called out to others who were close by. Within a few moments they all left.

Auditor came in before long and spoke with Doctor Gerould for a few moments before doing what she could to get Callimay ready.

"I love you," Callimay yelped as she gripped Destan's hand.

"Easy. Let your wrist have a break." He rubbed her hand and brushed the side of her face; doing everything he could to be strong for her. "I love you too. You'll be alright."

Auditor interrupted as she gave him Callimay's rings, "I'll need you to hold these, please. — We're all ready to go, Liaison."

"Alright. — I'll see you in a little bit, Calli. — Take care of her." Destan pleaded as he stopped Auditor.

"I promise I won't leave her side, Doyen."

ℬ

Seeing the look of fear and confusion in her eyes as she fell asleep; well, it crushed Destan. He was the one who did this. He hurt her… again. Yes, it was unintentional, but he was negligent: he didn't check.

Not but a moment later, he flopped into the closest chair and stared as his blood-stained hands; him beginning to realize how helpless Callimay must have felt when he was shot.

And recalling the few times he almost stabbed her neck and torso terrified him: had she not been ready for this or her wrists were worse… he could have very well killed her!

"You left this in your combat room," someone muttered as they came in and draped his veil over a chair.

"Leave me be, Fidus." Destan let out a growl of a sigh.

"I… I should've stopped you sooner than I did. I apologize."

Another growling sigh lingered in his chest as he bowed his head, "Just leave, Fidus. Please. Go tell Elder he got what he wanted."

He sat there and let his thoughts spiral into a bottomless pit of self-blame and depression; unable to allow himself the ability to be human. This error "could" have been deadly, but so could a thousand others he made prior to this; and he wasn't beating himself to a pulp for those.

His scolding session was already lengthy, but it's conclusion would have to be put on hold. A tapping noise started building, Destan eventually hearing it and whipping his head up. It was Auditor. She took her mask off and mouthed as she smiled and pointed to the door, "We're all done."

This whole time he spent staring at the floor — or at least that general direction — but now he wouldn't take his eyes off of Callimay. He didn't move until they started taking her out of the operating room; and then ran to where he could meet her.

She was still asleep; and this news didn't sit well with Destan at first, but what else could he do? And in fact, he knew a person coming out of surgery wouldn't be "awake". He knew the drugs working through her system were keeping her asleep like they were designed to. He just forgot because it was his wife who was affected.

Once everything was secured and doubly checked, Destan crept over and reached for her hand, only to be reprimanded by Auditor, "I think she would appreciate it if your hands were clean, Doyen."

"Oh. Well… I…" he looked dazed as he turned to look at her.

"There's a sink behind you," she gestured; sounding just as kind as the smile on her face.

At first it appeared he was just distracted, but Auditor could tell he was "lost". He'd become reliant on his wife for her constant help and encouragement to the point he couldn't function if something was wrong concerning her. It tugged at her a bit, but in a good way.

Unknown to him, he was going through a "lighter version" of what Callimay did when he was shot. Here he was, washing his hands and his wife's rings of her blood; emotionally at rock bottom. The main difference was he knew she was alright.

The water was warm, but the way his hands shook, you would've thought it was ice-cold. Part of him wanted to cry, but with Auditor still there he didn't dare show that much emotion.

He was weary from everything: dealing with the stress of his "job"; keeping his marriage strong; being a Godly, Christian man; and now having to protect the love of his life from things he never knew would be a danger to her. Destan was beginning to lose confidence in his ability to protect her; him second-guessing his decision to stay. It, in a way, felt as if someone were trying to wear him down by attacking her. But why would Elder want to get at him? What had he done? They were supposed to be on the same side.

At the coaxing of Auditor, Callimay opened her eyes but was still lethargic and confused; more confused than anything. With calm and reassuring voices from everyone telling her she was alright, she kept herself from flying off the handle. She settled down and relaxed; everyone leaving except for Destan. He was still sitting next to her, holding her right hand as his head rested on his other palm; him looking down at the floor. She was about to say something but heard: *…I don't know if I can take this anymore. I can't protect her while we're here like I thought I could. ~ But you didn't know about~ It doesn't matter. I think it's time for us to just go back to Rayleen. I know Elder's— Canary knows about him. She can deal with it.*

"We'll be leaving for Rayleen tomorrow, Destan."

"I'm afraid you'll have to put off leaving for a couple days." Doctor Gerould interjected as he came in. "And I'm afraid to say dancing is going to be on the no-fly list."

"Well… then I guess we'll get to 'rest' — quite literally — after the ball before we come back. That will be nice."

"She does have a point, Destan." Doctor Gerould agreed, seeing the disapproval in her glaring expression toward his last comment.

"When can we leave? To go back to the suite, that is." He mumbled without raising his head.

"Once we take one last set of vitals and fill you in on what to do to care for that incision, and as long as Callimay is feeling alright, you can go in probably fifteen minutes." Doctor Gerould glanced at the clock as he walked over to the machine she was hooked up to. "Pitcher should be by within that time with the medication."

Destan asked confused as he jerked back, "Medication?"

"She's going to need some pain medicine, just like you had after your surgery."

"Oh. — Calli… I'm so sorry I—"

"Do I get my reward? I think I deserve it after what happened. If for nothing else, I'd think it'd be a better apology than you carrying on like this. … Hum?" She tilted her head and tried to hide a smile behind the smirk that was falling apart.

It took a moment, but he caught on and popped up out of his chair, giving her a kiss, "Better?"

"It's a start." Callimay tried not to laugh.

"I'll take whatever I can get."

ॐ

Destan had a similar bout with Elder via Nexus' inquiry about his whereabouts not but five minutes after he got back to the suite. It's like they knew the moment he calmed down and was relaxed!

"Why doesn't the coward just ask me himself?"

"Don't shoot the messenger." Nexus snapped back. "I'm only doing as I'm told. … So what am I supposed to tell him?"

"Tell him… tell him that I won't—"

"He'll leave here in ten minutes, Nexus." Callimay spoke up; grabbing Destan's arm as he started to get up.

"Thank you."

Don't let him toy with you like this, Destan. We can't push on him too hard until we know what ability he has. I know your father wrote 'Origin' in that note, but what Elder did wasn't what that ability is capable of.

The sooner we get to Rayleen the better. He glared at the door; flipping as he sat down and stuttered, "If… if you feel like doing it and they're available… could you… see about getting with—"

"I'll call Redje and Tabitha as soon as I feel like it. What do I need to ask them to do?"

"Rej will know what's to be done. Don't worry."

"Do you have to speak at this one?"

Destan groaned as he ran his hand through his hair, "Oh great. … Yes. And Rocher's with me so—"

"Tell me what it's for and I'll see what I can come up with. I mean I did write the last one you gave." Callimay smiled as she brushed the side of his face.

His eyes got wide as he turned more, "That's right, you don't know."

"I was talking with Tabitha about it but she said it would be more meaningful if you told me. … What did she mean by that?"

"How many people with green eyes have you met before me?"

She looked at him with a suspicious eye, "Is this a trick question?"

"No."

Her eyes showed that her brain was flipping through memories as quick as a flash; her replying in a drawn out, puzzled tone after a few moments, "N… none?"

"That's what I figured. — Having green eyes, 'actual' green eyes, is rarer than being left-handed. If I'm telling you something you already know, well… you'll just have to listen to me." He winked his eye as he took her hands; sounding much more relaxed. "Yeah, the advanced terraformation of this planet did 'fix' the way this planet's atmosphere filters our sun's rays; but it also 'broke' it. Since people like me are so rare, the adverse effects weren't noticed for quite a while: people like me with green eyes are now extremely susceptible to going blind. Its fancy name is Irochromolysis: the destruction of the iris. But even though it surfaced, nothing was done about it because it was so rare. So, it became a 'death sentence' of sorts for us 'verdes'. My father had been doing primary work to help those who were already blind but switched and worked nonstop on a preventative treatment when he found out I had green eyes. He ended up developing something vaguely similar to contact lenses. Only these are implanted just in front of the iris to refract the rays that would 'dissolve' the green part — iris — of my eyes. I had the first ones implanted when I was three, and then replacements when I turned fourteen. Thankfully the double procedure doesn't have to be done now because they've developed them to 'grow' with the person's eyes. There's been leaps and bounds to help those who are already blind, but there isn't a fix-all remedy yet. — Enjoy your history lesson?"

"You mean…" she gulped as she pushed his hair away from his emerald-green eyes.

"You can't see them, but there are clear implants fighting and guarding me every day so I'm able to see you, Calli. I would've gone completely blind when I turned fifteen — twenty if I was careful, which Rocher swears I wasn't — if it hadn't been for my father's diligent work. Waking up and being able to see was something I was always thankful for, but getting to wake up and see you… it's something I treasure."

That's why Tabitha said it needed to be green.

"And I'm sure she told you it had to be a textured fabric." He finished; explaining when he saw the look on her face, "It's like that because quite a few who attend are blind. What they 'see' is what they 'feel'. And so, I've always done it so they feel included and are able to enjoy the evening a little more. … There'll be quite a few young ones there, too. I think the sound of them giggling helps those who are blind as well. I know it would help me."

Callimay sat there and stared at his eyes. She never heard about the 'disease' he was born with and couldn't imagine what it would be like to be blind — to never be able to see Destan's face. It put things as a whole in such a different light; her tone revealing she was a bit scared, "So, you're… for lack of better term, cured?"

He smiled and rested his hand on her shoulder, "As far as losing my sight goes? Yes. All the studies they continue to do have shown a one-hundred present positive prognosis. The lenses are able to refract normal exposure for the equivalent of one-hundred years before they start breaking down. So the only bad thing will be if I live to be a hundred and fourteen: I'll have to go get new ones. Now just because I'm safe doesn't mean I'm not affected by it at all. I'm still sensitive to bright light or sudden flashes of it."

"That's why you would always turn away when I'd open the curtains in the morning. I'm sorry!"

"Well… that was partially due to me being lazy and not wanting to get up because I'd stay up so late. And you know why now." Destan smiled as he reached out and calmed her. "Don't be sorry, Calli. It's not like you 'meant' to do it. You didn't know. I've opened the curtains many times and had the painful reminder that I wasn't thinking."

"So, being a shadow is actually a help to you."

"Working at night has its perks," Destan nodded; noticing she was still staring straight into his eyes. "They're not gonna disappear, I promise you."

"I'm just… I'd never heard of it. But there are so many things I haven't." She sighed as she hung her head.

"And you know things I have no idea about, Calli. Now don't go putting yourself down. … By the way, how did we get here from asking Rej to help?"

"I'm sorry."

"Now that's not what I— ugh. I'll be back in a bit and fix dinner." Destan threw his head back and sighed before looking at her and pointing, "You. Rest. 'In' bed. Got it?"

"Yes, Doyen." Callimay exaggerated as she nodded.

~ 12 ~

Having Destan with her when she called Redje and Tabitha was just as special to Callimay as it was a surprise to their two best friends. Their discussion took a hard right from its original purpose: why Destan was there and why they weren't back yet. He did his best to keep it surface-level and not go into everything, but Redje "and" Tabitha weren't having any of it.

From there it was a slew of questions to be sure Callimay was doing alright and to find out details about what happened, "Look, Rej, we'll talk more about it when we get back… okay?"

"How about I pick you two up when you get here? Which brings up: when 'are' you getting in?"

"I'm praying Tuesday works out, but we might not be there until Thursday night. I just don't know yet. — And I'm not opposed to the idea of be chauffeured at all. Thanks for the offer."

"Well we'll be praying with you for Tuesday." Tabitha nodded as she took Redje's hands.

ℜ

One day, two days, and then three passed by: Tuesday obviously didn't work out. There was still time to get back but they were on a razor's edge. Callimay prayed the whole way to the medical wing and while Doctor Gerould changed the dressing.

"Even though the it looks like it's holding, her muscles still need a few more days before she starts walking for long periods of time."

"But can we go? I… I won't walk that much. I promise." She pleaded when she felt Destan's reaction.

205

He did it with the amount of reluctance that could be likened to the time it took to get a cat into a bath, "It's in a fragile state right now… but you do need to keep moving." *And this is Callimay I'm talking to, 'not' Destan.* "Well… I guess if you limited your walking to extremely short distances, don't wear any type of heel, listen to your body when it says it's tired— and absolutely no running!"

"We're just going to a family-oriented ball, Lance. It's not like we're making a run." Destan chuckled as he got up and patted his shoulder.

Can you hear me? … Good. Let's go outside.

Calli can hear you— 'if' she wants to. Destan clarified as he followed him out. *She's not right now, but just so you're aware.*

I'm leery about letting you two go because of her. Now I know she'll take care of herself, but I just don't want you getting into trouble. It's no secret you've been preoccupied and at Elder's throat the past three days. I know you never truly got along, but your suspicions are letting things slip and get out of hand. Doctor Gerould warned as he glared at him. *Either accuse him and get things out in the open or learn to exist in the same room with him for the time being.*

I don't have any tangible proof yet. Destan sighed as he shook his head and leaned against the wall. *If I say anything now and nothing happens I lose the only shot I have.*

The Veil is 'your' base of support. You are the leader.

Oh really? Then explain to me why they're not supporting me when I'm driven half out of my mind with worry about Calli. Explain to me why even though I'm Doyen, Elder seems to be the one pulling all the strings. If you have any, by all means tell me.

You're worried about not having the final say and ultimate power, seriously? Doctor Gerould asked a bit perturbed.

I'm worried about losing a grip on keeping my wife safe while she's here, Mender. Part of that is having control of the Veil.

He hasn't changed any, Des—

"Destan?" Callimay called out as she opened the door, her breaths labored. "What's wrong?"

Don't you 'dare' say a word to Elder while we're gone or I swear—

Doctor Gerould gritted his teeth as he grabbed his arm, "What have I done to lose your trust?"

He sighed deeply as he groaned, "Nothing, Lance."

"Then 'don't' place blame where it doesn't belong or voice your concern about something you 'know' the other would 'never' do." He shoved Destan just a bit as he let him go. "Don't start acting like a spoiled child again. I'm getting sick and tired of being a father to you in that way. Man up."

"Destan?" Callimay repeated as she started to hobble over; causing him to run to her.

~ 13 ~

Impatient. Impatient and doubtful. Those were the top-billing emotions on Destan's roster for the entire evening. On one hand, they stemmed from him getting approval from Rocher to do a solo cross-country flight. While he wanted the freedom to fly without his teacher, that exact same point worried him: what if something went wrong? Was he ready for this? The old saying of "be careful what you wish for" began poking and prodding fun at him.

And then on the other hand was Elder and Trever… and whoever else they had in their band of Narks. What was going to happen while he was gone? Elder's conduct the past week was devolving into a brazen confession… almost. The way he worded things screamed to Destan that he was indeed behind what was happening, but he crafted it so no one else would be the wiser. Was it naïve to think there was any hope of this trip being enjoyable?

After someone mentioned Canary, it dawned on Destan what his father instructed him to do: he needed to somehow get in contact with her. This brought up another issue he wasn't thrilled about and was almost dreading. Communication with her was always one-way — her to them. How was he supposed to contact her? How did Trever?

But, when it came right down to it, Destan was just nervous that something was going to come up or happen to make it impossible for them to make it to the ball. And at times, he found himself doing nothing but waiting for things to fall apart.

"What are you bemoaning so deeply, Sir?" Rocher's brow was deeply furrowed as he laid a gentle hand on his shoulder. "Is Milady quite well?"

"I'm just…" he looked up and paused, taking a deep breath as he took the bowl of cut fruit from the elderly man he deeply cared about. "Worrying about what I can't do anything about."

"You and Milady have both struggled with much effort the past month with regards to your lifestyle changes. I applaud your progress and give my humble words of sentiment that bestow my deepest wishes that this furlough is rewarding."

"I'm not going to be convinced we're going until that hatch is closed and Raven's in the air." He tried not to grumble as he rolled his pen away from himself; picking through the fruit to find his favorite. "There always seems to be 'something' that comes up as of late."

"Far be it that such a thing would happen this time around, Sir."

"What makes you say that, Rocher?"

"Did you neglect caller's warning not but a moment before I came over? It is daybreak."

Destan sat there in a daze, somehow not believing what he was hearing even though he could see the sunshine.

"Is there a pressing reason why you are still here? Has Canary sent more word? I am of the firm conviction it has nothing to do with your solo. From what I gathered concerning the weather report you should have clear skies and tailwinds the entire way."

"I… it… you mean—"

"We'll see you in a week, Doyen." Fidus commented as he walked up and nodded.

"A week it is," Destan sounded so relieved as he shook Fidus' hand and then flew up the stairs.

Ϧ

He waited until no one was around and then jumped to the suite. It seemed impossible, but he was bursting with excitement; and this wasn't something that would ever be missed by Callimay. She tried to get him to calm and think about his wild idea of leaving right then, but he wasn't having any of it until she grabbed his hands and pulled him to her, "Destan! I want you to actually think before you answer me."

Unlike what her touch normally did, all of his jitter-joy drained in an instant. But this wasn't a bad thing. He closed his eyes for a while, taking a deep breath before he answered, "I'm sure I want to go right now. Our schedule's going to get thrown off again with us keeping regular hours when we get back so this will be an easier adjustment for me if I'm up longer. And if it weren't going to be an easy flight I would wait; but it's supposed to be easy. … I'm sure."

Silence filled the air, worrying Destan that Nexus was going to take this opportunity to but in like Rocher must have taught her to do; but Callimay smiled, "Let's go."

🄑

Destan grabbed his duffle bag and threw a few things in before he scooped Callimay into his arms. He didn't stop speed walking until they were at the control tower and he filled out the necessary paperwork; going over a few things with Rocher before leaving.

Watching Destan do the ground check in the hanger was odd enough with him running around, but then there was the fact he was doing it inside the hanger when it was light out.

But, this really wasn't strange. Everything outside "went to sleep" during the day for Shadows and Veils alike — like nocturnal plants.

Rayleen will be there if we're a few minutes late. Callimay chuckled when Destan ran back to an area he'd already run to five times. *And the ball isn't until tomorrow evening.*

He stopped dead in his tracks and looked over with wide eyes; his expression quickly melting as he smiled. This shift in how he was allowing his emotions to drive his actions was new… well, new as in the type of emotions driving him. As a knee-jerk reaction, he thought it was stupid for him to act like this, but being excited wasn't an emotion that was on the list of debunking his masculinity. If anything, it was another little ramification of his love for Callimay.

The second they got in the jet and the cockpit door closed, he breathed a long and deep sigh of relief, "We're going home, Calli. We're going home."

One of the first words which rattled out of Destan's mouth Callimay remembered being what was said right before takeoff. She nestled into her seat and started mouthing the words as he talked, not caring if he saw her or not.

210

Someone called Navigator was on the other end and did their part just as she remembered Kendal to — not that they were being graded of anything or that she was the authority on it.

Destan saw her out of the corner of his eye this whole time and chuckled to himself. He then took a deep breath and closed his eyes after he officially got the green light: *Do you mind?*

Huh?

Would you put your hand on mine like you would when I drove?

I don't want to distract him. ~ Yeah, dying isn't on my list of things to do today either. ~ That's not what—

"Calli?" Destan sounded worried as he leaned forward.

"I'm— I'm not gonna say that." She caught herself and tried to act uppity; them both laughing before she smiled, "Sure. I'll hold your hand. Just… just don't let me do something wrong."

He returned her soft gaze with his tender one as he put his hand on the throttle, "Just keep yours on top of mine and we'll be golden."

Things were going so smooth that it wasn't too much of a stretch to see it come to an end; Callimay gasping, "Oh no!"

"What?" Destan's hands froze as he whipped his head around.

"I forgot your speech. It's on the desk. I put it out so I'd—"

"Just give me a heart attack why don't you, woman! Geez!" He flopped his head back on the headrest and rubbed his face. "I'll call back and have someone send a copy to my computer at home."

"I… I'm sorry."

Destan wasn't about to let this slight miscommunication ruin the beginning of their furlough; taking a deep breath as he reached over and brushed her cheek, "Calli? Calli, look at me. … I know you were only reacting to what you know is a big deal for the ball."

Up, up, and away. It had been a while, but with the conversation just prior to takeoff clicking in her mind everything else fell into place: muscle memory really was a thing.

For about an hour there was nothing said of much importance; either that or they were both too tired to talk.

And to add to this thought of being tired, Callimay questioned where their little holographic jet was on the global map, "Why are we going north? Rayleen's south."

Well hello to you too. "Reeg," Destan explained as he flipped a couple switches and then watched a certain monitor for a few seconds before finishing, "They're a no-fly zone."

"What about going to the south instead? Wouldn't it be faster?"

"We'd be over water the entire time and I'm not technically cleared for that yet. It's splitting hairs since I will once I land, but I prefer to avoid water if at all possible anyway. It's only an hour longer this way."

Destan got on the com within a couple minutes and started talking with someone from Reeg, explaining every tiny detail about the flight plan: *Why didn't you just give him your birth certificate and our marriage license?*

It is quite a bit of info, isn't it? He chuckled as he went through his clipboard to find the number the man asked for. "Seven tree fower dash zero zero two."

He'd known for a while that she laughed at how he talked with others while flying, and had to work to control himself when he heard her: *And you make fun of Rose for mispronouncing words.*

Now listen here.

I know, I know 'it's to help make things clear' but could they just pick a different word that didn't sound like babbish? She huffed as she rolled her head over toward him. *You know, it kinda could be scary knowing some poisons cause you to do that.*

Well don't look like you just ate a prune, woman. I'm not the one who made this all up.

'It's from the Homeworld', I know.

Why don't you look for Berchshire out your side window? Destan shoed his hand at her as he continued to work.

O-kay. She exaggerated; him smiling which made her smile even more. *Just be glad I didn't get all worked up and think you were poisoned; talking like that.*

They chatted on and off for a while, Destan suggesting at one point she rest. With all that was going on and the fact they were together and alone — and away from Bulwark — she wasn't about to let one moment slip through her fingers. And what could he do? It's not like he could "make" her go to sleep; and he knew it helped her to be free to look around and see what was going on.

The sun was so warm and refreshing to both of them; giving them extra warmth as if to say it missed them and was so excited to get the chance to see them again. So, the air cooling system kicked in and kept this "excited" greeting at a comfortable level.

A peaceful hush softly blanketed the cockpit for a while, Destan for some odd reason sounding sad as he rubbed her hand, "Calli?"

"Yes Destan?"

"It's time for your least favorite part of everything."

"Well it's better than jumping out and falling down."

His smile still had a hint of concern in it, but he kept with the upbeat attitude she had and replied, "My ray of sunshine. — Ready?"

Callimay sighed heavily before replying, "As ready as I'll be."

"Okay." He nodded as he squeezed her hand; getting on the com with Kendal.

Destan was extremely nervous when told there was a strong crosswind at ground level but knew once he got down there it could be gone. At least that is what he was hoping and praying for.

They touched down without any major issues and just like that: they were in the hanger. For a split second all Callimay could remember was that day and how it felt like they went for a training flight and came back home — Bulwark, the Shadows, and everything else vanishing. What a liberating few moments those were. They reminded her that she hadn't lost her life with Destan; she hadn't lost him. Thing had changed but they weren't making her whole life so different that it totally lost what it was before.

Redje wasn't there yet, but Destan still had his paperwork to get done. Callimay sat by the door and stared at Kendal for a while, him taking a double glance when he realized, "What's wrong? ... Is there a spider on me or something?"

She looked around and then hobbled over, asking in a hushed tone, "If I said the word 'shadow', what would you think of?"

"Huh? Excuse me, what?"

"What does the word 'shadow' mean to you?"

No. That's what she said alright. ~ I still can't believe it.

He couldn't hold it back; Kendal belly laughing as he bent over and slapped the table.

"What's so funny? I… I didn't—" She whipped her head around to Destan who looked over from his paperwork.

Kendal tried to talk, but he couldn't get a grip long enough to say two words that were coherent. A few seconds later he had to leave since he was coughing. When he came back he took a deep breath and let one last chuckle out before answering, "Who's been her trainer?"

"What did you say, Calli?"

She faded to just about a whisper, "I… I just… I just asked him what a shadow meant to him."

If a cricket would have been by the door outside of the farthest hanger you "still" would've been able to hear it chirping.

Destan was staring at her as Kendal stared at him, "What's wrong with everyone? Stop staring at me!"

"Calli I…"Destan tried so hard not to laugh, but the moment he looked at Kendal he couldn't help it.

Once the two men exhausted all of the laughing gas — albeit fictitious laughing gas — in the air, Destan finally answered, "That's not how we signal other Shadows."

"But I didn't know if he was or not."

"What made you think he was?"

"You know him."

Both of the men bit their lips as they did everything they could to stay composed, "That's it?"

"Of course not, silly! You mentioned 'Grounder' a couple times as if you were talking about a person, and Kendal's the only one you've talked to this entire time. We're both wearing our ensembles and you don't have a problem with him seeing that; and then the fact his boots are made out of the same leather as ours added up to: he must be a Shadow. I… I just didn't know how else to ask him is all."

While this observation didn't surprise Destan, Kendal was taken aback, "My boots? How in the world…"

"The grade of leather used for our boots isn't like any I've 'ever' seen before. And then the square buckles look just like the handles of the throwing daggers I've been working with as of late."

That last comment made Callimay very proud. She was noticing the finer details like she'd been working so hard to notice.

Destan shrugged his shoulders and went back to his paperwork; Kendal left to mull through what he just heard by himself and Callimay left with her question still not answered… exactly.

℔

"It's good to see you two. Sorry I was late; had some things pop up at work last second." Redje slapped Destan on the back; grinning from ear to ear. "Doing alright there, Callimay?"

"Oh, I'm enjoying being pampered like this."

Destan and Callimay bickered with each other in hushed tones, so after they got in the car Redje laid some ground rules, "This is 'my' vehicle. I expect you to behave and show some decorum."

"Well," Destan labored a bit as they got settled, Callimay still stifling laughter. "Seeing as how Rose's car seat is still back here and the billions of toys you constantly are buying her, there's really not that much room for me to work with; let alone Calli."

"There's not 'billions'." Redje grumbled as he started the car.

"Whatever. — And my poor wife is injured. It would be best if she just sat on my lap instead of making her navigate the plush mine field back here."

"What mine field?"

"How can you 'not' call this a mine field? — What happened to you? You got married, had one kid, and poof! Became a slob? It seriously looks like a bomb went off back here. This is an issue vehicle, you know."

"You gave it to me as a wedding gift, remember? So that doesn't apply any longer. — You know, I hope you have twins: girls." Redje snapped back as he glared at Destan in the rearview mirror. "Teach you a thing or two about what's important, ole pal. You think Rose has got you wrapped around her finger… ha! Just you wait and see."

The back seat all of a sudden was as quiet as a library and felt as sad as a funeral.

"I'm sorry, you guys." Redje pinched his nose and groaned. "I went way too far with that one."

Nothing was said, no noise made. Such a joyous beginning to their trip brought back a devastating truth.

But Destan knew he walked right into it; it wasn't Redje's fault. Well, not completely. He learned the hard way it wasn't just him being affected by his ill-pointed banter.

I'm sorry, Calli. He grieved as he pulled her close. *It's my fault.*

Before too long, the air felt a slight lightening, so Redje tried to start some positive talk, "Tabby has your dress, Callimay. — She's actually had it for two weeks. — She's told me countless times she wants you to design her dresses from here on out."

No response.

Their expressions didn't hint toward them not wanting to hear him talk or objecting to any conversation, so he prodded just a bit more, "You've really got a knack for that sort of thing: designing dresses."

"That was actually my job." Callimay sounded depressed as she fiddled with the knife in her sleeve. "There was a smaller branch for the Maritime Fashion House in my hometown of Berchshire. My mother was a seamstress, so she taught me what she knew. I was always enthralled watching her turn my stick figure drawings into beautiful sketches and actual pattern pieces. — I was never the greatest when it came to actually sewing. — So, when I found myself in need of income, I fell back on what I knew and enjoyed. Because I didn't have a degree and didn't 'know' anyone, I was given a 'scrapper' job: the designs no one 'wanted' to do and the ones where the customers were so picky that no one could do what they wanted."

While her first little snippet was what he expected, her answer was what Redje was truly hoping for, "That would explain it. — So, what did you specialize in even though you kinda got whatever?"

Callimay shrugged her shoulders, not sounding much better, "I just did whatever was handed to me. There wasn't really one thing given to me more than another."

"Well, what did you enjoy doing most? I'm sure you didn't get those very often."

"Oh…" she sighed as she looked up and thought; Destan stroking her hair and cradling her close the entire time. "It wasn't men's fashion, I'll tell you that. You can only do so much with a pair of pants and a shirt."

"Guess that's true." Redje laughed as he glanced back.

"I guess I ended up liking those 'impossible' designs that no one could get. It proved to me I didn't need a degree to do what was asked of me." Callimay continued, sounding better with each word that rolled off her lips.

"How did that all work?"

"There were two different ways: direct consultation and written requests. Direct was just that: I spoke with the customer face-to-face and designed the outfit while they spoke. Those were… 'interesting' sometimes; definitely demanding. — Quite the eye-opener for me as far as people in the world and what they desire. Thankfully I didn't get those that often since the customer would often ask for your credentials and the company didn't want to get a bad name because of me. So, to keep me hidden they had me do most of the 'hard' written requests. The funny thing was though, those were only from top-paying customers: high ranking government officials, their families, and even some prominent social figures. As time went on, my name started popping up on those requests. No one ever told me why exactly. I'd like to think it was because I was consistently able to actually get the design concept from just what they wrote. — Granted, there were still those few times that what I thought and what they meant were total opposites."

"Which one really stood out to you? For whatever reason."

"There's a few…" Callimay started to laugh as she recalled. "Oh! There was a request for a horse's costume one time. It was masquerade season and so I didn't think anything of it and started working. I sent it out and the next day the customer actually came in. I thought it was to complain — a written order only comes in to complain — but he was laughing so hard I didn't know what in the world was going on. As it turned out, he wanted a costume for an actual horse!"

They all had a good laugh, Redje curious now, "So… did you do it?"

"I warned him, as did my manager, that animals weren't something our department did; but since they were a high-profile customer they weren't turned away. He was nice enough to come in a couple months later and thank me for the hard work I put in, and made sure to take my name down."

"Well," Redje offered as he pulled into the driveway. "It's impossible what's waiting for you is anything like that or I would've heard about it. — I'm sure there's quite a few people back there who miss having you around. It sounds like you were able to reach quite a few people."

"I just hope I did what I needed to."

"I'm sure you did. — Now you two are welcome to stay for dinner if you'd like. I know it's early but I doubt you really ate on the way here. It's not like there's an air insta-serve anywhere."

"That'd be a great innovation." Destan chuckled. "Thanks, but don't bother. We don't' want to put you—"

"Tabby's got everything ready, so I don't think you have a choice." Redje winked as he opened his door. "It's not really a 'request' if you know what I mean."

Destan got out of the car and grabbed Redje's arm, whispering, "How did you do that?"

"Do what?"

"How did you know how to get Callimay's mind off earlier?"

"I just did what I've done in the past to help Tabby when I'd stick my foot in my mouth about sensitive subjects. It's take a while to figure some things out, but this was one way that's consistently worked. — And look, I'm really sorry about—"

"It's my fault." Destan shook his head. "I should've just left well enough alone. … Thanks."

"Give it some time and keep at it. You'll pick up on things." Redje encouraged as he slapped his shoulder and turned to leave. "Like I said: I didn't know that one out of the starting gate and it took me a couple 'years' to figure it out."

"Papa! Papa! Papa!" Rose giggled as she ran to the corner of the yard and started bounding like a bunny.

"Hello Sweetheart." He scooped her up and threw her in the air. "Let's see what Mama did with your hair today."

While on a normal day she would go into a fifteen minute description of what her mother did, she was distracted because of their visitors; her twisting around and peaking over Redje's shoulder as she waved, "Desan! Cowimay!"

"Hello Rose." Callimay smiled as she waved back.

"Was wong?" She asked worried as she pulled herself up so she could see better. "You wearwing awl bwak."

"I left my clothes here when we left."

"Why?" Rose asked confused as Redje set her down.

"I didn't have time to pack." Callimay continued as Destan helped her sit in a chair.

"I hewp you pack dis time," she ran over and started crawling onto her lap. "You no needs to be so sad wooking a—"

"Rose!" Destan scolded as he ripped her away. "Don't do that!"

She wailed in a frightened tone, "But I no hurt Cowimay."

"I…" Destan paused, realizing she had no idea Callimay was hurt. "Come here, Rose."

She pushed away and clamored to accept Redje's outstretched arms.

"I thought I heard your voice." Tabitha said with a sparkle in her eye and excitement in her voice as she came out of the kitchen; stopping and sighing, "Oh Rose. What is it now, Sweetheart?"

"Desan mean, Mama." She cried as she pointed her little finger at him and then used it to rub her teary eye.

"Oh?" She asked shocked as she looked at him. "Why was he mean, Sweetheart? What did he do?"

"Desan gwab me away fwum Cowimay." Rose began to sob as she reached for her mother. "He yewl at me four twying to sit which hur."

"Oh Sweetheart." Tabitha consoled as she took her daughter's hands in hers. "He's just protecting her. Yes, he was very rough about it, but Callimay's leg is injured really bad and Destan just didn't want you to accidentally hurt her. He's not being mean, Rose."

"You weg hurt, Cowimay?" She whipped her head around and asked wide-eyed.

"Yes, Rose."

"I sowy, Desan." She cried as she reached for him; leaning over as far as she could.

He sighed as he took her back and held her close, "I'm sorry I scared you. I was way too rough."

She snuggled close and babbled to him for a few seconds; Destan closing his eyes and imagining having a little girl like Rose for his own. It sounded like such a wonderful thing but it just wasn't a possibility right now. He started to feel Callimay backsliding emotionally, so he set her down and walked over to where Callimay was.

"Rose? Go wash your hands, Sweetheart." Tabitha suggested to keep things moving in a positive direction.

"Desan—"

"Come on, Rose." Redje interrupted as he took her hand and started coaxing her down the hall. "Let's go do it together. I need to, too. See?"

"Otay, Papa." She grinned and giggled; running ahead of him.

"Hang in there, Destan… Callimay." Tabitha tried to comfort as she crept over; resting her hand on her baby bump. "The Veil isn't a life-sentence. And you know things are looking promising, Destan. Hold on to that beautiful dream you two have; don't let it die because of what's going on right now. … I'll be sure to have a talk with her tonight and make sure she makes herself scarce while you're here."

"Oh, please don't—"

"You're going to have more than your fill of interaction with little ones at the ball, Callimay." Tabitha shook her head as she raised her hand. "Believe me, I know. — And it's not that you'll 'never' see Rose. We'll just keep it at a bare minimum, okay? You two need some time to rest anyway, so it will help if she's away. I know my Sweetheart can drain the energy right out of you so don't feel bad."

"Thank you," Destan mumbled as he glanced in Tabitha's direction and then back to the floor.

"Speaking of the ball— your dress, Callimay! I didn't take it out to look at it and I've been 'dying' to see it!" Tabitha quickly changed the subject; her smile bursting forth. "Did you want to—"

"'After' dinner." Redje announced as he walked back in the room; shaking his head. "I haven't eaten yet and as head of this house I'm saying that dress is going to have to wait."

"In front of guests!" Tabitha scolded, throwing her fists at her sides.

"Mama and Papa pwaying." Rose giggled as she danced over to Destan's side and took his hand; calling out when no one said anything, "You turn, Papa!"

"You're not guests, are you, Destan?" Redje winked at him and motioned for Rose to come to him.

"Callimay mi— nope. No, neither of us are." He said more upbeat as he took a deep breath and stood; sounding puffed up as he finished, "We're like the younger version of you two when you were happy."

Redje winced as he turned away, "Ouch."

Callimay gasped as she slapped his leg, "Destan!"

"Pfft! See what I mean?" He continued as he gestured to her and then picked her up. "Does your wife hit you anymore? No. So obviously that mean's she's given up trying to change you; seeing you're set in your ways and unable to change. Hence: unhappy."

"Destan Quinton…"

"He did much worse than that when we would go out on missions, Callimay." Tabitha sighed as she rolled her eyes and ushered everyone into the kitchen. "I remember once he poked fun that we were a couple, while unbeknownst to him we actually were!"

"So that's why—"

"Yes it was, Destan." Tabitha cut off as she laughed.

"How long were you two…" he trailed off as they sat down.

Rose bounded back and forth between the table and Tabitha, helping carry what dishes were light enough; and then took her seat. She raised her hand and shook it a bit, but was reminded, "Let's thank God first, Sweetheart."

"Otay." She grinned as she took her hand and Redje's before bowing it; banging her legs on her chair as she swung them back and forth.

The second the prayer was done, Rose asked in a quiet voice as she tugged on her mother's sleeve, "Mama?"

"Yes, Sweetheart?" Tabitha smiled as she put her daughter's napkin on her lap.

"May I pweeze sit necks to Cowimay? 'Pw-ee-ze', Mama?"

Tabitha looked up at Callimay who was now smiling, and then replied, "You may go ask her what she would prefer."

"Otay Mama." Rose handed her napkin to her and bounced over, raising her hand and waving it so it could be seen.

"What?" Callimay asked with a bit of enthusiasm.

"May I pweeze sit necks to you and Desan? Mama said I cood but dat I had to ask."

Callimay's eyes darted back and forth for a moment, her mouth opening a couple times to say something but nothing coming out.

Destan took her hand, seeing her somewhat upset: *Don't feel bad, Calli. It's okay.*

"N… not tonight, Rose."

"Otay. Tank you." She nodded and bounced back to Tabitha.

ꝺ

Right after dinner was done, Destan caught Callimay dozing off. She objected, saying she would be alright — even going so far as to offer to help with the dishes — but they all knew she needed her rest, "I'll be by later this evening for Calli's dress. I'm sure it's in safe hands here."

"Tabby may hold it hostage until Callimay puts it on so she can see it." Redje pulled his wife's chair back and helped her stand.

"Really!"

"I'd hold out," he attempted to whisper as he shook his head.

"Could we for once just have a nice, civil, normal conversation?" Tabitha sighed as she shooed Rose into the living room.

"Where's the fun in that?" Destan asked a bit disgusted as he helped Callimay. "Be all formal and serious… like adults? Makes me sick just saying that."

"You'd have to be an adult to even know how to act like one, oh little one." Redje countered.

Destan scoffed as he snorted, "Little? Pfft! I could take you down in less than a minute and you know it."

"Well, first you would need to put Callimay down. That in and of itself would give me the advantage since you're in the middle of the room — not by a chair, mind you — and she can't really walk. Second, if she's all you've been using for your workouts then you're 'really' a lightweight. And third, Tabby would kill you if you tried… and you know she could. She did just clean everything today." Redje rattled off without a second thought; standing there for a while and waiting before reminding, "Umm… it's your turn ole pal."

"I'm tired," Destan deflected as he tried to think of a quip.

Tabitha shook her head as she opened the door, "Sometimes I won— you two are hopeless."

"Thanks for having us over, Tabitha… Redje." Callimay said as she tried to fight off a yawn.

"And me!" Rose chimed in.

"And you, Rose."

"You two get some rest and let us know if you need any help." Redje followed them out to the sidewalk, his bantering tone subsiding. "And we don't have anything planned for the evening so pop over whenever. — I see the Veil let you retire your father's veil. It was well-deserved."

Callimay was drifting off, so Destan glanced around and then said in a hushed tone, "I don't want to put you four in any more danger than you already are, but I've found out something about a Veil and at least two Shadows that's downright disturbing."

"Does it have to deal with Callimay's accident?"

"Yes, but there's more to it. I don't want to drag you back into everything. I know you and Tabitha got out for very good a reason. I—"

"All four of us can meet and talk, then Tabby and I can decide what we want to do. I'm not going to make any commitments either way right now."

"Bare minimum I just need someone to talk with; bounce ideas off of?" Destan sighed as he leaned his head against Callimay's before looking back to his best friend. "You know: make sure I'm not crazy."

"I'll ask her once we get Rose put to bed; hopefully have an answer for you by the time you drop by later."

SD

When they got back, the house was left just as it was when they literally ran out the door: the bed wasn't made, her gown and his tailcoat were still out, their shoes and accessories littered the top of the clothes chest and her vanity.

All of these little things compiled to bring back memories of what they went through; but somehow, Destan was able to find that silver lining — something he'd never been able to do before.

He lay Callimay down and started picking up things, having to search a few times to find where her things went.

Saved for last was her dress. The soft feel of the fabric and the scent of her rose perfume reminded him of the wonderful time they had at the ball: their secret wedding reception. Destan took it into the other bedroom and stared at it for a while; he wanted that kind of life back. He wanted to be free again. But he knew what he was doing — what they both were doing — was so their freedom would be more secure.

~ 14 ~

Destan had a flashback to the morning after the ball when he opened his eyes; running to the window as he tried to catch his breath. All he could do was pray he would find Rose outside playing.

He braced himself against the wall and closed his eyes, taking a deep breath as the curtain swished back and forth. The muted sounds of her joyful voice were a comfort to him, but by the way his hands shook it was easy to tell he was battling his emotions and memories.

After dragging his hands through his hair and looking out the window, he came back and collapsed on the bed: *I hope this goes away. ~ You've always been one to hang onto things like that. ~ That's what I'm worried a*— "Morning, Calli."

"Morning," she yawned while sitting up and stretching; looking over worried when it struck her, "When do we have to leave?"

He returned the yawn; his eyes looking irritated that he couldn't fight it off, "We should get there around two if we can. — I totally forgot to get your dress last night." *Why didn't Tabitha say anything?*

She waved her hand in front of his face, rolling her eyes, "I guess all you have to be is sleepy to be as distracted as me, huh?"

"What?"

"Could you get my medicine? I'd rather let it start working before I try to get up."

"Oh!" He popped up and rushed over to his duffle bag.

❧

"Callimay Rose Nevrille!" Destan gasped when he looked up and saw her; him shutting the door so it sounded just as shocked as his voice.

This sudden outburst caused her to lose her balance; proving to do nothing but cement the fear he had. He tossed the dress box to the floor and ran up to catch her.

Even though his hold on her was tender as he carried her into the living room and set her down on the sofa, she could tell something was irritating him; and it wasn't just her.

He turned to leave, and then threw his pointer finger back at her as his eyes began to flash, "Stay!"

She said coy as she cowered; clinching her arms across her chest, "A… alright."

"Oh, Calli." Destan sighed as he kneeled beside her; taking a deep breath before finishing, "Why were you doing that?"

"I heard Doctor Gerould say I needed to keep walking, even if for only a minute or so, so my leg muscles wouldn't get lazy. … But I guess the stairs weren't the best first place to do that."

"I just want you to be alright," he pushed her hair out of her face and rested the same hand on her neck. "Just… just do it while I'm home, alright? And please, 'not' the stairs."

"Okay. — I… is something else wrong, Destan?"

"Not really. At least not 'wrong'."

"It's okay." She smiled in a knowing way as she put her hand under his chin. "How about something to eat?"

There was a beautiful moment where the sun burst from behind the clouds as he looked over to her already glowing face, him sighing as that small smile couldn't stand being held back, "Sounds good."

As he got up, he snapped his fingers and motioned for her stay; him bringing the box he tossed away over to her, "Why don't you let me get breakfast started while you check it over, huh?"

He kissed her forehead after she nodded and then started for the kitchen; stopping short when he heard her yelp, "What?"

"Tabitha had them change the color. I know I said a hunter green. But she told them emerald." Callimay continued as she pulled the dress out and laid it on her lap; her hands beginning to tremble.

"I'm assuming those two colors don't look like each other?" Destan asked as he sat down beside her and pointed to what resembled more of a wad of green fabric.

"It… it looks like your eyes now." Her broken voice came out in utter shock as she looked at him; trying her best not to cry.

Destan just sat there and smiled.

"I love you," Callimay threw her arms around his neck.

"I love you too," he laid his cheek on hers.

☙

She took her banishment from fixing breakfast as well as she could, but when it came to cleaning up she was not to be denied. As they started working away — her at the sink and him walking back and forth to the cupboard — he had to admit he was wrong. This was something they still did while at Bulwark but it had a special meaning here… for some reason: *Maybe it's because we're not talking about 'work'. ~ Possibly. ~ What about the kitchen itself; maybe the dishes? ~ That's a possibility as well. ~ Okay, okay. I can take a hint. Why. ~ Look at her. … What's different? ~ No black. And her smile; it's changed. ~ Ex-actly.*

He glanced at the clock as they finished up, "Calli?"

"Yes, Destan?"

"I've got something really quick to take care of downtown today."

"Well, let me get my hair fixed and—"

Destan corrected in almost a mumble as he stopped drying his hands; looking worried, "I'm going by myself."

"Oh," she replied depressed as she stopped turning the water off.

"Just this once, I promise, Calli. I won't be gone long at all: an hour, two tops."

"Why bother asking me? I don't have a choice, do I?" She grumbled as she turned away.

"C… Calli, I…" Destan tried to appease as he reached for her arm.

"Just go!" She pulled away and hobbled out of the room.

Destan stood there for a little while, trying to think of how to make her happy while accomplishing what he needed to… but there just wasn't any way with the little amount of time he had left.

He dragged himself to the front door and saw Callimay in the living room, curled up as much as her leg would be allow on the sofa. The part of his heart that began to break begged for him to do something; him reaching out to her as he opened his mouth to say something.

Nothing came out as he let his hand fall beside him. He turned and picked up the keys… and left.

❦

When he got back, he started sprinting to the door, but stopped short and peaked in the window. Callimay was on the sofa with something in her hands. Destan strained to look as he got closer to the window pane and saw it was a stuffed dog. He listened to see what kind of mood she was in; and was crushed when he heard: *You've never given up. You've always been there. There's nothing that frightens you. Well, it's getting harder and harder for me to do this, you know—*

"Desan!" A joyous voice called out as she waved her hand over the fence and jumped up and down.

"Not right now, Rose." He shook his head as he stepped back from the window; sounding depressed. "Not… not now."

The door opened and yet he stood there, holding the handle: *Today was supposed to be a good day; and what did I do? ~ It needed to be done, you know that. Passage said it was either now or wait another four months.* "I'm… I'm back, Calli."

She turned around and sat up, moving the pillow closest to her, "Is everything alright?"

His agonized tone got worse as he bowed his head, "I… I'm sorry."

"For what?" She asked frightened as she hobbled to him. "What's wrong, Destan?"

"I heard what you said before I came in. That it's getting harder and harder for you—"

"Destan, I— that's not what I meant." She replied frantic as she reached out to him. "I wasn't talking about you! I mean I was, but… this is going to sound stupid, but when I said it's getting harder… uh… I… that was my stuffed animal talking. I was acting like I was talking with it. I know it's childish but that's how I've always treated the toy."

"But I…"

"You must've heard only part of what I said." Callimay sighed as she threw her arms around his neck. "I'm sorry I got so snappy before you left. I just wasn't expecting you to do 'work' things while we were home. I know when things need to be done they need to be done."

❧

Things took a gentle turnaround and continued to calm during lunch which Destan got while he was out so they didn't have to spend so much time fixing food and cleaning up. It was odd to sit on the sofa and eat, but this "lazy" feeling was also a small change that reminded both of them that they were home.

Doing this also gave him the perfect opportunity to find what she'd stashed under the pillow when he got back. At first she didn't notice, but she quickly shooed his hand away; this only making him try harder, "I know what's under there, Calli."

"Just leave it alone."

"You know I'm not ticklish. — But I know you are."

She screamed as she laughed and tried to squirm and wiggle out of his grasp, "Destan, stop! I can't breathe! Please, Destan!"

"Let me see the stuffed dog and I'll stop."

"Okay! Okay!"

Hidden with care was a stuffed white dog, "Is it one that Rose left?"

"No." Callimay huffed as she worked to catch her breath; hissing a bit as she rubbed her leg, "It's mine."

"Who gave it to you?" Destan asked curious as he flopped its ears and rubbed it against her face.

"I'm guessing my 'real' mother but I don't know." She became somewhat sad as she cautioned him, "Careful! He... he's is the only thing I have from my original life."

"I'm sorry," Destan laid the lush toy in her delicate hands.

"S... someone named Lanta gave him to me."

"How do you remember that?" He pushed her hair out of her face and began stroking it.

"I don't," she shook her head as she looked up. "I just remembered his name: Mr. Ruff. The tag is what gave me so much of what I have: my name, my birthday, the name of the lady who gave it to me, and then the nickname she apparently had for me."

"May I see?"

Callimay took a deep breath and showed the tag on the dog's collar. It was easy to see how she'd taken every effort to preserve the original

228

inscription on the small, heart-shaped tag; Destan knowing himself how precious little mementos were.

"No wonder you love roses so much. It's your nickname."

"I guess so," she took it back and held it close.

"I… I'm sorry, Calli."

"I just wish I knew who she was!" She sobbed as she leaned her head against his chest. "I just—"

"Shh." Destan calmed as he rocked her. "I'll tell you what. I'll do some digging when we get back to Bulwark and see if I can find out about anyone named Lanta around the area of Quaverly. Alright?"

"You think you can find something!"

"I can't guarantee anything, but I can look." He got up as the phone rang. "Hello. … That's right, I did and I totally forgot. I'll go check right now. … Oh, she's fine. … Yep. Will do. … You too. Bye. — That was Rocher. I forgot to download my speech when we got in. Oops!"

Callimay stifled laugher as he made a face and then disappeared around the corner into the hall.

He was gone for a few minutes and came back with a mesmerized expression; having nothing but praise for how she — once again — crafted a beautiful speech.

Of course she wasn't thrilled with it because she couldn't speak from his point of view, but Destan begged to differ. Yes, it was different from what he'd done prior, but he loved it so much.

She kept objecting, accusing him of being bias because she wrote it, and promised she'd try one more time. Destan wasn't about to budge, "It's fine the way it is. W— why don't you just give the speech?"

Callimay was shocked to think she would be allowed, her not able to get one coherent word out; prompting Destan to calm her, "I was only kid— you know what, that's actually not a bad idea. Why 'don't' you?"

"I… I can't do that! Are you crazy?"

"Why not?"

"Because… well because I—"

"You'd be amazing. I know you would."

This back-and-forth continued as they made their way up stairs and started getting ready. He finally won and got her to agree to deliver the speech herself. Her face was just as uncertain as her voice, but seeing the glimmer in his eyes left her with no defense. So, she went back to fixing her hair.

At one point she noticed Destan was sitting on the foot of the bed, arm wrapped around his leg he had his chin resting on… just staring at her. She knew she looked a sight: holding some hair in a specific fashion that had her hands just about pretzeled around each other and hair pins in her mouth. How could he keep such a straight face?

What? She looked in the mirror again. *Go ahead and laugh.*

"Oh, it's nothing." Destan responded in almost a daze as he tilted his head a bit.

Callimay kept working but couldn't help noticing how he wouldn't take his eyes off her if she moved, and he hadn't moved one inch from where he was originally sitting. For as much as this attention was sweet, it was making her efforts to concentrate almost impossible.

Enough was enough; she let go of everything and turned around, huffing, "Are you alright?"

"Never better."

"Are you sure?" She softened; almost sounding worried as she hobbled over.

"I'm positive." He nodded as his eyes followed her; him still not moving. "Am I making you nervous?"

"Well it 'is' a bit distracting." Callimay smiled as she flopped beside him. "I've never seen you do that before and so I wanted to make sure you were alright."

"You wouldn't allow me to for the last ball but— you mean you've never noticed?" Destan asked a bit shocked as he let his leg go and his foot slapped the floor.

"Notice what?"

"I've 'always' sat and watched you fix your hair and do your makeup. I thought for sure you saw me."

There was a striking silence; her taken aback as she tried to think, "I… I guess I missed that. I don't recall you ever doing it. — I'm not saying you didn't. I just don't remember. — Is it starting to look good?"

"It looked perfect before you even started."

Oh what a frustrating thing it was to have sweet moments like this always hampered by that one protestor who made sure they were heard: the clock being the culprit this time, "Speaking of hair, you better get yours 'fixed', Destan."

"Eh," he brushed off as he moseyed over to the door. "You know all I really need is a good raking… see?"

"Oh shush." She made a face and rolled her eyes. "Now go on! I promised Tabitha I'd let her see the dress before we go."

❦

It was beyond strange to drive all of seventy-five feet before stopping and getting out, but Destan wanted to limit how much Callimay walked, "It'll give a more dramatic aura to the dress reveal. And you know, it'd help me practice getting you out of the car."

"It's gorgeous, Callimay!" They heard Tabitha gasp as they turned.

He carried her up the walk and then set her down so she could give Tabitha a hug, "Thank you for changing the color."

"I knew once you found out you'd love it more this way. And now that I see it in real life, the fabrics you chose— what was the name of the velvet again?"

"Devoré. The process for making it is just mesmerizing. We'll have to go some time and watch. — Velvet was a great idea but I thought this might help keep it lighter. And with my injury this is so much better. … I'm so in love with how it turned out."

For as much as their small chit-chat was enjoyable, Tabitha had to address the elephant in the room, "Do you wear anything other than gray and black, Destan?"

He sounded hurt as he looked down at the dashing gray suit he had on, "I have a green square and matching tie I'll have you know."

Tabitha exaggerated as she acted like she was backing off, "Oh 'please' forgive me. I didn't realize."

"Ooo! Cowimay!" They heard Rose's shriek from inside the house; followed by the sound of little footsteps thundering in their direction.

"Now be careful, Sweetheart!" Tabitha reminded as she ran straight to Callimay.

"You still wook wike a pwinsess," she complemented as she took Callimay's outstretched hands.

"Thank you, Rose."

231

"Mama!" Rose gasped as she turned and offered the fabric that was clutched in her hand. "Cowimay's dwess ez so sof!"

"I know, Sweetheart." Tabitha calmed as she motioned for her to come back. "It's a lovely dress, isn't it?"

"May I has a hug, Desan?" Rose requested as she wiggled her outstretched fingers up to him.

"Of course," he nodded and kneeled to her level.

"I wuv you, Desan." Her loving and muffled voice vowed as she patted his chest. "Four ewver and ewver. I pwomise."

"I… I love you too, Rose." He said a bit grieved as he held her tighter and tighter; his eyes beginning to sting.

"You squishing me, Desan!"

"I'm sorry."

Knowing there was a type of tension in the air that was rooted in an equally beautiful and difficult matter, Tabitha sent Rose inside and encouraged, "Enjoy tonight. You've had a rough and hectic time the past month and need this 'alone' time. Remember to not forget each other, okay? … Good. — Redje's just come down with some kind of cold so the poor thing's lying in there dying… so he thinks. He hardly gets sick so when he does he feels like he's dying."

"Serves him right for last night." Destan scoffed.

"Let's not start that again." Callimay hushed as she turned to leave. "Tell Redje we said hi."

"I will." Tabitha waved. "Drive safe. And don't hurt yourself!"

"Bye, Cowimay! Bye, Desan!" Rose called out from the front window as she shook her hands in the air instead of waving them.

♔

Just like Callimay predicted, Sonnie immediately began asking if something was wrong when she saw Destan carrying her in. He looked like he lost a bet, but couldn't truly be upset that people who cared actually noticed something was "off".

Once that was put to rest, he let Sonnie know the car needed to be parked since Rocher wasn't with them.

It interested Callimay to see how this request was treated since she knew Rocher drove him all the time… but apparently this wasn't something "unheard of": *Rocher's usually with me, yes, but he told me early on that he saw this ball as some kind of 'therapy' for me. For the longest time I had no clue what he was talking about, but I've realized that this ball was pretty much the only one I showed any type of vulnerability through the amount of emotions I expended; and then the fact I have to admit I have what most consider a disability… even though technically speaking I'm cured.*

Rocher's really sweet even if it takes him fifteen minutes to tell you, and another five days to understand it. Callimay smiled as she leaned her head against his chest. *I can tell he cares about you so much; like you care about others.*

He's not bad. Destan chuckled as they came into the ballroom. *And maybe I did rub off on him a bit, but he was like that all along. — Well… here we are. Looks like Rej did a great job, but how about we do our own check?*

"It's going to be a wonderful night. I just know it. — Now I can lean on the tables if you want to go check with—"

"Absolutely not, woman!" Destan tightened his grip on her. "You're staying with me."

Rectangle tables were set in long, straight rows on the main level; the balcony closed for the evening. The décor and table centerpieces were done in all different coordinating hues of green; everything showing that pristine attention to detail in the range of texture from the napkin rings to the usage of placemats.

One thing that looked lackluster in this finesse was the place cards, "How will people who are blind know where to sit?"

"Oh!" Destan stopped and leaned over. "Pick one up, any will work. … Are there what feel like bumps on the lower left hand corner?"

"Umm… yeah. I guess so."

"They are kinda small, aren't they?"

"Wait. Is… is this… oh, what is it called?"

"Braille." Destan nodded.

"Do you know how to read it?" Callimay asked as she set the card back down; fussing with it so it was perfect.

"Somewhat," he shrugged his shoulders as he started his inspection again. "I couldn't sit and read a book of it, but short things like names I can. I'd need a little refresher, though. — Could you check to make sure the menu has it, please?"

"You don't have to carry me everywhere. I can walk for a little while so you don't get tired. I won't last greeting everyone, b—"

"I'll have them put a chair out at the front for you."

"I'm going to look like a little child next to you if I sit down! I'm already over a foot shorter than you and I can't wear heels right now. They might actually think I can't stand if I'm sitting down all of the time and then you carry me." She objected vehemently, but tried to work with him instead of against when she saw his face, "Why not have a high stool of some kind for me? Surely they have some of those."

"Well, there's one way to find out." Destan looked around and then started over toward a staff member.

After a brief discussion, the staff member said they would be sure to have something available. — Quick fix. Good — So, they turned their attention and checked on a few more things before going to the lounge to relax and wait. But instead of Destan getting all worked up, Callimay was the one worried.

Her being quiet was rather odd, but what caught his attention was the fact she was wringing her handkerchief so much it was probably about ready to rip in two, "Calli? What's wrong?"

"I've never addressed a crowd before. What if I mess up?"

Oh, my Calli. Destan comforted as he put his hand under her chin. "You have too, silly woman. Remember when you 'broke' into Deep Dark? You spoke to a group then and you didn't come across the least bit afraid. I don't know that I've ever seen someone — other than myself — get in Elder's face like that. You've got a fire in you."

"There was only a handful—"

"That you could see."

"What?" Callimay jerked back, her eyes bugging out.

"I didn't— ugh!" Destan said defeated as he threw his head back.

"I'm not supposed to know. I understand." She closed her eyes.

"I wish that this were—" *No, I promised myself I wasn't going to talk about that. That's all put to bed.* "You'll do just fine, Calli. And you

234

don't have to do it like Rocher and I do — have it memorized. You're not going to be graded or even kicked out because of it. I'll make sure everyone knows I pinned it on you last second."

"You're sure?"

"Calli. Just speak from your heart like you always do. I 'know' this speech is no different. Everyone'll love it, I know they will. And they'll love you too. No more of what happened at the last one, I promise."

ॐ

The majority of guests who first arrived were forty and above; all of who were blind even though some could see faint shadows and such due to the continued advancements being made based off of Destry's early work.

As much as she knew to expect it from what Destan told her, it was a terrifying shock for Callimay to see what this "disease" — as she referred to it — did. Until it was gone, she didn't know how much the appearance of the humanity of a person rested in the iris of their eyes.

It was a battle for her to remember this wasn't an actual disease — the kind you could "catch". She scolded herself for thinking of these individuals as "unclean". How could she even think such a thing?

They all were beyond sweet to her; everyone overjoyed to find out Destan found someone to marry. It took no time for all the questions to start, as well as requests for hugs which fed a part of Callimay that she had no clue had been starved for so long.

In their own ways, each person would comment about the textures of her dress and ask if she could describe it to them. Her ability to paint such a vivid and beautiful mind-picture blew Destan away; him closing his eyes at one point, only to see her exactly as he knew she looked.

As if planned that way, the next wave of individuals who arrived were the group around Destan and Callimay's age. While there were a few in this group who were blind, a majority of them were unaffected.

The different hues Callimay saw in their eyes amazed her, but in the end, none of them compared to the pair that looked at her with such tenderness and love. Yes, they could flash and glare, but no matter how they might ebb and flow in their moment by moment emotions they loved seeing her as much as she loved seeing them.

Even though the ballroom was pretty full at this point, people continued to stream in; this next group being teenagers.

While the common nature of teenagers was apparent — rebellious and demanding freedom from their parents' oversight — they overall were civil and mature in their demeanor. It was then that Callimay understood why Destan called those at the Society "kids". And yet she had to admit these individuals in front of her right then were much more mature as a whole than those she'd spent time with at the Society.

She glanced back at one point and frowned.

What is it, Calli?

Did they set out too many tables?

Destan nodded in the direction of the elevators and smiled: *No.*

Sure enough, a handful of families were standing in the hall by the elevators; them waiting for some reason.

Little children flocked together and started racing around, looking out the glass wall as well as looking through their feet and screeching in delight.

Once a couple other groups came along they started in the direction of the ballroom, Destan played with them by "opening" and "closing" the door for a little bit. He'd laughed so many times before, but his laughter right then was so much different. Their giggles and squeals had to be fueling this change.

They all flocked to him when he was finished, most of them calling him by his name.

It melted Callimay's heart all over again to see how much he loved children… and how much they loved him. He kneeled down and paid such close attention to each child as they spoke; hugging the girls and giving a high five or fist bump to the older boys.

All this joyful interaction was beautiful, but it wasn't lost to either Destan or Callimay that there were a few who hung back by their parents. He popped up and calmed them all before going over and introducing himself to the parents of the more timid children. They smiled and spoke for a moment, having their child make some effort to at least say hello. A couple of them refused to even look at him, but most of them warmed up immediately and ran to him, unable to stop mentioning how he had the same color eyes as they did.

There was one little girl in particular who just couldn't get over the fact he looked like her… though she was meaning his hair color more than his eyes.

This grabbed the other timid children's attention so their curiosity was perked to the point they ventured over with one of their parents.

Destan glanced over and saw Callimay's glassy eyes and loving smile. He knew it was hard but he also knew she loved it at the same time. Even he had to admit that for as much as he was enjoying himself he was beginning to feel that tug on his heart.

With his new little "family members" now comfortable, he came back to the large group. They all in unison glanced in the direction he was looking, and then immediately back as he spoke with them.

The second he stopped speaking, a tidal wave of children rushed to Callimay. It took every ounce of strength she had to not break down. They all clamored for her attention and were instantly smitten with her dress, whether it was the girls saying things about how it looked or the boys about how it felt.

One by one, they became quiet when they noticed she was just staring at them. She could barely comprehend the emotions that came over her; all these precious children seeing her as the most important person in the world… if even for only a few moments. What it must feel like to have even just one do that all the time!

The feeling of someone taking her trembling hand made her flinch, but when she looked up she saw Destan's smiling face; him giving her hand a gentle squeeze as he leaned his forehead on the side of her face for a moment.

With this reassuring and encouraging gesture, Destan made a face at the gathered children to which they all responded in their own ways, "Thank you Misses Callimay!"

Overcome, she dropped to her knees and wrapped her arms around as many of them as she could, "You're so very welcome."

Her heart couldn't do it anymore. It was too much to take. She got to her feet and excused herself before darting out.

When she closed the door of the lounge, she crumbled to the floor, wailing. Tabitha was right when she said she would be overwhelmed. She was that and even more right now: grieved to see those who were going through life without something she'd always taken for granted, comforted by the genuine thankfulness from others close to her age, reassurance that there were still parents out there training their children to be respectable people, and overjoyed to see the purity found in such young ones who saw with their hearts.

And then on top of everything she was in agony; Callimay was reminded she might not ever have a child of her own who would look at her the way all of those young children just did. She couldn't hold onto them for as long as she wanted. It always had to end with her sending them back to their mother's loving arms. They would never call her mother, mama, mommy; that wasn't her role in their lives.

She'd thought through what her and Destan decided early on and had come to terms with it, but now she had her doubts. The decision was made for every good reason and purpose, but it couldn't quench the God-given desire she still had and now couldn't see past.

Ᏸ

Destan finished greeting everyone as fast as he could and jogged out to find Callimay. As he tried to open the lounge door he looked down and saw fabric from her dress and heard her crying. He kneeled and bowed his head; tears welling in his eyes as he with a gentle touch laid his hand on the door, "Calli? Calli, please let me in. … Please."

A minute later, he saw the fabric slide away. He slowly opened the door and then rushed in and shut it.

Callimay was still on the floor, almost convulsing as he offered his warm and loving embrace; her looking up in agony and reaching with her trembling hands. How could he not sound choked up with seeing her like this?

"I'm so sorry, Calli. I… I didn't want to cause you any emotional pain by having them— I thought it was a nice—"

"It's not your fault. It's just been such… such a whirlwind: feeling guilty for how I acted at first, relieved there are people still out there who are grateful and appreciative for even the simplest things in life, and being both joyed and tormented by the children. I… I just can't get over how you love them so. It melts my heart but breaks it too. I know we can't… can't…"

"When Mrs. Manning broached the subject, I had to admit to myself that I 'wanted' children. — Another desire my Doyen self saw as being a sign of weakness. — I know we talked about it and all, but I just want to… I want to give our children a life we don't have right now. It's hard enough to know you have to go through it. I really don't know how I'd handle having a baby with everything going on. I know I can't eliminate every danger that might come into their lives, but there is a major one we are dealing with right now that I 'know' I have a strong chance of eliminating. — Calli? Calli, I know this is hard. When we were getting ready to leave and Rose said she loved me… for that split second I was imagining her being 'our' little girl. And Calli? Calli, it felt so— if you hadn't been standing there when I looked up earlier I might have walked out."

"Y… you want children too?" She asked wide-eyed as she looked at her husband who was now the one crying. "It's not just something you want because I do… you really 'want' children?"

"I think just about as much as you do. I know I never said anything before. I just didn't know how to or whether or not it would help any."

"Oh, Destan." She sighed as she wiped the tears from his face.

He helped her to her feet and took a deep breath as he smiled, "It's alright. I guess God used this to show us something else we've never truly talked about."

"At a rather inconvenient and embarrassing time." She sniffled as she brushed out her skirt. "Everyone's got to be wondering why I ran out and why you left."

"Eh. They're probably already eating. — How do I look?"

"Probably not even half as bad as I do."

"You look just fine." Destan hugged her from behind as he looked at her reflection. "Maybe a little pink in the cheeks and nose, but I doubt anyone will notice. Me on the other hand…"

"Oh, you're fine." She fussed as she turned, grabbing his arm and double over from pain as she hissed.

"Calli!"

"I — ouch! I just irritated it. … I'm fine now."

"There's no discussing this, Mrs. Nevrille…" Destan ordered as he scooped her up. "I'm carrying you and that's final."

"Yes, Doyen. — Destan! I mean Destan!" Callimay gasped as she clapped her hand over her mouth.

"Woman!" He tried to act upset, but couldn't hold it. "My poor Calli. You finally get it down and everything changes."

ᛒ

They weren't able to slip in entirely unnoticed — the occasional person taking a double-take when they saw Destan carrying Callimay — but there wasn't an uproar about their absence.

He got her chair for her and made sure she was alright before taking his seat at their table which was set off to the side, somewhat hidden. The warm candlelight was the only light in the entire room which gave her the added comfort of knowing her flushed face was "hidden" by the shadows that came with this kind of lighting.

Callimay and Destan would start to reel again when the sound of children laughing or giggling could be heard above the muted music, but they remembered what a blessing each child was to their family. In a way, knowing both their hearts were pricked helped them strengthen themselves to keep going.

Unlike the first ball, this one didn't feel like one. It seemed more like a normal evening family meal. Even the menu choices agreed with this thought; them being on the "normal" side. Destan's conduct was even different: he dug right in after he made sure her meal was to her liking.

But, for as much as this break from formality was refreshing, there was a looming reality that Callimay wasn't quite at peace with: it was soon going to be time for the speech to be given. In a way, she knew why Destan wouldn't eat: *He doesn't get nervous though. ~ I'm sure he does to 'some' extent. ~ Well that's just because I was around. ~ How do you know that?*

Seeing her so distracted, he had a flashback of sorts to their time at the Society; specifically when they were at lunch after Toreon had his fun tormenting her. Destan began to wonder if maybe he should give the speech himself. He didn't want her to miss out on enjoying herself and it was quite apparent all she could think of was somehow failing, "Is the cheesecake not good, Calli?"

No response.

"Two people whom I love deeply told me if I kept focusing on the bad of what might be that I would miss the good of right now and be putting the future in jeopardy. … Everyone loves you, Calli. And what you have to say will show them how much you love them 'and' me. I'll stay with you the whole time; I'm not going to leave. But, if it will help, I'm more than willing to give the speech myself."

Her glazed-over expression began to fade as she listened. She looked up glassy-eyed and gazed into his soft and loving eyes for a while; still not saying a word.

"I'll give you fair warning, though: you'll have a captive audience of the younger children who will sit right in front of you and listen. At least that's the way it's always been for me. If you don't want to, I can give the speech so you can stay here."

She fussed with the pocket of her dress as she took the pages out, mumbling, "I… I'll do it."

"Are you sure?"

"I… I'm sure."

A few children laughed, Destan seeing the pain in her eyes flare, "I'm sorry I didn't say anything sooner, Calli. I knew children were so dear to you ever since we moved here. I just— I didn't know how to ask you or what to say. I still don't now, so that's not a good excuse. Huh? — Where are you going? Aren't you going to finish your dessert?"

"Isn't it time for—"

"You enjoy your dessert first. This evening is pretty laid back. Really they all are. The last one was— well you know."

Once he was satisfied and she said she was ready, he headed over to made sure things were ready. He stopped Percivon who nodded and came back with the stool she'd used before as well as a companion for it. This all perked the interest of the children; especially when Destan strolled over and leaned over the back of Callimay's chair, "Ready?"

"I think so."

The music drifted away as they came up to the stools, the stillness catching the attention of every child under the age of ten. Most of them scrambled to where Destan and Callimay were, sitting in a semicircle on the dancefloor; eyes shining to show how mesmerized and full of excitement they were. And then a second wave of the children who were still unsure came and formed their own little group on one side; their eyes wide as their heads bobbed back and forth between their parents and the two of them.

Destan glanced at her to make sure she was holding up alright and then took the microphone and smiled, "It's so good to be with you all tonight. I apologize I had my plans ill-timed last fall so I had to cancel. And can't begin to say how much I appreciate your openness and acceptance with these alterations. This evening is always the highlight of the year for me, and for those who are new to our 'family', I hope you come to love this fellowship as much as the rest of us do. — Now I know the little ones won't understand and some of you teenagers might be repulsed by this, but I've come to have a deeper appreciation for the blessing of sight because of my wife: my Calli. While things have been hectic for us both recently from her getting injured and me busy with work, the speech for this year is going to be a bit different. Calli, like she always does, jumped in while I was busy with my work to help where she knew she could: writing the speech. And I thought it only proper since she wrote it that she also deliver it. So, without further a due, please give a warm welcome and your undivided attention to my wife: Callimay Nevrille."

Everyone applauded as he took his place beside her and handed her the microphone. Callimay gulped as she took hold of the slender metal device; the only sound picked up being faint breathing.

This hesitation caused the gathered children to scoot closer; as if they were afraid they couldn't hear her. Destan put his arm around her to support her, nodding her on.

"I'm going to have to apologize, I've never given a speech like this before." Callimay said rather quiet as she tried to keep the pages from quivering like they were.

"Tell us a story, then!" One of the young girls called out.

Everyone laughed, Callimay having a feeling of calm come over her as she looked at the girl, "Some people might call this a story, really… even though it's what really happened."

"Oh goody!" Several of the children responded joyfully as they squirmed around and got comfortable.

Speak up just a bit, Calli.

Oh. Okay. "I… I grew up in a vastly different world than Destan. I had no knowledge of what Irochromolysis was; let alone the profound impact it will forever have on his and your lives. — And I do apologize if I mispronounced it. I don't mean to sound ignorant or rude. — Even as I wrote the speech I didn't understand; I can see that now. I didn't understand until I saw and met you all because sight was something I had. There was never any fear in me of waking up and it being gone, no extra precautions I had to take each and every day to protect it because I viewed it as a given, not a gift. It has become crystal clear to me that I have been ungrateful. I've now found a part of me that has neglected to be thankful for what God has blessed me with. Every inch of our being is a gift — yes, even green eyes. Knowing this reminds me, and I hope you, that there's nothing 'wrong' with being born that way. It's just another way God is showing the world that you are so uniquely you. It's outside factors or other individuals which you don't have any control over that attack it as a blemish or defect in one way or another. Don't ever view yourself as being a burden or worthless because God chose to give you green eyes. And don't give up fighting just because it gets hard. Fight harder. You never know if someone else might see you and take courage to keep fighting through what they are dealing with. — I guess I got off on a tangent there, didn't I? I'm sorry. … When I met Destan," Callimay paused as she looked over and smiled in a nervous way; his sweet smile calming her. "He was the first person I'd met who had green eyes. I had no idea for so long that there was a daily war being fought so he could keep his precious eyesight. They caught my attention so quickly when I saw him — as they still do — because I could always see his emotions so plainly in them. And yet, I couldn't see the warriors that guarded them every second. It actually wasn't until a couple weeks ago that I found out those striking green eyes were still there for me to see because of the diligent work of his father, Destry Nevrille. I never met Destan's father, but I know how much he loved him by the hours of lost sleep, moments of frustration, and stretches of despair I am convinced he had to endure to save the only son he had. If you don't mind my asking — though I am not requiring any replies — how far are you willing to go to protect those you love? What are you willing to give up so they have a better life? … I know the answer to those is yes for each person here because… well, you're here. — I 'am' speaking as someone on the outside looking into this lifestyle; someone who will admit she still doesn't understand everything you go through; especially those here who have lost this gift. As much as I grieve for you I take courage from how full of life you are and how you do not let this defeat you. You show that you do not throw your hands up in defeat because you lost something. No. No, you show those around you who live in fear of one kind or another that hardships are only a training ground for your courage. Thank you. — To those who are old enough to understand what a gift this treatment has been: live each day like it's your last. Don't go through life just sitting on the ground looking up. Get up and go! See what there is to see. Enjoy the beauty of everything. Help others enjoy it. — To all the children, I want you to think really hard for me. Think of something your mother and father have done to make you happy. Think of the most amazing thing they've done. … And try to understand that what they did by making sure your eyesight is protected is just as amazing as that. Make sure to tell them thank you; give them a hug and kiss. — Mothers and fathers love those just as much as you do. — I know this was nothing like what I had written, but like I said: I didn't even have as much of an understanding as I did when I met you. Thank you so much for opening the eyes of my heart to see what a joyous and marvelous gift I have myself as well as in Destan. Thank you for being strong, caring, loving, selfless, and… just thank you for being you."

She thought about going on, but the hush in the room kept her from it. Part of her was scared to, but she looked at Destan, only to see the sweetest smile on his face and what looked to be stains from a couple tears on his cheek.

I ruined it all, didn't I?

Out of the awe-struck silence came the methodical and strong applause of a single, elderly gentleman in the back. Within moments, everyone was on their feet and applauding; even the children.

What she'd intended to be a casual conversation turned into an outpouring of her bottled emotions; each linking arms with the other in a focused effort to convey what her heart was weighed down with. And yet, in her special way that could sometimes wander while not losing its way — what was so personal to her was turned into an expression of what it appeared everyone in the room felt.

The orchestra began playing as the applause faded, the children running up and hugging her before scurrying back to their families… though some of them stayed right by Callimay, clinging to her dress. Some families came up right then to thank her for what she said as well as some individuals; one of them being the elderly gentleman who rose first to offer his applause, "You did a world of justice with what you said, Mrs. Nevrille."

She took his outstretched hand, him kissing it, as she bowed her head, "I appreciate it."

"Your name is Callimay, is that correct?"

"Yes sir."

"Very good. — She is a rare jewel, Mr. Nevrille." He turned his head in Destan's direction as he patted her hand. "See to it she doesn't become tarnished or lost."

"I'm trying my best, Mr. Erwin. Every day, I am."

"Good," he repeated a few times as he nodded and turned to go back; sounding like he was carrying on a conversation with himself.

A young girl about seven who's hair looked every inch like his own walked up to Destan, her hands behind her back. She avoided his gaze as she asked, "Could I dance with you?"

He looked to Callimay who nodded, but warned: *If I do this, you're going to be asked.*

I've been resting this whole time. I should be able to make it a few dances before I'm tired.

I meant—

I know. … If you want to I'll be fine to do it too.

You're stronger than you give yourself credit for, Calli.

Destan turned back to the little girl and escorted her out to the dancefloor and really just stood there while she twirled around.

Callimay smiled as she watched with a torn and yearning heart, but couldn't neglect this repetitive tugging that was becoming stronger and stronger. She looked behind her and saw a little boy standing there, probably four, holding a fistful of her dress.

He dropped it a second after and froze with fear.

"I'm Callimay," she offered her hand to the little boy as she smiled.

"I… I'm Winston." The boy stuttered as he backed up and stood stiff as a board, but finally darted up and took her hand. "I… I wanted t… to ask you. Would y… you dance with me?"

"I'd love to, Winston."

Destan looked over when he noticed what he knew was her graceful movement: *Please be careful.*

I promise.

Calli? He asked worried.

I'll be alright, she fought to sound happy.

Seeing her made him a bit choked up and put him in the position he knew she was just a minute ago. Even though she was so good at hiding it, he could tell her heart was breaking with each passing moment. — How could she be enjoying herself; putting herself through this kind of torture? — But, she kept on and swayed back and forth ever so slightly as Winston's hands directed her.

At one point he stopped and grabbed her skirt, swishing it back and forth. He motioned to her with his finger and then got on his tiptoes as he cupped his hands around her ear.

Callimay's smile got brighter as she nodded. She let go of his hands and twirled around so her skirt flared out and then wrapped itself around her before spinning back out. Winston jumped with glee as he took her hands again and started swaying to-and-fro.

As any sudden movement or audible reaction did, the attention of many of the little ones — even the girl with Destan — was diverted. Seeing her skirt unfurl the last little bit was all they needed; them running over and pleading for her to do it again.

Callimay wanted to appease them, but looked over the small gathering of children to her husband who was still standing a little ways off.

He rushed over and worked his way through the little crowd and thrust his arm out for her to take.

Yet, unlike what he was expecting, once she steadied herself she did it again for her little audience. They all were ecstatic and asked her to do it again, but Destan stepped in and replied no: *I'm not about to be chewed out by Lance for not making sure your leg had time to heal.*

They all looked to Callimay with wide-opened eyes, as if begging; her pouting: *Just a short dance? For the children? Then I'll stop.*

I… but I don't want… he tried to refuse, but just couldn't when he saw the look in her eyes. "Alright. One short dance and then I'm carrying you back to our table. Deal?"

"Deal."

Part of him kept saying this would end bad — Doctor Gerould's booming voice echoing in his mind — but he shooed the children back and began to slowly waltz around.

The one-shoulder evening gown flared out and flowed like a fountain to the floor; it swishing and swaying as Destan tenderly caressed and led the beautiful woman wearing it. He spun her out once, allowing the layers of various emerald green fabrics to roll and wave in their own unique ways like grain fields in the breeze. The undivided attention they gave to each other was so beautiful to see and wasn't bothered by the commotion from the children around them.

Finishing what barely began with a peck of a kiss, Destan scooped Callimay into his arms and took her back to their table.

The still didn't sit well with him for long since he'd been up and moving, but he forced himself to wait a while so she could rest.

"Why are you fidgeting?"

"Oh. Sorry."

"What is it?" She looked at him out of the corner of her eye.

"How about we go talk with everyone?"

I never would've guessed. "That sounds wonderful." She nodded as a couple children darted over to them, all of them having the same question. *I know, I know. I promised.*

If you just stand there I guess it'd be alright.

How about I hold your hand and let them take turns?

I can work with that, Destan nodded as he helped her up and ushered the children back to the dancefloor.

They switched partners every minute or so, and before long satisfied every child under the age of ten, "'Now' let's go see everyone."

Her bickering didn't detour him from carrying her — him not caring if someone asked — but let her walk at a snail's pace when she was beside a table.

While Destan usually held more of a casual conversation, Callimay asked an array of questions that always came with the disclaimer of her wanting to help by understanding. Their responses were always jovial and open which reminded her again how she was around a group of people who appreciated such outreach and weren't ones to jump to "nasty" conclusions.

Since this ball was done with families of younger children in mind, it didn't last nearly as long. And so to her, things began to wind down practically the moment they began. Everyone made the extra effort to speak with Callimay and thank her for making the evening so special for everyone; welcoming her to their "family" and giving their well wishes until they would see each other again the next year.

"Will you be moving it to this time of the year on a permanent basis?" One of the fathers asked as he shook Destan's hand.

"Once everyone's had time to soak in tonight, I'll send out some kind of questioner to see what everyone prefers."

"I wouldn't expect anything less from you; it's a great idea. — Then I guess we will be looking forward to seeing something from you in the mail soon."

"Absolutely. Drive safely."

❦

Since it was still rather early, Destan drove out to the waterfront on the northwest side of Rayleen. He'd been meaning to take Callimay there when they first arrived, but there were so many things that it got shuffled back… and then forgotten.

The moon was almost full in the black sky, only a select few stars being allowed to shine. Similar to when they were traveling down from Faberton after escaping the Society, the seemingly endless water before them looked somewhat like a black mesh with glittering moonlight bursting through the spaces. There wasn't a hit of salt in the air or the noise of the oceanside to tie this place to such memories; it having a clean slate begging to be filled with page after page of warm and wonderful times.

Destan let her walk for a little bit, but Callimay mainly stood there and stared up. She'd missed seeing the stars at night like this.

"Someone told me that back on the Homeworld they map the stars into groups called constellations." He cleared his throat while rubbing his neck, sounding rather embarrassed. "She also said that they seem to shine brighter in the colder weather."

Callimay stopped and whipped her head around, "You… you remember me saying that?"

"I paid attention to everything you said… to one degree or another. It's just that I didn't always respond."

Chapter one, page one of this place's book was going to hold nothing but her mind's picture of what Destan looked like and the sweet things he said he remembered. What a wonderful way to start things off.

A soft and cool blanket of calmness caressed them both with such a tender touch that they couldn't help but feel content.

And then something strange happened, "What's wrong, Calli? Is it crooked?"

"No, silly." She sighed as she almost yanked on his tie so he'd lean over, allowing her to kiss him.

"You could've asked." He faked a cough as he tugged on his collar.

"Where's the fun in that?"

Destan laughed for a bit and then rubbed her hand as his tone softened, "I know tonight was difficult, and so maybe this will sound stupid… did you like it?"

"Tonight was exactly what I needed. It's helped me, us… 'God' helped us."

He took a deep breath as he wrapped her in his arms, her finishing, "And thank you for bringing me out here. It's such a quiet and peaceful place. There's no rush to go anywhere or get anything done. It's just… so nice, Destan. So nice."

~ 15 ~

The next morning dawned with Destan sitting in bed, hunched over and staring at his hands that looked to be resting on the bedspread. Callimay took a deep breath that ended up as a yawn and reached over to get her medicine but found it wasn't there; grunting as she pulled herself up. Without any concern, she reached over and laid her hand on his shoulder.

He didn't acknowledge her or react to her touch.

This instantly triggered a flashback to the last ball and what all transpired the morning after. And yet her wild eyes were able to find the real reason for this distance before she said a word: he had the Shadow Box opened and the picture of the two of them when they were so young carefully held in his hands as he rubbed the edge of the glossy paper. Callimay breathed a shaky sigh of relief, "Oh D—"

"You've never changed," his voice cracked as he took his first breath since she woke up.

"I have. Maybe you just haven't realized it. … I must say I'm very thankful you have."

Destan cracked that tiny smile for a moment, but it was quite apparent her jovial comment wasn't going to help much. What was bothering him had too much of a hold on him. He hated their joyful times had to be cut short, but at least this interruption wasn't going to be life-threatening like the times before.

He heard hard breathing and wincing which slapped him with the realization of what he forgot; him jumping out of bed, "I forgot again."

She grabbed his arm and pulled him back to her, "We've got five days to do this. Let's rest today. Our emotions need time. … Destan?"

Doyen was fighting hard, but seeing the look in her eyes gave the deciding blow, "How about we go for a drive after breakfast?"

Relieved it worked, Callimay smiled as she rubbed the side of his face, "I'd love that."

ℬ

With her medication on board, the pain was nothing more than awkward pressure; Callimay able to get up and about without help. And yet this didn't give her a green light for the stairs, oh no. Destan wasn't having any of that.

As he fixed breakfast, he was sad to a certain extent when he didn't see Rose poke her head around the corner of the window or ring the doorbell. But, looking at Callimay and remembering what he even felt the night before, he knew it was for the best: *I'm not so proud as to ignore the fact Tabitha was right. ~ You're a humble soul, Boon. ~ Oh shut up.* "Calli? Breakfast's ready."

"I'm already in here, remember?" She called out from the dining room, laughing.

"Oh. Right. My bad." Destan rolled his eyes as he came in; smiling as he set a small bowl beside Callimay's plate, "And… just because."

"Well what in the world did you do wrong?"

"Nothing! I just wanted to fix it for you." He huffed as he plopped onto his chair.

"Calm, down. I was only joking."

"We'll need to work on your timing and delivery. You were a bit 'too' convincing." Destan pointed out as he took her hand. "There is a code of conduct in the realm of banter, woman."

"I 'beg' your pardon."

"Much better."

~ 16 ~

Quick as a flash, they found themselves with only two days left to go through everything Destry had. — So much for spreading things out so they weren't rushed. — But who could blame them for taking their time and enjoying the life they loved for as long as possible?

It was dark in Destan's office as they came in, the Shadow Box sitting right where he left it. While it always was a point of confusion as to why he kept it so dark, knowing what she now did about his eyes made everything clear.

But did it? If he wasn't in danger of losing it, why take these extra precautions? Was he deep down scared of losing his sight still?

Those thoughts were all but a flash in the pan when she sat beside him. Callimay wanted to curl up on his lap but with her leg being extra tender that day she couldn't.

"I'm just upset because I don't feel g— what 'are' you doing?"

"I've only used this when I was too exhausted to go upstairs while waiting for a response from a Shadow or Veil." Destan answered cryptic as he started tossing things around in one corner of the room. "But, now I see it has a very good purpose. … There! Now all I have to do is unplug a couple things over here and tell the computer to do something it's never done… and… oh come on. I know you can you stupid hunk of—" *Oh for the love of—* "There we go. — Now you can sit with me and I can still work."

They got comfortable and then tensed up the moment he put the drive in the computer.

The screen went off!

Don't worry, Calli. It's supposed to do that.

"Program activated. Initiating secure voice recognition." The computer's AI said. "Name?"

"Doyen."

Destan's voice was repeated by the computer, it taking a few moments before saying, "Voice recognized. Content unlocked, Destan."

To this response he even flinched, and yet he didn't say a word. The screen began to come back on but it wasn't what he was expecting: it was a video beginning to play.

An older man was fiddling with the camera, mumbling to himself for a while before sitting down and taking a deep breath as he looked straight at the camera.

"I… I always thought I'd know what to say. … But how are you supposed to tell your son you're still alive after he sat there at five years of age and cried over you, thinking you were dying? And worst yet, have to tell him even though you're alive you're never coming home again. That you've died a second time." Destry struggled to say, him looking everywhere but at the camera now and fiddling with anything he could get his hands on. "I… I know I've caused you so much grief, Destan. I'm sorry for every, single, rotten, selfish, idiotic mistake I've made. I'm sorry I put you and Ly— there's not a day that goes by that I don't wish I would've gone into hiding with you and refused the Shadow's offer. I should've had the strength of will to lay aside what I wanted and kept the two most prized possessions I had safe. I should've listened to your mother 'and' you: your pleas for me to choose you. I should've valued you more. I should've taken my Jewel's advice and left the moment I started doubting. I should've been a man!"

Both of them jumped from the pounding sound of him slamming the desk; his raw emotions demanding their attention with the fear of consequence as if he were in the room with them.

And then it faded; muffled sounds of sobs bringing this climactic display crumbling down.

"I'm hoping you can learn from my mistakes, Destan. Don't shrivel up and die inside because of what I did. Please don't get so lost in yourself that you lose sight of what's happening to those around you. —I… I want to come back, I want it more than anything, but I have to right my wrong. I have to… I have to face up to my mistakes and be willing to do what I must to make sure no one else suffers. The reason you're even looking at this is because of the monster I created." He took a deep breath, glanced around him, and then continued with a kind of determination that Callimay had also seen in Destan himself, "When I first started working with the general — you'll know him as Elder if he still goes by that title — I could sense he was power-hungry. Aside from his work to rise in rank within the Shadows, he'd worked years and years to get the title he did in the Faberton government. Not to say it was wrong for him to do so, but his focus was solely to see how much control he could gain over others and situations. And yet he had such a passion and zeal for protecting and aiding people like you that it put my immediate knee-jerk reaction to the wayside. I should've kept that initial observation in mind when he asked about my serums. But I was caught up in my pride and let him have all the information I gathered. If there is any saving grace for me, I 'did' voice my concerns with how they weren't stable for practical usage, but he assured me he wasn't going to run headlong into something insanely dangerous; he only wanted his nephew — Baleck Lenön Willgun — to look them over and give me a fresh perspective. Lenön, as he preferred to be called, was like Elder in so many ways: power hungry, money driven, and self-centered. And yet his thoughts, for the most part, were quite eye-opening. That was probably nothing more than a ploy to sucker me in, but he 'was' knowledgeable… 'very' knowledgeable. But for as much as I came to value his opinions, he kept prodding me with the idea of mixing them. This was something I didn't even consider from the start and in no way wanted to even try seeing as how there was no way to control how they would be altered. It was a recipe for disaster in my opinion. — Before I knew it though, processing began. The work hours got longer and longer with each week; errors compounding from the lack of sleep on everyone's part. Elder played his part beautifully by heeding my concerns so I would trust him and divert my attention from what he was actually doing; realizing what was going on once it was too late. I came in that morning and found the processing room used for two runs, but they covered all of their other tracks. It was stupid of me, knowing what serums were administered, but I stormed into Elder's office and confronted him. But, as any 'good' liar would, he admitted to what did but created another fantastic story that justified the betrayal he committed. I did right one wrong by not believing him. It was probably because I was so furious, but had I not been, I'm sure he would've talked me down. — Your mother was about half out of her mind when I burst into the house just an hour after leaving for work, but she was right to be worried about what was going on and upset with me and what I'd done… and not done. I… I…"

Destan leaned forward, so enveloped in this that he felt his father was right in front of him. All he wanted to do was comfort him. He knew somewhat of the agony of losing the woman you love so dearly. For his entire life he never knew his father to be this kind of a man: emotional. He'd never seen a tear fall from his eye, never heard his voice break from the emotional weight on him, and until now never knew or understood how much his father loved his mother.

"I regret raising my hand against her like I did." Destry confessed as he buried his face in his quivering hands; unable to go on for a while. "I… I just… I didn't— wasn't th… she got everything packed and I sent Rocher ahead to the train station to get whatever tickets he could. We both knew you understood something was wrong, that there was this tension between us, but it didn't stop your mother from keeping you occupied the best she could. — We were out in the hall discussing things right before we were supposed to leave when you started playing something I don't ever remember you playing before: the song your mother played the night we met. Everything froze for a moment and things seemed as they were supposed to be. I looked at my wife for the first time in over two years for the beautiful and precious woman she was. She let me hold her as she cried, but rushed in when you kept playing the same chord over and over again… just like you always did when you wanted her attention. — Yes, I knew you were faking when you did that; well, most of the time anyway. I'm sure she did too, but she enjoyed being 'asked' to play with you. — I was going to follow her, but I heard a knock at the door and assumed it was Rocher. — What a stupid lapse of judgement that was on my part. — Baleck was reasonable at first, just trying to get me to calm down and come back, but that was just a smoke screen to get me to let my guard down enough so he could force his way in. The second he found his opening he took it; lashing out and demanding for the rest of Challenger's information. There was no way possible he could get it out of me, so I held out; hoping Rocher would be back soon and slip in the back way to get you and your mother to safety."

Another pause filled the air, Destry laboring to take a few breaths as he rubbed his face.

"Destan please stop it. You need to—"

"Calli I can't." He flashed his eyes, gritting his teeth. "I… I'm s—"

"If I only would've stopped and held onto what I knew, I 'know' I could've avoided what happened! I know I could've! … He threatened me, saying he contained both Origin and Dreamer — the 'dream team' as he loved calling it every, single time he talked about it with me — but the scars from the electrodes for cementing were absent. I know you've read what paperwork there is on some of the serums, so hopefully you know what I mean by my last statement. One thing you may not know is there was a period of time required to 'discover' one's ability, but because he knew about it I'm sure he would've begun training as soon as he could stand it. But he wasn't showing any signs of either ability at all. Well, not until he told me to call for Lylah; and now I know it wasn't even him doing it. — When I first confronted him I thought I saw someone in the back seat of the car, but at the time they were the least of my concerns. Turns out 'she' was the one who was given Dreamer. As innocent of a child as she was to begin with, she's now as close to a Strigidae without being one: a stone-cold heart with a thirst for sport killings. She hangs off of Lenön wherever he goes: Ginger Lanphren is the name she usually goes by. Watch for her and never trust what you see; she's powerful. — Back to what I was saying: him burning my face or breaking my arm didn't work," he gestured to his eye patch, sounding more enraged. "So he called for Lylah himself after 'she' created some kind of dome by the stairs. I waited and prayed she was already out of the house with you and Rocher. He kept calling, and just as I was about to take a sigh of relief I heard her running down the stairs. I tried to scream out for her to leave and that I was alright, but Dreamer can, in essence, create an alternative reality where even sounds are controlled. All Lylah could see when she bolted down was what looked like me lying on the floor… dead."

Even though there was no way for Callimay to read his mind, she knew what was going through his: he was reliving that memory and it was ripping him apart inside. What made this almost unbearable was him going through this without a single soul to turn to at the time; he was staring at an inanimate object: a camera.

"She was so hysterical and horrified as she gathered what she thought was me into her arms. That's a haunting image I will take with me to my grave, but it doesn't compare to the one that still jolts me awake at night: her turning the gun Lenön threw by me on herself while she kept screaming for someone to stop her and that she didn't want her baby to die… and then pulling the trigger. — I've since found irrefutable evidence that Lenön shot her: she was 'taking too long' and Ginger made it so I didn't see him do it, but I just can't… " he trailed off into a mumble before looking straight at the camera with tears in his eyes; confessing, "Yes, Destan. Your mother was expecting at the time. It wasn't long enough for us to know if it would be a girl or boy so we didn't bother saying anything to you until we knew."

Part of Callimay wanted him to stop because she didn't know how much more Destan could take. His knuckles were starting to bleach themselves as they clung to the sides of the screen and he was breathing so heavy. But did she dare say a word?

No.

"Lenön let me go but it was too late. Had I have not looked back at him to tell him what I thought of him when I did, the shot he fired would've killed me instantly. I was in shock and didn't find out until later that you came down and saw everything. I'm so sorry, son. I… as hard as this pain is for me to carry, I can't stand knowing what you've gone through. I wish there was something I could do to make you forget it like you did other things." Destry's focus began wandering again; it slowly settling as he continued, "Canary stopped by since she was in the area and ended up saving my life; pulling me out and doing what she could to tend to my wounds. I remember she told me she was glad her trip was successful in that she saved someone's life. She was so relieved to find out you were safe… a cruel irony. Canary got home early the next morning only to find her family had been massacred the night before. Had she taken the nonstop train she would've made it home in time to save them. — I still don't think my life was worth saving compared to her children. — After our emotions had time to settle, her anger with me and my guilt, we worked together feverishly to figure out what happened. Me telling her what I knew at the time convinced her both attacks were connected… and we needed to keep a low profile. — Report after report kept coming in about an arson mercenary with the same descriptive titles: demon ghost, invisible man, or just devil. The only thing was, these attacks were against Syndicate individuals as well. They'll go to great lengths to cover some things, but this was a red flag. When they had a Nark of any kind in the past they made a public spectacle of it. Burning the individuals to a cinder wasn't keeping with their 'style' and the people targeted were as loyal as they came. So, with this in mind, Canary used her connections to uncover the fact Lenön was receiving large payments from both extremist groups in Faberton as well as the Faberton government. The payment dates were staggered, but there was still a pattern that couldn't give any other answer than he was the one making these hits. It wasn't a surprise to me or Canary that Elder sanctioned some of Lenön's hits; hits which were against those he swore to protect: left-handed individuals. Something wasn't sitting right about that all so I kept digging. Those assignments from Elder weren't actual hits: they were capture missions. I found several of these individuals were held by various governments for vicious behavior that was sometimes deemed 'unnatural'. — Not but a day after I got that information, Canary was assigned a black widow mission within the Syndicate… cutting my ability to getting further information from her contacts. I tried to turn to others I trusted, but everyone in Deep Dark began to turn on me in one way or another; Elder the most hostile one. During one of our 'altercations' I noticed he bore scars from a cementing process."

Yet another pause came as his eyes began to dart around; him checking his watch as his voice dialed down to a whisper and was rushed, "Challenger is the only serum able to come close to what Elder's concocted for himself. But for Challenger to work it needs the right person. I hate that I'm saying this but it needs you, Destan. This is the last thing I want you to do but I just— I don't know another soul on this planet who would be compatible with it. But from what Rocher's told me, your emotional state isn't getting any better. Yes, it's stable, but it by no means has a good 'foundation'. Now I'm not saying this just for the sake of your processing, I'm saying this as a concerned and loving father: find some way to move past the pain and forgive me. Find closure in the memories of your mother and myself that were good. Maybe you don't think right now there are any since the bad ones are so shocking and prevalent, but believe me Destan: they're there. You just have to look for them. I need you to learn to forgive me for what I've done, learn to forget the painful memory you don't think you can let go of, learn to not want revenge for something that was beyond any of our control, learn to not hate me for staying away this whole time… and learn to stop hating yourself. Alcohol isn't going to fix it. I've tried that already. Get out of it right now before it gets worse. Son, you were only five at the time that all happened. There was nothing you could've done to change a single, solitary thing. It was 'my' fault. 'I' am the one who's to blame. Hate me if it helps for right now, but I'm begging you by repeating this: please forgive me. Please forgive yourself."

"I don't hate you, father. Not… not now." Destan mumbled under his breath; tears streaming from his closed eyes as his grip lessened.

His father was doing what Callimay usually had to do!

"No one without some type of ability can even 'think' of standing against Elder." Destry's voice sounded panicky. "But you have something he doesn't have: you have a heart that cares about others. I'm going to contact Creigam Freigh to see if he'd be willing to help; getting everything ready for you to undergo processing. — Now even though I've told you this all, it's your choice because it's your life. No one else, not even me, can 'make' you do anything. You don't have to become Challenger. You don't even have to become a Shadow, let alone Doyen like Commander has planned. Everything is your choice, Destan. And know that no matter your choice I support you. I believe in you. You're my son and I'm 'so' proud of you and who you've become so far. — I… I wish I had more time, Destan. I need to tell you about the picture and Callimay, but I just— if you find her, keep her safe. Find Canary. I love y—"

The screen cut to black; the computer saying as a loud pop was heard, "Content security level critical."

For as long as he could remember, one major thing Destan wanted was to hear his father's voice one last time; to see him under different circumstances. But now that he had, part of him wished it never happened. Seeing his father's face disfigured like it was, coupled with the wrenching emotions he was going through, "Why did you do it? Why did you put yourself through that? Why! … W… why did you lie to me, Rocher!"

And yet, in all this turmoil, he felt the tender and loving touch of his wife's hand against his tear-stained face. He turned to her and pulled her close; the thought of running away and hiding becoming more and more lucrative. Now that he understood just who Elder was he wanted to do what his father regretted not doing: keeping the one he loved safe.

But what would that do? Destry said no one without abilities could ever think of besting him; his reign was an invisible one. Those in danger were far more than just Callimay; how could Destan tuck tail and run?

Meanwhile, Callimay was scared about something else. Destry intended to explain everything about her but something happened. What? Why did the video cut out? Did he do it? Did Elder find out? Did he already know what was on this stick? How did Destry know her? "Why" did he know her? Who is Canary? Why does Destan have to get them to each other?

Destan let her go and left the room; the sound of his footsteps letting Callimay know exactly where he was. She heard a door shut — not slam — followed by the fading sound of steps that became slower and slower… and then nothing.

While she wished he would've stayed, she knew he wasn't prepared for this. Seriously, he was handling it much better than she imagined.

Well, that was until she felt an enormous spike from him. Callimay started to run, but fell against the wall as she cried out.

The next thing she knew, Destan was beside her, helping her up, "Are you alright?"

She took a deep breath as she swallowed hard, "Not really, but I'm more worried about—"

"I'm fine."

"Destan?" She pushed back to see his face; his tone worrying her.

"I've decided we're going to Trawnvane — tonight." He picked her up and brought her back in his office.

"Excuse me, what!"

"We're going back to the Society."

"But why?"

"Creigam Freigh." Destan said determined as he picked up the computer and walked back to his desk. "My father said he was going to get with him about processing me. If he did in fact get with him I've got to know. The whole Rogue thing was a hoax, so Elder and Willgun must've concocted it to get him under their control. ... And yet, if he knew all this, why allow me to undergo processing? Why allow you to be my failsafe? — I've got to have answers, Callimay. I've got to know where I stand at in this fight with Elder."

"O-kay. But it's more than a day's ride by train and we—"

"Raven can get us there in just about four hours. I'll check flight conditions and see if it's going to work." *It's got to. God please!*

"Destan?"

"What?" He whipped his head around and glared; softening when he saw the fear in her eyes, "I'm sorry, Calli. ... What's wrong?"

"What if they're still there? I mean the Rogues or whatever you want to call them. W—"

"Like I said, that all was a hoax. The Rogues never existed. There was no band of individuals out there preying on human kind with reckless abandon. Elder somehow got to Creigam Freigh and made him believe it for whatever reason. — And as far as if anyone is there at all: the Society was shut down and deemed a contaminated zone. At least that's what Willgun led everyone to believe was the reason for over half the student body dying in such a short timeframe. So with the exception of some vagrants, there shouldn't be anyone there. But even if there is, I'm not going to let anyone touch you. I promise you that."

"But I... I can't run, Destan. I can barely walk now. What if... if something happens and we get separated?"

He paused for a moment, as if realizing why she was so concerned, "You could just stay here. We've already tested and you can reach me from anywhere. And with it—"

"I'm not letting you go alone!"

"This has got to be done before we go back." Destan argued as he shoved his chair back. "We can't do anything while we're there."

"Why not? What's to keep Elder from knowing what's going on here? If mine can reach however far I need it to then why can't his? And why right now?" She stood her ground, knowing good and well his emotions were blocking his better judgement. "Elder's had his run of the Shadows and Veil for how many years? What's a couple months going to matter? He doesn't know we're onto him, does he?"

"You said you saw him, Callimay!" He continued to argue, getting louder and louder as his eyes began to burn with anger. "And you said he knew you were aware of him and what he was trying to do. Things can only get worse after we get back. I can't wait! I've got to get this done now!"

"You don't know that for sure, though! Maybe he just thinks I'm strong-willed. Maybe he's using all of this to trap us. Maybe—"

"Callimay shut it! You overthink everything! That's what got you almost killed when we were at the Society! And now all you can think about is having a family. It's impossible, okay! We're never going to have a family. So stop thinking about yourself and just let your stupid fantasy go!" Destan bellowed as he grabbed her by the shoulders and shook her; shoving her aside as he stormed out of the room.

By the time the initial shock wore off, she hobbled to the front door, only to hear the car revving. She rushed out to the gate, screaming in pain, "Destan!"

While a couple's spat wasn't something she liked to get into, Tabitha who was standing out in the yard couldn't help but think something more sinister was going on, "Callimay? Callimay, what's wrong?"

"I've got to get to him." She cried as she hissed and moaned. "He's spiraling out of control and heading for the airstrip. If he tries to fly Raven he'll kill himself!"

Oh God please no! "Come on." Tabitha grunted as she leaned over and put her arm around her. "You can take our car… that is unless you need someone to drive you."

"I'll be fine."

"Are you sure?"

"Yeah," she nodded; mere moments before she fell to her knees.

"Come on. I'll drive."

Tabitha helped her to the car and then corralled Rose inside the house and grabbed her keys and purse.

ℬ

"Voyager? Find Wolf and patch me into his coordinates." Tabitha said not but a second after she started the car.

A few moments later the car replied, "Wolf's signal is scrambled."

"Destan, I swear…" she grumbled under her breath, finishing in a firm tone, "Run a parallel scramble then."

"Still nothing, Helpmate. It could be Wolf has been deactivated."

She tapped her fist on the steering wheel as she bit her lip, and then sighed, "I… I'm pulling a blind guard, Voyager."

"Are you sure that is necessary, Helpmate?"

"Hack into Wolf, Voyager! Doyen's life depends on it!" Tabitha sounded terrified as she threw her hands up. "I missed my— ugh!"

Even though Callimay was in quite a bit of pain, she knew what the car's AI was saying wasn't good. And it kept getting worse, "Doyen must have put a failsafe into Wolf's programing that I am unaware of. I cannot get in."

"For the love of… Destan!" Tabitha yelled as she punched the gas; spinning the tires and drifting through the rest of the turn she was making. "Patch me through to tower control."

After a couple rings, they heard, "What's up, Helpmate?"

"Grounder? Doyen's a-wall. I don't want to, but by what Liaison told me it needs to be done: I calling in a solid blockade. Do 'not' let him get airborne. Do whatever you have to until I get there."

"If he shows, I will." Kendal answered a bit confused. "Do I need to pass the word along to anyone else?"

"What do you mean he's not there?"

"Just what I said." Kendal turned and looked out the window at the hanger. "Wolf isn't in the lot and Raven's still tucked away. I just got back in from making rounds. What's going on, Helpmate?"

"But I know I didn't pass him…" Tabitha said under her breath.

"He's at the plant!" Callimay blurted out. "Destan's at the old abandoned plant."

The car made cringe worthy sounds as it skidded to a halt, Tabitha fuming as she finished, "Just keep your guard up until you hear from me. And do 'not' pass this on yet."

"That's a five-by-five, Helpmate."

The plant was only about two miles off when Callimay doubled over and wheezed; reaching out to grab something.

"What's wrong, Callimay? Callimay?" Tabitha asked terrified; her focus bobbing between the road and her best friend. "Callimay we're almost there. Hang in there."

She started shaking her head furiously; her screaming out, "Destan don't! P-l-ease!"

Tabitha shrieked as she looked back at the road; her gripping the wheel and slamming on the breaks.

The car came to a stop inches from Destan who didn't look the least bit fazed or worried.

"Don't get out of the car, Tabitha. Whatever you do. He's mad at me. I don't want you to get hurt."

Tabitha said out of breath as she watched her open her door, "Where are you going?"

"To save my husband."

Destan's green eyes were burning just as much as the last time she saw him; he never took his eyes off her as she hobbled farther and farther from the car, keeping her hands in front of her like she were calming a rabid animal.

His chest violently recoiled from his heavy breathing and his fists were white. It took her every ounce of strength she had to not run; knowing all too well what happened the last time he looked at her like this: *It'd be worse if you did. ~ How did he slip this far this fast?*

Seeing her gave Destan enough strength to open the door in his mind; even though he was drowning inside of himself.

Destan please come back to me. Fight this. Don't let it consume you. Make your ability bend to 'your' wishes. I know you can. You've done it before. Please don't give up. ... You promised you'd never leave me and I 'know' you want to keep that promise. ... Destan 'please' remember!

"You!" He sneered as he lunged at her; throwing her to the ground and wrapping his hands around her neck.

"Destan don't!" She squirmed and fought to breathe; frantically trying to pull his hands away and get him off her.

"Callimay!" Tabitha screamed as she threw her door open.

"Get back in the car!" She scrambled to reach for Destan's arm; him letting her go and turning around. "Tabitha!"

She yelped when she looked up and Destan all of a sudden appeared beside the door; grabbing the pistol out of her purse and pointing it at him, almost crying as she pulled the hammer back.

"Destan! Leave her be!" Callimay coughed as she rubbed her neck; struggling to get to her feet. "Stop this! My Destan wouldn't 'ever' hurt someone. Especially not an unborn child! This is the demon the Society created. Fight it Destan! I know this isn't you!"

Knowing that talking alone wasn't going to get through to him, she resigned to the fact she was going to have to fight him. Her leg poked her as if to say what she was thinking was impossible, but her mind started running through what she needed to do while Destan lunged at her again.

She was able to evade him… but that only fueled his anger. There was no way he was going to let her get away with that again. He cornered her and started taking shots at her, quickly finding her weak spot. In no time at all he had her on the ground in a chokehold.

Callimay was desperately trying to get him to listen this whole time but nothing was working. It were as if he wasn't in control anymore; as if her Destan had drowned.

In a terrifying moment, Callimay "saw" what was happening: *Elder!* *You've got to get out of here, Tabitha. As far away as you can!*

I'm not leaving you! She yelled out as she reached for the car door again. *Let me help. I'll just wing him, I promise. He'll be alright.*

Don't you dare— keep that door closed! I'd never forgive myself if anything happened to you or the baby. This isn't just Destan I'm fighting. … I know of one way to get this to stop, but the problem is I don't know how to control that ability. I don't want to harm you in the process. Callimay explained as she finally got in a good position to get Destan off her. *Get. Away. From here. Now!*

But—

Tabitha, get as far away from here as you can, as fast as you dare.

Destan looked over at Tabitha as she left, to which Callimay called out, "You want me, Elder. Not Helpmate. … Or are you scared of me now that I can 'see' you?"

"You are the one who should be scared." Elder said as Destan had a fiendish smile come across his face. "Terrified, actually."

"Leave. My. Husband. Alone!" She screamed as she put her hands out and braced for Destan to run into her.

ℬ

"Calli? Calli, can you hear me?" She heard over and over again as someone rubbed her face.

It took her a while to gain enough consciousness to open her eyes. She jerked back as she kicked and punched him; scrambling to pull herself away as he fell to the side.

"He's gone, Calli." He winced as he reached out to her. "I'm sorry. I… I know I hurt you."

"Destan?" She worked to catch her breath, tilting her head so she could look in his eyes better.

"It's me, Calli. I promise."

She wasn't convinced for a minute or so, but then sighed in relief and collapsed.

He was just as terrified as she was about everything; part of him not sure if he was "safe" or not. This proved Callimay's point: Elder's reach was just as powerful as hers was. Being home in Rayleen wasn't any safer for them than Bulwark. It also brought back the horrific reality that Destan could reach a point where her pleas weren't enough to bring him back.

Things were still fuzzy, but he did remember telling her that them having a family was a "stupid fantasy" that she had to give up. Why would he say that? He didn't feel that way at all.

It was then he decided he needed a second stopgap, a failsafe that wasn't Callimay… or another person. There needed to be something he could keep with him at all times that would keep him grounded no matter what.

But as he kept thinking of this all, he remembered what Callimay said to Elder when she was defending him in Deep Dark. It wasn't her doing what she did that alone saved him time and time again. He had to choose to listen. He had to choose to see her as more important. Was the love he had for her beginning to fade?

Destan knew the answer was no. Why did he even bother? He loved her more than he loved his own life; him willing to give up his so she'd be safe. He knew that.

The only thing this all proved was it was that his ability to control his emotions wasn't anywhere as strong as it needed to be. And he was struggling so much more than he realized with the idea of having a family. He was fighting with himself; Doyen against husband. His head was telling him one thing while his heart was pleading the opposite; it not wanting that light to be snuffed out for good.

And in the midst of all this, he was reeling from everything his father said, reeling from seeing his father and hearing his voice, and reeling from knowing he couldn't have it back. The video was gone forever, just like his father was.

Aside from everything, Destan's plan to go to the Society wasn't abandoned. If anything it was even more cemented: *Elder can't afford for me to go… which means there 'is' evidence to be found. Willgun slipped up. I've just gotta beat the people Elder will send to 'clean up'.*

There was a problem though: how could he appease Callimay while keeping her safe? Would her staying behind even be safe? What if she stayed around him? Could he ensure he wouldn't fall for whatever trick Elder used this time?

The red marks on her neck from where he tried to strangle her glowed in such a way that he couldn't stand to look at her. Destan said grieved as he pulled her closer, burring his face in her unruly hair, "I'm so sorry, Calli."

"You didn't know."

"Yes I did. I knew 'exactly' what I was doing. It were as if I didn't care… as if I 'wanted' to kill you!"

"That was Elder telling you that, Destan."

"But I was the one thinking it."

She took a hard swallow and then gripped his arms, "Maybe I'm overthinking this or maybe I just don't know enough to have a clear picture, but it sure looks to me that he manipulates people's thoughts.

Remember how he tried to get me to let go when we were on the cliffside? He was taking the fact that I was exhausted and thought I was going to die used it against me. The only reason I knew it was someone else saying anything to me was because I could hear his voice. It was the same voice I heard that day when I almost committed suicide. I know it was him. I saw him when I pushed him out, thinking it was Baleck. He did the same thing to you, Destan. It's not any different."

Silence. But the type that was still unwilling to forgive self.

"I… I don't know if what I did right now helped you in the long run or not." She sounded depressed and lethargic from the pain. "And about earlier, I should h—"

"No!" Destan corrected in a desperate voice as he jerked back to reality, reaching out to her, "Calli I'm sorry. I wasn't going to— Calli!"

"Just leave me be. Please." She cried as she curled up on the ground.

"Calli I won't hurt you. Please." He put his hand on the barrier she put up around herself. "You had every right to remind me at the house that you were in no shape to be doing what I asked of you. And I shouldn't expect you to be fine with sitting on the sidelines and not worrying. The Doyen side of me is kicking in so hard, because of what my father told me, that I'm struggling to keep him in check. You're right: trying to do everything while here isn't going to solve anything. It might help keep questions from being asked by others, but you 'are' right: Elder's ability is far-reaching." *'Way' too far.* "I have no excuse for shoving you and yelling at you; or storming out like a spoiled brat. And I most certainly had no justification for doing what I did to you just a few minutes ago, regardless of whether or not Elder had a part in it. I'm sorry, Calli. So very sorry. … Calli? Are… are you alright? Do you need me to call—"

She put her hand out like she would when her head felt like it was killing her, him bowing his head and letting his hand fall to his side.

Other than her wheezing, it was dead silent for several minutes. Not seeing her face or being allowed to help tortured Destan, but he knew how paralyzing a near-death experience was. She needed time.

The barrier finally vanished. She was breathing much easier, but he didn't dare move since her emotions were right at that tipping point. He didn't want her to run off and hurt herself more than he had.

Destan?

Yes Calli? He answered without any hesitation as he whipped his head up.

Y… you need to call Tabitha and let her know everything's okay. She… told Kendal something about a blockade? I'm not sure—

I'll take care of it. He brushed off; not budging from where he was. *Calli? … Calli?*

Please go take care of that. I— please, Destan.

At first it looked like he was merely cringing from being pushed away a second time, but when he stumbled after putting weight on his one leg it was quite apparent: *I'm sorry.*

Don't ever be sorry for protecting yourself, Calli. He did his best to sound calm and loving. *Not even when it's me you're fighting. 'I'm' the one who should be sorry.*

There were a few moments of silence as he kept walking to the car, him sensing someone was rushing up behind him. Before he could react, Callimay plowed into the side of him; wailing, "It was the hardest thing I've ever done, Destan. I didn't know if I could bring you back. Elder's hold on you was so strong."

Usually he would stroke her hair and hush her hysterical rambling, but he couldn't bring himself to do it this time. Really? He was just as terrified as she was: *I pray it's something you never have to do again.* *God? Please help me fight harder so I don't keep putting her in danger like this. … Please.*

❦

The drive home wasn't enjoyable by any means: silent, disconnected, and tense. Destan wanted to help her when they got back but she darted past him and slammed the door in his face. And if that wasn't enough, his scolding continued when Redje stormed over, "What happened out there?"

"I let things get way out of hand, but we're alright."

"Tabby told me you said something else happened. — Has this got to do with what you were asking me about last week?"

"Yeah… but—"

"Why button up now?" Redje asked irritated.

"Because I don't have any hard proof, okay? Everything I do have tangible is the word of someone who's dead now. No one is going to take that as a valid charge."

"My wife and child were put in harm's way today." Redje fumed as he wagged his finger at his house. "I'm not leaving until you tell me."

"C… can we at least go inside?" Destan tried to calm; giggling the door handle. "Calli? Calli unlock the door. … Calli?"

🕭

This emotional tug-a-war continued as Destan tried to juggle discussing things with Redje while not upsetting Callimay. It was understandable that Redje was so upset, but he backed off when he realized what else was going on.

Without asking another question, he left for an hour or so; Tabitha accompanying him when he came back.

They talked for over an hour; every nitty-gritty detail discussed to the point nothing felt real anymore, "I'd say I am shocked, but I am well past that."

"Do you understand why we can't let you help us, Rej?"

"Why wasn't he doing anything sooner?"

"I… I don't know." Destan answered flustered; Callimay leaving for the fifth time without saying a word. "I don't know if he's— I don't know if he's making his move because the Eclipse is coming or if it's because Calli came along. I… I just don't know. I'm hoping that by going back to the Society I can find that answer."

"So, you're taking her on a mission?" Tabitha questioned as she got up, hearing Callimay crying.

"No. We're just going to collect info. Nothing else. Easy in and out. There shouldn't be a soul without twenty miles of where we'll be."

~ 17 ~

To say they had a rough evening was an understatement: Callimay snuck out and slept on the sofa in the living room. But in contrast to what they'd done before, they spent the next day together with friends; after which they spent just as much time with each other talking things through — alone.

They came to terms with what happened and started the process of healing. While it wasn't the greatest circumstance to test this new depth to their relationship on, it was telling of Destan's desire to change as well as Callimay's resilience and deep-seated trust in her husband.

Come evening, they sat on the deck that after dinner looking on as the sun bade farewell to the day.

Before long the darkness snuffed out the last bit of light, leaving the moon to fend for itself. But it wasn't that helpless: it was full that night. Thankfully, the forecast for where they were flying to showed overcast skies. Destan was hoping this held true because as confident as he was that this would be an easy in and out like he told Redje and Tabitha, there was that part of him — Doyen — that kept prepared for the worst. While he admitted this was the same line of thinking Callimay had at times, he always saw it being different because he was watching out for who he'd known to be his most dangerous enemy for so long: the Syndicate. It wasn't like he was just fretting over an engine knocking out or something like what she'd done in the past.

After finishing their nightly routine, they scurried upstairs and started getting ready.

"How many throwing knives did you bring, Destan?" Callimay asked shocked as she looked in his duffle bag at the three soft cases which each held of a few dozen hummingbird and assorted small throwing knives.

"Do you know how many your boots will hold?" He half-laughed as he started laying them out.

"Why do I need them at all?"

"It's… it's just in case, Calli. And really, your hummingbirds are so light you probably won't be able to tell the difference. Better safe than sorry, right? … Are you sure you're well enough to wear these?"

"If you're alright helping me around for most of the time I should be fine for short distances."

"Alright," Destan nodded as he took her boot and started working.

"Aren't you taking any?"

"They're already loaded." He corrected as he bent over. "See?"

Hidden with such perfect camouflage were a single throwing dagger and four Kunai; all arranged so he could grab them all at the same time under the folds in the leather of his boots. Ingenious design! Not even the handles were visible!

"They've always been loaded — even while we were at the mansion. My veil normally is, but I admit I took them out so you wouldn't notice. … It's expected of everyone, but especially as a Veil you 'never' unload your ensemble. You never know when you'll need them."

"What's this?" Callimay asked as she picked up a leather envelope that looked odd.

"I was waiting to give them to you for a 'graduation gift'." He sighed as he took it from her and started to unfold it. "You favor these quite a bit so I got you your own set. You're not 'technically' supposed to have them until you've received your beacon; but I could really care less about formalities right now. — You know how to use these, Calli. I know what happened at Bulwark is still fresh but don't be afraid to use them. Remember they are only as deadly as the person wielding them; that they by themselves can't do any damage to anything. Respect yourself, your capabilities, and them. Use them wisely and carefully. And if the need arises: protect yourself as God would want you to."

Nestled in this leather envelope was a set of Seaxes; there was no mistaking the silhouette. She took a firm hold of one and removed it from its "fresh" smelling black leather sheath.

The handle was of the same resin design as the ones she found belonging to Destry; the only difference being the addition of fine lines of orange that crisscrossed it like veins in marble. The spined side was engraved as well. After reading the one she had, she quickly took the other one.

"Fight if you must so you can come back to my arms..."
"...and always remember you are my life and my love."

Granted she read them in the wrong order, but even then, it blew all of the stress and fear of what happened the day before away. At least for the time being. A few tears jumped from her eyes and splashed against the matte carbon steel. To most wives, a set of knives wouldn't be considered a special gift, but to Callimay it meant the world.

"Do you like them?"

If actions speak louder than words then she was screaming: laying them down and hopping up so she could reach to clasp her hands around his neck.

Destan's face melted into a warm smile as he held her close. The necessity of her needing those bothered him so much, but at the same time he was glad there was something she could keep with her to help protect her if he wasn't around: *They won't help with Elder's abilities... but I guess in a way they will.*

She glanced over and saw what time it was, rushing to finish her hair and get her boots on, "Destan?"

"Hum?"

"You never did tell me what your knife is you normally use. I know you said you don't like to carry one, but I was curious. So far you've used a different one each time."

"Actually, the one I carry isn't really a knife." Destan answered as he pushed his veil back and gripped a handle on his right hip. "It's 'classified' as a knife but acts as a dagger. There's no spine on this, and since the three blades twist like they do there's a complete three-hundred and sixty-degree range of strike from it."

"I've never seen this one before? And I thought you showed me all the knives there were to choose from."

"Commander left me this. It was hers: one passed down through her family to the eldest child. It was her way of showing she was passing the title of leader to me; even though it was given to me after she passed. That's partially why I don't use it: knowing it is a reminder of her — and her death — to Rocher. … That and spiral daggers don't have handles that make them good combat-type knifes. — At least in my opinion. — That's why I have the larger throwing knives."

"Or why you just use what your opponent has."

"Exactly. Now, put this on." Destan handed her what looked like a belt; pointing as he explained, "It's a homing device that's specifically programed for you. Again, you're not supposed to get this until you finish, but so what if Elder complains. If we do get separated and you can't talk to me in any form — for God forbid whatever reason — I can find you through it; and vice versa. And if you have any ancillary items like I do, they fasten to it so they're easily accessible. — Let me call Grounder really quick and then we can leave."

℔

It looked like sunrise when they got to the airstrip; the moon so bright. Kendal was a bit confused still about what Tabitha said, but let it slide for more current matters, "Whatever you're up to, Doyen. I just hope you have a canopy. The moon's going to be your enemy if not."

"Even if it is, Grounder; what we're doing shouldn't require a run." Destan responded as he checked a few screens before turning a dial. "We should be back in about seven hours. Eight tops." *Hanging in there, Calli?*

Yep.

I love you. Destan smiled as he took her hand. *Everything's gonna be just fine.* "Remember to let Teralyn know about the vehicle drop off time and location."

"Yep, that's all squared away. You're cleared for takeoff." He sounded chipper; the sound of a book slapping shut in the background as his tone changed, "Don't make me scramble a scour team. You've got ten hours before I do."

"That's a five by five, Grounder." Destan sounded direct and stern. "Ten hours."

274

The flight was something Callimay found so different. With it now dark out the world beneath them looked so different… no good way to tell where the world ended and the sky began. The only help was the orientation of the jet and the small yellowish orbs and lines that glowed from street lights, buildings, vehicles, trains, and the like that spread out in every which direction like webs.

Not too much longer, a fluffy layer of clouds obscured their view of everything… every, thing. Destan tensed up as he spoke with Kendal, and then before long they popped out into the clear night sky; both their emotions leveling off.

Unlike what she assumed, the night wasn't at all boring. Watching the glowing clouds below them was almost mesmerizing; or maybe she was just that tired because of what happened in the last thirty-six hours. — The latter sounded more realistic.

They dove into the clouds again and continued for what felt like forever; Destan just as nervous as she was. She was adjusted to how bright it was on the way there that when they broke through the bottom of the clouds it felt like they were in a different world: it being so dark out.

Destan reported to the office for a little bit after a near perfect landing and then came back with a set of car keys, "Now don't you dare huff. This isn't easy for me, either. I've had to keep my eye on the skies and instruments for the past three hours and fifty-two minutes… and not you."

Callimay bowed her head, sounding ashamed, "I guess I—"

"We'll be back home before you know it." He assured as he stroked her hair; lifting her chin so he could see her eyes. "I promise."

Б

When he got to the drive for the Society, he turned the lights off and tapped into his night vision ability: *Just in case, Calli. Okay?*

While his words were a comfort, when they got to the gate even he was concerned. Only one side of the gate was closed… the other was mangled beyond recognition.

He had her stay in the car as he got out and looked around; saying in a hushed tone as he opened the door, "There's no one here."

"Something doesn't feel right, Destan." She rubbed her arm; her voice starting to crack as she pointed, "What… or 'who' did that?"

"Calli? Look at me. … I'm not going to let us get separated."

"O… okay."

The clouds began to break up, allowing the moon's light to shine through. And with that, revealing some of what happened. Destan had seen places like this before but Callimay only heard of places that were warzones at one time; and yet this fit the bill: abandoned so the chaos could remain as a constant reminder. Glass shards crunched under Destan's boots from the broken windows, shattered pieces of furniture and computers created a minefield he had to maneuver, every type of school book ruffled with an empty and horror-ridden sound from the soft breeze that swept through. She remembered what the place looked like not but a Homeworld's year ago and couldn't believe what she saw.

Something sneezing startled the two of them, causing Callimay to activate her barrier as she held onto Destan tighter. He whipped around only to find it was a dog who made the noise; and a beautiful one at that! Its coat was such a pure white that it looked like it was glowing in the moonlight.

This innocent sight calmed Callimay so the barrier vanished. The fluffy creature just stood right outside the gate, crooking its head at them as its tail wagged.

"Well hello there." Callimay reached out, her voice so soft.

Destan was as stiff as a board, his eyes as wide and wild with fear as ever: *Don't. Move.*

"But h—"

Quiet!

He crept backward, never turning his back to the animal; and then as he got up on the sidewalk he glanced behind him before jumping.

Why was he so frightened? It was just a dog and not doing anything aggressive. In fact, it looked friendly. It was probably just lost, poor thing. But was Callimay about to say anything about it?

Absolutely not. The way Destan's emotions flipped terrified her; yesterday's events too fresh in her mind.

Not wasting any time, Destan got to the first door that led to Mr. Freigh's office. He took the time to make sure Callimay was alright and then started working on his computer to hack into the security system.

The darkness of the night couldn't hide the whispers of the wind; the most eerie of sounds wandering down the empty halls and through all the broken glass, just waiting for the perfect moment to jump out and grab Callimay.

A stench of the most pungent yet awkward kind coated her nose; the only things she recognized being soot, smoke, and bad pork.

The cloud cover broke again, allowing the moon to reveal the shadows that were there the whole time watching their every move… and something else altogether more terrifying: bloody handprints, footprints, smears, and puddles literally everywhere. Granted it was dried by this time, but there was no mistaking what it was. Callimay yelped when she saw the large handprint of blood right beside her where she was leaning against the wall; gaining the condemning glare of her husband: *Hush!*

I… she did her best to catch her breath without losing her balance at the same time. *But… Destan!*

Seeing this made her begin to grasp the chaos Dakoe talked about. Callimay took a hard swallow as she reached out, now clinging to Destan's arm.

What's wrong?

The stupid thing can't find the system. It's invisible. — But that's impossible! He fumed as he kept his focus on what he was doing. *I was able to get into it—*

The power's not on.

Destan froze when he saw what Callimay was pointing at; rubbing his face and muttering as he put his computer back on his belt. The light that was always a solid red or green on the door lock wasn't on at all: *Great job of overlooking the most obvious, Boon. ~ Shut it.*

There was a couple seconds where he stood and stared "through" the door, and then opened it; turning back to pick up Callimay.

It was going to take too long to navigate the hall that was half caved in from the fire damage done, so Destan looked around and then jumped straight into Mr. Freigh's office.

While he could see without any issues, Callimay had no idea what was going on. And all she could hear as he walked was glass hissing and cracking: *The windows are broken. ~ That smell is worse in here. ~ I know. I sure hope this doesn't take too long.*

Knowing it was getting to her, Destan found a chair and had her sit down and handed her a handkerchief.

Not but a couple seconds later, he had his computer out, its minimal glow only lighting his face: *The auxiliary power is still active, but from what I'm seeing it's not based here. — Why not? … We need to go.*

Where?

Where the faculty stayed. Now come on. He grunted as he picked her up. *What's wrong?*

Doesn't that smell bother you?

Yes and no.

What is it?

There was a long pause, followed by Destan sighing: *Rotting flesh.*

What! She started squirming and fell out of his arms.

We don't have time. It'll be better when we get out of here. His voice sounded more understanding as he reached out in the darkness.

She started panicking as she felt around her, but calmed when she felt a hand: *There you a— why is your hand so cold? And it's s— it's not yours, is it?* "Destan!"

Shh! He clapped his hand over her mouth as he kneeled beside her; jumping again.

The horror inside her couldn't be relieved by her screaming inwardly; her running and pinning herself against the closest tree.

"Calli," Destan whispered as he ran up and tried to corral her flailing arms. "Calli, I need you to calm down."

"How in heaven's name do you expect me to calm down! That was a human being in there… dead!"

"I know it was!"

"How can you just say 'I know'!" Callimay said disgusted as she pushed him back, wheezing as she sniffled, "Don't you care? That was a human being!"

While he knew she needed to vent, he knew they were in a tight spot and needed to get this done and over with as soon as possible,

"Yes, I 'do' care. But I also know there's nothing we can do for them. …
And if we don't hurry we'll be joining them."

"What!" She yelped as he took her hand and jumped again.

He started breathing heavy, Destan realizing he had to stop using
his abilities or things would go from dangerous to deadly.

And yet he didn't get much time to recover when he heard his wife
wheezing and sobbing.

"Calli? That dog wasn't a 'real' dog." He paused when she whipped
her head up, her now wild eyes burning with fear. "They're called
belvederes: a hybrid animal machine used by the Syndicate to hunt
down Shadows. They 'never' go far from their keeper, so either a high-
standing Informer or Falconer is close by. Either way, we've got to find
what we came here for and get out as fast as possible."

"But I… I thought you said— how did they find us?"

Destan gritted his teeth as he went to the closest window and peeked
out, "We've got to work quickly. — Come on."

It was definitely better smelling here, but what struck Callimay as
they crept along was, "Why isn't anything damaged?"

Remember what Dakoe said about being here to 'stay safe'?

Why are we in this house specifically? She took his hint as he
opened a door.

*This is where Willgun lived. And as it turns out, this is the source of
that energy signature I was picking up. … Go over and see if you can
get the computer to turn on. I can search through everything by myself
but I don't know how much there is to go through and we don't have
much time.* He sounded concerned as he pulled the curtains in the
room and took his computer out.

They both started working — Callimay following his instructions —
but after a minute and no leads his emotions began spiking.

Destan?

Just keep going. I'm sorry. Just… just keep going.

The majority of what Callimay was searching through was video
feeds: nothing helpful.

"There's got to be something!" Destan said frustrated when his
search showed the same result; him slamming his fists on the desk.
"That's the only reason Elder would've sent someone after us."

"Did you already check these two drives? A and B?" She asked in a sweet and calm voice as she pointed.

"Drives A and B don't actually exist, Calli. They were meant for an ancient type of memory drive and no one's ever bothered to change it."

"Then why are they showing up?"

Upon opening the two drives it was a hot bed of nothing but communications between Baleck and Elder: *Got you now. You can try to cover things up but you'll never erase the truth.*

All our information is here! … And look! There's an entire list of those labeled 'Cliffhanger'.

I'm grabbing them too. … Alright. We've gotta go.

Destan cut the power and let her get out before he opened a vial and dropped it into the room; running and shutting the door behind him. He closed his eyes and turned his head away until a crackling sound accompanied by a bright light flashed out the bottom of the door.

"What in the name of…" Callimay gasped when she saw what was outside the far window.

"They don't even have respect for the dead." Destan muttered under his breath as he wiped the doorknob. "Okay, let's go."

"How could they…"

They're barbaric mercenaries, Calli. — I shouldn't jump right now, but maybe I'll be able to run when we g—

Do what you need to, Destan. She stopped and pulled on his arm so he'd look at her. *I trust you. Trust yourself. … Please. I understand how dire this situation is now. I… I'm sorry for flying off like I did.*

₳

As they came in view of the front gate he started to tap Toreon's ability so he could pin-point his jump… but a blinding light flashed right in front of them. It caught them both off guard, of course, but Destan tumbled to the ground as he yelled out in pain.

Just like the last time he came to a dead stop while running so fast, she was launched into the air. What brought her seemingly endless tumbling to a stop was one of the willow trees. As if the pain Destan was experiencing was bad enough, she just "had" to hit her injured leg on the tree. Of course!

She struggled through the pain to get her bearings; only to see what caused the light flash, "Justice Wan?"

And then there was the belvedere: standing right next to him, letting him pet it. It looked harmless… that is until he spoke to it and pointed to Destan. Its white coat darkened to a midnight black and it began snarling and growling. — Was it foaming at the mouth, too?

Destan still couldn't see and had no idea what was going on. He was completely defenseless!

"No!" Callimay screamed as she scrambled to her feet, only to fall because of the pain from her leg.

Her kneejerk reaction was to grab her leg, which also reminded her: *My hummingbirds!*

The belvedere just started to attack when she calmed enough to throw the knife. It landed right in the creature's shoulder, causing the belvedere to fall when it tried to put weight on that leg.

Oh good.

This creature was indeed tough. That perfect hit wasn't enough to keep the blood-thirsty Belvedere from getting back up.

Destan had gotten to his feet but he was still disoriented and unable to see; groaning and hissing as he stumbled into the wall.

Still unable to get up, Callimay grabbed another knife and threw it, hitting the belvedere in the loin. It yelped and fell again, infuriating Justice Wan, "Take her down you stupid— go!"

To that order the belvedere turned its focus and ran toward her.

For as scared as she was she knew she couldn't run… she had to fight. She threw a few more hummingbirds but the belvedere caught them in its mouth and tossed them to the side; never missing a stride.

The ground shook and rumbled from the creature's fast and focused movements toward its prey.

Right as the creature jumped to make its attack — bearing its fangs as is snarled — Callimay drew her Seaxes and then instantly let all her training fly out the window.

All she could think to do was cross them in front of her.

"Calli!" Destan called out in horror.

$$\mathfrak{SB}$$

After a few seconds and nothing happening, she quickly looked back and saw she put up her barrier. The belvedere continued to growl and claw at it, furious it couldn't satisfy his hunger. Callimay looked at the etchings in her knife blades, remembering what they said: *Deep breath. It's just an animal. ~ Well, part animal anyway. ~ Surely it's able to be taken down like a real dog. ~ Oh why didn't Destan tell me about these things yet? Wha… what do I do!*

Seeing the belvedere's ears perk and it turn to look at its keeper, Callimay panicked. She knew good and well she didn't know how to control her barrier ability, but somehow she got it to disappear when she needed it to.

Heaving and whimpering, she rushed the creature. Her bulldozing into the side of it caught the creature completely off guard, but as it went down the belvedere reached back and growled as it bore it's fangs at her. It reverted to its white appearance and fell limp.

Callimay was worried it wasn't dead, but seeing and feeling Destan taking a beating meant she couldn't wait.

It was painful — to say the least — for her to run, but seeing her husband struggling so much kept her going.

And yet, just about ten feet away, her leg gave out.

Come on, girl. It's no worse than your migraines and you've fought through those for Destan. She coached herself; gritting her teeth as she stood. *Just a little bit further, Rose Petal. Come on!*

Crying out again, she forced herself to her feet and rushed up.

He turned his attention toward the commotion, but not in enough time: Callimay turned her Seax and used the pommel, expending as much energy as she could to make hard contact with his kneecap.

That got him to his knee and gave her enough time to hobble over so she was between him and Destan, "What are you doing!"

"Getting my pound of flesh." Justice Wan grimaced as he looked up at her and spat at them.

"But you told us you were against everything the Society stood for?"

"Just because I thought 'they' were responsible for my daughter's death. But I've since come to find the actual truth: 'you' are the ones responsible for my innocent daughter's death."

"We didn't kill, Hyra."

"That's not what I heard from a certain Strigidae whom we both know. — And it doesn't matter that you didn't pull the trigger yourself. You're responsible."

"It was in self-defense." Callimay pleaded as she took a couple steps back, now standing right in front of Destan. "As a justice you know it's within anyone's rights to defend themselves."

"Not when it's my daughter who is dead." Justice Wan fumed as his eyes narrowed and he took a combative stance. "And not when a Derelict is involved."

"What?" Callimay gasped in horror as she glanced back to Destan who was reaching out to take her hand.

"I'll admit Destan's extremely good at diverting people's attention when he's writing. Even though I knew to watch for such things I fell for it. But I noticed how clumsy he was when signing your marriage license and his temporary passport. Not even an injured person would be 'that' bad. And he didn't strike me at all as the type to be so careless with their penmanship."

"Well, if you knew, why didn't you do anything then?"

"When I saw the shape you two were in and found out Hyra was still alive I… I let my hatred of them burn deeper; putting my mission aside. … But now I have no reason since you lied."

"Why are you doing this? Working for the Syndicate? What are they offering you that honest work won't?"

"Money." Justice Wan answered a bit perturbed, but without a moment's hesitation. "No 'honest' man can make a decent living. Not in the world we live in. — They were willing to pay handsome amounts of money in exchange for just a few thieves I knew quite well."

"Thieves?"

"You're all thieves: 'protecting' those who are violating the Law and stealing money from those who need it. Do you know that just a single bounty or standard reward could support someone for almost a year?"

"We're all human beings!" Callimay screamed as she shook her fists; tears of anger bursting out of her eyes. "Quit calling us Derelicts. Quit dehumanizing us. We're not the evil disease that's plaguing this world! It's the sinful desire for money that people like you grovel in; 'that's' the problem! That's the disease! If anyone's a thief its 'you'!

You're stealing the most basic right of life from someone who's no guiltier of what caused the Homeworld to sever ties than yourself."

Her echoing cries appeared to silence Justice Wan; and yet the gleam that started to build in his eye hinted otherwise, "'We'? 'Us'? … So, 'you're' one too?"

Destan finally got to where he could function again, so he took hold of Callimay and jumped.

Not wasting any time, he opened the door as he heaved, "Calli, I need you to drive. I can't see that well."

She helped him in and then ran around; pausing for a moment when she heard thundering footsteps nearby: *But I—*

What are you doing! Get in!

Her skin was crawling as she jumped in; it taking her every ounce of self-control she had left to keep from screaming.

That thought became the least of her problems when a stabbing pain came out of nowhere.

"I'm… I'm sorry, Calli. I'm trying." Destan hissed as he rocked back and forth; reaching over when she went to turn the car lights on, "Fox? Run mode."

"Run mode transition in progress." The car's AI replied.

The windshield and windows turned opaque for a moment, and then Callimay could see everything around her in various green hues. She threw the car into reverse just as Justice Wan got to the gate; her tearing down the drive just like the faculty did when they left.

🜔

When they got to the base she could sense something wasn't right. But what? She looked both ways to see if she could turn, asking worried, "Why are those lights down there red?"

"What!"

"There are car lights to our left—"

"Syndicate sc— we've gotta head up the mountain." Destan growled as he tried to keep as calm as possible. "Turn right, Calli."

They both could feel the fear in each other, it doing nothing but making their own fear worse. — Her ability was working against her "and" him.

Callimay's only driving experience was on the straight and flat roads of Kerogen, so it wasn't a surprise to find this mountainous and curvy terrain throwing her for a loop: *If those lights behind us weren't so... ~ Ominous? ~ Why do they 'have' to be red? And why are they getting brighter so fast? ~ Really? ~ I don't wanna hit someone coming down the mountain! I don't have my lights on.*

"Fox? Scan the area for other vehicles." Destan calmed as he reached over and took her hand.

Before she could say any word of thanks, the car informed, "The only vehicles within five miles of our current position are behind us, Doyen. A squad of standard Syndicate vehicles."

While that last little bit wasn't the greatest news to hear, the fact was they had a clear road ahead of them. She could go faster, but there were still limits; and Destan knew this. He wasn't about to be angry.

They reached the peak where the road leveled off for a longer distance, so Callimay floored the gas petal; the smell of burning rubber building in the car.

Being able to see more road in front of her calmed her, but it didn't last, "Two squads of Syndicate vehicles in range, bearing 0012."

"Stop the car." Destan braced his hand on the dash. "Now Calli!"

It wasn't the best reaction, but being terrified and then hearing him yell… stomping on the breaks achieved what he asked for; but what a blessing it was that she didn't cut a tire and flip the car!

A few terrifying seconds later they came to a stop; them jerking back against their seats as they stared at a slew of red lights in front of them. Destan took off his seatbelt and ran around to her side; her arms frozen stiff just like her hands on the wheel.

He almost snapped at her, but took an extra breath and urged, "Come on, Calli. We've gotta go."

Having the moon's light flood through the opened door brought her back, her fumbling to get her seatbelt undone as she cried, "I'm trying."

Destan hunkered behind the door and helped her; keeping an eye on the vehicles that just came up behind them as well as the welcoming committee in front of them: *Well it looks like they learned their lesson: a squeeze only works if you've got enough people to do it. And yet they still have more to learn.* "Fox, wipe it clean. Condition critical."

"Wipe initiated. Ten seconds to completion."

Destan helped her out of the car, her skin as pale as the moon and her eyes as terrified as he ever remembered seeing them. It wasn't what he was hoping for, but then again he expected it: her body couldn't take any more emotional strain. He caught her and gathered her in his arms; taking off down the steep embankment.

Not but a few moments after he did, the car exploded. Looking back could keep him from getting hit by shrapnel, but if he didn't watch where he was going it was just as dangerous. And to add to everything: he really didn't need to see three squads of Falconers scaling down after them. In fact, that was the worst thing he could do.

So, onward and forward!

His eyes were doing much better, but the terrain was still too steep. If he were by himself he would've used his ability, but he wasn't about to risk anything.

As it turned out, where they ended up put his trajectory just north of the outer perimeter of the Society. And within a few more minutes his emotions were much more stable and the slope of the land was to the point he felt safe taking the risk.

While it wasn't the greatest feeling — running under a full moon with little to no cover — it was the only way he was going to get to the airstrip ahead of the Syndicate… providing those they saw were all Elder sent after them.

Taking the time to look down to see Callimay's face helped him stay stable, but he knew he wasn't going to make it the whole way with just that. So, he stopped every minute or so to catch his breath and allow his emotions to calm so he could keep going.

℥

The parking lot looked clear of any Syndicate vehicles, so he strolled into the terminal like nothing was wrong; all the while keeping a keen eye out for anyone who looked the least bit suspicious.

It was the wee hours of the morning so the only people there were ones waiting for connecting flights. And where he was going was empty of anyone except staff. He was given a waiver for the ground check since it hadn't been but two hours since they touched down,

"Really? Huh. … I guess I didn't think about the trip falling into that timeframe."

"Short trips do have that small perk." The man smiled as he reached to take the paperwork from Destan.

"But," he kept his hand on it. "I… I'll go ahead and do it." *The Syndicate could have tampered with something.*

"A true pilot," the man nodded as he pulled his hand back. "I appreciate you valuing safety over convenience."

He poured over it with a fine-tooth comb and sure enough, Destan found where the jet had been tampered with. It was so blatantly obvious and easy to fix that he was puzzled why they chose it, but then again: it was something Rocher said was easily overlooked by most pilots when they were in a rush… because nothing was ever wrong with it.

Once satisfied, Destan climbed in and started waking Raven up; but stopped short when he saw Callimay: she was still out cold. The poor thing was going straight from one emotional trial to the next without any break.

But they were so close that he couldn't give up now. What they found there was going to be the death sentence needed against Elder, he knew it. Destan just didn't know if she could make it through this last stretch. It wasn't going to be easy at all.

ℬ

As he started his ascent, he glanced over and saw a thin smoke stream rising from one of the Brussel Mountain peaks: where Fox was. The Syndicate wouldn't want to draw attention to what they were doing, but pulling a fire out didn't erase what happened.

He sat back and smiled, but then sighed as he groaned: *Why didn't I pick up on Justice Wan— what did I miss? There had to be 'something' there. But I looked! … At least Calli didn't call me by my title. ~ Everyone at Bulwark may scold her for messing that up but it was a huge help. Every little bit counts. ~ But everything else is gone: my 'real' life is going to be destroyed before we even get back to Rayleen. And it's going to be 'so' wonderful to deal with that when we get back to Bulwark. — I'm sorry, Calli.*

The flight was turning into one of the easiest ones he'd had; giving him time to realize how alone he was. For so long he enjoyed being alone, but he couldn't function like that anymore. Callimay was sitting right next to him and yet she wasn't: she wasn't looking at everything, asking him a million questions about what was what or why he was doing what he was doing or what different screens or dials were. She wasn't constantly telling him to "keep his eyes on the road"; in short, she wasn't there.

This was revealing something that almost scared him: this was the first mission — though it never was intended to be — that he was reacting to. He wasn't sure how this whole emotional roller coaster worked in this kind of situation. Not that it was much, if any easier for Callimay, but she understood it more. He needed his helper.

꒰ꕥ꒱

The sun rose without any knowledge of what happened in its absence, it flooding the landscape below with warmth and joyful light without any concerns or questions. And yet, even though it was wonderful to see the world below and remember the blessings he had, Destan was missing his sunshine: his Calli. She hadn't moved this entire time: around five hours.

"Cutting it kinda close, are we?"

"Sorry Kendal." Destan sighed as he rubbed his face.

"Tetralyn said her Fox wasn't waiting for her. What happened?"

"Nothing's come out yet?"

"Excuse me?"

Destan took a sigh of relief, "I'll explain things later. Get with the hub in Yergo and have them send her a replacement last night."

"Will do."

꒰ꕥ꒱

As he pulled the jet into the hanger, which faced into the sun, Callimay began to moan and move. Destan finished everything as fast he could and then got to her side as she opened her eyes, looking around for a bit until she got her bearings.

"Destan?"

"We're home, Calli."

"Home?"

"Yep." He sounded chipper as he helped her unfasten her seatbelt.

"Why am I so tired?"

"You needed that rest." Destan leaned back on his heels and then got up and grabbed his clipboard. "And really, I could use some right now. In a way I was kinda jealous."

"Are your eyes alright?"

He heard her wince, prompting him to drop his paperwork and whip round, "I guess I didn't think about bringing your medicine."

"Medicine?" Callimay asked in a disoriented mumble.

"And my eyes fine now. I promise."

꤮

After he finished talking with Kendal and making sure his paperwork checked out, Destan carried Callimay to Wolf. He was concerned when he saw she was still lethargic and disoriented, but her also showing signs of frustration reminded him of what she did when they got back from the plant, "You're in shock, Calli. Don't try to figure things out right now. Just rest."

She nodded as she closed her eyes, giving him the added confidence he was right. He shut the door as soft as he could and then jogged around to his side; wincing each time he put weight on his left leg.

Right as he opened the door he heard her scream out, him climbing over to her as he gasped, "What's wrong?"

"Why does my leg hurt?" She argued as she threw her head against the seat's headrest.

A moment of shock washed over him; a horrible thought crossing his mind, "Calli? Calli, did the belvedere bite you?"

"Did the 'what' bite me?"

Not wasting any time, he checked her arms and legs. Nothing to suggest the creature got her. He did, however, see a metallic purple streak on her pants leg near her Seax, so he pulled it out.

"Calli?" Destan's voice began to crack as he reached over and took her other knife out; it being coated with the same thick, glistening fluid. "Where did you hit the belvedere with your Seaxes?"

"My 'what'?"

"Your knives! Calli where did you stab the belvedere!" Terror began creeping into his voice as he threw them on the floor.

She looked up for a while and then replied, "You mean the dog? Uh, I don't remember."

I should have killed the thing myself when I saw it that first time. "Calli, you need to drink this."

"Why?"

"Calli, please! Just drink it!" He popped open the vial and forced her to take the black liquid.

To say he started panicking was conservative. Why wouldn't he since she lost consciousness and stopped breathing? He rubbed the side of her face, "Calli… Calli, wake up. No. No, I'm not losing you! Come on, Callimay. Fight! Please. Calli, please. None of this is worth anything if I lose you. Please! — God please don't do this! Not again! I can't do it, I can't take it. Stop! Please!"

Kendall dashed out, hearing Destan's frantic yells, and got him to calm enough to get her inside so they could check her vitals.

Even though he didn't know exactly what happened, the black stain on her mouth told him everything as he started hooking her up.

He knew it wasn't any use — the antidote needed time to work — but hated to say anything or stop what he was doing. Yes, Destan knew good and well if someone lost consciousness there wasn't anything that would bring them back, but how could Kendal remind him of that?

Destan was hysterical; still trying to get Callimay awake.

Something had to be said or done. Letting him keep on like this wasn't going to do any good.

The device he was holding vibrated, him sighing when he saw what it said. Kendall laid his hand on Destan's shoulder and bowed his head.

"Calli," he sobbed as he threw himself across her. "I… Dear Lord, 'please' let me keep her. Please. Pl…"

His broken voice gave into his violent sobs; his hands having a death grip on the woman he loved and lost. — How many times does he have to go through this? What is he supposed to be learning?

"Why do I have this rancid taste in my mouth?" A feminine voice puckered as Destan felt movement. "Oh, that's dis-gusting!"

"Calli!"

"Yeah. Destan are you alright?"

"It… you…" he fumbled as he looked back at Kendal and then to her. "H… how?"

"I'm sorry I didn't reply. I was trying but I all of a sudden got so tired." She soothed as he wrapped her in his arms as tight as he dared; her cradling his head against hers as she finished, "It's alright, Destan. I'm here."

Kendall was standing there, staring at her; but left not too much later to give them some space: *This doesn't make a bit of sense. How in the world did she come back?*

"Are your eyes doing alright?"

"But I—" Destan caught himself as he pulled her back. "Yes. Yes, I'm fine."

"Are you sure?"

"Yes. Yes, I'm fine now." Destan assured as he put his hand over hers and took a shaky breath.

🕉

Once things we calm and stable they headed back; them doing nothing but listening to each other's thoughts the entire way.

When Destan pulled in, Redje, Tabitha, and Rose were just leaving Mrs. Manning's. The elderly woman waved in the manner he knew too well; groaning as he got out of the car. Had it not been for Callimay's encouragement he would've ignored the well-meaning gesture.

"Land's sakes alive what 'are' you wearing, my child?" She sounded shocked as she pointed with her cane. "My goodness what… what happened to your face! And why are you— I… what have you two been into? You both look like you have had a fight with each other."

"We're fine now, Mrs. Manning." Callimay replied; a sweet smile on her face.

"You just miss bwekfass! Is so-o good! — Mammy? Cowimay's weg ez hurt, you no dat? Dat why she no stand." Rose tugged on her sleeve as she rubbed her own leg. "She say it hawd two sweep beetus it huwt. — You just tyward, awen't you, Cowimay? Dat why you wook wike dat. White?"

"Not r—"

"Like Callimay said, Mrs. Manning: we're both fine now." Destan evaded even what Rose was suggesting.

"Come on, Sweetheart." Tabitha took her daughter's hand and rushed off without even saying hello.

"Very well," Mrs. Manning sighed; taking the subliminal hint as she walked back inside her house and shut the door.

"Not an easy in and out, was it?" Redje asked rather flippant as he pointed to the streak on Callimay's leg. "Why in the world was a belvedere at the Society?"

"The man who helped us escape: the one who married us?" *The cruel irony*— "turns out he's working for the Syndicate."

"I thought you said he didn't have any money?"

"He didn't when we saw him, what… seven months ago?" Destan looked to Callimay; her nodding. "So he either was in for a while prior to us ever meeting him or came into some money just recently."

"Falconer or Informant?"

"I don't know." Destan shook his head. "He seemed like both at different moments."

"I noticed Rose and Tabitha left quickly." Callimay interjected; trying to keep things calm. "I'm sorry we're—"

"We're both leery to some extent, still. But as far as that goes, Tabby was just getting Rose away so she wouldn't touch what's on your pants' leg there."

"What are you—"

"Calli don't!" Destan gasped as Redje grabbed her arm.

"Belvedere blood is dangerous, Callimay." Redje warned as he let her go. "You haven't started your run training, have you?"

"No."

"Look, I'd like to talk, but I need to get Calli's—"

"Just— don't… don't kill yourselves." Redje sighed as he tried to find a better way of putting it. "This isn't worth your lives. We'll make it like we have been if need be. Elder can't be 'that' powerful."

"But it's not just—"

"I… I know." He rubbed his neck, sounding desperate. "Just— you two don't have to do this alone."

"I don't mean to sound rude, but who else can help us?" Destan asked point blank. "Just keep praying. That's all we can ask for right now and we all know prayer is powerful. And believe me, if something does come up where I 'really' need you, I'll let you know."

℔

By the time they got up to the bedroom, Callimay was hissing through her teeth. He kept apologizing for everything; her having the same, calm, sweet answer each time. For as much as this "down playing" of what happened annoyed him, he knew she was only trying to keep him calm. The pain she was in didn't need any help from him.

Once she was as pain free as humanly possible, he started taking off her boots, "You're going to need a new ensemble when we get b— I know it's only on your pants, but I just don't want to risk it."

"So just touching it can kill you?" Callimay asked worried; her whipping her head around and looking at her sleeves.

"Actually, touching it only burns you. It's when it that glittering poison gets into your bloodstream that it wreaks havoc: progressively deteriorating your heart's electrical function and eventually causes cardiac arrest. A bite from a belvedere will do the same thing."

"Is that why you were so worried earlier?"

He stopped what he was doing for a moment and then took a deep breath as he looked up, "At first I just thought you were in shock from everything, but you kept getting worse. — You didn't just pass out like last time. You kept getting more and more disoriented. — And you weren't bitten so I was even more confused. I saw your Seaxes were covered with it but had to let the 'how' question go. All I 'needed' to know was that it was in you. — That horrible taste in your mouth was the antidote we've developed. Come to think of it, Canary was actually who got us the info on it."

There was a pause that was awkward enough, but the look in his eyes told Callimay everything.

"I'm okay. You figured it out, and that's what's important. Right? … Destan? … How about I go get out of this all and into something a little more comfortable? Sound good? … Do you need to change?"

"It'd probably be best." He sounded dazed as he watched her get up.

It was always a chore for Destan to keep belvedere "blood" contained, but he was even more nervous with Callimay being responsible for keeping it contained. He trusted her, but he didn't want something to happen. And to make matters worse: she'd been in the bathroom for quite a while, "Calli? Calli, are you alright?"

There was an immediate gasp in response to his knock, soon followed by, "Umm... yeah?"

"Calli, what's wrong?"

"When are we leaving?"

"Well... I guess as soon as you're ready." Destan sighed as he jiggled the door handle. "Calli can I come in?"

"Just give me a moment. ... Alright."

It was apparent she tried her best to cover it up, but she didn't quite get the one towel into the hamper. Seeing the blood-stained fabric made Destan whip his head over, "Oh Calli!"

"Well, the mystery of how the belvedere's blood got in is solved." She half-laughed while she kept tending to her leg. "With all the pain I was in already I didn't notice my skin was burning."

Her comforting words fell on deaf ears, Destan dropping to his knees in defeat.

"Now don't go blaming yourself. You didn't know this would happen. ... Neither of us did. — Are your eyes doing alright?"

It took her question a moment to register, Destan blinking a few times as he nodded, "Yeah, I'm fine. Do... do I need to get you something? Is it still burning?"

"No. It was just that one spot and I cleaned it as much as I dared. That's why I asked when we were leaving. ... Destan? Destan I'm okay. A little worse for wear, I won't deny, but we've both been through the wringer in our own ways." She smiled as she finished securing the bandage and then reached over to brush the side of his face. "Scars fade with time. Maybe they won't disappear, but it's not like I've never had any my entire life. This big? No. But it's not like there's anything I can do to change it."

"I just hate that y—"

"I'd like to take some clothes that are more comfortable with me." She forced this change to keep his emotions under control. "While my ensemble 'did' do a good job of concealing the pain since it was compressing everything, I don't think I could get it back on for a while without screaming."

Destan nodded as he got up and then picked her up. "I'm sure Lance won't clear you so it's not like it'd be a big deal anyway. … While we're on the subject: would you mind if I asked you to bring your perfume with you?"

"What subject is this?" Callimay chuckled as he set her down.

"Being comfortable," he struggled to get out as he turned away, rubbing his neck. "Would you?"

"Alright." She shook her head and chuckled to herself as she started going through her clothes; stopping when she glanced out the window at movement that tugged at her, "Destan?"

"Yes, Calli?"

"Do… do you think we'll ever be able to have a family?"

He looked back and saw Redje with Rose, almost groaning when he put her bag on the bed and opened it, "I… I don't know, Calli. As long as I'm Doyen I really don't see it being an option. Plus, there's all the unknowns with our abilities that we've already discussed. And t—"

"But those files you got had to have our medical records. Well, I guess— why wouldn't they? Maybe Doctor Gerould could figure out a way if something might not b—"

"Calli," he interrupted, sounding equally depressed and grieved. "I… please don't torture yourself thinking about it right now."

"I… I just…" she tossed her clothes aside and shoved the bag off the bed. "I just want to know there's more to look forward to! I've been doing so well, but then we got back and— I've tried so hard to keep myself from thinking about it but I just can't, Destan. I'm sorry. Please don't get mad at me again. I… I don't know what's come over me. I should be perfectly content with it just being the two of us. I don't love you any less or—"

"Shh." He ran over and pulled her close, stroking her hair. "We're so close, Calli. Don't give up on me now. Please. … I'll… I'll go ahead and tell you. — Maybe it will help give you a thread of hope to cling to.

— It may not be too much longer that I have to be Doyen. There may soon be no need for the Shadows at all… hopefully. Please, Calli. Help me. I've been wrestling with it too. But if things work out like they've been planned to, maybe Lance 'can' make sense of what we got and we'll be able to, if nothing else, know for sure. All we can do right now is keep working and pray: pray like we never have before."

"No need for the Sha— but how can that be! As long as the International Law is in place we're in danger."

"Please, Calli. Please help me. I need you to help me stay focused so we can have a shot at this dream. I know it may seem like you're telling me quite often or I may start to get irritated by you saying it again and again, but believe me when I say I 'want' to hear it. I need to hear it. Often. I need to be reminded there's a goal for the two of us — aside from just being together — so I don't give up working as hard as I can to lead us to that."

"I… alright."

"We're going to make it, Calli. I can't give up hope that we will. We're so close. So very close. Just don't give up. As long as you can keep going, I can. … Please."

ℬ

Laundry was finished, goodbyes were said, and right after lunch they were headed back out to the airstrip.

"Do I have to get new knives?"

"No. They just have to be sterilized. Same for the ensembles, though I have a bone to pick with Outfitter about yours."

"Why?"

"Your sheaths are placed right next to the seams." Destan explained as they walked across the apron to the jet that was already out of the hanger and ready to go. "They shouldn't be anywhere near the sheaths. — I know, I know: you're shocked I know 'anything' about clothes. You can pick up your jaw. … Now don't get me wrong, I look at them. But I look at them according to function. I think my ensemble proves 'looks' mean practically nothing to me: function or nothing. And this ensemble of yours is 'severely' lacking in that department. — The only thing left I can't figure out is why your leg wasn't bleeding through." *I'd know.*

"Well it was keeping it compressed: it's pretty much skin-tight."

It's probably that new fabric Outfitter's been gloating about for the past year or so. ~ Maybe it wouldn't be a bad idea to get a new one.

"What about your veil?"

"What about it?"

"Will it get… sterilized?"

"Yep."

"Have you ever had to use the antidote personally?" Callimay asked out of the blue as she looked up to him, having to corral her hair since it was so windy.

As with every time he wasn't prepared for a question, he hesitated as he kept on walking; finally stopping right by the stairs and sighing, "Quite a few times, actually. — I knew exactly what you meant when you said it tasted horrible. — You'd think knowing that would've kept me a bit more vigilant so I wouldn't need it time and time again… but."

"Destan!"

"It's not like I was 'trying' to get bitten."

"But you could've—"

"It's alright, Calli." Destan smiled as he held her closer. "I always caught it really quick obviously. I wouldn't be here if I hadn't."

♬

After making sure she was comfortable, he ran to finish his paperwork and check on a few things. He was grumbling with himself as he came back, but let it go when he came in the cockpit, "Since your leg is back to square one just about, we'll focus your regimen on the other areas you may not have noticed me utilizing when we were out and about. I know you need your rest but I don't want you falling behind."

"And let me guess: a certain someone contacted you and started complaining. Right?"

"I don't know why he bothered," he began to fume as he flopped onto his seat. "He knows what happened. … Calli? You alright?"

"Yeah," She sighed as she looked over and away from him.

"Are you sure?" Destan brushed the side of her face.

"You said we're close. I don't know the relative meaning of that: weeks, months, or years. But as long as you can keep going, I can too."

~ 18 ~

It appeared the weather was doing everything it could to keep them from getting back to Bulwark — and oh what a tempting thought it was to turn around and stay one more day — major turbulence over Indalla, storms over the Faberton/Ferdinan boarder, and then overcast skies with a slight fog around Bulwark.

When they were flying around the first storm it was especially amusing for Destan to listen to Callimay talk on and on about it. In a way he felt he was listening to Rose; but just because she was in such awe about something he'd never seen much "beauty" in... and it wasn't something demeaning. In fact, it was quite the opposite.

She did her best to hide it, but he noticed her bandage wasn't holding up any longer, "How long has it been like that, Calli?"

"Not long. Maybe a couple minutes." She was quick to explain as she jumped; pulling her skirt to the side so the blood stain was hidden. "I know we're almost there so I didn't bother saying anything."

"Gazer? This is Doyen. Do you copy? ... Notify Outfitter and Mender to meet us when we touch down."

ℬ

After they landed — which was one of his best to date — Destan scooped Callimay into his arms and made a beeline for Doctor Gerould. Outfitter met them first and was extremely apologetic for the error he made, saying he'd see to it they were fixed as quickly as possible.

Doctor Gerould was less than pleased when he saw Callimay's leg but this didn't surprise Destan after the stern warnings they'd been given before leaving.

But this was an accident.

"I'd love to be able to treat you like an adult for once. — I thought you said she wouldn't have to run." Doctor Gerould cornered him; his scolding tone sounding just like it had many times before.

"She didn't."

"What about the belvedere burn? Don't assume I 'missed' that."

"I wasn't expecting that at all. I was literally blindsided by that. I'm still seeing flashes every now and again."

"You just don't— what did you say?" Doctor Gerould paused, sounding concerned.

"It was night and the belvedere's keeper blinded me. In fact, I'll still see flashes similar to it every once in a while. It doesn't hurt. Just a nuisance, really."

"No pain?"

"Not now. Why?"

"Just…" Doctor Gerould hesitated when he saw the fear wash over the young man in front of him. "Let me know if it does or the flashes get worse."

"Is something wrong?"

"Bursts of intense light can do damage to anyone. Your eyes are close to a hundred times more sensitive."

"You don't think I'll—"

"It all depends. … It all depends." He gripped his shoulder as he sighed; finishing in a more chipper tone, "Once Pitcher gets done and I have one last look at it, you should be able to take Callimay back. — But if anything, and I mean 'any'thing, changes find Oculus as fast as you can; I won't be far behind."

⹄

It was just about sunset so it was time for him to leave and see to his duties. Pulling a double shift wasn't what he was expecting to do, but there wasn't anything that could be done about it now.

He was hoping it would take longer so he could spend some time with Callimay, but things just didn't work out that way: Outfitter showed up with Destan's veil and a fresh ensemble — made from the new fabric — a couple minutes after they got settled.

~ 19 ~

Thankfully the flashes he was having did turn out to be nothing but a warning to Destan. It did, however, bring to light his "disability" wasn't hidden. The Syndicate had that personal info about him and would do their best to use it every chance they got. Of course they didn't know it was "him" — Doyen — but what did that really matter at this point? Anyone not expecting that bright of a light to shine out of pitch black darkness would be stunned.

In an effort to get things set in place on the off chance something would happen, Destan sent word to the University of Kerogen to see if there was anything they knew of to help downgrade or subdue the severity of bright flashes of light; but was told in no uncertain words they were no longer honoring any ties to him since word was released to the public that he was a Derelict and would notify the authorities he contacted them: *Oh please. You think I'm stupid enough to call from a phone you can track?*

Even though it was a logical thing to consider — Justice Wan in his rage would do whatever he could to bring "justice" to those who he blamed for his daughter's death — he didn't want to tell Callimay what was going to change now as far as their "normal" lives. And yet he knew all too well he couldn't keep her in the dark.

Of course she took it hard, but started working to find what good she could from it.

An urgent phone call came in about the same time. While Destan was initially irritated Nexus interrupted him, when he heard who was calling he calmed down: Redje and Tabitha were beyond concerned that word had gotten out so quickly.

"There was just a report about the balls. Every one your father or your name is attached to has been indefinitely canceled." Redje sounded on edge. "Journal couldn't get with me until the report was almost over. I guess the Syndicate decided to spring it on everyone at the same time."

"How are things there?"

"So far the worst thing is I've been getting questions from a select few at work. Just pray for me to handle it like I need to. — I've sealed the vault access in your house and removed everything I could find."

"Did you check for belvedere—"

"It's clear. The towels still had some residuals on it so I put them in the vault. — Ulysses has already said he and Raina would take your place. … It's gonna be strange not seeing you."

Destan sighed and groaned as he ruffled his hair, "Rej, I— what am I doing wrong? Why is everything falling apart this close?"

"I think you know the answer to that."

Elder.

It's satan, Destan. He's using Elder, but it's him. He knows what good's going to come out of this all and he wants it stopped.

I… I know. "If there is even a hint of something starting, get out. The mansion's a no-go even though a tag's never been found on it so head for—"

"We've got an evac plan in place. Don't worry. Things are creeping in that direction, I won't deny, but we're praying it doesn't come to that." Redje calmed as a little voice could be heard in the background. "I'm not downplaying or ignoring your help, I just don't want 'you' to worry about things that are what they are. We signed up for this and are going to have to face the consequences of those decisions we made ourselves. But no matter what, we're ready, Destan. God's got this. We've just gotta keep doing our part."

"Keep in touch as much as you can."

"I w— just a sec, Destan." Redje chuckled as his voice faded out.

"Desan!" A joyful voice jumped through the phone to give a hug.

"Now what are you doing up at this hour, Rose?"

"I heawred Mama and Papa tawking so I comes to see wha going on. I so gwad. You otay?"

"You sound awfully awake for just coming out." Destan questioned, sounding suspicious.

"I tawk which duh moon fwum my bed since I tant sweep. I miss you awlweady! When you come back?"

There was a crushing moment of pause that only the adults on both sides knew about, "I don't know, Rose. I just don't know. Hopefully it won't be very long."

"Wewl…" she sounded a bit upset, but tried to be happy. "You stiwl cawl, white?"

"That I can promise."

"I awow you to stay away den. Nigh night, Desan!" She kissed the phone. "Say nigh night to Cowimay four me! Bye-e!"

~ 20 ~

Callimay's regimen was very subdued for the next month. Well, just about nonexistent. While having the time to rest was nice, it was torture in a way: pushing back everything that much longer. If Elder kept this as his backup plan it worked perfectly.

To keep things semi-productive, Destan would take her on a walk for about an hour, always making sure she got outside for fresh air and some sunshine. He more times than not ended up carrying her, but it didn't bother him. After what happened in Rayleen he needed to repair what trust he'd lost with his wife.

They would talk some about what she would be doing next with her regimen during these walks, but Destan wanted to leave that be as much as possible. He was already bringing work home since they were living there; talking about it only was going to prove nothing but be the vice that would start choking their marriage again.

At times while they were inside, those they would pass would more times than not stop and stare at Callimay. Her appearance was odd and not "up to code" but Destan was glad she was different. He was made fun of by some and ridiculed by others for smelling like roses, but being reminded it was there brought a smile to his face.

It was actually comical to a point for him to see their reactions: confusion or irritation. Some stayed long enough for him to explain but others merely voiced their displeasure and left.

Playing this waiting game was doing nothing but putting Destan on edge. What was Elder gaining by being understanding and tolerant — even supportive — of his decisions all of a sudden? Then again, Elder was smart. He'd placed himself so well with the help of the abilities he contained… no doubt. Why did he need to rush? Waiting only helped him: Destan "and" Callimay were right where he wanted them.

While his father fell for this and trusted Elder, Destan wasn't going to allow himself to.

And then it hit: Elder's limit was reached. Destan already had the week for the next ball off and had every intention of taking it. Elder led the charge that since it was canceled due to his negligence that leaving Bulwark was a risk they could not afford.

This went on for a while, but he won the dispute since he reminded them they were flying from one Shadow airstrip to another. He did concede returning to Safe Haven was a security risk so he would have to make other arrangements for housing, but he wasn't letting go of his ability to move when and where he wanted.

❦

One evening while they were out, Destan commented, "I know there's not going to be a ball, but there 'is' a formal dinner coming up. Well, I call it a formal—"

"Oh! Where at!" Callimay asked almost giddy as her eyes got wide with joy.

"Well," he stopped and rubbed his neck. "It… it's here."

"Alright." She smiled; her joy not wavering. "When it is?"

"A few weeks."

"What is it for? Can I dress up?"

"It's the annual celebration of when the Shadows was formed. You can wear whatever you want, though I'd said you'll want it to be—"

"Black?"

"Yeah."

"Oh that's not a problem," she clapped her hands in front of her and tapped her chin. "Hum… what are you wearing? You don't have any suits here… well, at least none I've found."

"I hide them from your critical, professional eyes, woman." Destan joked as he tapped her nose. "I'm just kidding. I'm going to wear this."

"Oh," Callimay said a bit deflated.

"What?"

"I… it's alright."

"Calli, what is it?" He took her hand and turned her around.

"I'm not going to complain." She refused as she looked away from him, her cheeks puffing out a bit.

"Callimay Rose Nevrille." Destan said firm, but with a smile, as he leaned over so he could see her face. "You know you're going to tell me if I keep pestering you."

"No I won't."

"Pfft! You know I can just listen to you, right?" He kept egging on.

"I… ugh! I just miss seeing you wear something other than 'that'. Not that you don't look handsome in it. I just… well I like seeing you wear a suit or a polo and slacks."

Guess 'I' should've packed some clothes too. "Why didn't you say anything, Calli?"

"Because you're pretty much 'on-call' twenty-four seven. I didn't think you'd ever be able to."

He thought for a little while and then took her in his arms, "Tell you what. I'll get with Outfitter and see what he can get together in time. Sound good?"

She asked surprised as she ran her hand across his veil, "You don't 'have' to wear this?"

"Nope."

"Really?"

"Really."

"So… I can have Outfitter make a dress? Or is that against code?"

"I'll drop you off before I leave." He put his arm around her as he started walking; him looking worried, "Do you need me to carry you?"

"I'm fine." She smiled as she took his hand. "Did you make sure to leave the door unlocked?"

"Umm… yes." Destan hesitated as he looked up. "It's unlocked."

"You're sure?"

"Positive." Destan nodded as he laughed.

🕉

"Doyen! It's a pleasure." Outfitter said a bit shocked as he came out of the back room. "What can I do for you today? There's nothing wrong with Liaison's ensemble is there? I—"

"The anniversary dinner is coming up and I was wondering if you could make a suit for me."

"A… suit. O-kay?"

"You heard me right: a suit like normal men wear to a dinner."

"You're not— but you've always worn your ensemble. You always told me t—"

"Things change, Outfitter." Destan made a face as he cut him off. "This is just one of the million and some things that's changed in the past year."

"Alright. — So… what kind are we looking at?"

"I'll let Calli go over that with you." Destan glanced at his watch; turning his attention, "I've gotta go, Calli. I'll see you in the morning."

"Okay," she beamed as he gave her a hug.

"Love you."

"I love you too. Be safe."

He kissed her and then smiled, "I will."

Callimay sighed as she turned back, only to see an utterly shocked Outfitter standing there with jaw on the floor, eyes as big as dinner plates. For a split second she thought something was wrong, then chuckled to herself. Many must be like this: unaware Destan just didn't get married, he loved the woman he was with and wasn't afraid to show that to anyone.

"So…" she took a deep breath as she swung her arms back and forth as she walked over. "Let's work on the suit first, shall we?"

"Whatever you would like." He threw the shirt he had in his hands over his shoulder.

"Let's go with a— you know? Actually, let's pattern it more after a tuxedo. It won't have the traditional earmarks, but being a rebel is who Doyen is, right?"

"You know about the earmarks of a tuxedo?" Outfitter asked as if hit with a second wave of shocking news.

"My job was as a fashion designer before I met Doyen."

He perked up and grabbed a tablet and pencil, "That's fantastic! … What were you thinking?"

She grinned as she took the pencil, bowing her head before jumping into it: *You know it's been almost a year since I've done this. ~ Oh stop.*

You haven't forgotten. "How about a grosgrain shawl lapel for the jacket. Jetted pockets. ... Match the grosgrain on the pants' leg stripe like this. ... For the waistcoat let's see what a deep-U one looks like."

This extended pause proved Callimay already had a good idea of what she wanted and Outfitter wasn't able to keep up with her "real-time" drawing she was making: *I guess I didn't forget, huh? ~ And it appears your skills are indeed better than most. ~ Oh come now. It doesn't sound like Outfitter gets many requests in this fashion. There's a science to doing it this way.*

Once he was caught up, she nodded as she looked over his sketch, "That's looking perfect. I like how you've made sure to account for his long torso. I sometimes forget that when doing men's suits. — Now! How about for the waistcoat we do it in satin to add a bit of contrast."

"Are you wanting just a standard worsted wool for the body of the jacket and pants?"

"I think so. Let's keep 'some' normalcy so people aren't completely shell-shocked."

"Black?"

She sighed a bit as she agreed half-heartedly, "Yeah. ... Let's come back to that, thought. Now I know he prefers a narrow tie so we'll go with a satin one. And try to keep the pleats on the pants to a minimum since he has such long legs. And... well... maybe it shouldn't... do the dress shirt in black broadcloth?"

"The 'entire' tuxedo in black?"

"It does sound a bit bleak being all black, doesn't it?" Callimay sighed as she doodled on the corner of the page. "But this is a dinner 'for' the Shadows and it's nothing but black here. White's going to look like a slap in the face: Syndicate. Right?"

"I see your thought process." He nodded as he adjusted his glasses; stroking his beard. "Maybe... maybe forego the waistcoat if you go with a complete black look."

They stared at their own drawings as they went back and forth, altering it a few times before Callimay picked it up and said pleased, "I think this will work perfectly. Let me see yours. ... No, I 'know' it will. Doyen will love it. It's a perfect fusion of traditional and modern. I even think I could see Roc— Sentinel wearing this."

"It's nice to work with someone who has a working understanding of, well, everything. Thank you for giving me time to catch up. Let me put this over here so I don't lose it— would you mind if I kept yours? I enjoy looking at other designers' sketches."

"Of course I don't mind." She smiled as she scribbled her mark in the corner and then handed it to him. "I know what you mean: every person has their own style. Like you: your male 'models' are so much crisper than mine. See how your lines don't curve like mine? They look more masculine and better proportioned."

"Well thank you. I appreciate that." He cleared his throat as he looked over what she pointed at. "You have a distinct eye for fusing aspects of polar opposites into a seamless look that is recognizable and yet so distinct. And the way you draw the give and tucks in fabric… well it looks real."

"I don't know about you, but it sure sounds like we're having a melding of the minds, doesn't it?"

He thought for a second and then belly-laughed, "You're so right! It has been quite a while since I've had this kind of 'deep' conversation. — Now! What about you? I'm assuming by what Doyen said that you'll be wanting something as well."

Callimay fiddled with her pencil, biting her lip, "I've had this thought but I don't want to step on any toes. It popped in my mind not but a second after Doyen mentioned the dinner… but I don't want to get in trouble."

"Well, there's no evil in getting your ideas on paper. And if there's any question about what's permitted and not, I'm glad to assist."

She glanced around, as if worried Elder or someone else who wanted to find some reason to hate her were standing there, and then gave in as she took over and started sketching, "So, here's what I was thinking: a square-neckline sheath dress with thin shoulder straps. Not spaghetti thin or too far to the sides, mind you. And there's a good reason for that. … Floor-length of course with a blush-length train; maybe none. I'll leave that up to your better judgement. Now I don't know if you have any access to brocades, but I had in mind a black one with silver accenting for the body, the same satin as Destan's tie for the lace up portion in the back and other trims. I know brocades need extra support, so a bit of blocking won't bother me." *Lace up back? Are you sure? ~ Oh yeah.* "Have an invisible zipper behind a row of the loops."

"Make it a pseudo-lace. Got it." He nodded as he watched in awe as her hand flew across the paper. "It'll look much cleaner with the zipper hidden rather than splitting the panel in the back."

"Exactly. — And then to finish, a cape that would mimic the look of a Watteau train. It would have a choker-style neckband and cold-shoulder cutouts; which is why I said the straps need to be placed just right so they aren't visible."

"You could forego the straps—"

"I prefer to have straps." She shook her head; sounding determined but kind.

"Understood." He nodded, gesturing for her to continue.

"I'm still not quite sure about the fabric for the cape. Maybe a black silk? I don't think chiffon would be good because I want it to be solid. … And then how about some jewels around the neckband to resemble an actual choker necklace?"

She slid the paper to him after she jotted a couple notes down and waited. He looked baffled as he turned the page toward himself; but the kind that stemmed from being impressed, "I must say… this is an absolutely exquisite design and beautiful sketch. I honestly haven't seen someone sketch that fast and precise in years. Your rounded and curved style lends itself beautifully to women's fashion. — Brocades aren't an easy find, but it 'just' so happens I have some I've stored away for such an occasion as this. Now the jewels I'm afraid I won't be able to help with. I had enough of a time getting those brocades in here. — And let me add I 'do' like the veil referencing with the cape."

"That's what I'm worried about."

"Why are you worried? I see it as a respectful nod to your husband's position. It has the feel of it without being anything close to it. Can I one-hundred percent guarantee it won't ruffle anyone else's feathers? No. But I'm more than happy to take the brunt of any comments made since I'll be the one making it."

Her jaw hit the floor: *Did he just say that? … I c—* "You would?"

"I don't make anything I'm not comfortable with and that I know violates Shadow or Veil codes. There isn't a single thing in your request that breaks anything. Let me go dig up the brocades I have and let you pick the one you want."

Callimay nodded, but couldn't wrap her mind around the fact he was so supportive and helpful. But then she was ashamed: *I'm acting like I did at the Society. I need to stop it. Not everyone's mean in this world, and people here just need time to adjust. Once I prove myself to them they'll come around. I know they will. I mean, Destan did.*

℈

Keeping occupied was usually easy for her, but it was easier when she could go wherever she wanted to and didn't tire so easily. She did a few knife exercises and went over some notes Destan left for her, but after a half hour went back to the suite to rest.

After reading some, she sat by the window and looked out at what stars she could see. The moon highlighted the foam of the ocean waves as they broke and rammed into the cliffside while every once in a while she heard voices and footsteps pass the door.

If it weren't for these two things everything would have appeared to be fast asleep — like any normal place would be at this hour.

Bored, Calli? Destan asked softly.

More tired than anything right now, she sighed as she leaned her head against the wall.

Get things straightened out with Outfitter? ... Are you nodding?

Oh! Sorry. — Yeah.

Do I get to see this dress when you get it or do I have to wait until the day-of? — Remember, Mrs. Manning isn't here to help.

You can see it when I get it. Her laugh trailed off.

Destan sounded pleased and relaxed, *Miss you.*

I miss you too. ... Is everything going alright?

Destan said cheerful as he sighed, *Kinda slow right now which is n— I shouldn't have said that. Ugh! I'll see you in a bit.*

~ 21 ~

On the night of the dinner, Destan was sitting in his armchair dressed to the nines in his tuxedo — his veil draped over the back of the chair — staring out into the darkening world while he tapped the armrest in a slow, methodical manner. Callimay knew he was frustrated about what happened concerning the balls, and even she had to admit she was sad about it all, but they still had each other. And there were still opportunities like this dinner to have a special evening.

"At least when we go to Rayleen we won't have to worry about leaving a day or two late." She leaned over the back of the chair, putting her arms around him and resting her head on his shoulder.

A growl of a sigh rolled off his lips as he pulled her arms away, "We can't go back to Rayleen."

Oh. That's right. She scolded herself before snuggling her head closer to his. "Well, it'll be nice to go back and see the mansion."

"We can't go there either." Destan continued in his monotone voice as he leaned away.

"O… okay."

The silence was starting to become murky with his simmering emotions. While she of course didn't want to set him off, Callimay was determined to have a good evening. Her training regimen had just gotten back to full force and things weren't going so well. She was starting to drain emotionally and needed this night to help. So, she came around and sat in front of him on the floor, "So… it's a surprise?"

"I guess you could call it that." Destan responded rather depressed as he rolled his eyes before looking at her smiling face and glistening eyes. "I'm… I'm sorry I'm not in a very good mood tonight."

"Is there anything I can help with?"

"No."

"Please don't!" She pleaded as she gripped his hand. "Please don't push me out like this. I know things are hard right now and most of it you can't tell me, but… but we're doing this for a better future, right? A shot at making our dream a reality? Remember? … One setback doesn't mean its game over. We just have to adjust and keep going. Let me help. Tell me what you need from me. Tell me what you want."

"I just want this all over." He rose from his chair as his eyes began to flash, him jerking his hand away from hers.

"What do you mean by 'this'?"

"The Shadows, the Veil, the secrets, the uncertainty, the waiting, the wondering…"

His ramblings were the last warning she needed: *Destan? Just calm down. Take a deep breath and look at me. It'll be alright.*

"Will it?" He snapped at her as he stopped and whipped around to glare at her. "Things are falling apart and it's 'my' fault."

She reached out to take his hand, trying to find something to say, but he ripped his hand away and stormed out of the room; slamming the door behind him.

"Destan," Callimay cried in a whisper as she leaned her forehead against the door and put her hand up to it.

On the other side of what felt like an entire universe and not just a door, Destan still had a death grip on the handle. His emotions were beginning to boil over and yet he didn't give into his desire to storm off.

As if he couldn't let go of the door handle because something was keeping him there, he turned and leaned his forehead against the door; then slammed his fist against it.

The desperate sound of Callimay's yelp frightened him so much that he jumped back across the hall. He could see her standing there, one hand against the door and the other clutched to her chest. Her head was bowed and she looked to be in so much pain while she cried.

She fell to her knees and clutched both hands in front of her; Destan falling to his as he buried his head in his hands while listening: *I'm just doing what you asked me to. Maybe I was— I don't know what to do anymore! I thought things were going so well. We finally started addressing problems we didn't know were problems but were subtlety tearing us apart. We started trusting each other, 'really' trusting each other. I just— what happened! Is this Elder? Are you just on edge since things have been so quiet? Do you 'need' something to be wrong? Are you making something out of nothing? I know it's hard to enjoy the peace and quiet. I've been leery too. But don't cause chaos just because it's what you're comfortable with. — Please, Destan. Come back. Talk to me again. Please don't stop loving me. Please.*

"Calli." His broken voice whispered, him still having his head in his hands. "I… I still love you. I'm sorry!"

When he dared to look up she was gone. He scrambled to his feet and yet hesitated when he grabbed the door handle.

After calming himself, he cracked the door open. It was faint, but he could hear her sniffling even though he couldn't see her.

As she threw some of her clothes into a bag, she saw him stop at the door. She didn't want to say a word but stifled a sob as she explained, "I'm going home. Whenever you decide you're done here, you can come for me."

"Calli… I…"

"I can't take this anymore, Destan! I can't take this constant emotional push and pull from you. I've put up with it for so long but I just can't anymore. Things usually get easier for me, but this just won't… and I don't think it's supposed to. — I try to do what you tell me to and end up getting yelled at for it. So I clam up and don't say anything… and then get scolded for never telling you. I… I don't know what to do anymore! Things seemed to be going just fine and th— what happened today? It's like you can't stand being happy. Like you have to make something go wrong so you can fix it and feel like you're in control. It's like you enjoy fighting. Well I can't fight anymore, Destan. I can't fight you 'and' everything else at the same time. I'm not strong enough. I'm giving—"

"Please don't, Calli." He begged as he ran to her and threw his arms around her. "Please don't give up. Please don't say that. Please! … I guess you are right. I 'don't' know how to relax. I don't know how to function when nothing's wrong. I guess my mind just doesn't know how to function in the still and peace; it thinks something's wrong if it is. Things in Rayleen seemed calm when we first moved there, but I was dealing with all this to some degree. You didn't know because I kept it from you. I'm sorry. I'm sorry I keep slipping up like this. I try so hard and… I hate it when I realize I'm not doing things right. I don't know how to navigate these emotional roller coasters. I'm sorry. Please don't leave, Calli. Please. I wouldn't know what to do with myself if you did. I'd miss you so much and wouldn't be able to do anything. I need you with me. The only reason I've made it this far is because of you."

"Tell me what is going on if you love me that much!" Callimay cried as she all but pounded her fists on his chest.

Destan reached over to a panel and hit a few buttons before looking back at his distraught wife and confessing, "While you were finishing getting ready tonight I got a message from Canary. She said we needed to meet but that it had to do with Gathering Night. That mission is just about to move to the final phase: Total Eclipse. Everything I've told you hinges on it… 'every'thing. So, I'm terrified she's got news that'll set everything back; possibly lose everything my father, Rocher, Doctor Gerould, and everyone else has worked so hard to accomplish. — Gathering Night has been the original focus of the Shadows since they were founded thirty years ago. Mrs. Jackman — Commander — still had strong ties to the Homeworld from her and her husband's families, so she began gathering funds from individuals who wanted to help when every governing body backed out in support of her plan… even though they agreed she was right. She had several contacts in high standings of various governments here and began building enough support so a legal storm could end the Syndicate's reign of tyranny and reverse the International Law that's legalized genocide and forced the two of us into seclusion. — Shadows take care of the temporary fix of getting lefties to Safe Havens while Veils work around the clock to make it so no left-handed person has to live in fear. Those in the Veil are the only ones who know about this. … So, for Canary to say she needs to meet about this, I'm worried I've caused something — Justice Wan — which has blown any chance we have to win."

"What!"

"You've known all along there's been something else going on. I knew that because I kept dropping hints here and there." Destan admitted as he sat down and slumped over, sounding completely defeated. "I— Tabitha was right in advising me to tell you everything from the start. Calli I was just trying to slowly bring you in. You were so terrified at first, and then things got so dangerous I just didn't feel like I could tell you. And then I didn't want to disturb our moments of peace and quiet with it. — Yes, I backed out when I had a perfect opportunity right before we came back; I let Doyen win that battle. I'm sorry, Calli. I'm sorry I have to keep saying that. My heart wants rest from everything, it does. Most importantly, it wants it for you. You've been through so much from me and because of me. It's the least you deserve. … Calli? Calli, I'm telling the truth. There are no other secrets I have hidden from you about who I am or what I do. If you want to know anything just ask me; I don't care what consequences there would be from the Veil if I told you. I'm done keeping things from you. I'm done with holding this false belief that you're safer not knowing. I'm done locking you out of my life. I'm done letting others, memories, or emotions control me. Please, Calli. Please stay. Please don't give up. You said you could last as long as I do. Well, I'm not willing to stop yet. I've gotten so close a few times — like tonight — but you've reminded me as I asked you to about why I'm even here at all. You were even reminding me before we ever talked about having a family."

"So, you've been at the head of this all — working to reverse the International Law?"

"That's why the Veil is so strict and secret about what we do."

"Your… 'job'. It's to free us? To take down the Syndicate?"

"Yes."

"You were mad tonight because of Canary's message?" Callimay continued as she braced her arms against his chest.

"It wasn't the only reason, but it was the final straw."

"What did she say?" A terrified look washed over her face.

"I needed to meet as soon as possible with her because of Gathering Night. Which is odd the more I think about it."

"Why?"

"When I left the morning of the ball last week I met with one of the few individuals I know that has contact with her. I told them I needed to see her… and yet she never mentioned that in her note."

"Well… when are you going?"

"Not me, 'we'. You're why I got in contact with her. — I was just going to wait until we left next week."

"You mean I'll get to meet her?"

"Yes." Destan sounded loving as he put her at arm's length; warning as he looked her in the eye, "You've got to follow 'exactly' what I say. One false move and Canary's cover could be compromised and it'll turn into a recovery mission. I don't want her 'or' you in that situation."

She took a hard swallow as she nodded, and then started wandering toward the window, mumbling, "I'm going to find out who I am?"

"I'm hoping so, Calli." Destan sighed as he framed her face. "Calli I'm not forgetting what happened. I… I'm sorry for lashing out. I know things are hard for me in that area, but it doesn't give me an out. Please don't leave."

"You told me the only way I could fail you was if I gave up. I… I was willing to do that just now." She closed her eyes and tried to keep from crying. "I was just going back home to wait, but that's still not right. I swore never to give up. I… I'm just so tired."

He took her in his arms and grieved, "I know it seems like you can't catch a break. And I know I'm to blame for so much of that. I 'am' trying, Calli. It might not seem like it at times, but I 'am' trying to make a better life for us. I'm trying to keep you safe and protected; be the husband I'm supposed to be. — I'm sorry I've pushed you this far so you'd break. Please let me pick up the pieces and fix this."

"I just want to go home and rest. I just want 'us' back."

"I'm sorry it feels like you've lost me, Calli. What do you need and want me to do?"

"Talk to me and listen to me. Those are the only two things, Destan. As far as I can tell every problem we have stems from our lack of or assumptions when it comes to us communicating. I'm not saying 'I' don't have to work on it because I know I do. I just… just let me help."

And there it was… again. The exact same thing she would plead for each time it got this far; the same advice those who knew him best would give time and time again.

His heart ached because he realized he wasn't truly paying attention to or understanding what was being said. What was going to keep him on track? He'd been looking and looking for a stopgap to help him, but now it was do-or-die time.

A hairpin in her hair caught on his wedding band as he stroked the side of her face. His eyes widened as he spread his hand out to look at the band of metal he so oftentimes forgot he had on: *It's been there this whole time but I was oblivious. I... I forgot 'why' it's there.*

Unbeknownst to Callimay, Destan had his ring engraved after they moved to Rayleen. He had the inscription put there to remind him of his devotion and love for her. This band of metal he'd had on his hand for close to eight months? This was the stopgap he'd been looking for.

Even though he was scolding himself for forgetting such a blatant symbol of his love, he found comfort in the fact his quest to help him remember was accomplished. He took a deep breath and stepped back so he could see her face; him wiping the tears he could see, "Calli? What can I do right now to help you?"

"Now? I—"

Heavy footsteps came thundering down the hall, them stopping outside as the person knocked. She cringed as she turned her face away and let her arms fall away from him.

"Calli. I'm not leaving until you tell me."

"Doyen?"

"Fidus is waiting," she sighed as she bowed her head.

"He can wait." Destan shook his head as he got down on a knee. "I need to know what you want. I want to know what you need."

"Doyen!" Fidus' voice became more worried as he knocked louder.

"Calli please." Destan began to plead as he took her left hand and rubbed her ring.

"Doyen, open the door!" Fidus started pounding on it, causing Callimay to jump.

"I'd rather him break that door down and just try to take me away from you than me go answer it of my own free will and leave you. ... Please tell me what to do, Calli."

"You just did." She kept repeating as she began to cry; dropping to her knees and reaching out to him.

It was obvious he was confused by what she meant and why she was crying; but it all of a sudden struck Destan: he'd made the choice to ignore everything around him and ensure his most prized possession was being properly cared for and given the love she deserved. The love he had for God was being extended to her like it always was meant to. He was putting Doyen in his rightful place and letting Callimay take her rightful place of honor and importance.

This whole time Fidus was trying to get in through various means; him now ready to body-slam the door. It opened at a slow rate as he got ready to try again, him looking half-crazed when he saw how calm the two of them were, "What took you so long! Why didn't you respond?"

"This is my private suite, Fidus. 'Not' an office. Not anymore. This is my home. As long as I'm in here everything else will have to wait its turn. Now what is it?"

"Why did you turn your connection to Nexus off?"

"Like I said: this is my private suite, my home. I don't see any more explanation being necessary."

He took a moment to regain a normal breathing pattern as well as calm his emotions before saying what he originally intended to, "You're past due."

"I'm well aware of that." *Do you still want to go, Calli?*

Don't you have to?

No.

Well… could I have a couple minutes before we go?

Of course. "We'll be there momentarily."

"I— very well." Fidus sighed when he saw the look on Destan's face.

☙

The moon was just rising as they started making their way; it bathing the hall with its soft light. It was making her hair look even more glossy than usual; it highlighting the silhouette of her face. Her gown would shimmer every now and again when she would take a step forward.

While things were much more stable than earlier, there was still this lingering silence that hinted to the upheaval of not even an hour prior. The fact Callimay had her head bowed couldn't help but solidify this.

He couldn't let this go on. Destan stopped and put his hand out, taking her by the wrist.

She turned to face him, her eyes full of confusion.

He hesitated for a moment before resting his hand on the side of her face; covering her scarred cheek. The look on his face reminded her of when he proposed. But unlike then, he didn't let her go or back away. He wasn't uncomfortable or embarrassed. This feeling he felt wasn't wrong. It was beautiful and he wanted this feeling to stay. He wanted her to stay just as she was: *I love you, Calli.*

🕈

When the door opened, Callimay expected to hear chatter of some sort, but there wasn't one whisper to be heard. Nothing. This silence worried her but Destan's smile comforted her. While it was a rather dark room for such an event, the lack of light wasn't out of place.

As they made their way toward the front, they caught shocked stares from some, gentle smiles from others, and then of course there were those who glared. — What is wrong with some people?

On their left was a platform where a single, long table with chairs on one side was; it and all the other tables bathed in black. No surprises there. By the look of those seated at that lonely table, that must be where those in the Veil sat.

The closer they got to the platform, the less Callimay recognized the people — newer Shadows were seated closest to the "front".

Destan helped her up and then took her arm as he made his way to take his central seat; him pausing when there was no place for her. He turned to Elder — who was seated to his left — infuriated.

Callimay followed his suggestion and stood behind him; him just about to say something when the cold voice of Elder commented as he refused to look at them, "She's not a Veil, Doyen; and as such is not privileged to be seen among us at such an event. … There 'are' rules."

"We discussed this, might I remind you. Callimay's my 'wife'. And as such her rightful place is beside me." Destan tried to stay composed.

"Once she completes her regimen, and providing she is allowed into our ranks, 'then' she can. But for now she can be seated with the other trainees — where she 'be-longs'."

"You agreed—"

"How else was I to get you to quit squabbling over this insignificant and meaningless venture?" Elder turned to him and sneered. "What's done is done. I expect you to take your medicine in its full measure and act accordingly… 'Challenger'."

While he could very well be alluding to Destan's old title, Callimay knew good and well he was referencing his ability. Elder knew how to manipulate his weakness and the thought passed her mind that she still wasn't sure if what she did was enough to help Destan to at least be able to "see" him. Things could escalate from this tense exchange to a full-out brawl, or worse, if he slithered back into Destan's mind.

After a few moments of stewing, he took a deep breath and replied in a cruel tone, "Very well. Have it your way. — Let's go, Calli."

Destan, we don't have to leave.

You spent so much time getting ready and I know you've been looking forward to this. There's no way I'd let Elder have that victory by just putting up and giving up. Come on.

Even though he was angry at Elder, his tone with her was so soft and caring. — He was controlling it.

He guided her to the main floor and over to the lonely spot at the far end of the table — farthest from where he would be: *Figures.*

There were hushed comments by some of the trainees as the two of them walked over, and even more when Destan sat down.

What are you doing? Callimay whispered as her eyes darted back and forth.

You don't want to sit?

On your lap?

"Woman, are you going to sit or am I going to have to make you?" Destan whispered as loud as possible; his eyes dancing with delight.

"Okay! Okay!" She appeased as those sitting at that end of the table began laughing.

This laughter faded out; only to be replaced with shock as the news of what Destan did rolled like a wave from table to table until everyone knew. Callimay was uneasy about the way things were going, but this feeling stopped with her; Destan was completely calm and aware of how to control the situation. Even Elder storming over didn't faze him, "What is the meaning of this? 'This'… is 'not' your place."

"I must say thank you for reminding me that my place is with my wife. Here I was, expecting her to come to me, when she shouldn't have to do anything of the sort. It's my job to be with her wherever 'she' is." Destan reminded as he glanced at her and kissed her cheek.

"This is absolutely preposterous." Elder scoffed as Callimay got up and Destan guided her behind him.

"And you know what else you've helped me realize? I can better enjoy my time by getting to know the newest members of our team. Again, thank you." Destan replied in a loud and clear voice as he gestured to those at the table with him. "I believe it's better this way. We do have a hierarchy, I don't deny, but I think it helps encourage the ones who do not have as much experience, or even influence, that those over them do not see them as inferior or useless. The more we are willing to share with each other the stronger our trust in each other will end up being. — I would suggest to all those sitting at the head table and even those in the back of the room to think about moving to another where you don't know that many; or inviting someone you are not familiar with to yours. Talk with them. Get to know them. Find where they're struggling. Listen to see if you can help. Let them talk about where they're excelling. You might be able to learn from them. None of us are beyond the capacity of being a student; even the most learned people are referred to as scholars... which means to be a student. We each need to know who we can call on if we find ourselves in a situation that requires a certain set of skills we don't have ourselves. Leaving that knowledge to a select few isn't helpful. What if something happened to them? Then where would you be? ... We function as one unit and so we need to know how well-rounded our unit is. If something's missing, we need to know so we can find the individual who can fill that void. Maybe they're ready and willing but have no idea they're needed. We've got to be open and vocal about this. Without them we won't succeed. Every individual here matters."

Rocher stood and offered his approval by picking up his chair and moving down to the other end of the table Callimay and Destan were at. Doctor Gerould and a few others followed suit and spread out to other tables; soon almost half of those in the room playing some odd form of musical chairs.

Elder stood there, blistering with anger. And yet he couldn't refute what Destan said. There was too much wisdom in every truth he spoke.

And so, he left.

At first he sulked in his seat, but finding himself the only one left at the table reserved for the Veil, he begrudgingly took his chair and went toward the back of the room.

Destan sat back down, smiling. He'd won the battle of showing privilege and placing value. It was something you gave to those around you as a gesture of thankfulness for their guidance and generosity — not place as a requirement on others to give you so you puff yourself up. It wasn't even something that was only given to those in authority; anyone was capable of having a talent or learned skill that surpasses those who had a title of authority.

A good leader — even a husband — never had the right to position themselves as one aloof of those under their authority.

Callimay was left speechless as she sat back down. He always said he struggled to convey his emotions but what he did right then was a testament to his calm and thoughtful side bursting forth to express what he so deeply thought. And then add to that how he was able to control his emotions so he could defuse the situation without coming close to resorting to blows; let alone raised voices and emotions? This proved yet again that the battle being raged inside of him was coming to an end: with God's help he was winning.

His off-the-cuff comments were deemed the opening speech for the evening, so everyone started filing toward the buffet; Destan and Callimay waiting until the end to join the line. And yet she went the opposite direction, "Where are you going?"

"Everyone is going to need the silverware and glasses they left."

He smiled and followed her to where the empty table was; helping her distribute the utensils and such to their respected new places: *Happy you get to help?*

Very, she grinned; looking so content as she worked away.

You look beautiful tonight. And I've heard everyone else thinks so too. … That and they're shocked I don't have my veil with me.

Who told you that? I've been with you—

*No one's said it out loud." Destan chucked as he put his arm around her. *I listened because I was curious what everyone was thinking. — Now I know it would be practically impossible for him to do it, but just to be safe, whatever you get I'll eat. I just don't want to risk anything like last time. Okay?*

But then you'll be—

Elder's not going after me. If something's wrong, he'll find a way so I'm not able to eat it.

A… alright. Callimay sighed as she picked up a plate.

Fidus was upset Destan was beginning to rebel like he was, but was taken aside and reminded the stipulation was that he was not to neglect his role within the Shadows and Veil. When his presence was required, or just requested, he was always there. Standing up to bullying she was suffering and being strong-willed when it came to how he was training his wife didn't nullify his dedication to his work.

Seeing his argument wasn't finding any foothold, Fidus ended his comments by warning, "Elder and some of the others are beginning to take up arms against you again. — Against Liaison."

"I'm well aware of that. But them just thinking it or squabbling over it amongst themselves does no good and puts them in contempt of what they accuse me of all the time: Veil codes of conduct. They have the responsibility of coming and telling 'me' there's a problem. Remember: I'm not asking you to be the go-between. I can handle them."

Shadows and Veils alike would leave for short periods of time throughout the event. While it struck her at first as being rude, she took a step back to remember where she was and what was going on: there was no time to sleep when it came to organizing the type of coup Destan explained to her was building.

These thoughts were ones to ponder, but seeing certain individuals glance at her and then make hushed comments to those around them made her uneasy being where she was: on Destan's lap. It's not that she didn't want to be right next to him, but there was a chair — his chair — still sitting at the abandoned table: *If people would just mind their own business it wouldn't be such a big deal. I mean it's not like we're doing anything rude or—*

I'll be back, okay? He smiled as he gave her a quick hug.

Huh?

Get up, woman so I can get my chair.

Oh!

As he made his way up to the table, it struck Destan how yet another facet of Doyen had been altered. This dinner wasn't anything like the cold, formal, detached meal he always remembered it to be. In a way, he felt like he was around family; what he knew Commander intended it to be all along even though her way of doing it wasn't what most people attributed to a family get-together: *Commander wasn't always right. There are traditions that need to change, that need to be lax and informal. That's what makes 'real' life real.*

This inner reasoning was abruptly cut short when he turned back and saw Elder leaning over and talking to Callimay. He rushed down and stepped in between them, "What do you want?"

"I was merely commenting on the attire your wife was wearing."

"Alright. You've said it. Now go."

"I find the referencing to a veil a 'bit' presumptuous, though." Elder commented as he took the black silk fabric in his hand; also catching a lock of Callimay's hair.

"I would appreciate it if you would leave my wife alone." Destan gripped his hand and yanked it away; him being reminded too much of how Toreon would torment Callimay even when he was with her; almost spitting in his face as he whispered, "Don't 'ever' try that again or so help me—"

"Watch your step, 'young man'." Elder spoke in a hushed tone as he passed; a smug smile creeping across his face. "If you truly love her you need to learn to control your temper. Things can get dangerous very quickly with what demon you now contain. You might even hurt her, strangle her. — Even though she's able to walk and has that type of dress on, she can only cover up some of the bruises around her neck."

Like a whip with embedded daggers, Destan whipped his head over and revealed his flashing eyes to Elder. While this nonverbal show of force would most often demand a submissive attitude on the part of the one receiving the look, Elder knew good and well he'd hit a raw nerve. This is exactly what he wanted; and left the impression he was still going to try to use Destan to kill Callimay.

And so, there went the evening. It had a rough spot already — to put it lightly — but now? Why did this have to happen? Then again, they knew this was going to happen at some point. What a blessing it was that he was only toying with them and not actually putting a knife to their throats.

But did he just toy with them? As Destan turned to Callimay, he saw her hands were trembling and her eyes were almost glazed over. He dropped to a knee and took her hands in his; the look on her face bringing back so many disturbing memories.

Salvaging what he could, Destan gave her a kiss and smiled.

"Please don't leave again." Her voice quivered in a whisper that was barely audible.

It wasn't what he wanted to hear, but at least she said something, "I'm sorry, Calli. I'm here now. And I highly doubt he'll come back. Not while we're in here, anyway."

Keeping to his word that he spoke at the beginning of the evening, when she had time to recover Destan took her and went from table to table to speak with different Shadows and Veils. He always made the effort to introduce Callimay; hoping the encouraging comments from others would help her push out what happened.

There was one table in particular he refused to go to, though. Those who sat with a certain someone at this table didn't surprise Destan at all. They were the only unhappy people left in the room and the ones who had shown the most contempt for Callimay.

Someone asked if Callimay had met one of the individuals at that table; suggesting she go meet them as they gestured in that direction. Needless to say, her reaction wasn't supportive of the idea. She wasn't brazen about her distain and fear, but Destan could feel how she was seizing with it, "I… I think we're going to head up top. We haven't had much alone time for a while, so this would be a perfect opportunity with everything being pretty confined."

❦

It was so peaceful and calm out; only a slight breeze and the moonlight to welcome them as they came out into the wooded area. The shallow breeze was capable of catching a few strands of hair that evaded being tied into Callimay's bun; pushing them where it pleased.

They wandered where they usually did; enjoying the blissful silence of night. She seemed so much better, but something was still lingering.

"Is there anything I can do, Calli? Anything at all?"

"Remind me when we're leaving for Rayleen… or wherever."

"The end of next week. Ten days. … Which brings up: I 'do' need to figure out where we're going. Do you want to know once I do find a place or would you like it to be a surprise?"

While the chipper tone in his voice usually lifted her own, it was just as heavy as the air was, "I guess a surprise."

"Okay." Destan tried to encourage as he took her hand. "It's hard to see all the stars when the moon is out, isn't it?"

"How much longer is my regimen going to take?"

"Well… with how well you learn it's almost hard to tell. But with us only getting half-days in it kinda evens out. — The next portion is very physically demanding. That usually lasts two months, but it can take up to three if you're not able to meet the criteria. Then that's followed by your run training. It's a set amount of time since it's a series of so many runs you have to complete. The good thing is you've done all the 'book work' required so you can skip right to runs. — The stuff I'm giving you right now is just so you're not bored while I'm gone. — So, with that all figured in, it would cut things down to just about four months; late-December if everything goes at the rate it is."

Four months? That seems like such a long time. ~ It's an eternity.

"That's not that much longer than the time we spent at the Society. And we'll have each other in a way that we didn't back then." Destan tried to console, his voice starting to sound desperate. "What can I do to help you, Calli? How can I make things easier for you?"

"I… I don't know."

"Tell me if you think of anything. Anything at all. — I'm going to fight through this and I 'will' win. This change 'is' sticking."

She stood there for a little while and then opened her mouth to say something, but stopped short.

"What is it?"

"I… I know there's no music. … But… could we dance?"

They swayed to-and-fro in a small circle for nearly an hour, and yet it didn't take half of that time for Callimay to forget where she was.

Before long, Destan slowed and rocked her; holding her close as he let himself be lost in this precious and tender moment with her.

~ 22 ~

With their latest "growing pain" fresh on his mind, Destan would get with Redje as well as Mr. Utree on occasion and ask what their opinions were on different issues. It was reminded to him that he needed to include Callimay in his thinking; but his outreach for counsel was always well received and encouraged.

These slices of deep, honest conversation were a welcome break from the fake calm that was still lingering. Elder continued with this unnerving attitude of acceptance and tolerance… even after the words they exchanged the night of the dinner.

While it could've been so easy to "listen" to what Elder was really thinking, Destan was in no way wanting to risk what almost happened the last time their two minds were connected. And he wasn't about to have Callimay do it. "Normal" people had to use their instincts, all their senses, physical investigation, and use what some called technologically primitive techniques to figure out what was going on around them and what people's intentions were. He did so much of his work in this fashion before "the Society" happened so there was no reason to say he couldn't do it now.

♃

After talking things over, Destan got word back to Canary about when they could meet. Her answer was almost instantaneous which put him on edge a bit, but then again he was pleased the short notice worked.

In fact, her response sounded overjoyed to see him and "the parcel" he said he would be bringing.

Maybe he was wrong about her having bad news for him.

With this confirmed, Destan made the last-second change of where they would be going on their furlough. Part of this included going over things with Callimay to make sure she was aware of how things would go so there would be the least amount of stress possible… and keep all three of them safe.

❧

And so with everything planned and ready to go, all of the other things that were bothersome felt like they faded away. But, after Callimay and Destan had a breaking point or scare, things always turned out like this… no matter what the "bothersome" things were. She was hoping and praying it would stick this time like he promised.

Her breaking point being reached reminded him of this fact: it wasn't enough for him to say he was trying and then "try". No. No, he had to "do" without thinking about things not working. His confidence needed to be bolstered like never before. No matter what his "work life" was like he had to keep pressing on.

Thinking back, he knew he had the capability to: *Our time in Rayleen was working so well. I need to get back to that again. I need to focus on Calli more. And focus on her just because of her; not because of what's been going on. That feeling was wonderful. And now I know it was more than just a feeling: it is the way things are supposed to be.*

Every time he'd leave for the night, he'd take his wedding band off and read — out loud — what was engraved inside it. Doing this helped remind him what he did everything for… and who mattered so much to him. Second only to God.

"I promise: 'till my dying breath, Calli"

~ 23 ~

*S*o, what's the name of this vehicle?" Callimay scoffed as a high-end sports coupe opened its doors when they got close enough. "I can't see this one not having a name. I mean look at it."

"Chet," Destan chuckled as he helped her in.

"Yes, Doyen?" The car's AI, a deep male one, responded.

"It's nothing, Chet. Ignore. — And before you ask, it's short for Cheetah." Destan made a face as he smiled. "This kitten can go from zero to one-hundred in less than six seconds. So obviously it needed a name that matched such a trait. But… I didn't want to say such a long word constantly, so I shortened it."

She had a question to ask, but he shut the door before she could; so, Callimay waited until he got into his seat, but not a moment longer, "Cheetah is a 'long' word? Seriously? … Land sake! You'd need it to be as fast as it is because of how loud the engine is."

"I can turn that off. — Chet? Calm things down. — Better?"

"You said 'constantly'. What about Wolf?"

"Technically speaking, Wolf is Rocher's. He was given Commander's Viper when she passed, so he let me have Wolf for the time being so I'd have a sedan." Destan explained as he pulled out of the parking lot. "Apparently he thinks they're safer."

Well they're a whole lot quieter and 'mature' if nothing else, I'll say that. Callimay rolled her eyes as she looked out the window.

"Hey, I heard that, woman."

"And what are you gonna do?" She taunted as she made a face.

"I guess just put up with it." He shrugged his shoulders; gaining some unwanted "affection" from that comment. "Hey! What's—"

329

"Now we're even."

"What? So this is a competition?" He glanced over, looking shocked. "When did you start keeping score… and what is mine so I know?"

"Har-har. Very funny."

"I'm serious! Tell me so I can keep up."

"No you are not." She slapped his arm again, trying to keep from smiling. "Now focus on where you're driving. This is an actual road. Not the sky."

❦

They drove for an hour or so, the terrain changing from the flat lands of what was Southern Faberton to the mountainous terrain of Indalla that was at one point galactically known for its pristine runs and top-of-the-line long ski craftsmen. She knew this change in where they were going was coming, but it still struck her as odd to be somewhere so close to where she grew up and yet still such a foreign place.

When they got to the border she was struck again, "Wait just a second. I thought Indalla was a closed country?"

"Yeah," Destan waved to the man who opened the gate.

"Oh for the love of— if you have Shadows everywhere why didn't you just have them take care of things so we didn't have to worry about so much when we left the Society? We might not have run into Justice Wan at all."

There was a pause of striking silence as he rolled up the window and kept going, followed by a sigh, "I wasn't thinking clearly. Between my 'anger' and it being a while since I'd been shot, I was having a hard enough time making sure I kept myself where I could watch over you like I needed to."

"I'm sorry." Callimay said ashamed as she bowed her head.

"Hey. Let's not start things off on a sad note. I 'was' struggling when we got to Brigon, but when I saw that young woman I knew I had to fight through for you. Now I'm not saying you couldn't protect yourself at all at the time, I was just trying to fulfill my duty. — Which then reminded me I'd just gotten married. — I had a wave of terror wash over me; the emotional stress more than enough to keep me awake."

"You mean you didn't want—"

"That's not what I said. It was stressful because it wasn't how I wanted it to be. We'd only been engaged for a little over two days to that point; blindsided by the fact things had to be done right then. … There was never a doubt in my mind that I wanted to marry you, Calli. Okay? I can't say for sure it was true love I felt when I first saw you, but if it wasn't it was the closest thing possible to it. … Now. That's the past. There's no reason to worry about it anymore, right?"

She nodded as she settled into her seat, and then sat up, "Wait a second! You've been shot before!"

You just 'had' to say that, didn't you? "Calli, I—"

"But— why are you stopping?"

He put the car in park before turning to his wife and calming her, "It can't be 'that' surprising to find out, knowing what kind of life I've lived up to this point. Can it? … Can it?"

"I guess not. But that still doesn't mean—"

"I never meant you 'had' to be okay with it. Being shot isn't really 'that' painful compared to other things. A broken rib? Ho oh brother! Don't get me started."

"Broken rib!"

Would you just shut up, Boon. "I— let's try this again: Indalla is a closed country. Yes, we have a border gate we pay for like we do in a majority of countries so we can move freely. I wasn't thinking about that when we escaped because I was too focused on you; the woman I've always wanted to marry. … Calli?"

The tanker he passed five miles back rumbled past them, slapping her back to reality, "I guess I never quite put the dots together, huh?"

Destan smiled as he sat back, "It's alright. — Ready to go?"

❦

Getting to what looked like the top of the mountains wasn't nearly as long of a drive as she thought; before she knew it, Destan pulled up to a small cabin.

It was almost the end of August and yet it felt like December when she got out of the car.

She clutched her arms in front of her and sounded surprised, "I understand why you said wear my warmer clothes!"

"Let's get in and then I'll come back for my bag."

Without a second's hesitation, she scurried over to his side and nodded like Rose sometimes did: *Why in the world did I think it'd be warm? ~ I don't know. Why did you? ~ I... I'm just talking. I'm not expecting you to answer. Ugh!*

Now well-versed in the extent of the Shadows' reach, finding the main floor's fireplace lit and the room warm wasn't a surprise at all. In fact, it was so welcome to see and the first thing she visited.

As she turned around toward the rest of this compact area, Callimay was confused by what she saw. It took her the whole time Destan was gone to come to terms with what she was seeing, "I don't think you can get much smaller than this."

"This isn't that big, is it?"

"Compared to the mansion this is just a closet! But I love it."

"Oh, you want to move here?"

"Do you see all that snow out there and it's the middle of summer?" Callimay walked into the dining area and pointed out the window. "You know cold and me don't get along very well. — It's a wonderful place to visit but I'd rather 'live' in Rayleen."

"You'll need to get comfortable with the cold somewhat, at least."

"Why?"

"We perform runs through all types of terrain — even mountains like this. And all year round. Granted I really hope you don't have to 'use' that part of your training, but the fact is you've got to get through it because your schedule is going to put you smack dab in the thick of winter weather." Destan sighed as he came over and took his veil off. "I'll say this much, though: being a Veil has the added benefit in cold conditions of having this layer of leather. And if all goes according to plan you'll be even better equipped because you'll have sleeves on yours. — It can make things rather miserable when it's hot, but there's always cons to anything if you look hard enough."

"So," Callimay tapped her lip as she sat on his knee. "Since you 'obviously' can handle the changes so well — as I recall you saying at the Society — you 'intentionally' didn't have your suit jacket on when you came for orientation, didn't you? It wasn't because you were hot from wearing the black, am I right?"

His face started to flush as he laughed and scratched his head, "Well… that was mainly me just not wanting to look like the rest of the guys there: I didn't want to be lumped with them. I snuck up and looked in a few minutes before anyone saw me and couldn't help but notice how everyone was dressed. Needless to say they repulsed me on that front alone. — But, I'll admit it was pretty hot for a wool suit. And it was nice not having a tie on since I had a lump in my throat from being nervous."

"Nervous? 'You'?" Callimay did her best to not laugh. "I mean, I kinda thought you were, but you didn't actually show it."

"What's so amazing about that? Any guy who would see you would be a complete idiot if his heart didn't start pounding out of his chest and his palms didn't get all sweaty."

"So 'that's' why you didn't shake my hand!"

"And now the 'big' secret's out." Destan exaggerated to hide him blushing. "I wasn't about to be embarrassed on top of everything else!"

"I would have 'never' guessed!" Callimay smiled as she leaned her head on his shoulder; looking peaceful and happy… but then had every ounce of it drained, "Am I going to be alone during all those runs?"

"What happened to this being a vacation?"

"We're meeting Canary."

"Point well taken."

She made a face, finally having to say, "Well…"

"Alright, alright. — You won't run solos until your last month. And those will be closely observed so you won't ever technically be alone. The vast majority of the time I'll be right in step with you."

"You'll be with me the entire time?"

"As much as I possibly can."

"But wait… if I have to go through four months of this, how do the people you go get on a run survive? They're not trained."

He gestured for her to get up and then the two of them started up the stairs, "Funny thing is: the purpose of runs have constantly changed over the years. At first, entire families were being run to Safe Haven, so only short-distance circuits were used; and obviously it was contained within the borders of Ferdinan solely. The families were given explicit instructions of meeting locations and it was their job to get there on time and be ready to move. Fast forward to the time my father was in and they were apparently nonexistent: the political side was being pushed so hard that the 'little man' was getting shoved aside. — And with Elder coming to a more prominent role during that time it kinda makes sense now. — Commander realizing this has been used to explain why she committed suicide, but both Rocher and myself know she was not that type of woman. In her culture rituals, to end one's life without resolving the wrong you committed was to bring dishonor upon you and your entire family: past, present, and future. … Anyway. That discussion's best had at a later time. Fast forward a couple years and smaller sized Safe Havens started functioning at full tilt in key areas around the world to make it more feasible for those without the capability for such long treks. And then when I came along, runs had morphed into individual pickups with the intention of that person becoming a Shadow. Families and groups would have arranged pickups in public places that are so well hidden that the Syndicate has no idea. And now. Well, there are still some who are in remote places and 'closed countries' , like Indalla is, where runs are necessary. — Make any sense?"

"So that means when you went to get Tabitha, it was done with the intent of her joining the Shadows?"

"Her father didn't want her to, but she was bound and determined to get her pound of flesh."

"Did she?"

"You know her, Calli: fiery redhead who'd never give up her Salvation. She was younger at the time and 'really' wanted her revenge, but also knew it was going to do no good. Her mother and sister were gone. Him and his belvedere dying wouldn't 'fix' anything. — But, he did get his due. Tabitha had a secret price put on her by that Falconer and so one night while she was out on patrol he found her."

"And?"

"And so Redje did what he had to, to protect her." Destan sighed as he got up and leaned over the landing's railing. "She was doing well with fending him off, but poor thing froze like a block of ice when she saw that belvedere. — They might all look the same at first glance, but this one was a golden: drop ears, champagne color, and a shorter coat.

— I know she didn't 'see' her mother and sister die, but what she saw and heard was more than enough. And the aftermath? … Triggers come in all forms, and that creature was hers."

She was shell-shocked: *No wonder she didn't want to talk about it.*

This silence caused Destan to turn around, "Calli? … Calli are you alright? — Easy! It's just me."

"I…" she tried to catch her breath as her eyes darted to-and-fro. "I didn't… I…"

"It's okay." He calmed as he ran his hand through her hair; his smiling face tainted with worry. "You didn't know that's what really happened. I know she wouldn't blame you."

"It's just I—"

"Just take a deep breath, Calli." He hushed as he took her quivering hands. "How about I get out of this absurd uniform and into something more becoming of 'vacation' attire. Huh? … Alright."

ℬ

Once their self-guided tour, early dinner, and personal discussion time was over, Destan went out to the car and brought back a large box.

"What's that?"

"Rej told me late last week that Sonnie started finding letters addressed to the Conflux; the problem being there was no 'attention' additions or return addresses. I think he said they started a month ago. Anyway! They kept piling up, making her curiosity burst. And it's a good thing." He huffed as the box made a muffled boom sound as it hit the floor. "Turns out they're all for me."

"What! But why?"

"Why don't we read and find out?" He smiled as he leaned over and opened the lid, handing her the first one he grabbed.

While she wasn't sure what to expect, what these letters turned out to be floored her… and him. They were all in support of Destan amidst the uproar of the shocking discovery about him being a Derelict. Most weren't signed and they were typed and printed on plain paper in black ink; but Destan wasn't the least bit put off. The only clues were some made mention of the last ball; referencing Callimay's speech: that there's nothing evil about him being left-handed.

One letter in particular caught Destan's attention. It "was" signed and written by hand on watermarked paper.

As it turned out, it was from the elderly gentleman who first stood for Callimay's speech and came to speak with them afterward.

She stopped the one she was reading and listened to the voice of an older man who sounded like the perfect grandfather type. In a formal manner similar to Rocher, he said he was grieved such "savage oppression" was being placed upon them because of the humiliating and heinous label those in society had deemed him being "worthy" of. And beyond that, he personally wanted to extend his support for the two of them; leaving his contact information and saying if there was anything he could do to help, to contact him.

It was such a breath of fresh air to hear such words, but Destan's reaction wasn't quite what she expected. He jumped to his feet, his eyes sparkling as he fumbled to say, "Th… this is too good to be true."

"What?"

"Brigon is the last country we haven't been able to get any contacts in since its government is a monarch. His name? Calli this is the 'king' of Brigon himself!"

"How did you not know that all this time?"

"The name he used wasn't this one; and I can name a few reasons off the top of my head why he wouldn't use his real name." Destan's joy kept building as he paced back and forth. "This is just amazing!"

Seeing him so overjoyed was wonderful and usually she'd be right there with him, but Callimay wasn't so trusting of individuals anymore, "What if it is a trap?"

In most circumstances that would've taken the wind right out of his weathervane, but the hope inside Destan couldn't be quenched, "I'll admit there's that chance. And let's face it: 'all' of them carry that chance. But I'm clinging to the hope this is true." *Oh God please let it be!* "I'll send this to Fidus and see what he can find out."

Even though she didn't know everything, she remembered what he said before, "Is that the last thing needed for Gathering Night or whatever you called it?"

"One of the last… and one of the biggest ones we need for Gathering Night: Total Eclipse."

~ 24 ~

Under the overpowering silence and still in the night air was the soft crunch of snow as Destan came out on the balcony and sat beside her, "Calli. Why are you out here?"

"I couldn't sleep."

"Did you get 'any'?" He sounded worried as he brushed her cheek. "Calli you're ice-cold!"

"I'm fine. I got some sleep." She sounded melancholy as she looked over and did her best to smile.

He wasn't thrilled with how she looked, but he made the best of it and tried his best to make things positive, "Tonight's going to be a big night. I'm interested to see what Canary has to tell you."

"I'm scared, Destan." She sniffled as she looked down at the picture of the two of them. "I don't know if I want to know what she can tell me. I… I have great memories of the childhood I had. Maybe I sho—"

"I know there are so many unknowns, Calli." He comforted as he pulled her over to him. "And believe me when I say I know how hard it is to find out a part of your childhood wasn't what you thought it was. It's hard but at least for me it gave me closure. I never thought I needed it but it turned out part of me was begging for it."

She stifled her sniffles and clung to him for a while.

He brushed the snow off her shoulders and hood as he smiled, "How about I fix you a good warm breakfast to go with a mug of piping hot tea, as Rocher would say."

"Sounds wonderful," Callimay sniffed as he helped her up.

𝕯

After about three hours later they were down in a valley, passing the same border gate.

As they came into view of what he knew was the meeting place, Destan turned off the car lights. Callimay started to get nervous again, so he did his best to help her stay calm and focused. Well, as much as possible. This was an extremely risky thing they were doing. The role Canary had within the Syndicate didn't afford her much freedom because of the lockdown nature of the Syndicate with its leadership. While this may sound strange — the leaders being locked up — it was showing who they were: deep down they knew what they were doing was wrong and the silent majority hated their guts. They were scared.

Destan parked Chet at the edge of the woods where there was an orchard not too far from a brightly-lit spacious house made of red stone and surrounded by a wall made of the same stone.

Callimay got out and felt like they were being watched. Destan was his usual calm, Doyen self, so she began to wonder if it was just her being paranoid about everything.

They stayed there for a little while and then Callimay heard rustling behind them. She whipped around and saw a belvedere standing not too far off, looking just as innocent as ever but completely black; its green eyes fixed on them as its tail wagged. She gasped and threw her arms around Destan, her activating her barrier ability.

"It's alright, Calli." He walked toward the belvedere, sounding soft and tender. "Canary told me she'd send her belvedere to escort us."

"Are you sure?" She asked terrified.

"I told you about this. Canary set it up this way. Remember?"

"But it's black!" Callimay whispered as loud as humanly possible as she grabbed his arm and pulled him back.

"I know it goes against everything you've learned, everything I've said about the creature, and even what you saw that one time," Destan sighed as he turned to her and stroked the side of her face. "I was a bit shocked by her saying this is what she'd do, but remember: belvederes are under the complete control of their keeper and Canary's calling the shots for this entire meeting. And a belvedere can attack just as much when they're white and innocent looking as when they're midnight black and growling. You know that."

"How do you know this isn't a trap? You've said yourself you've never met Canary. How do you know she isn't a double agent of some kind? What if she's in cahoots with Elder?"

"She saved my father's life, Calli. No matter how long she's been off the grid or who she's been around for the past fifteen-so years, that one act in and of itself gives me reason enough to trust her. … Please, Calli. Trust me."

"O… okay."

Destan turned back and nodded to the belvedere, gesturing for it to lead the way. It turned and took off as silent as ever; them beginning this last leg of their trip to find answers.

And yet, with each step she took, Callimay wanted to leave; she didn't want to know what Canary had to tell her.

It turned out this orchard was a sea of apricot trees. It was late in the season for them but oh did the wafting breeze smell delicious.

As they got to the edge of the orchard Destan was confused. There was a barren stretch of about a quarter mile between them and the closest structure; the wall that matched the house only stretched across the side that was against the road.

The belvedere began circling and pawing at the ground beside one of the trees, so Destan kneeled beside it and felt around. Not too much longer he lifted a trap door; the tunnel he revealed was pitch black, the belvedere disappearing when it jumped in.

After looking around, Destan motioned for Callimay to jump in.

I'm not getting in there with that creature!

You promised you'd do 'exactly' as I said while we were here. This isn't easy, but trust Canary and me. … Now get in the tunnel.

Everything inside of her screamed to run, but being separated from Destan wasn't an option in her eyes either. So, she forced herself to his side and let him help her down into the tunnel; him following suit not but a moment later.

❧

They inched along for what felt like an eternity; Callimay not being able to see a single, solitary thing and questioning where to take the next step even though Destan was guiding her.

Finally! They heard soft clacking noises that sounded like the creature was going up something metal. There was a pause and then a thud from something hitting the wall before the clacking noises started again and the creature nudged Destan's hand. His jerking and rapid breathing reminded Callimay this wasn't easy for him either. He'd never been in a situation where the creature could be trusted.

It's alright, Boon. Calm down. … What was that noise? … Oh! *That was just the trapdoor hitting the wall. Remember her mentioning that?*

It was beyond unnerving to be so close to the creature; the belvedere's tail thumping her leg as it stood there pawing at the door.

Destan took a deep breath and had her stand against the wall, him opening the door just enough for the creature to squeeze its head through. It bolted around the door and left them.

He froze as he shielded Callimay, but relaxed when he heard a cheerful female voice, "There you are! Did you have fun?"

There were a few moments of silence, him pushing his hair back behind his ear and waiting. He then pushed his hair back again and smiled as he took a deep breath: *Wait here until I come for you.*

Alright. She said nervous as she gripped his wrist. *Destan?*

Yes Calli?

I… I love you. Her voice trembled just as much as her hands.

I love you more. Destan smiled as he gave her a kiss. *I'll be right back. Stay here.*

ᚦ

The room he found himself in as he made the sharp left turn like the belvedere did was a lavishly decorated sitting room with three beautiful bay windows on the north side and two flanking an oversized granite fireplace on the other. Destan took a quick surveillance of the area and then rested his attention on the only person in the room. The belvedere was sitting next to an armchair where a lady, presumably in her mid-sixties, was sitting cross-legged.

Upon seeing him, she stopped petting the creature and rested her fingertips of one hand against the other in front of her. She was wearing all black just like Destan; her veil of a very distinct fashion: *Armenian? ~ That'd explain the apricots and tuff stone everywhere.*

"My how you've grown, Doyen. You look just like your father." Her alto-toned voice smiled as she rose from her seat. "It's so good to see you again."

"It's an honor to finally meet the woman who saved my father's life." He kept a firm and yet kind tone.

"Good. You found his Shadow Box." She said relieved as she offered her hand.

"It was quite a bit to take in."

"I'm sure it was. — I'm so glad you were able to make it tonight."

"It wasn't the easiest thing, following that creature." Destan nodded in the direction of the belvedere that hadn't moved.

She chuckled as she turned and motioned for the creature to come to her, "I didn't think it would be. But if anyone was going to be able to follow my instructions I knew it would be you."

"Tonight's the blood moon. I take it that wasn't by accident?" He gestured out the window.

Canary smiled as she turned and strolled to the window, "So. It wasn't a fairytale I heard about you getting married."

Destan confirmed, suspicious of why she was avoiding his question, "What has the blood moon to do with Gathering Night?"

"Where's Emissary?"

"He's out on run detail in Gastonia. He wanted Indalla but things just didn't work out. Why?"

"Did you see him before he left?" Canary asked concerned as she rushed up to him, looking him square in the eye.

"I sat in on his debriefing." Destan answered slowly.

"Why did he leave his mission?"

"He was pulled by Elder. Emissary said—"

"Elder!" She hissed as she stormed to the window.

"Canary, why are you avoiding my questions?"

"Where's the parcel?" She said in a raised tone as she glanced over her shoulder and tapped the window pane. "Let me see it first and then we'll discuss everything."

"Tell me about Freigh. 'Then' the parcel." Destan refused. "And didn't you get my initial message from Passage?"

"Didn't you know?"

"Obviously not," he sounded half perturbed, half worried.

"Passage was killed five months ago. Syndicate web."

Then who~ Elder. ~ I know that. Who was it I talked to!

"Someone met?"

"All they could've found out was I was wanting to meet 'soon'. I didn't give exact dates to them."

Why didn't news get back about Passage? … Elder. "Let's pray that is all they got." She sighed as her shoulders dropped; turning to face him, "In regards to Freigh I have good and bad news."

"Canary I'm sorry. I didn't know. No one knew."

"I'm not blaming you, alright? What's done is done."

"H… how did you know to warn me?"

"There's no good way to say it. I was in the meetings Baleck had with the Monarch a few months ago. He kept alluding to information he had about a certain Derelict who was more than just a nice payoff. He dropped hints about Kerogen and a wealthy individual… so I made necessary conclusions. As time wore on and more details came out I found out I was right." She turned back and sat down. "Do you want the bad or good news first?"

"Bad."

"Freigh is dead."

"And the good?"

He could feel her emotions tearing her apart as she admitted, "No matter what they did, he never let out your location. I… I was there the entire time for his interrogations. I don't know how he did it. I thought him losing his wife hit him hard enough that he would give up, but he fought to the death defending you."

"Slight correction, Canary. His wife was murdered. Murdered by Baleck's swain."

"I knew there was something disturbing about her." She tapped her fist on the armrest as she gritted her teeth. "Now enough stalling. You know I don't have much time. Show me the parcel."

Destan sighed as he turned around, catching her attention, "Where are you going?"

"To get the parcel. It's not the type I could carry on my person."

Canary motioned for him to go on, but looked puzzled.

$\mathfrak{B}$

"Destan!" Callimay clamored to put her arms around him when he came around the corner.

"Ready?"

"No. … But there's no going back now."

"It's going to be fine. Just remember to follow our instructions."

She nodded as he took her hand and started back.

The door closed as soon as she walked out; the "door" looking like it was just a part of the wall! Seeing that made her stick to the back of Destan, her screaming to herself: *I wanna go back. I changed my mind!*

Hearing his voice made her freeze, "You spoke of me being married, Canary. Well it just so happens she's the parcel. I found—"

"It can't be!" Canary gasped as she stumbled back; yelping as she missed the bay window seat and fell.

"I had no clue until I found the Shadow Box about two months ago about my father telling me to find her and keep her safe so I could get her to you." Destan continued as Canary calmed her belvedere and stood back up. "And then what Emissar—"

She ran over and took Callimay's hands in hers, then framed her face, and finally wrapped her in her arms while she repeated, "Is it you? Is it 'really' you?"

"I'm sorry?" Callimay looked at Destan for answers.

"W… why are you wearing—"

All of a sudden they heard voices and quick footsteps from the direction they came. Destan whipped his head around to Canary for instructions, seeing her seize with fear; pulling Callimay behind her.

"This way, Doyen. Hurry!" She took Callimay by the hand and began running.

She signaled the belvedere to follow as they entered a side hall on the other side of the room. Toward the end, she darted into an open room, barely evading the people who were following. Canary locked the door and ran to a small table.

Clinging to Destan's arm, Callimay asked, "What is going—"

"Hush, child!" Canary warned as they heard footsteps converging on the room they were in.

"Atlanta? Atlanta, are you alright?" A man's voice called out as he pounded on the door.

Canary put a bracelet on and tapped it, causing her entire outfit to transform into a pure white version of what she had on — even her hair changing to a stark blonde shade. She took a deep breath and signaled the belvedere to follow her.

Not wasting any time, Destan took Callimay and put her in a darkened corner of the room that would be hidden by the door; shielding her with his body.

Destan? She looked up at his chiseled, serious face; her voice trembling. *Did I do something wrong?*

No, Calli. He stroked her hair and then wrapped his arms around her. *Just stay perfectly still and quiet.*

Callimay could feel Destan's heart pounding as he pulled her close. His hands and arms felt so strong and sure, though. It amazed her how he kept his emotions in-check during moments like this.

"What, is it?" Canary sounded irritated as she threw the door open.

"We were signaled by the belvedere that you were in distress."

"Well as you can tell: I'm fine." She assured as she petted — more like slapped — the creature. "He may be due for a tune up."

"He must be. The point of origin was the sitting room."

"Well then I agree he is due."

How could someone act so collected under such pressure? She was keeping such a perfect façade for the sentries to see. Callimay and Destan both could hear her inner terror and fear practically screaming.

"We'll sweep the area just to be sure." The man replied as he nodded to the others who then left; and started into the room himself.

"Excuse me. I said I was fine." Canary put her hand up and stopped the man.

"My orders were to make sure you are secure." The man shook his head as he saw her fingers beginning to tremble.

"And I'm telling you I am."

"Why are you in full dress?"

"Because I couldn't sleep. What is it to you?"

"I'm having a look."

Without a second thought, Canary threw the man against the wall.

Destan ran to help but found she was quite capable of taking the sentry down herself.

She glanced out in the hall and then shut the door while Destan dragged him to the other side of the room and tied him up.

"Stupid creature." Canary snapped as she glared at the belvedere, causing it to cower from her. "I'm sorry, but you two have to leave. I value your safety more than information."

"We can't leave you here." Destan said in his authoritative tone. "There's too much for you to explain. You're coming with us."

"Why did I have to be right?" Canary mumbled in a defeated tone as she took the bracelet off, returning to her actual appearance. "Fine. I'm in no position to argue. But first I've got to get something. I'm not leaving without it."

"Where is it?" Destan asked in a whisper as he cracked the door open to see.

"Back in the sitting room. —I… I'm sorry you're having to see all of this." Canary grieved as she took Callimay by the hand. "Doyen? The others won't be back for a minute or so, we've got a small window of opportunity but that's it."

Destan nodded and then checked the hall again. He looked back at Callimay who was terrified and brushed the side of her face: *Calli? Calli, I'm here. Nothing's changed. Just follow my lead.*

She took a hard swallow and then nodded as she let out a shaky breath. He took her other hand and then they ran to the sitting room… Destan stopping short when he heard voices. They were saying Canary could not be trusted and orders from the Monarch were to treat her as they would a Veil. He whipped his head over to look at Canary who cringed and closed her eyes.

After a moment, she leaned over to her belvedere and gave it an order while she pointed to the room. It then pranced in ahead of them.

"Close your eyes." She warned in a whisper as she hugged Callimay.

Some asked why the belvedere was alone, and then soon there was a great deal of commotion followed by complete silence.

Callimay could still see a flash even though her eyes were closed, and was worried what was going on: it was the moment when there was the most commotion and then complete silence.

When she was let go she looked to Destan: *Are your eyes alright?*
I'm fine.

Canary was the first to go in. She started looking at the mantel of the fireplace but was becoming frantic when she couldn't find what she was looking for. Destan and Callimay soon followed and found everyone in the room lying on the floor, the belvedere still glowing.

While he respected her wishes, the growing amount and volume of voices made it clear, "Canary? I'm sorry but we've got to go — now."

"I can't leave without it!" She demanded as she continued to look.

"What 'are' you looking for?" Callimay asked, Destan not allowing her to leave his side.

"It's supposed to be right here!" Canary rambled in a shrill tone as she furiously shook her hands at an empty spot on the mantle.

Destan shoved Callimay to the window as a few men rounded the corner. Canary abandoned her search to help him but didn't notice the ones who were knocked out were beginning to come around.

Callimay stood there trying to find something to say to warn them, but they weren't listening. She began to panic and ran over, doing what she could to buy them some time. That sudden movement caught Canary's attention, her groaning as she watched Callimay.

Now with the last one subdued, Destan gritted his teeth, "Canary, it's not worth it. We've got—"

"This 'is', Doyen!" She argued as Callimay ran to his side. "You have 'no' idea how important it is! Gathering Night will fail w— where was it? Did I move— I did."

Canary grabbed a small box that the belvedere had in its mouth; it standing beside an opened bookcase. She flew past Destan and Callimay down the same hall they came from just a few minutes earlier; her belvedere hot on her heels as she ordered them to follow her.

Before they could, several men came in the room. The men yelled out and then raised their weapons.

Destan gasped and shoved Callimay in the direction Canary ran.

Shots rang out, them barely missing Destan as he threw himself over her. He scrambled to his feet and scooped her into his arms, following after Canary who turned to her left and headed up a flight of stairs, not looking back or waiting.

The men Canary and Destan took down were coming around and Destan knew the others were going to be only seconds behind them. So, he tapped Toreon's ability and jumped to the stairs; then started running, making sure to shelter Callimay as shots continued to pepper the wall around them.

❦

When they got up to the other floor, they saw Canary was messing with something on the wall almost at the other end of the large room. The belvedere ran to them, causing Canary to glance over. She waved for them to come and kept working.

Destan was a bit concerned that the belvedere was staying so close to him. He tried to detour it a few times but it ran right back.

Canary stepped back and looked up as he came up beside her. Something snapped and part of the ceiling began to move away, revealing a passage. Destan set Callimay down opposite the belvedere to which it ran around and sat practically on her leg; trying to snuggle its nose under her hand as it wagged its tail.

"Keep her safe, Doyen." Canary said in a hushed tone as she laid the small box in his hands. "Everything the two of you need is in there."

There was a painful pause from him before he asked, "What was it you were going to tell me?"

"Elder's got to be disposed of before The Arena." She grabbed him by the shoulders; her eyes wild with fear. "Do 'not' let him live, Challenger. You're our last hope. … Please! Don't let your father and my sacrifices be in vain."

"How did you—" Destan asked in shock as a single shot rang out, followed by glass shattering.

The computer Canary was working on was obliterated by the high caliber shot. She looked up in fear, seeing the door begin to close.

"May the new moon continue to rise on you." She sniffled as her eyes welled with tears and she drew her weapon.

Destan nodded; cringing as he closed his eyes, "May the stars welcome your presence as guide and guardian."

After a moment of silence, he jumped up through the closing hole and set the box down so he could reach back. His voice popped and skipped as he stretched out as far as he could, "You've gotta jump, Calli. Now!"

She jumped as high as she could, barely catching his wrist and dropping back down. The look of terror in her eyes as she slipped out of his grasp took his breath away… in a bad way. He scrambled to see if he could stretch out any further, him able to get her the second time.

"Callimay!" Canary yelled as she moved in front of her, taking a bullet to the shoulder.

"Canary!" She screamed as she reached back.

"Calli, you've gotta hold on tight or I'll lose you again!" Destan strained, sounding desperate.

A moment later, Canary pulled herself up and shooed her on, "I'm fine, Callimay. Go on."

"Calli come on!" Destan yelled, the door closing more and more each second.

It wasn't what she wanted to do, but hanging where she was wasn't going to help anyone. She looked up and gripped his hands tighter so he felt safe in pulling her up to him.

What a relief it was to have her in his arms.

But it was short-lived when Callimay pulled away and frantically tried to keep the door from closing; calling out to Canary to jump.

Destan kept trying to pull her away but she refused to let go.

"I can hold it open long enough." She cried, the belvedere whining and barking as it tried to reach her hand. "Just give me your hand. I know it's going to hurt, but please try!"

"Doyen, get her out of here!" Canary fired her weapon a couple times, it clicking the last time.

"Calli, we've gotta go!" Destan pulled her away. "This is how she wants it."

"No!" She screamed hysterical as she fought him. "We can't leave her. — Canary!"

"Stay safe my Rose Petal. Mr. Ruff will keep you safe. Remember that. Mummy has to go be with Paba and your brothers now. Eat your Tsiran and remember I will 'always' love you." Canary smiled through her tears as she looked up to Callimay and the door closed.

The End

Then that means— no!